Vicious Circle

Arlene Hunt is originally from Wicklow, but now lives in Barcelona with her husband, her daughter and a mêlée of useless, overweight animals. *Vicious Circle* is her first novel.

ARLENE HUNT

Vicious Circle

Hodder
LIR

First published in Ireland in 2004 by Hodder Headline Ireland
A division of Hodder Headline

A Hodder/LIR paperback

3 5 7 9 10 8 6 4 2

ISBN 0340 832630

Typeset in Plantin Light by Hodder Headline Ireland

Printed and bound by
Clays Ltd, St Ives plc

Hodder Headline Ireland
8 Castlecourt Centre, Castleknock
Dublin 15, Ireland
A division of Hodder Headline
338 Euston Road
London NW1 3BH

To Kitty and Peter McWilliams

Prologue

It was 3 a.m. before he made it home and stumbled up to the front door, clutching the broken fingers of his right hand under his armpit. As he turned the key and inhaled the familiar scent of home, the panic began to subside.

Once inside, he bolted the door behind him and leaned against it, breathing heavily. His ears were cocked for any strange sounds. Had the big man followed him? He didn't think that was likely; he had taken the longest possible route. And if they had followed – well, what would he do about that?

He shook his head to clear it and hauled himself up the narrow, threadbare stairs. Every step was agony, jarring his body and sending shock-waves of pain through him in ways he hadn't thought possible.

He made his way across the landing to the bathroom without the need for light. He closed the bathroom door with his hip, leaned over the hand-basin, vomited until his stomach dry-heaved. Then he wiped his mouth on his sleeve, turned on the tap and ran cold water over his wrists. Apart from the fingers, he had lost two teeth and he knew his right eye would be closed for a few days. He didn't think his ribs were broken – bruised badly, but still in one piece. He ran the fingers of his good hand over them, but the pain made the walls of the tiny bathroom blur and he had to sit down heavily on the stained rim of the bath to keep from passing out.

After a few minutes he regained control. He pulled his shirt open and felt around his ribs, pressing gently, trying not to suck air in too deeply. Maybe one or two had snapped after all.

He knew he should have gone to the hospital, but he couldn't risk it in case they asked questions. His breath hitched and he steadied himself with his good hand. No, he'd have to grin and bear it, eat the pain right up. Maybe it was a sign – a sign that he must suffer for all his sins after all.

He blamed himself for his sorry state: he should have checked first, should have taken more care.

He stood up slowly and tiptoed across the landing, past Mother's door, to his own bedroom. He hardly ever used this room any more – not like before, when he had spent every waking moment here. Now he preferred to sleep downstairs on the pullout sofa in the front room. It was easier that way. He could come and go as he pleased without disturbing her. She had *explained* that to him *very* carefully. She did not like to be disturbed.

The curtains were drawn and the grubby mattress smelt of mould and damp. He grimaced as he pulled the curtains open to let in some street-light. God, how he had always hated sleeping in this little shoebox.

Not that he slept much any more. Nightmares – he'd been having the nightmares again. They taunted him, woke him in sweats night after night, making him cry out, unable to hold back the swell of terror as he came screeching back into the waking world.

He closed his eyes, trying to concentrate on the here and now. First things first: he had to do something about this hand. He dropped to his knees and pulled a metal toolbox out from under the bed, propped the lid open against the bed and dug out a roll of masking tape. He stretched out his rapidly swelling hand and, using his aching teeth to tear the tape, taped the three broken fingers together. Sweat gathered on his forehead and dripped down his face as the pain cut through him. Dark spots danced before his eyes, and he had to drop his head onto his knees and take deep gulps of air until the worst of it passed.

After a few minutes he regained enough control to risk moving again. He pulled out an old bicycle-repair kit and flicked it open. He had stashed some of the pills the fat bastard doctor had prescribed for Mother in here. She hadn't missed them. He popped five of them into his mouth and dry-swallowed.

The dull glint of the wedding ring on his left hand bothered him. He popped the finger into his mouth, licked the ring loose and sucked it off, careful to avoid his broken teeth. He spat it into his hand, wiped it carefully against the front of his shirt and dropped it into his pocket. Mother had given it to him as a gift, after her hands had shrunk so much it slipped off every time she reached down. He wore it to reassure the women he was a happily married man.

Appearance was everything.

Appearances were deceptive.

Why did you do it?

He sat up. There was that fucking voice again, the one he thought he knew. He strained to hear which direction it came from, ready to move towards it, to smother it out. But the only sound was the distant drone of the night traffic.

He had made a stupid mistake tonight, assuming the bitch had been working alone.

He'd made a serious error in judgement.

The pain in his hand began to ease slightly. It was amazing how well the pills worked. He smiled and rolled his tongue around his mouth, tasting the sharp, coppery tang of blood. He pushed his tongue through the gap where his teeth had been, wiggling it one way, then the other, savouring the salty taste and the velvety flaps of his gum.

The lesson had been a valuable one.

1

Amanda Harrington stood on the steps of Kilmainham Courthouse and smoked her third cigarette in twenty minutes. She kept her gaze low to avoid any accidental eye contact with the assorted degenerates congregated out there with her. The last thing she wanted was a conversation. She needed time to think.

She scanned around, keeping a wary eye peeled for any of the photographers who sometimes visited the courts if the day's news was slack. She hadn't spotted one, but that didn't mean they weren't there; and discretion was proving difficult. She hadn't worn a tracksuit and didn't own a Puffa jacket or hoop earrings, which were very obviously the fashion for lower-court appearances, and at five foot ten even her height marked her as unusual. She leaned into the grey wall, frozen by the vicious March wind that howled up the steps of the court, and cursed under her breath again. She wrapped her black velvet coat tighter around her body and shook her head in weary resignation.

To her left, a scrawny, unkempt lad of about sixteen picked at his spots and coughed. He seemed impervious to the cold; he was wearing a thin cotton T-shirt, the sleeve rolled high to show off an ugly tattoo of a woman coiled around a knife-blade. Amanda glanced at his hands; he wore a massive sovereign ring on his left pinkie, and each knuckle had a black dot tattooed over it like a badge of honour. He noticed her looking as he finally hacked up whatever was caught in his throat. He curled his lip into a sneer and spit. A yellow ball of phlegm hit the wall near her boots and slid down slowly, leaving a faint silver trail. Amanda turned away and concentrated on studying the graffiti.

Another wave of angry self-pity hit her. This was a farce, a total farce. The Gardaí had no right to drag her and Marna to this godforsaken hole. They weren't criminals – not like the scum she had witnessed pleading their innocence before the judge today: shoplifters, alkies, smackheads, crack-heads, people who would rob the sight out of your eye if you weren't careful; junkies, granny-bashers, joyriders and vandals, thugs and scumbags, the dregs of Dublin. What the hell was she doing here? She didn't belong with this crowd.

Unfortunately, the bitch judge hadn't seen it like that. In fact, to Amanda's growing anger, the judge had taken one long, condescending look over her steel-rimmed glasses at the two women standing before her and had deemed them not just criminals, but criminals of the worst kind.

She had thrown the bloody book at them.

Despite the protests of their two-hundred-euro-an-hour solicitor, the bitch had imposed the maximum fine for a first offence, *and a conviction*. Even Michael Dwyer, the detective sergeant presenting their case, had looked shocked at the severity of her ruling.

Amanda flicked the cigarette butt down the steps, stuffed her hands into the pockets of her coat and brooded over the injustice of it all. Deep in thought, she didn't notice Fergus Collier until he was directly in front of her.

A handsome, cheerful man in his late fifties, Fergus found himself mildly bemused by his surroundings. It had been a long time since he had been to a district court, and he hoped it would be a long time before he was there again.

'Well,' he said, absentmindedly searching for his tobacco pouch in his many pockets. He found it and stuffed his pipe full of Condor tobacco. Only when a puff of pale-blue, aromatic smoke escaped skywards did he continue.

'Well,' he repeated, 'that was interesting. I don't remember her being that moral before. She was quite severe, very intolerant. I really didn't think she'd be that vocal on the subject. My, my … very surprised, I am.'

Amanda pushed herself off the wall and laughed bitterly. 'I fucking knew that was going to happen, I just *knew* it! As soon as I heard we had that bitch, I knew we were bloody screwed. I told you this would happen. Trust me, Fergus, I knew it.'

Fergus puffed on his pipe and eyed his client with a certain amount of pity. She was right, of course: if she had been lucky enough to get an old boy as her judge, she would probably have got off with a slap on the wrist.

'This is bullshit, Fergus,' Amanda fumed. 'What harm are we doing, eh? This fucking backward country … Hypocrites, the lot of them. What – do they think we drag the fuckers in off the street with a gun to their heads? It makes me sick.'

'You were unlucky, my dear,' Fergus said. 'Operation Tailcoat threw out the net to catch the big fish, and unfortunately you little minnows were reeled in with them. It's the nature of the business you're in, I'm afraid. Still, damned unlucky getting her as a judge.'

'It galls me when I think of all the other fuckers who've gotten off for the same shit.' Amanda lowered her voice as she noticed the spotty boy listening with open curiosity. 'I'm talking about guys who were running big places with tons of girls working for them. Only last week Tom McCaul got off with a fine – and he had three places. Where's the justice in that? Where's the Northern prick with the stable of East European girls working twenty-four-bloody-seven? Don't see him sweating his arse off, do you? What about Paul McCracken? Where's that vicious little bastard?'

Over her shoulder, Michael Dwyer emerged from the gloom of the courthouse foyer and squinted into the light. He spotted Fergus and ambled down the steps to join them, clutching his files tightly to his chest. He was a tall, lanky man in his early forties, with thick black hair, a bushy moustache and a perpetually mournful expression, like a hound dog that has lost a scent. Despite appearances, however, he was easy-going and friendly, well-liked and respected on the force.

Amanda Harrington despised him. To her, he might as well have been the Devil himself.

'There you are.' He nodded to Amanda. 'Well, at least that's all over. There's nothing worse than having these things hanging over your head.'

'Are you for real?' Amanda said in disbelief. 'Thanks to you, I'll have a criminal record for the rest of my life. Thanks to you, I've been humiliated and treated like a fucking scumbag – but, yeah, it's best not to have it hanging over my head. Congratulations, Sergeant, you must be *very* proud of yourself: justice has been well and truly served. Excuse me.'

She brushed past him and trotted back up the steps into the court to search for Marna Galloway, who was now, quite literally, her partner in crime.

Michael watched her go, his forlorn expression deepening. 'You know, I didn't have any choice about bringing them to court,' he said to Fergus. 'The directions came back from the Director of Public Prosecutions. It was completely out of my hands after that.'

Fergus chuckled and sucked on his pipe. 'She's

very angry about the whole carry-on. Although I must say I thought old Judy was very harsh on them.'

'You can appeal against the ruling, you know – maybe get the fine lessened.'

Fergus cocked an eyebrow. 'I don't think the money is bothering her, do you?'

Michael's moustache drooped further. 'No, probably not.'

'It was very good of you to give them a few days' notice before their actual arrest. I gather that's not standard practice.'

'I didn't think it was necessary to send squad cars to get them this morning. I knew they would turn up.' Michael sighed and shifted his weight from one foot to the other. 'I mean, let's face it: they're hardly Dublin's most wanted.'

'Indeed. Still, it was good of you, and I'm sure they appreciate it.'

'I doubt it.'

'They will when they cool off a bit,' Fergus said. He sucked on his pipe again and gave Michael a thoughtful look. It could have been an act, of course – members of the force were, in his view, consummate actors – but the Garda did seem genuinely sorry.

A few minutes later, Amanda and Marna Galloway appeared at the main door together. They were deep in a huddled conversation, and, as Michael watched them, he was surprised to see Amanda laugh. Marna glanced at him and dug

Amanda in the ribs; Amanda stopped laughing and looked at Michael with such contempt that he felt deeply annoyed. After all, it was hardly his fault they were prostitutes. He glanced down and studied the ground for a second. He didn't know why Amanda Harrington affected him the way she did.

At thirty, Marna was a year older than Amanda. She was tall, curvaceous and very striking; with her pale skin, high cheekbones and wide almond-shaped eyes, she could easily pass for a Russian. Her long blonde hair was swept into an elaborate up-do (she'd had it done in the hairdresser's that morning, especially for her court appearance). She wore a long, cream cashmere dress and a soft black leather jacket trimmed with fur. Expensive gold jewellery glinted every time she moved. She oozed confidence and style. Every head in the place turned to watch her as she slowly made her way towards Michael and Fergus.

'Now that is an ordeal I don't want to repeat in a hurry!' she declared, making direct eye contact with Michael. 'That old judge of yours was a pure cunt. You sure can fucking pick them, Detective. Did you see the way she looked at us? And what about the fines? A grand and a half … each! Can she really do that, Fergus?'

Fergus shrugged. 'I'm afraid she can.'

'Typical. We had to get a bloody woman who wants to make an example of us. What the hell was her name again?'

'Judy Hanrahan,' said Michael.

'Judy Hanrahan – that's a name I won't forget,' Amanda said softly. She looked at Michael through cold grey eyes. 'I can add it to my list of people not to send Christmas cards to.'

'Michael here says you can appeal if you like,' Fergus said.

Marna snorted and patted her hair. 'Bollocks to that! Why would we bother? Unless you're going to say that you made a mistake when you raided us, mixed us up with someone else. If you're not, then I don't see the point in going back into a courtroom to be sneered at by some bitch in dire need of HRT.' She smiled at him. Her green eyes crackled with sudden mischief. 'Oh, go on, Mickey, my boy – are you going to say you made a mistake?'

Michael looked even more uncomfortable. 'I can't do that,' he said.

As fast as she had switched the charm on, Marna switched it off, managing to look completely bored in an instant. 'I didn't think so.'

Amanda shook her head. 'I can't believe she turned us down when we offered to donate the money to the court poor-box. What did she say again? She wasn't accepting "contaminated" money.'

'Contaminated! What did she think we were going to do – yank the money out of our fannies and drop it into the box? Contaminated, my arse. If it was that dirty, why do we have to pay a fine at all? Where does she think we're going to get the cash for that? From our trust funds?'

'I imagine she thought you could well afford a hefty fine.' Fergus pointed at Marna's heavy gold bracelet with his pipe.

'I did tell you to dress down,' Michael said quietly.

Marna turned to him in amazement. 'Why should I? I've earned the right to wear what I like! Just because I have to visit the sewer doesn't mean I have to dress the part.' She glanced around. 'Anyway, I don't think I *have* anything like what passes for clothes here.'

'I'm just saying that, for the purposes of a court visit, it might have been—'

Marna ignored him. She wrinkled her nose and shrugged deeper into her coat. 'Fergus, honey, can we get out of here now? This place is making me depressed.'

Fergus patted some more pockets, searching for keys. 'I'm ready whenever you are.'

'Then let's go.' Marna turned to the detective and jabbed him in the chest with her finger. 'Next time we run into each other, you'd better have an appointment. No more sudden arrivals, right? We were good girls; we co-operated fully with you, for all the good it did us. Now it's your turn: you've got to stick to your word. No more fucking raids! You've done us now, right?'

Michael Dwyer sighed heavily. 'Don't worry, you won't be getting any more unexpected visits. I hope you both realise I was doing my job. If it was up to me, you wouldn't be here at all.'

Amanda shot him a filthy look. 'Oh, sure,' she said. 'That makes everything all right, then. You feel bad. We understand.'

Marna placed a restraining hand on her arm and smiled sweetly. 'We do understand. As long as you realise that we're doing our job. Anyway, what's done is done – no point in crying about it now. Fergus, let's get the hell out of here before we're robbed again.'

Fergus and Michael exchanged firm handshakes. 'It was nice to meet you, Michael, even if the circumstances weren't the best.'

'You too.'

Marna stuck out her hand. 'See you, Mickey boy. Don't worry about the fines too much.' She winked at him playfully. 'Sure, it's not even a week's wages.'

Michael laughed and shook her hand. She was such a cheeky miss, it was hard not to like her. He turned to Amanda and held out his hand. She snorted, turned on her heel and walked off. She wasn't as forgiving.

Michael watched the trio climb into Fergus's silver Mercedes. The truth was, he didn't feel particularly good about bringing them to court. They weren't pimps; they didn't make money from anyone else. They worked for themselves, and both women seemed to have a handle on what they were doing. As the car pulled off, he wished to God he could leave as well, but unfortunately he had three other cases to present. Reshuffling his files, he climbed the courthouse steps with slumped shoulders, resigned to the long day ahead.

Fergus Collier drove slowly along the canal, listening with mild amusement to the women bitching with gusto about their treatment at the hands of the court.

'It's fucking stupid! If I'm working on my own I'm not committing a crime, but if I'm working with Amanda we're running an illegal business. It doesn't make any fucking sense.'

'It is the law,' Fergus said mildly.

'I don't know why you're so fucking friendly with that prick Dwyer, Marna. He really stuck the knife in today. I mean, did he really have to tell the old bitch about my client in such detail?'

Marna laughed. 'Come off it, Amanda. What the hell did you expect? Jesus.' She shook her head. 'I thought her eyes were gonna pop out of her crusty head when he was describing the harness.'

'Why did he have to tell her about the gag?'

'As far as I can tell,' Fergus said, 'Dwyer wasn't exactly overjoyed about bringing you to court today.'

Amanda snorted with derision. 'Give it a rest, Fergus. Don't tell me you fall for that sorry shit. He's wearing his nice face today, like he did to get a fucking statement out of us. Honestly, he makes me sick! Apologising one minute and sticking the knife in the next.'

'There's no point in being angry with him.' Marna turned around in the front seat to face her friend. Ever since the raid Amanda had grown increasingly angry and tense, nothing like her usual good-natured self. She was jumpy and often took days off at short notice without any explanation. They used to meet on Sundays for a cocktail or two; now they never did. Amanda looked tired and drawn; Marna was beginning to worry about her. 'You know he's the monkey, not the organ-grinder. His boss was at the back of the court – I saw the little gnome there, slinking about. How do you think it would look if Mickey went easy on us? Like the man said, he's just doing his job. Look, Amanda, we knew this had to happen sooner or later. And, on the plus side, every cloud has a silver lining.'

Marna started to laugh, and Fergus looked puzzled.

'What's so funny?' he asked. He glanced at Amanda in the rear-view mirror. She wasn't laughing; if anything, she looked even angrier.

'Don't ask me,' she said. 'Ask Miss Easily Entertained here.'

'Do you remember when we were standing up in the front of the court, while that wretched bitch was tearing strips off us?' Marna said gleefully.

'Of course.'

'While she was droning on, I had a good look at the other members of the Vice team. You know, know thine enemy.'

'Indeed.'

'So I'm looking about, and next thing you know, I saw a face I thought I recognised from somewhere. Now, there's nothing odd in that, but he was doing his level best to hide from me. So I knew he was a bloody client, right?'

'Ah.' Fergus nodded.

'I thought to myself, Don't embarrass the stupid git by making it obvious I've clocked him. So, after that judge bitch finished her little speech, I deliberately avoided eye contact. Until, that is, I saw Michael "please forgive me" Dwyer handing him a file.' She laughed again. 'That stopped me dead in my tracks! No wonder the fucker was trying to avoid me. He's a Vice cop.'

'Really?' Fergus said with a shocked laugh. 'Are you sure he was a client?'

'Positive, although not a recent one – he's from a while back. But I never forget a face. I saw Dwyer go outside, and I went straight over, grabbed your man by the arm and asked him if I could have a quick word in private – and, Fergus, I'm not joking, he nearly shat himself. Of course he said yes, so out we went into the foyer. I swear, I nearly throttled him with my bare hands. "You could have bloody warned us, you prick!" I said to him. "I didn't know it was you," she mimicked, falsetto. "'Oh, please don't say you know me, please." You can imagine what I said to him!'

'Oh, I can imagine,' Fergus said.

Marna laughed nastily at the memory. 'I said I'd

think about it, and that my thinking would be greatly influenced by a lack of future police presence. Then she came in.' Marna jerked her head in Amanda's direction. 'All fire and fucking brimstone.'

Amanda snorted in the back seat. Fergus almost felt sorry for the man.

Marna ignored her. 'She had him totally freaked out.'

'Marna gave him one of our business cards and says, if he has any more questions, give her a call,' Amanda finished. 'It was all very civilised.'

'Well, I always say keep your friends close and your enemies on the hop,' said Marna, admiring her nails. 'You never know when you might need a little help from the cops. Better to have them on side.'

'On side! There's no such thing as on side with that lot. You shouldn't have messed with him. Those bastards are dangerous.'

'Amanda, lighten up. I was only teasing.'

Fergus shook his head. He wasn't a criminal lawyer; his sedate world revolved around accident claims and property. These rare adventures into the murkier side of life on Amanda's behalf never ceased to both amuse and repel him. Just when he thought nothing else could surprise him, something invariably did.

'Fergus?' Amanda said. 'Will you drop us off in George's Street, please? I need a fucking drink. You want to come with us?'

Fergus declined with some regret. 'I can't, I'm afraid; I've got to get back to the office at some stage today. But thanks for the offer.'

'Any time, pet, any time.' She gave him a warm smile and patted his shoulder. She had a genuine fondness for Fergus; he had never judged her, and they went back a long way. 'Maybe next time.'

'I'd love to.'

Fergus dropped them off outside the Globe pub and watched them stroll down the street. He didn't know Marna that well, but he knew Amanda. She was a nice woman and he admired her. But sometimes he wished she'd put her intelligence to some better use than prostitution. If she put her mind to it, she could do anything she liked. Surprised at his paternal feelings, he switched on his indicator and pulled out into the heavy traffic.

2

Sandy Walsh painted her toenails lilac. Little white puffballs of cotton-wool separated her toes as she carefully applied the lacquer. She held them out to admire her handiwork, pleased that the colour looked well against her lightly tanned skin.

She checked her watch. She had about half an hour before her last appointment of the day – plenty of time to relax a little and grab a bite to eat. Walking on her heels into the little kitchenette, she boiled the kettle for a cup of tea, rummaged about in the fridge and grabbed a low-fat chicken supreme, which she popped into the microwave to heat up. When everything was ready, she went back to the sofa and flicked through the magazine she had been reading earlier.

Her daughter's confirmation was only a few weeks away, and she had spotted some nice outfits that didn't cost a fortune. She was determined to look well for her little girl's big day. After the amount she'd spent on her daughter's outfit, she deserved something special for herself.

Sandy smiled as she thought of her kids. They were the pride of her life. It hadn't been easy bringing them up on her own, but she had managed. Sandy's husband had walked out on her when her daughter was a year old and her son on the way. Darren Walsh had left her with no money, mortgage arrears, unpaid bills and little self-respect.

The bastard, Sandy thought smugly. But she'd had the last laugh. The last time she'd laid eyes on Darren Walsh had been the previous Christmas. The bastard had come home, for the first time in years; he was sitting in the lounge of her local pub like a bloody lord, nodding to people, head held high, as if he had never abandoned his wife and kids and run off with a fucking tart. Sandy had watched him from a snug, biting back her anger, refusing to fly across the room and scratch his eyes right out of his head. But the longer she'd sat there, the cooler she'd become.

Darren had changed. He was no longer handsome and whippet-thin. His clothes were cheap and fitted badly, and his hair, his pride and joy, was receding – she was pretty sure she could see his scalp under the dim bar-lights. Confident that she was holding the cards, she had said goodbye to her friends and walked past his table on her way to the door.

Sandy had taken great pleasure in cocking her nose that inch higher and saying, 'Why, hello, Darren, Imelda! Enjoying your Christmas?'

When he'd realised it was her, Darren Walsh's jaw had almost hit the ground. He'd spluttered

Carlsberg into his glass and had a coughing fit. The bitch he'd left her for had almost shat herself too; the look of sheer loathing on her pasty face could have soured milk at ten yards. Sandy had smiled then. It had been worth the wait, worth every insufferable client with rough hands and bad BO. The look on her husband's face, as his beady little eyes travelled over her freshly styled hair and her best suit, had wiped away every bad moment in an instant. And when he'd asked her if she wanted a drink, and got himself a dig from the greasy bitch he was shacked up with, Sandy Walsh had almost whooped with delight. Her polite refusal before she sashayed out of the pub and back to her beautiful little house had been twice as cutting as any swear-word she could have come up with.

The annoying trill of her mobile phone brought Sandy out of her memories with a bang. God, she had been lost in thought. She answered it with her heart hammering in her chest.

'Hello.'

'Hello there, heh, heh, heh, Sandy. Is that yourself?'

Sandy recognised the loud country accent: Paddy, a good, but highly annoying, client.

'Howya, Paddy. Sure, of course it's me. Was it not my phone you rang?'

'Well now, pet, sure as eggs is eggs, you can't be too careful these days. All this newfangled techno-no … oligy. Heh, heh, heh. Now, listen till I tell you

– I'll be up that way on Thursday around lunchtime. Any chance I can call in to see you then?'

"Paddy, you just let me know when you want to call. I'll be waiting for you,' she answered sweetly.

'What about two o'clock? Would that be all right for you?'

'Two would be perfect, Paddy.'

'Great stuff, heh, heh, heh. So that's two o'clock on Thursday, then.'

'That's right, pet. I'll see you then.'

'Right so, Sandy, that's perfect. Bye-bye, God bless. So it's two o'clock, then. On Thursday.'

Sandy rolled her eyes skywards. 'OK, Paddy, see you then. Bye.'

'Bye, pet. See you on Thursday. At two o'clock.'

Sandy hung up. Poor old Paddy; he really was a nice old devil, but he drove her mad. She knew that he was coming up on Thursday, and at what time. It was the same appointment he had every week. She knew he had to ring to confirm it. It was all part of the game to Paddy. The call somehow made it more official, like he was going on a date.

She shook her head and chastised herself. She had no right to be impatient with the poor old cratur. So what if Paddy repeated himself? It was hardly the worst thing in the world to put up with. If half her clients were as decent as Paddy, she'd be on the pig's back.

She stood up and stretched. Her client would be there soon, and she didn't want to look like she had been slobbing around all day. She picked up a make-up bag the size of a small handbag and started to apply some frosted pink lipstick.

She had no right to get annoyed with any of them. If it hadn't been for them, she would have been rightly screwed by now. Some of them, like old Paddy, had been visiting her for years. They treated her well and they were loyal – better than any boyfriend, that's for sure, she thought sourly. One of them, Barry the mechanic, had even paid the deposit on this little flat for her.

True, it was small and a little bit dingy. But it meant that she'd had somewhere to work after that bastard Tricky had chucked her out on her arse last year. And at least it was in a basement, so it had its own front door. Sandy could come and go as she pleased without the neighbours watching her every move. Best of all, it was easy to find. Clients didn't like to drive around looking for a place; nothing spoiled the mood faster than that.

She had thought it would be hard to work on her own, after the company of the women in the parlour. To her surprise, it wasn't. She had a television, a radio and peace and quiet. It suited her to come in and spend a few hours working without talking to another soul. It suited her to work whenever she saw fit. If a day was slow and she had only a few appointments, she could go home early. In fact, she often wondered why she hadn't started working alone before she had been forced to. At least she couldn't be arrested for working this way. With two kids to think of, she couldn't afford to have the police on her back or her name in the papers.

She was about to sit back down when the doorbell rang. Sandy glanced at her watch; her client was early. 'Bollix.'

Smoothing the silky nightie over her hips and fluffing out her hair, she hurried to the door. She stopped and checked her reflection in the hall mirror, tilting her head this way and that. Sandy couldn't resist a smile. Not bad for a woman fast approaching forty. She opened the door. 'God, you're an eager little fella to—'

The man standing on the doorstep was not her client. Sandy's smile faltered for a split second. He looked familiar, but for the life of her she couldn't place him. He was tall, in his early thirties, medium build and average looks. His dark hair was too long and a hank of it fell over his eyes. Sandy looked at him closely. As he lifted his hand to push his hair back, she clocked the wedding band and relaxed. Married. What was she worrying about? He had 'client' written all over him.

'Sorry, love, appointments only.' She stuck her head around the door, concealing her body. There was no point in giving him a free gawk if he wasn't staying.

The man smiled shyly. Sandy noticed he was missing a tooth on the left side of his mouth.

'I'm very sorry. You were recommended by a friend.'

'Yeah? Which friend would this be?'

The man shuffled his feet. 'His name is John.'

Sandy cocked an eyebrow. 'Yeah, well, that narrows it down a bit. And what's your name?'

'John.'

Sandy stared at him for a few seconds and he stared right back. It was an obvious lie, and it wasn't the first time she'd heard it, but normally they laughed a little when they said it; this guy didn't even crack a smile.

'Whatcha looking at, John?'

'Your hair. I like your hair.'

'Thanks.' Sandy stared at him a little longer. He was definitely familiar; maybe she'd looked after him before. 'All right, you may as well come on in now, since you're here. I can't give you the full half-hour, mind. I've an appointment in twenty minutes, so it'll have to be a quick one.' She opened the door a bit further.

He didn't move an inch. 'You have an appointment?'

'Yeah, I have.' Sandy felt her irritation grow. She wondered if this was going to be a waste of her time. Sometimes the fuckers liked to talk on the step, then head off and wank in their cars. 'You coming in, or what? Can't stand here all day.'

'I don't want to be rushed.' John looked at his watch and scratched his head. 'I could call back in a while.'

Sandy chewed on her lip as she thought about it. 'I'm heading home after my next client,' she said.

John shrugged and gave a quick nod of his head. 'All right.' Abruptly he turned and walked away.

Sandy calculated rapidly. If he wanted to stay for an hour, she could charge him about a hundred and twenty. That would bring the day's money up to almost three hundred. With the confirmation coming up, she would be a right eejit to turn it down. Who knew, what with all the bleeding raids going on, when she would make this much money again? She made her decision.

'Here, John, wait!'

He turned back to her straight away.

'Listen, love, I've got to take this other client now. If you want to call back in about an hour's time, I'll wait for you. Then you can stay for the hour with no rush. Is that any use to you?' She beamed at him, easing one breast around the door and into sight. 'If you do call back, I'll make it worth your while.'

John stared at the barely covered breast and blinked hard. 'I promise I'll be back in exactly one hour.' He took another quick look at Sandy's breast, turned away and bounded up the basement steps.

As Sandy watched him go, she tried to remember where she'd met him before. It wouldn't come to her, no matter how hard she tried, and she gave up and closed the door. How was she supposed to remember every client she had ever looked after? Even the name – John … honestly, couldn't they ever come up with anything original?

Sandy's next client – Larry, a tax inspector from Mallow – arrived right on time. Sandy spent most of the half-hour fussing over him, listening to his woes, boosting his ego and fondling his flaccid dick. Sandy felt sorry for Larry and he was definitely her easiest client. Most of their time together was spent bitching about his wife, who'd run off with a meat-packer from Belfast the year before. Sandy didn't blame the woman – not that she ever let on; why would a wife stay with a man who couldn't rise to any occasion?

As Larry was leaving, he leaned across and gave her a kiss on the cheek. 'Here's a little something for the kids.' He pushed a twenty-euro note into her bra and kissed the tops of her breasts.

'Ah, there's no need,' she said, grabbing the money as fast as she could in case he changed his mind. She shooed him out the door and hurried back into the warmth of the sitting room to add the unexpected tip to her steadily increasing funds.

She was delighted with herself. The day was turning out well. The new guy was due back soon, and with his money under her belt she might be able to afford new shoes, too. Sandy brushed her hair and applied fresh lipstick. This John wasn't a regular of hers, but, if she gave him a really good time, he would be. That was the one thing she was confident of: she was damn good in the sack.

When there was no sign of him after the hour

was up, she wasn't too bothered. It happened sometimes. If you couldn't take them straight away, they went off to another place. The money would have been nice, but Sandy had been too long in the business to worry about things she couldn't help.

She began to tidy up the flat, getting ready to head for home. Her thoughts turned to the outfit she was going to buy. She deserved to get something really nice for herself.

She was getting into her street clothes when the doorbell rang. Sandy slid her jeans off, fluffed out her hair and ran for the door. It was John; he hadn't found someone else after all.

'Come on in, love.'

'Thank you for waiting.'

He stepped into the small hall, carrying a sports bag over his left shoulder. Sandy tried to remember if he'd had it with him earlier. She noticed the wedding ring on his finger and smirked: another 'happily married man' with time on his hands.

'Ah, sure, I know, love; parking anywhere in the city is impossible these days. Sure, you're here now.' She showed him down to the bedroom. 'Do you still want to book in for the hour?'

'I don't have the time,' he said apologetically. 'I have to get back home soon.'

Sandy shrugged. 'Sure, love, I understand. Would you like to have a shower first?'

'Yes,' he said, looking around the room. He

dropped his bag onto the floor and turned back to her. 'This is a nice place; it's … very homey.'

'Ah, thanks, love. I do my best.' Sandy watched as his eyes roamed her body, and decided to get her money in case he was just a looker. 'John, I don't mean to be rude, but can I get my money now? No offence, but I prefer to be paid up front, if you don't mind.'

'Oh, of course you do.' He reached for the inside pocket of his jacket and pulled out his wallet. 'How much do you think I should give you?'

'That'll be sixty quid.'

He opened his wallet and extracted the money, carefully counting it out on the bed before handing it to her. As soon as the cash lay in Sandy's hand, she relaxed a little. 'Now, pet, how about that shower?'

'Please, can you give me a few minutes to prepare?' He smiled shyly and pushed his hair back off his forehead. 'I'll be ready in a few minutes.'

Sandy nodded. Sometimes they were shy; he probably didn't want to get undressed in front of her.

'I'll tell you what: there's a shower room just through that door over there – shower gels and everything at the ready. You work away, and I'll be back in a few minutes.'

The client nodded. 'Thank you.'

Sandy closed the door and went back into the sitting room. She checked the money carefully against the light before she slipped it into her bag. She had to be careful; there were a lot of fake twenties floating about. She grabbed a fresh towel from the hot press and a condom from her bag and went back to the bedroom.

'Now, love, let me just ... Oh, you're still dressed, then?'

John was exactly where she had left him. He hadn't taken off his jacket or moved an inch. His head was cocked as if he was listening to something.

'Are you all right there, love?'

'I'm sorry, I thought I heard something.' He shrugged and stared at her legs. 'I'm very nervous.'

'Ah, Jaysus.' Sandy sighed and took a step into the room. 'You've got nothing to be nervous about. You're in good hands.' She laughed. 'Or, at least, you will be when you get your kit off. Want me to give you a hand out of those pants?'

John shook his head. 'No.' He began to remove his jacket. 'I suppose it has to be this way sometimes.'

'Eh ... yeah, sure, everyone gets nervous.' Sandy went past him to get a hanger from the wardrobe, but she suddenly felt uneasy. There was something off about the way he was watching her every move. Gut instincts, honed to near-perfection after years on the job, began to kick in. Maybe he was nervous, like he said – lots of first-timers were – but there was something off-putting about him.

'If you want, you can hang your clothes in

here.' She passed him a hanger for his coat. There it was again – nothing much; a look. She would feel a lot better when he was naked. At least she'd know he wasn't a reporter or, worse, a bloody cop. She went back to the bedroom door and reached for the handle.

'It has to be this way. I understand that now. I didn't before.' He said it softly but clearly.

Sandy's shoulders stiffened; she began to turn. 'Here, listen, John, don't be too hard—'

He lunged at her, grabbed her by the hair and slammed her head into the doorjamb. The impact split Sandy's eyebrow open. Stunned, she tried to turn around. Blood ran into her eye, and when she lifted her hand to her head she was horrified to see her fingers covered by the dark, warm liquid. Instinct told her to run, run and scream the place down. She drew a deep breath and opened her mouth.

This time he hit her in the face with a closed fist, as hard as he could. It smashed into her cheekbone and Sandy's legs buckled underneath her. The whole attack had taken less than thirty seconds; but Sandy already knew she had wasted her one chance to get out. With a terrified moan, she slid down the door and onto the floor.

'John' gently swayed with excitement. He poked her crumpled body with his foot to make sure she was completely out. Satisfied that she wouldn't be going anywhere for a while, he grabbed his sports bag, opened it and checked inside. He had everything. He pulled on a pair of surgical gloves and, turning back to the prone woman, grabbed her by her ankles and hauled her across the floor. Quietly he stepped over her, opened the door and slipped silently out into the hall.

He was sure she worked alone, but he had fallen for that trap before. Moving stealthily up the hall, he paused and listened before gently pushing the sitting-room door open. He stuck his head around the door and breathed a sigh of relief. He scanned the room quickly, taking in everything at once. Sandy's bag stood on the little coffee table. He picked it up and tipped it out onto the floor. Lipstick, tissues, keys, all the usual crap that cluttered a woman's handbag tumbled out. Nothing of interest.

Why did you do it?

He ignored that fucking voice, squatted down on his hunkers and let his gaze roam the room. His eyes rested on the sofa. He reached out and lifted the first cushion: nothing. Lifting the next one, he found a wallet, a mobile phone and a notebook. He opened the wallet first. A photo of two little kids smiled out at him. He ignored them and extracted both his money and whatever else was there, slipped the cash into his back pocket and tossed the wallet among the contents of her bag. Next he turned his attention to the notebook.

He flicked through it quickly. His eyes narrowed as he read names he was already familiar with, complete with phone numbers and addresses. He stuck it into his pocket. He ignored her mobile phone, didn't want to touch that.

After a brief search of the flat, he was certain that he had everything of value. Now all that remained was to take care of the whore.

Sandy was still unconscious. Blood had seeped from the deep gash over her eye into her hair. Her cheek was beginning to swell. John grabbed her by the hair, yanked her head around and stared at her for a few seconds. Her eyes flickered, and with a grimace he dropped her head back to the floor. He knew he didn't have much time; the last thing he wanted was for her to wake up and start screaming the place down.

He opened his bag and took out the rolls of cling-film and an old-fashioned nylon headscarf, the type that older ladies wore to church. This one was navy blue, with a gold Celtic-style trim and a print of a horse's head, also in gold. He placed these items gently on the bed and turned back to Sandy.

He was repulsed by the look of her. How could this bitch have thought that he would pay her to put her disgusting body anywhere near his? Even now he could barely bring himself to touch her. They were plague-carriers, infectious, germ-ridden, dirty whores. And this one had been so eager for him to return – showing him her disgusting, saggy tit like that. He trembled and took a deep breath.

Why did you do it?

'*Shut up!*' John stared at Sandy. Had she said that? Did she know about the other voice? She hadn't moved; he hadn't seen her mouth move. He was certain she couldn't have said it. But who knew with these whores? They were capable of anything.

He ripped off Sandy's nightie, leaving her exposed on the ground in her bra and knickers. He picked up the first roll of cling-film and began to wind it around her feet, binding them tightly together, then around her hands. He continued to wrap until the roll ran out at her waist; then he tossed the cardboard tube aside and calmly started the next roll, covering her head this time. He knelt on Sandy's chest and wrapped the clear plastic around her head, overlapping the layers slightly to be certain they were secure. He left her mouth and her hair free. He had to be quick, though; she was starting to come round, he could feel her starting to move, and he didn't want to hit her again.

He stood up, admired his handiwork and smiled. She wouldn't be going anywhere now.

He scooped up the used condoms he had found in the bin and put them next to her.

Sandy moaned softly, and for a second he froze. Then he grabbed her hair again, yanked her head back and wrapped the rest of the roll around her neck until it reached her chin. He picked up the used condoms, grabbed her lower jaw and violently wrenched her mouth open. He stuffed the condoms into her mouth one by one, making her gag and retch as he pushed them down her throat. She struggled to push them out with her tongue, and he used his fingers to wedge them further into her mouth. Forcing her mouth closed, he grabbed the plastic and wound it around her head, covering her mouth, until he finished the roll and he could not see her features clearly any more.

'It's good that you swallow the filth; you need to swallow, or you will die.'

John waited. He watched as the whore struggled to free herself. He felt her body double up and knew she had vomited. It was unlikely she would be able to swallow now. It didn't matter. After a few minutes she didn't move any more. The plastic around her mouth stopped sucking in, and she was quiet and still.

John stood up and stretched. His back was aching. He'd give it a few more minutes to be on the safe side. He threw the empty rolls into his sports bag and sat on the side of the bed, watching the still shape on the ground, a dreamy calm on his sweating face.

After a few minutes, he leaned forward and nudged Sandy with the toe of his boot. When he was certain she was gone, he pulled her body back across the room and hoisted her up onto the bed. He propped her up against the headboard in a sitting position, pulled the sheets back and carefully laid them across her lap, tucking them in around her. She looked so peaceful and quiet it almost broke his heart. He stood and gazed at her with tears in his eyes; then he picked up the headscarf and arranged it carefully over her blonde hair, tying it in a neat bow beneath her chin.

He stepped back from the bed and stared at his creation. He tilted his head and frowned: she wasn't quite right. He undid the headscarf and tied it behind her, at the base of her neck. Now, now she was perfect; now he had created perfection. His tears flowed freely as he sat back down on the side of the bed and whispered to her, resting his head on Sandy's cooling fingers. Her words echoed in his ears.

I'll make it worth your while.

He smiled and nuzzled closer to her. She certainly had.

3

Amanda Harrington sat at an antique walnut desk and drank her second cup of coffee. She watched a weak sun try to penetrate the early-morning fog. Dublin was awakening to another miserable spring day.

She was in her favourite old leather wingback chair, dressed in a grey tracksuit and a pair of runners that had seen better days. She had gone out early to get the papers, to check if her name appeared in any of them. She hadn't spotted any reporters at the court the day before, but that didn't mean she and Marna were in the clear. It would be typical of her luck if someone had rung the papers to give them their names in exchange for a few quid. People were vicious that way, in her experience.

She picked up the phone to leave a message for Marna and was surprised when her friend answered after the third ring.

'You're up early.'

'Yeah, don't I know it. I'm on my way out for the papers.'

'Don't bother. I've already checked. We're not in them; they must have missed us.'

'Thank fuck for that. Let's wait and see if we escape the Sunday tabloids before we start patting ourselves on the back.'

'Fingers crossed, Marna, fingers crossed. Go back to bed; I'll see you in the office.' 'The office' was their name for the two-bedroomed apartment they rented on Mount Street, a five-minute walk from Stephen's Green.

Amanda picked up her cup and went to the French doors that led out to a pot-filled balcony. She opened them wide and stepped out to breathe in the cool morning air. At this time of year it was barren out here – she had cut all the plants back – but in the summer the terracotta pots were filled with large mop-headed hydrangeas and geraniums, plants that even Amanda couldn't kill too easily. Still, the view alone was worth coming out for. She leaned against the railing and stared out over the city.

Amanda had bought this penthouse overlooking the River Liffey a few months before the property boom exploded in 1996. Initially she had wanted a house, but she had fallen in love with the place as soon as she viewed it. It was close to everything. She could walk to the city centre in five minutes. And there was the size. The apartment had been built before space became a valuable commodity; it had three bedrooms, and the master, with a bathroom en suite, was almost as large as the sitting room in her last rented apartment. There was a second bathroom across the hall, off the sitting room. The kitchen was smallish, but fully functional – not that it mattered; Amanda didn't really do much cooking. The real selling point had been the split-level sitting room, with its wall of exposed brick, its large French doors and its balcony overlooking the Liffey. As soon as she had clapped eyes on the view, she had known that it had to be hers. If there was one good thing about the business she was in, it was that money was seldom an object.

Today, however, the view was not worth the freezing, so Amanda made her way into the kitchen to get a bowl of Sugar Puffs. She poured the milk over her cereal, plugged in her mobile phone on the counter by the microwave and left it to recharge.

Bowl in hand, she went back into the sitting room and switched on the TV to catch the eight o'clock news on Sky. But her mind wandered, as always, back to her situation.

They had escaped the papers. Other girls she knew hadn't been so fortunate. Only last week she had spotted two separate reports on people she knew by name, outed in the tabloids. One poor cow had been photographed leaving the court, and her picture had appeared next to the headline 'Brothel Madam Faces Conviction'. The woman, as far as Amanda knew, wasn't running a brothel at all. She worked with two girls in a crummy flat off Dorset Street. Not that it mattered: innocent or guilty, they were all tarred with the one brush in the eyes of the law. And the fucking tabloids and the useless hacks loved a whiff of sex and scandal. It sold papers. Fuckers, she thought sourly.

The doorbell rang.

Amanda kept her private life and her business strictly separate; they never crossed – with the exception of one man. And, at three minutes past eight, the exception had rung her doorbell.

Colin O'Riordan was a short, pleasant, insignificant-looking man in his mid-fifties, who worked as a financial advisor with a large independent bank. He was also the father of three adult children and the husband of Grace, a housewife with whom he had a successful twenty-four-year marriage. He was a likeable man, well respected in his work for his even temper and sharp mind. His wife still found him attractive, even after years together. He didn't smoke, drank socially, and the only drugs he abused were Rennies and Anadin. He was happy and content-ed, an advert for the good life. His only vice was the one fetish he couldn't resist.

Every Tuesday and Thursday morning, Colin left his detached house in Dublin's leafy south side and drove the two and a half miles into the city centre. There, he parked his deep-green Volvo estate in the underground car park nearest to his office. He said a cheery good morning to the attendant and rode the lift up to the street level, as he did every morning. But on Tuesdays and Thursdays he emerged onto the street and, instead of turning left towards his workplace, turned right and made his way back down along the quays. He walked briskly to the front of Amanda's building, keyed himself in with the security code and rode another lift to the top floor. On the way up, he examined his appearance in the tinted mirrors to make sure he was presentable.

He did this twice a week, every week, unless he happened to be away on holidays. He never changed or varied his routine. Routine was very important to Colin. It formed the basis of the man he was.

At the sound of the bell, Amanda got up from the sofa and made her way down the hall. She opened the front door wide and signalled the little man in without a word.

Colin bounded into the hall. 'Good morning, Madame. And how are we feeling today?' he inquired, beaming at her. 'I hope you slept well. You look wonderful.'

'I'm wearing a tracksuit.' Amanda closed the door and glared at him. 'You're late.'

The effect was immediate. Colin's smile vanished, replaced by a crestfallen expression. 'Oh, no, Madame … I am so dreadfully sorry. I know you don't want to hear excuses, but really, the traffic was appalling today.' He wrung his hands frantically in front of him. 'Oh, please, Madame – it won't happen again, Madame. I promise. You must forgive me.'

Amanda exhaled deeply and brushed past him

on her way back to the sitting room. 'Get changed. I don't have all day, you know.'

Colin slumped against the door with relief. 'Yes, Madame. Thank you for being so understanding, Madame.'

He scurried off into the spare bedroom, muttering under his breath, apparently furious with himself for his tardiness.

Amanda went back to the sitting room, lit a cigarette and settled back down on the sofa to watch the news. Five minutes later Colin, resplendent in a PVC French maid's uniform, came tottering into view.

Colin loved this uniform. Sometimes he dreamt about it in his sleep. The day Amanda had thrown him the brown paper bag containing it, he had almost fainted with joy. He would have kissed her, if she had allowed that sort of thing. The dress was perfect. It was black, bottom-skimmingly short, with white puffball sleeves and a lacy white collar; it even had stiff underskirts to hold it in its proper position. Over it went a white PVC apron, which he tied in a neat bow behind him. On top of his grey head sat a cap of white lace, pinned with great aplomb. Opaque stockings adorned his skinny legs and, on his size-ten feet, a pair of black court shoes completed his immaculate image. Colin preferred to wear stilettos, but the clicking of heels on Amanda's wooden floors annoyed her so much that she had banned them. Colin had duly obliged and reluctantly replaced them with rubber-soled court shoes. While he rather felt they spoilt the look, they were far more comfortable and practical.

'What would you like me to do first, Madame?' Colin asked, frowning at the cereal bowl and the overflowing ashtray perched on the arm of the sofa. It horrified him that Madame had such bad eating habits. He had offered to make her breakfast once, only to be informed that she could light her own fags.

'There are clothes in the linen basket that need washing. When you're finished that, you can tidy up my room,' Amanda said without a glance.

'Very good, Madame. Shall I make you fresh coffee before I start?'

Amanda passed her cup to him. He turned on his heel and bustled off into the kitchen. When he returned, he placed the cup on the table in front of her; but, unlike Amanda, he used a coaster. 'Madame, I do wish you wouldn't leave your cup down on the wood; you'll ruin your table that way,' he said. 'Look, you can see the rings already.'

'Colin, if I want a lecture I'll whip it out of you.'

Colin tutted under his breath and hurried off to begin his chores, thrilled with the thought that she might just do it. Unlike other Mistresses he'd had in the past, Madame Amanda had just the right element of danger.

Over the next twenty minutes, Colin tidied the apartment and loaded clothes into the washing machine. He had just finished making Amanda's bed when she came into the bedroom. She pulled off her clothes and let them fall until she was completely naked.

'I'm tired, Colin. I could do with a bath. When you finish in here, run one for me, will you?'

Colin grinned like a Cheshire cat. He loved it when she asked him to do more personal things for her. Sometimes – only if she was in a good humour, of course – she let him blow-dry her hair, a job he did with the utmost care and attention. He was very conscientious in everything he did for Madame. He idolised her. He loved that she walked around naked in front of him so casually; he worshipped her; he could look, but he could not touch. She knew him so well it made him tremble.

Amanda was the only woman who truly understood him and his needs. She treated him like a proper maid; she never laughed or tried to be overly familiar with him. With her, he knew his place, and it was far beneath her. She held his fantasy in perfect balance.

He was eternally in her debt for allowing him to come to her private residence to play his role – something he knew she had mulled over a great deal before agreeing to. Colin would have followed her to the ends of the earth if she had asked. Amanda was well aware of that. It made her all the more powerful.

The twice-weekly visits made Colin's life whole in ways he couldn't explain. Whenever he felt he was being smothered by his pleasant, banal life, he thought of this apartment. It never failed to restore his good humour instantly. If work was hectic and people made a lot of demands on his patience, he could close his eyes and feel the smooth PVC encasing his body, the high shoes, the tights that rode high on his narrow waist …

He realised Amanda was staring at him, waiting.

'I hate to disturb your daydreams. Now, are you going to run me that bath or do I have to do it myself?' She was tapping her foot impatiently.

'Certainly, Madame. Forgive me – I seem to be very distracted today.' He blushed slightly and hurried out of the room. He had a tremendous hard-on that he would relieve in private as soon as his mistress was reclining in her bath. That was their arrangement: he would never ejaculate in front of her, couldn't even imagine such a grievous sin.

By nine o'clock Colin was smartly dressed in his civvies. His work done, his seed spent, he was ready to face the world. Amanda walked him to the door, wearing the fluffy bathrobe that she had 'borrowed' from a hotel one night while on a callout. Colin paused and waited patiently for his dismissal.

'Now, Madame, your smalls are on gentle spin in the machine and I've given the sitting room a good dusting. I will Hoover the whole apartment on Tuesday, so, please, don't do it over the weekend. You leave that to me. I hope you are satisfied. Will that be all, Madame?'

'That's fine, Colin, thank you,' said Amanda, starting to open the door. 'You worked hard today. Sometimes I don't know what I'd do without you.'

Colin's face lit up. 'Thank you for saying so, Madame – you're very kind,' he gushed, blushing again. Madame hardly ever gave compliments. To receive one was truly special.

'And, Colin ...'

'Yes, Madame?' He was still flushed from her praise.

'Don't be late on Tuesday. Or I'll get rid of you and find myself a new maid – maybe a younger one with bulging muscles.'

Colin's face grew serious. 'I wouldn't dream of it, Madame,' he said earnestly. 'I'll leave earlier and make sure I'm here at eight.'

'Good. Bye, then.' She closed the door in his face.

'Goodbye,' he said, staring wistfully at the closed door. Then he set off to his office. He had a full day ahead of him. He wasn't about to be late twice in one day.

As Colin headed for his other job with a jaunty step, Amanda went into her bedroom to get dressed. Before she did, however, she went to the head of her bed and lifted one of the recently plumped pillows. From underneath she extracted four crisp fifties, left there by her discreet maid. Colin never paid her into her hand; it ruined the role-play. Shaking her head slightly, she folded the cash and threw it into the top drawer of her bedside cabinet.

If only their wives tried to understand them like she did, there'd be a lot more happy marriages. She pulled on a fresh pair of knickers and thought about that for a second. Nah ... on second thoughts, if their wives understood them she'd be out of business.

4

Michael's legs were cramped from sitting in one position for too long. He twisted and turned in the front seat of the unmarked Corolla, but, no matter which way he moved, he couldn't straighten out fully. At six foot two, he wasn't designed to sit in small spaces for hours at a time. Every muscle creaked, and his back and shoulders ached. There was nothing for it but to get out and walk about for a few minutes; maybe that would get his circulation going again.

'I'm going to nip across the road for some coffee,' he said. 'Do you want some?'

Gerry Cullen nodded. He was slumped in the passenger seat, his feet resting on the dashboard. He was unshaven and crumpled and also in need of a damn good shower. Michael had been sharing a confined space with him for the last two hours, and the smell of stale sweat was another reason he needed to stretch his legs.

They were parked down the street from a plain red-brick apartment block on Aungier Street, watching the comings and goings of every man and woman who crossed the threshold. Inside the nondescript building, one of the top-floor apartments was operating as an escort agency. The team knew which one it was and who worked there; they even knew who owned it. Now they needed to prove it. So they waited, gathering their information, looking forward to the night when they could make their presence felt.

Surveillance was the most tedious part of a cop's job, Michael thought. Night after night, sitting in the dark, bored and tetchy, willing the time to move faster, looking forward to the end of the shift when they could go and have a pint or five. Michael glanced at the upstairs window of the Red Hot and Blue Agency and wished he had X-ray vision. The blinds were never up, not even for a split second, so they had never confirmed a visual. The girls worked twelve-hour shifts and never left the building together. Michael wasn't sure he'd recognise one of them if she stood in front of him. And that was a problem. Without their constant vigil and the steady traffic of the clients, they would have nothing to go on but a few complaints from irate neighbours.

Michael got out of the car and stretched, enjoying the cold air on his face. He crossed the street to Joe's Café, returning a few minutes later with two Styrofoam cups of bitter coffee. He got back into the car somewhat reluctantly, passed one of the cups to his partner and slid behind the steering-wheel, placing the small but powerful Nikon camera on his lap.

Gerry accepted the coffee gratefully. He kept his eyes on the main apartment door and yawned loudly. Michael glanced at the young man and almost felt sorry for him. Gerry had recently become the father of twin girls, and he had three other children, all under the age of six – a hefty load for a young man and his even younger wife. And, while Gerry was crazy about all his kids, shift work, late nights, and babies who never seemed to sleep were beginning to take their toll. An in-house pool had developed on who would catch the young man dozing at his desk this week, head down in the middle of his paperwork. The squad had fifty quid riding on it and were forever bursting in on Gerry unannounced, trying to catch him off guard. Gerry was pissed off with the buggers scaring the crap out of him every few minutes, but what could he do? At eight weeks old, the twins still showed no interest in sleeping for any longer than three hours at a time, and their father was beginning to look ragged around the edges. Next week the squad were going to double the stakes. Gerry's exhaustion was going to make someone a hundred quid richer.

Michael had no such problems. At forty-three, he had been a widower for almost ten years. He and his late wife had never even had the chance to start a family. His house was the very model of peace and quiet. Gerry claimed he was jealous of Michael's tranquil home and regularly offered to swap places with him for a few weeks. Michael laughed, but privately he doubted Gerry felt any such jealousy. In fact, he knew the squad found his silent, immaculate home, still decorated in the style chosen by his late wife, a little off-putting. That suited him fine.

'Heads up.' A sharp nudge from Gerry jolted him out of his reverie.

'We have a live one?' He put his coffee on the dash and grabbed the camera. Gerry squinted and, after a moment, nodded slowly.

'I knew that little bollix was scoping the place out. See that guy over there, the one in the tan raincoat?' Gerry indicated a nervous, gawky man in his fifties. 'That's the third time he's walked past the door in ten minutes. Look, see him studying the window of the carpet shop? He must know the display by heart now.'

'Maybe he's window-shopping.'

'Go fucking in, will you? You know you want to.' Gerry scowled and glanced at Michael. 'Man, I'll be so fucking glad when I'm back on regular duties. This is the worst assignment ever.'

'Tell me about it.'

They watched the man loitering around the door. His nonchalance was so forced it was comical. Michael grinned as the man looked in every direction before approaching the door of the building. Talk about signposting yourself.

'Bingo,' Gerry muttered under his breath.

Hoisting the camera up to shoulder-level, Michael stared through the lens, zooming in to capture the number on the button the man pressed. After a few words into the intercom, he was buzzed in.

Click, click, click … In less than half a minute, Michael had all the information he needed. The client might have thought he was being casual, and to the untrained eye maybe he was; but to Michael Dwyer, it was like shooting fish in a barrel.

Gerry scribbled the time and details in his notebook. 'How long do we give him?'

'Thirty minutes, max. These girls don't hang around.' Michael took a quick glance at his watch. 'Not when there's money to be made.'

'Do we pick him up?'

'Nah, tomorrow we come back with a warrant. Then we can pick up anyone we catch. We can't have these girls tipped off, like the last time.' He shook his head in disgust at the memory. 'No way. This time we do it by the book. Clients, girls, whatever – we hit them at the same time. No mistakes, no early warnings.'

Gerry nodded in agreement, but he couldn't hide his disappointment. Snagging clients after they left the premises was his favourite part of the Vice job. He loved their sheer panic when he rested a hand on their shoulders and asked them for a moment of their time. He enjoyed the act that followed, the protest and the bluster, the sheer terror. Most of all he loved the look of resignation when he explained to the trapped men that their every move had been recorded.

It never failed to amaze him how quickly these men went from cocky to humble. Once they were in the back of the squad car, reality hit them hard. They babbled and cringed, divulging everything, anything, spilling their guts to the bemused gardaí.

Gerry excelled in his role as father confessor. Head tilted sideways, he listened intently as the men offered the information he required, and some he didn't. With his wavy blond hair and soft, kind features, he was the soul of sympathy, always understanding and never judgmental. Nine times out of ten, the men were married. They twisted their wedding rings round and round, pleading with the officers for leniency. 'It was my first time!' they cried, their eyes darting from one garda's face to the other. 'Please, I'm a married man!' Gerry would nod, compassion etched across his face. 'I know how it is,' he'd confide, keeping his voice reassuring. Sometimes he flashed his own wedding band. 'Sure, we're only human too. Look, fellas, it's not you we're interested in. Tell us now, and we'll let you get on home to your family.'

The clients would offer tentative smiles, and soon they would answer any questions Gerry asked. With the demented look of a trapped animal, they spilled the beans on the girls they had been with. They embellished details in an effort to appear more helpful. When they finished purging themselves of their secrets, they would swear, promise, pledge, never in their lives to do something so stupid again.

Gerry always let them squirm for another few minutes, his face strictly impassive, giving nothing away. The sense of power was so strong that sometimes he wished he could make it last longer, but Michael was starting to question the need for such cruelty. Finally, much to the relief of the men, Gerry would release them and send them home with little more than a mild admonishment.

The free men would thank him profusely before scurrying off into the night with a newfound respect for the boys in blue. The clients kept their promises for a while, at least until the memory of the snare became distant and their hormones began to dictate their lives once more.

'Are you coming for a pint after work?' Michael asked.

Gerry thought about it for a second. He knew he should really go home and help Ellen with the kids. The thought of his tired, snappy wife with her swollen face and cracked nipples and his screaming children decided it for him.

'Fuck it, why not? I could do with a drink.'

They settled back in, waiting for their next photo opportunity to present itself.

5

The problem, as far as he could see, was the husband, a heavy man who drove a taxicab by night and sat on his vast arse watching a massive wide-screen TV during the day.

He waited in the park and watched the back of the house, ignoring the heavy rain that saturated his coat and hair. From his vantage point he could see right into Tessa Byrne's kitchen. He could see her sitting at her kitchen table, reading her paper, drinking cup after cup of scalding tea. He knew it was scalding because he knew that she didn't take milk and that she drank her tea within seconds of adding the boiling water to the Lyons tea-bag. He knew she liked to walk her eight-year-old daughter to school every morning, even though it was only half a mile away and the kid could surely make it there unaided. He had followed them, and he knew she and the kid chatted non-stop until they reached the school. He knew that she hated saying goodbye to the kid, that she kissed the kid every day outside the school, that the kid said 'Mam!' and laughed, pretending to be embarrassed.

He knew she listened to Gerry Ryan in the

morning while she made breakfast for the fat man. He knew she made the beds for her daughter and fat husband at eleven every day. He knew she normally went to the shop at twelve-thirty to buy fags, milk, one paper and a loaf of white sliced bread. He had studied her carefully over the weeks as he waited for his injuries to fade. And now he had her movements down pat.

The problem was the husband.

He shifted from one foot to the other, imbued with an overwhelming sense of impatience. He had others to attend to, others whose movements were also etched in his brain. And time was pressing on; he should have been through with this one. Was God not protecting him? There had been no mention of the other one, or the botched first. Surely that *meant* something.

He turned the collar of his jacket up and felt a slew of freezing water run down the back of his neck.

Why are you doing this? Please don't hurt me.

'Not this time! I know you can't talk,' he snapped at the tree he sheltered under. 'I am *so on to you*!'

Although she could not have heard him, Tessa Byrne looked up from her tea and glanced out her window into her dreary, mud-splattered garden. From his vantage point, high on the bank of the park that ran behind the row of terraced houses, her watcher curled his lip and spoke to himself gently, warning himself against talking trees. He studied her soft, curly brown hair, her clear, peaceful expression and her dimpled cheeks, and marvelled at how so perfect a surface could hide so much filth and rot.

She had such a smile, this one, such a beautiful smile. Such perfect teeth. He liked her teeth.

He would press on. Tomorrow he would finish this one, husband or no. He would time it for the morning, after she dropped the child off. He had the card the husband used to advertise his business. He would use that to lure the fat man away from the house. After that, it would be simply a matter of timing.

6

They waited for the go-ahead. Gerry was fidgeting and impatient; Michael was calmer, anxious to make the swoop, but willing to wait for the order. Their boss, Jim Stafford, was on his way, and there was little they could do until he got there.

This part of the job made surveillance worthwhile. They had the pictures, they had the details of the rental agreement, they had earlier nabbed a client and taken a sworn statement from a very shaken and tearful young man who was studying law in Trinity. He was being held in Harcourt Street, lest he make a call and warn the girls that a raid was imminent. Now, at last, after a week of sitting about, they would make their presence felt. They were going to break up this party once and for all. Paul 'Tricky' McCracken was going down. And once they had him, his other agencies would fall with him.

They were using Ed as a client tonight. Of all of the Vice officers, Ed Cairns looked the least like a cop. He was tall and lanky, with fuzzy, sandy hair and a goatee of indeterminate colour, more bumbling academic than law-enforcement officer.

'What's keeping them?' Gerry looked at his watch again.

Michael didn't answer; he was wondering the same thing himself.

After another twenty minutes of sighing and drumming fingers, the back door of the unmarked car opened. Jim Stafford eased his stocky body into the seat behind them, closely followed by Sergeant Miriam Grogan. Michael groaned under his breath. Whatever chance they had had of co-operation from the girls inside the apartment had just vanished. Miriam Grogan was rude, bad-tempered and bitchy, with delusions of power and a beaky nose permanently sniffing the air for the first hint of trouble. She was extremely ambitious, and Michael knew full well that she would use any available means to rise to the top – and that included taking praise for work that was not entirely her own, and stiffing her fellow officers for any mistakes they might make.

She had a remarkable effect on prostitutes. They hated her on sight. Ten minutes in her company, and they hated her even more. Not that Michael blamed them too much. The hookers expected Miriam, as a woman, to have a scrap of understanding for them, some insight into or per-haps empathy with their plight. What they got was disdain and undisguised contempt. It was an explosive combination, indignation fuelled by superiority.

'Anything doing?' Jim Stafford nodded towards

the front of the building; he never wasted time on pleasantries if he could avoid it. He was a short, bullish Cavan man of forty-eight, with a thatch of dark hair that, despite his years and occupation, showed only minimal amounts of grey. His small eyes, almost lost beneath caterpillar eyebrows, darted around, unable or unwilling to settle on any one thing. He was gruff and uncompromising – exactly the sort of man needed for detective work, but all wrong for the arse-licking and brown-nosing needed for further advancement in the Garda Siochána. Not that Jim Stafford gave a toss about advancement. He claimed a desk job would be the death of him.

'No, sir. Mind you, we've only been here for about an hour.' Gerry checked his watch again. 'Sometimes business takes a while to rev up.'

Stafford grunted and glared at the main door of the building. 'Right, then: we wait it out. You know who owns this fucking place, right? That slippery fucker McCracken, that's who. I want to catch somebody actually on the premises, preferably cock in hand. And don't forget, those girls have been well coached by that prick. Word is he's using his foreign contingent to man this place. They know what to do in a raid. Half of them will pretend they no speak the fucking English, and if they don't talk we've got fuck all. Immigration have been briefed on this fucker McCracken, but so far no one's put in an official complaint and we've never actually got close enough to talk to the workers.

Now, I don't want to waste any more time on this place than I have to. If we can catch some poor bastard with his trousers down, then we do it. Hard and heavy. Got me?'

'Yes, sir.'

'I don't want any fuck-ups with this lot. I'm sick of freezing my arse off while that fuckin' *slibhín* laughs at us from whatever rock he's under. We close him down. Got me?'

'Yes, sir.'

'As soon as a punter sets foot inside the place, you radio me. We'll give him about ten minutes to get his kit off, then we're going in. Right?'

'Yes, sir.'

'I'm going back to the van. Eddie's up there now, waiting for the go-ahead. Now remember, give the punter time to get his kit off. I don't want any fucking bullshit about him being in the wrong place or any of that shite. Kit off, girl on, money exchanged. That's the way I want it. Got me?'

'Yes, sir.'

With another frown at the building, Stafford slid out the back door and hurried back up the street. Miriam Grogan trotted after him like a little dog on a short leash.

As soon as he was gone, Michael and Gerry let out a shared sigh of relief. Gerry shook his head in frustration. 'Did he say *he's* sick of freezing his arse off?'

'He did.'

'Who's he trying to kid? He arrives for the last

day, all bloody gung-ho, and then tries to tell us he's sick of freezing his arse off. The man should try doing it for a week or more.'

Michael grinned. He could understand the young man's frustration, but he was also aware that Stafford was under pressure himself. McCracken was the biggest fish the operation was after, and so far they had missed him every time. It was becoming a bit of a joke, and he knew Stafford was starting to get a complex about it.

'Don't let it bother you, Gerry. Stafford's not the worst of them.' Michael rolled his neck to ease the tension in his shoulders.

Gerry grunted and resumed watching the door. It was thirty minutes before the next piece of bait arrived. The two gardaí sat up and watched as a well-dressed old man parked an ancient pale-blue Mercedes on double yellow lines, heaved his Oswald Cobblepot body out from behind the steering-wheel and waddled over to the front of the building. He rang the bell of number 17 without any hesitation and roared into the intercom, 'Howyiz, is Jade there?' so loudly that Michael and Gerry could hear him across the street.

'Jaysus Christ, look at the state of him. He's fucking seventy if he's a day! I doubt he's seen his mickey in twenty years,' Gerry said, his lip curling in disgust. 'How the fuck can they bear touching old lads like him?'

Michael shrugged. 'I don't think that comes

into it. Most of the women I've interviewed said they preferred the older clients. Reckon the younger ones are more hassle than they're worth. The old boys are grateful for any attention, even though they're paying for it.'

Gerry shook his head again. 'Can't imagine any woman in her right mind would prefer that fat lump over a young fella with a good body.'

'It's business. I don't think they really care what the men look like.'

As soon as the old man swung his bulk through the front door, Michael radioed the rest of the team. In exactly ten minutes Ed arrived to take up his role.

'It's showtime.' Gerry rubbed his hands together and licked his lips.

Ed pressed the buzzer and waited.

'Yes?' a soft female voice answered.

Ed made a conscious effort to sound nervous and excited. 'Hey, there. Can I come up? I rang yesterday and made an appointment.'

'Pardon?'

'I have an appointment. I called yesterday. C'mon, love, it's freezing out here.'

'Name?'

'Ed,' Ed said truthfully.

'Come up. Top floor, left as you come out of the lift, end of the corridor.'

The door buzzed. Ed shot a quick thumbs-up to Michael across the street, stepped inside and slipped a newspaper under the door to keep it ajar until the team reached it. The squad would go up to the top floor by the stairs, in case anyone was watching the lift, and wait in the stairwell until Ed got the apartment door open.

Ed rapped on the door of number 17 and waited. He knew he was being scrutinised through the spy-hole, so he fixed his hair and tried to look like just another nervous client. Eventually he heard the latch click, and the door swung open.

A drop-dead-gorgeous blonde of about thirty stood in the doorway, eyeing Ed up and down. She wore heavy eye make-up and a sheer black dress with a side slit that showed a lot of slim leg. She was barefoot, and her toenails were painted deep red to match her fingernails. Her honey-blonde hair was piled on top of her head and held in place by a silver butterfly clasp. She had wide hazel eyes that held no trace of warmth.

'Hi, there, can I come in?' Ed offered his big friendly grin, something he'd practised especially for these moments. He glanced at her chest and the grin widened of its own accord. Jaysus, she has some rack on her, he thought.

The hazel eyes narrowed; she seemed to be suspicious of something. Ed kept the stupid grin on his face, although it was getting slightly strained.

'Well, is there a problem?' he asked. 'I've got an appointment, made one yesterday.'

'I don't think so.' The woman had a gentle, soft voice, the one from the intercom.

Ed took this to be a good sign. He was surprised when she held out a hand, palm out.

'No, I mean I don't think so.' She stepped back and began to close the door in Ed's face.

'Eh? What do you mean? Why not?' He had to act quickly. He stuck his foot in the door and used his shoulder to barge it open further. The blonde squeaked and threw herself against it. His patience gone, Ed shoved as hard as he could, sending the woman sprawling backwards into the hall. She tripped over the hem of her dress and went crashing to the floor.

'What the fuck do you think you're doing?' she yelled, trying to get to her feet to block his entry. Ed noted that the soft voice had vanished.

He clamped his hand to her mouth and shoved his ID card in front of her startled eyes.

'I'm with Vice, love. So shut your gob and let me do my job. Don't bother trying to give any warnings.'

Her eyes widened as, behind Ed, more figures crowded through the narrow apartment door. Michael was first, followed by Gerry. Ed gave them the nod and they brushed past, rushing up the hall.

Four doors led off the narrow hall, but only two were closed. Behind these was where the action was presumably taking place. Michael stopped outside one, Gerry outside the other. Michael signalled, and they flung them open simultaneously.

'Stop, you fucking bastard!' The blonde woman struggled to escape Ed's firm hold. 'Get your bloody hands *off* me!'

Michael stepped into the room. It was empty, the bed neatly made, a table lamp casting a warm glow. Turning quickly, he yanked open the doors of the wardrobe, expecting to find the old man hiding inside. What he found was rows of neat clothes and a few pairs of shoes on the floor. A brief glance under the bed revealed nothing more than a suitcase and a pair of slippers. He stood up and gave the room his full consideration.

It was a neat room, painted a pale, crisp blue, with pale-blue-and-white curtains to match. There was make-up on the bedside table, pictures on the walls and a collection of CDs stacked on the windowsill next to a small, neat stereo.

There was no talc, no oil and no tissues, no towels and, most importantly, no client.

Gerry stepped into the room behind him.

'Well?'

Gerry shrugged and looked around, perplexed. 'Empty. It looks like a spare room or something. The bed's not even made up. This definitely a two-bedroom apartment?'

'That's what it says on the lease.' Michael ran his hand over his face, suddenly feeling a little queasy. 'Go check out the sitting room.'

In the hall, the outraged woman was back on her feet. Jim Stafford identified himself by pushing a search warrant under her nose and ordering her to stop wailing like a banshee. The blonde snatched the warrant from his hand and read it carefully, taking her time, absorbing every word. When she finished, she slowly balled it up in her hand and flung it in his face.

'You must be fucking joking!'

'This is no joking matter.' Stafford straightened out the warrant. He had little time for histrionics. 'You and I are going to have a chat. Got me? So you'll do a lot better if you stop all this drama and work with me. Go better for you in the long run.'

He stormed up the hall, followed by Ed, who was doing his best to haul the furious woman with him.

Michael crossed the hall into the bathroom. It was small, but tidy. The peach and white tiles gleamed under the soft central light. Two hand-towels were folded over the sink, and one large towel hung drying over the shower-rail. Michael opened the medicine cabinet above the sink and took a quick look. Toothbrush, half-empty bottles of cough syrup, make-up remover, Disprin, cotton-buds and tampons – everything you'd expect to find in a woman's bathroom. He closed the cabinet and took a long moment to stare at his reflection in the mirror.

'Shit!'

Back in the main bedroom, Gerry searched frantically through the wardrobe. He knew he was wasting his time. The apartment was empty except for the woman who'd answered the door. How had they done it, though? Nothing suggested to him that this room was used for anything more than sleeping in. He was looking through the neatly hung clothes when Michael re-entered the room.

'Gerry, go and get Stafford down here before he starts throwing his weight around. We have a problem.'

The atmosphere in the living room was rife with tension. The blonde had recovered from her shock and was busy yelling legal threats at Stafford, jabbing a highly varnished fingernail into his chest with each threat. The detective's blood was beginning to simmer. He wasn't used to being challenged, especially by women. Miriam Grogan and Ed Cairns watched as their boss's face grew darker and darker.

'Look, drop the act,' he said when she paused for breath. 'We can do this the hard way, or we can do this the easy way. It's your choice. The more you co-operate with us, the better it will be for you. So why don't you do your good self a favour and calm down?'

The blonde snorted. 'I'll calm down when you tell me what the fuck you and your fucking idiots are doing in my home!'

Stafford glowered at her. 'I told you to drop the act; you're fooling no one. Got me?' He raised his voice, hoping to intimidate her, although he suspected a stampeding rhino couldn't have done that. God almighty, the last thing he needed was this shit.

He gave the woman his best attempt at a smile. 'Look, I know you've had a fright, but acting like this isn't going to help your case one bit. We know what goes on here.' He waved his arm at the sofa. 'C'mon, now, there's no need for this carry-on.'

'Go fuck yourself.' She remained standing and crossed her arms.

Two spots of colour flared high on Stafford's already pink face. He was going to enjoy taking this one down a peg or two.

He was about to read her the riot act when Gerry popped his head around the door.

'Sir, can I see you for a moment?'

Stafford raised his hand impatiently. 'I'm in the middle of something, Sergeant.'

'Sir, it's important.'

Stafford bunched his hand into a fist and fixed the blonde with a cold stare. She returned it. As he turned to leave, he heard her mutter, 'Asshole,' under her breath.

Turning to Miriam, he smiled. 'Watch her, will you? Not that she's going anywhere tonight except down to the station. Make sure she understands just how long she'll be there if she doesn't cop herself on.'

'Of course.' Miriam straightened to attention and glared at the blonde with cold relish.

The blonde's head snapped up higher. 'You can't bring me do—'

'I think you'll find we can do whatever we like,' Stafford said with a smile, and left the room.

'What is it, Gerry?' He stomped down the hall after his sergeant. 'What the fuck couldn't wait two minutes? Did you hear the way that little ma—'

'Sir,' Gerry interrupted, 'we've got a problem.'

Stafford's eyebrows jiggled alarmingly. 'Don't tell me – we've snared someone important?'

'No, sir. You'd better see for yourself.' Gerry pushed open the bedroom door.

Michael sat on the bed waiting for them. He looked up and swallowed. This was not going to be pleasant.

Stafford shoved Gerry aside. 'Well, what did you find?'

Michael glanced up at his florid face. 'Nothing.'

Stafford frowned. 'I don't understand. What are you saying?'

'Sir, there's nothing here. Nothing at all – no clients, no girls, nothing. This doesn't even look like a working apartment.' He waved an arm about the room. 'Least, none that I've seen.'

Jim Stafford's left eye twitched, and when he spoke his voice dripped sarcasm. 'What do you mean, you found nothing? Explain that to me, Sergeant. I'm getting on a bit, so explain it to me slowly.'

Michael shifted uncomfortably. 'Sir, there doesn't appear to be anyone here other than the woman in the living room. The rest of the apartment appears to be empty.'

'Appears to be …' Stafford stood with his hands on his hips and stared at Michael for a long moment. A sharp ache in his gut indicated that his ulcer was listening to the exchange. He took a deep breath and tried to remain calm.

'This is the right address, isn't it, Mike?'

'Yes, sir. Number 17, sir. We've been watching it for two weeks now. We have photographs of the clients ringing the buzzer downstairs. This was the number the old man rang earlier, sir.'

'And he definitely came up? You saw him come up with your own eyes?'

'Yes.'

'So where the bloody fuck is he now? Where are the other girls? You told me there were at least three on every shift, Mike. What do you think happened to them? Is there a trapdoor? Are they under the fucking carpets, in the back of the wardrobes? Maybe they disappeared into thin fucking air. Did you check the other rooms?'

'Of course we did!' Michael gritted his teeth. 'We' – he indicated Gerry with a swipe of his finger – 'sat outside that front door for almost two weeks. This is the apartment in question, sir. This was the address we were given when we rang the advertised number. For Christ's sake, she buzzed Ed in when he rang the doorbell!'

Stafford struggled to keep his temper under control. 'No wonder little Miss High-and-Mighty was smirking at me back there. She's made a fucking eejit of me.' His head whipped around and he jabbed Gerry, who had edged out of the room slightly. 'Gerry, what are you standing around for? Search this fucking place properly, top to bottom. We've got a warrant. Mike, you come with me. Something's not right about this. Something fucking stinks, and I want to know what the hell is goin' on here.'

'Yes, sir.' Michael stood up, towering over the furious man.

'Nobody makes a fucking eejit out of me!' Stafford muttered under his breath. 'Especially that bastard McCracken.'

He practically ran up the hall and burst through the sitting-room door. Everyone jumped. He glanced around the room, went through into the tiny gallery kitchen and opened a few presses and the fridge. The kitchen was clean and tidy and showed few signs of use. The only items in the fridge were a carton of milk, some low-calorie spreadable butter and a mountain of takeaway boxes. There was nobody living here, that was for sure.

Stafford slammed the fridge door closed and leaned against it, breathing hard. He was beginning to get an idea of how fucking clever McCracken was.

He came out of the galley kitchen and stared at the blonde. She smirked and shrugged one shoulder. Stafford felt his blood flip from simmering to boiling.

'Take a seat.' Stafford pointed to the sofa. This time it wasn't a request.

The blonde noticed the change in his voice and folded her arms defiantly. 'You see, I to—'

'*Sit down*!' Stafford roared.

Startled, she sat. 'Don't you dare shout at me!' Her voice was raised, but lacked some of the conviction it had held before.

Ed glanced nervously at Michael, and Michael shook his head. There was nobody there. Somehow, either they had got the wrong place or the agency had got a tip-off. He glanced at his boss. Stafford's jaw muscles were bunched and his eyes almost lost in a sea of black eyebrow. A thick vein snaked down the middle of his forehead. Michael knew his boss was heading for a blow-up. The blonde, too, seemed prepared for a battle. He recognised the confident set to her jaw and knew they had been played somehow.

Michael perched on the arm of the sofa, waiting to see the outcome of this battle of wits. They needed to find out what was going on, and he hoped this woman would be sensible about it.

Stafford pulled up a chair and sat down facing the blonde. He was red with temper, but he held it tightly in check. She wasn't going to get the better of him. He was like a snake, poised, ready to strike at the first sign of weakness. And there would be a weakness, he would see to that.

'Right, what's your name?'

The blonde picked up a packet of Rothman's cigarettes from the low coffee table to her right. She lit one, inhaled deeply and blew the smoke directly into Stafford's face.

'So now you want to know my name?' she said

coolly. 'It's Emma Harris. You'd better give me yours again, Detective. I'm going to need it when I contact my solicitor to tell him about this fiasco.'

'Tell him what, Miss Harris?'

Emma Harris laughed and waved her hand around her. 'Let me see now … where will I start? Breaking and entering, trespass, assault, threatening behaviour … That should do to start with, don't you think?' Her hazel eyes held his without wavering.

Stafford stared back at her. She thought she was so clever, this one, thought she had it all sussed out.

'Won't do you any good. We have a warrant to enter and search the premises.'

She raised her eyebrows in surprise, shaking her head slightly as if she had misheard him. Michael almost laughed. She was a good actress, but not that good.

'Premises? This is my apartment, Detective, my *home*. I think you may have made a mistake somewhere along the line.' She exhaled grey smoke and smiled at him again. Casually she folded her legs under her, exposing a rather nice slender thigh. Michael saw Miriam Grogan pull a face, and mentally gave the blonde a delighted grin.

Stafford ignored the flash. 'How long have you lived at this address, Miss Harris?'

'About three months now. Why?'

'Miss Harris, cut the crap. You know exactly why we're here. We have reason to believe this apartment is being used as a brothel. A complaint was made by a concerned member of the public, and we're here to investigate that complaint. We spent a few days watching the place. Do you know what we saw?' He leaned forward in the chair, scrutinising her face, his eyebrow pulled so low his eyes almost disappeared under it.

'No, do tell.' Emma Harris leaned forward too, until her nose was inches from Stafford's. 'I'm dying to hear it.'

'We have observed a number of men coming in and out of this apartment.' Stafford smirked slightly. 'Many of whom we stopped and questioned. They all tell an interesting story about what goes on here.'

'Really?'

He sat back. 'You want to keep up the performance, be my guest. But this is going to look bad when you go to court. Judges frown on smart alecks.' He shrugged. 'So, do you want to be clever? Or do you want to dig yourself out of the hole you're in?'

Emma Harris gave a long, theatrical sigh. 'I don't think I'll do either. As far as I can see, there has been some dreadful cock-up here, and now you want me to pretend that I know what you're going on about. Well, I'm very sorry: I won't.' She ground out her cigarette in a heavy Player's ashtray. 'You can sit there and witter on all night, and I still won't have a clue what you're talking about. And I think you know that.'

Michael's heart sank. That proved, at least in his mind, that she knew exactly why they were there, and that they were wasting their time in trying to get her to talk.

Jim Stafford, on the other hand, loved a challenge.

'Oh, sure. I find people often have difficulty understanding me. That comes with the job. But they usually come round after it sinks in how much trouble they're in. Got me?' He glared at her, taking his time, letting her see that he wasn't a man who suffered fools gladly.

Emma Harris smiled coldly. 'Thank you, Detective, for making that clear. Now, if you could tell me what I'm supposed to have done, then maybe I can help you in some small way. If you can't, then get out and let me get back to watching telly. *CSI*'s about to start, and if you miss the beginning it's very hard to work out what's going on.'

'Do you know a man by the name of Paul McCracken?' The question was fired at her suddenly, to catch her off guard.

'No. Should I?' She arched one perfectly sculpted eyebrow.

'You should know your own boss. Most people do.'

'My boss?' She laughed. It wasn't a genuine laugh, but Michael knew she was comfortable with the question. Stafford wasn't troubling her in the least.

'Oh, I know my boss, Detective, and his name isn't Paul … I'm sorry, what did you say his last name was again?'

'McCracken.'

'McCracken. Anyway, as I said, his name is not McCracken.' She glanced over at Michael and gave a little shrug, as if to say she'd never heard anything so ridiculous in her life. 'Never heard of him.'

'I'm glad you're looking at Mike,' Stafford said quickly. 'See, he's one of the two men who've been camped on your doorstep every night for the last two weeks. He might be the very man to help you with your understanding of the situation. Mike, why don't you try and explain to this … lady what's going on?' With his best patronising smile, Stafford leaned back in the chair. 'She obviously has some difficulty understanding me.'

Michael cleared his throat and did his best not to look annoyed. He doubted this woman was going to offer them any information. Whatever was going on here had obviously been well planned in advance. He knew they were at the right address; of that he was certain. But they needed proof of illegal activity before they could do anything, and so far all he had seen was a neat, well-kept home with no visitors bar the gardaí stomping about it. They'd been had; he didn't know how, but they'd been had.

'Miss Harris, my colleague and I have been watching and recording the seemingly endless traffic of men coming into and out of this apartment. Are you trying to tell me that you deny this place has been used as a brothel, or as an escort agency?'

'Absolutely. I don't know what you're talking about.' Her voice was indignant.

Michael reached up to his shirt pocket and pulled out his notebook. He flipped it open and flicked back through a few pages. He glanced over the top to see if this provoked any reaction. If she was concerned by written proof, it didn't show.

'Last Saturday, 12 March, at 11.35 p.m., my colleague, Sergeant Gerry Cullen, stopped and questioned a man as he attempted to leave these premises. When questioned about his reasons for being here, the man stated that he had called on appointment, for the purposes of sexual gratification in exchange for money. Furthermore, it was not the first time he had received such a service at this address. When questioned further, the man revealed he had spent in excess of two hundred euros on the night in question, and that he had paid this money to a girl by the name of Jade. However, before this man had picked "Jade" he had been offered the choice of two other girls, one blonde and one brunette. He believed the girls were Eastern European.'

He paused, studying the blonde to see if any of this hit home. 'Does any of this sound familiar to you, Miss Harris?'

Her eyebrows arched again and her mouth twitched with mocking disdain. 'Maybe he was drunk? Or maybe you were.' She waved her right hand around. 'Look around you. Don't you think that, if this were an escort agency, it would have escorts or whatever they're called? Do you see any girls here? Eastern European – good Lord, whatever next? Maybe I've hidden them in the presses or something.'

'Why don't you stop messing us around? You're only making it worse for yourself, you know,' Miriam Grogan snapped suddenly. 'We know you're hiding something!'

Emma Harris eyed the garda with barely disguised contempt. She opened her mouth to respond, then changed her mind, preferring to ignore her.

'Did this man mention me, Sergeant? Did he claim to have met me?'

Michael looked through his notes. 'No, he didn't.'

'Well, then, you've obviously made a mistake. This is my apartment. I think if some man were here I would have noticed. Or he would have noticed me.'

'Can you explain why, if I were to ring the number of Red Hot and Blue Escorts, I would be directed to this address?' asked Michael.

'You wouldn't.' Her eyes twinkled with amusement.

'Ed, do you think Miss Harris was the woman you spoke to on the phone when you made your appointment?'

'Positive, sir,' Ed said with a deep nod.

Stafford nodded. 'Do you have a phone, Miss Harris?'

She tutted in annoyance and waved a bare foot at a bog-standard phone on the sideboard. 'Of course I do. Why? Is that a crime too?'

'Can I use it?'

'Work away.' She lit another cigarette.

Stafford took note of the number on the handset.

'Mike, do you have a copy of the advert for the agency with you?'

'Yes, sir.' Michael flicked through his notebook and grinned. Stafford was a wily old bastard, no doubt about it.

'Dial it.'

Michael used his mobile to dial the agency number. Emma Harris blew a perfect smoke-ring and watched him carefully out of the corner of her eye.

Jim Stafford tipped Miriam Grogan a wink. Once that phone rang, he was going to take great pleasure in arresting Emma Harris and hauling her ass down to the station. He wondered what he would charge her with first – maybe obstruction of police business. He was thinking of adding resisting arrest when he saw Michael frown.

'What is it?'

Michael glanced at him. 'It's ringing, sir.'

Stafford looked at the phone under his hand and snatched up the receiver. He got nothing but the dial tone.

'What the hell do you mean, it's ringing?'

'Hold on … Hello? … Hi, how are you? I'm wondering if I have the right number. Is this Red Hot and Blue? It is – I see … Well, where are you based? I'd like to call in to see someone in the next hour or so … Pardon? … Why not tonight? … I see – everyone is booked up? … Right, I understand. Maybe I can call tomorrow? … That would be fine. Tell me, are you still at the same address? … You are? That's great. What was it again? … Oh, why not? … Sure, I'll give you a call tomorrow.'

Michael hung up and glanced at the darkening face of his boss. There was going to be trouble now. He looked over to the sofa at Emma Harris, who was cool and composed once again.

'Ed, go and get Gerry,' Stafford said.

Ed hastily did as he was told. Stafford turned back to Emma Harris, who was leaning back on the sofa and watching him with undisguised amusement. He sat back down in the chair directly in front of her and clasped his hands together between his legs. He was afraid that if they were free he'd wring her neck.

'Tell that prick he might think he's clever, but this doesn't stop here.'

'Tell wh—'

'And as for you … you mark my words, we'll meet again very shortly. You think you can fuck us about and we're going to let the matter drop? Let me assure you, we will be doing no such thing. Got me? Now, is there anything you would like to tell me? Before I get really pissed off?'

'Yes, actually, there is something I'd like to say.' Emma Harris eyed him coldly through another stream of smoke.

'What is it?'

'Don't let the door hit you too hard in the arse on the way out.'

Jim Stafford sat in the front seat of the van and waited for a reply from Harcourt Street. Ed waited, perched behind the wheel, for the order to pull off. Miriam Grogan coughed nervously. Nobody dared open his or her mouth.

'He says it's definitely that apartment, does he? ...Yeah, let him go. Don't do anything else, just let the little shit go.' He snapped the phone shut and ground his back teeth together. He was baffled. Two of his best men had watched the place night after night, he had a sworn statement from the man they'd yanked earlier, he had a copy of the lease. They'd made an appointment, for Christ's sake. And yet here he sat, humiliated and under serious strain.

How had he fucked up? Where had the old man disappeared to? Where were the girls? How had it gone from a run-of-the-mill raid to such a spectacular cock-up?

One thing was for certain: somewhere McCracken was laughing his arse off over this one. Stafford rubbed his stomach. His ulcer was killing him.

'How do you suppose we made such idiots of ourselves tonight?' he asked eventually, turning in his seat to face the others. 'Dammit to hell! We watched the place for two weeks, took photographs – we even have a statement, for Christ's sake. And for what? To be made complete gobshites by that little bitch.'

He slammed his fist against the dashboard hard enough to make Miriam jump.

'Right! We're going back to the station to sort this out. I don't give a shit how late we work tonight, got me? We are going to get to the bottom of this.'

Ed started the engine and pulled out into the street. Stafford cast one last baleful look at the building that had so messed up his evening.

In the unmarked car, Michael followed them back to the station house. He was developing a headache and was in no mood for the bollocking he would most surely receive. Stafford would have his guts for garters.

'It's going to be a long night.'

Gerry groaned. 'Shit, Mike, if Stafford doesn't kill me, the wife probably will. I promised her I'd be home early for a change.'

Michael grimaced. 'I know, I know … but come on, she's bound to understand. Nature of the job.'

'Yeah? Try telling that to Ellen.'

Emma Harris watched from the window until the van and the unmarked car pulled away. When they were gone, she lit another cigarette and, with as much composure as she could muster, walked quietly down the hall and took a set of keys from the hall table. Her heart was still pounding in her ears as she opened the door and peered down the hall. She had seen them pull away, but why take the chance?

Satisfied no more gardaí were lurking about, she stepped out and closed the door gently behind her.

Directly across the hall was a door exactly like hers. She gave two sharp knocks, paused, then gave a single knock, followed by another double. The door opened immediately, and a young Algerian girl with a bad dye job peered at Emma from behind a thick fringe of hair. She was eighteen and tiny, with huge black eyes and small, high breasts, barely covered by the strip of pink gauze she wore as a top.

Emma glared at her. 'Close the door. Where's the old man?'

The girl shrugged one bony shoulder. 'He gone. Left back.'

'Good.'

'We work now?'

'No, not today.'

The girl scowled. 'We not work?'

'I said no, didn't I?' Emma marched up the hall and into a smoke-filled living room. Four other girls watched her entrance from under their eyelashes. Emma threw herself into a chair and rubbed her hand over her eyes. She knew they were bored and fed up. They were here in Ireland solely to make money, and losing a day was as good as being robbed.

Thank God the bloody phone divert had been on. Imagine trying to wiggle out of that … She thought about the look on Stafford's face when the phone had been answered – priceless. It had been close, though; they should have had more than a week's warning that the bastards were going to raid.

She felt some of the tension ebb from her body. The fucking gardaí could raid all they liked. No girls, no sex, no brothel, no matter how much the bastards tried to convince you otherwise.

She dialled Tricky's number. He answered on the first ring.

'They've been and gone.'

'They find anything?'

'No, just little old me and a whole lot of *shocking abuse*.' Emma laughed. 'You were right – that fat one has a real hard-on for you.'

'Bastard.' Tricky snorted softly. 'You're fucking off the wall letting them snag you, though; should've skipped out.'

'What, and have the fuckers call back? No, Paul, this will make them back the fuck off for a while.'

'Man, you're something fucking else. Dunno what I'd bleeding do without you.' Tricky sounded genuinely awestruck for a change.

'Tell you what – I'll meet you at the Shelbourne in an hour. You buy me a dinner and a good bottle of wine, and I'll tell you all about the poor widdle stupid gardaí and their poor widdle crushed faces.'

'Darling, you're on,' Tricky said. 'Got me some good news earlier, too.'

'Yeah?' Emma glared at the girl nearest her. She was cutting her fucking toenails, and pieces were pinging all over the place. 'What? It can't be better than my news.'

'Nah, babe, but fucking ace all the same.' Tricky laughed nastily. 'Remember that cunt Amanda?'

Emma rolled her eyes. 'Oh God, you're not still going on about that bitch, are you?'

'She was in court. Her and the other whore got done.'

'Really? I didn't hear anything about it.'

'Jammy bitches – fucking papers missed them. But they were done all right.'

'Wow. Then perhaps we need champagne instead of wine?'

'Yeah. Tell them birds to take a breather for tonight. If there's shit later I'll spread 'em out in the other places, but the shifts are covered for tonight and I don't want to be seen moving 'em.'

'OK. See you in a while.' Emma hung up and watched the girl hack away at her feet.

The little Algerian was conversing with one of the other girls in a French dialect. Emma didn't pick up the words, but she knew the tone perfectly. They weren't happy.

'You got a problem?' Emma called over to her.

The Algerian looked loftily at her. 'We here work. No work, we no need here.'

Emma smiled. 'Listen, you dumb bitch, save your United Nations speech for someone else. You're here because some guy – maybe your brother, maybe your father, I don't know and I couldn't care less – sold you on to Tricky. So do yourself a favour: shut your yap and take a night off. You go somewhere, he'll find you. And then you won't be able to work. Not here, not anywhere else. *Comprende?*' Emma stood up and grabbed her coat. 'No one wants damaged goods, baby, no one.'

A group of tired, despondent gardaí sat drinking coffee around a chipped Formica-topped table in the station-house canteen. It was eight in the morning, and none of them had got much sleep. The news of the murder had filtered through to them at 3 a.m. After their disastrous raid on the apartment, it was like salt being rubbed into their wounds. Worse still, the murder had occurred on their patch.

'Why did he cut all her fucking hair off? What the fuck's that about?' Gerry Cullen asked no one in particular.

'It's like he took it as a trophy. The poor sister, finding her like that … terrible,' Michael said. He rubbed his eyes and tried not to yawn. Every bone in his body seemed to throb.

'It's got to be a punter.' Miriam Grogan sipped

coffee so strong and hot the little white plastic spoon had bent in two. She read the preliminary report on her lap. 'No sign of forced entry, she's in the nip – it's obvious. It has to be someone she trusted enough to let in.'

Michael Dwyer lifted his head from his paper. 'You're making a lot of suppositions.'

'Maybe it was some kinky game, went wrong.' Miriam shrugged and went back to the report. 'All I'm saying is a punter would have access to her. There's no need to bite my head off.'

Gerry yawned and scratched his stubble on his chin. 'She's got a point. We're probably looking for a client.'

'Yeah, well, God knows how many of them there are. If we're going to bet on it being a client, then we give ourselves half the bloody male population of Ireland to work from. Somehow I can't see them racing forward with information, can you?' Michael tilted his chair back and stared at their faces. '"Excuse me, Officer, I'd like to help. I think I slept with the dead woman. Yes, I am a married man. No, I don't mind giving my name, not if it helps in any way …"'

'What about the other women?' Gerry was trying not to spill tomato sauce from his breakfast roll onto the front of his shirt.

'They're as reluctant to speak to us as the clients are. Let's face it, we're not exactly up there as confidants. You know what they think of us.'

'Yeah? Well, tough shit. They're not going to

have a lot of say in it now.' Miriam closed the report and slid it across the table to Gerry, who looked like he had slept in his car. 'If the call comes down that we can get in on a murder case, I don't give a shit whose toes we have to tread on, I want in. So they'd better start talking. I've a pain in my arse trying to tiptoe around these whores. It's like trying to get blood from a stone with some of them. The murder team want our help to interview hookers, and I for one am not going to fuck around hoping I don't offend one of them with my questions.'

'Did they get to talk to the husband?' Gerry asked.

'He lives in England. Someone's going to call him later.'

'England?'

'Yeah. I don't know much, but apparently the woman had two kids she was supporting on her own.'

'Not much use to them now, is she?' Miriam said. She tossed the last of her coffee down in one scalding gulp.

'Miriam!' Michael snapped, and even Gerry looked shocked. 'Don't you have a shred of compassion? Jesus, the poor woman is dead.'

'She probably wouldn't have been at risk if she hadn't been selling her fanny, would she? That's all I'm saying. Play with fire, you get burned.'

Michael felt his face warp into a mask of dislike, and he fought to control it. Her attitudes sickened him. He had to work with this woman for at least another three months; he couldn't afford to let her know how much he despised her.

'Even so, I don't think you should be so flippant about it.'

'Oh, please!' Miriam gave a sharp snort of derision. She crumpled up her cup and tossed it expertly into a nearby bin. 'Don't go wasting your sympathy, Mike. Look, nobody held a gun to her head. Lots of people are broke. They don't all resort to prostitution, do they? Being dumped by her husband ain't no excuse either. Lots of the ones we've interviewed are married, aren't they? And they're still hooking. Why should a man respect a woman if she has no respect for herself in the first place? Honestly, prostitutes give women a bad bloody name. No wonder nobody takes us seriously.' Miriam stood up, scraped her chair back and marched out of the canteen.

Michael watched her retreating back and shook his head. 'And she wonders why people don't like her.'

'I don't think she gives a shit if people like her or not.' Gerry belched and stretched. 'She told me once she was only passing through. Reckons she's gonna be the first female Commissioner.'

'With that mouth, she'll be lucky if we don't find her dead with a hatchet in her back someday,' Michael said, and shook out his paper.

'Oi, oi. Here comes the lord and master.' Gerry wiped his mouth with the back of his hand.

Michael looked up in time to catch a very bleak and washed-out Jim Stafford barging through the canteen doors.

'Well, we're up to speed. The woman's name was Sandy Walsh, definitely a prostitute, no previous arrests but she'd been in the game a long time.' Stafford dropped into the chair Miriam had vacated and glanced at Gerry with undisguised animosity. 'Where the fuck are the other two? I thought I told you to fucking wait here for me. I don't want to go repeating myself. Got me?'

'I'll go get them.'

'Aye, you do that. And while you're at it, go clean yourself up a bit. You're like a fucking tramp sitting there. Do you not have a clean shirt?'

Gerry flushed slightly and left as fast as his dignity would allow.

Michael looked at Stafford. Something other than Gerry's shirt was eating the little man. 'What?'

'Upstairs wants us in on the case. We are to *collaborate* with the murder team. Give them the benefit of *our expertise*.' Stafford made a face. 'Fucking showboating, that's what it is.'

'Who's heading the team?'

Stafford's face went through an alarming series of twitches and spasms. Michael stared at him, wondering if his boss was having some kind of seizure.

'Robert Scully!' Stafford spat the words across

the table. 'They've asked Robert fucking Scully to head up the investigation.'

'I don't think I know him.'

'He's a jumped-up little bollix with his nose always up the fucking Commissioner's arse. Prick!'

Michael nodded noncommittally, but his heart sank. Clearly Stafford had a history with this Robert Scully. This day, he thought, can't get any worse.

7

As Amanda made her way home from work that evening, the sky opened and the rain pelted down. Head down against the wind, she tried to sidestep pedestrians clogging the footpath. It was no use, and when some fat man nearly took her eye out with the corner of his umbrella she decided enough was enough. Diving into the nearest coffee shop, she brushed her damp hair back from her forehead and ordered a cappuccino. She took a window seat and moodily watched the crowd, waiting for it to clear a little before she went back into the fray.

The waitress brought her the coffee, and she lit a cigarette and relaxed. She was about to take a sip when her mobile rang. She fumbled around in her bag, trying to locate it and switch it off, then realised it was her personal phone and not her work phone. She cursed softly and answered it.

'Amanda?'

'Jesus, Marna, I haven't even reached home yet! What is it?'

'I've just had a weird call from Grapevine Paula. She's on her way here now.' Marna's voice sounded odd. 'You'd better come back.'

'What for?' Paula owned and worked in a run-down brothel near the city centre. She was not Amanda's favourite person.

'I don't know. She wouldn't say over the phone.'

'Why not?' Amanda's heart sped up a little. 'Is it something involving us? Are we in the papers?'

'I don't know – I don't think so. But Paula sounded really upset. Will you come back?'

Amanda checked her watch and sighed. 'Yeah, give me ten minutes.'

Never a dull moment; that was the problem with this job. There was always some crisis or other. It must be big if Paula didn't want to talk about it on the phone. That woman was never off the bloody phone.

Amanda took a deep gulp of coffee. Two things had to be said about Paula: she was generous with her information, and it was usually correct. Through a seemingly endless series of calls, the busty blonde was guaranteed to know exactly what was going on in the vice world at any given moment. They had all worked together at the Red Stairs years before; Paula had been the first one to strike out on her own, taking half the clients and some of the best girls with her.

Amanda gulped down the rest of her coffee, left the money on the table and hurried out the door into the crowd. As she swerved and sidestepped her way back to the office, her mind worked overtime trying to figure out what was wrong. There was always a good selection to choose from

– raids, newspapers, landlords trying to get more money, bad or dangerous clients, other brothels trying to get you closed down, vindictive girls, vindictive ex-bosses, vindictive current bosses … the list was endless.

As she reached Mount Street, her pace slowed to a crawl. Did she really want to hear this? Did they not have enough problems of their own without hearing more bad news from Paula?

Taking a deep breath, she let herself into their building and climbed the stairs to the first floor. As she entered the apartment hall, she heard raised voices coming from the living room. Paula, it seemed, had already arrived.

As soon as Amanda opened the living-room door, she knew the news was bad.

Paula – as always, bursting out of a dress that could have been sprayed on – looked pale under her fake tan, and she was smoking, even though she'd given up three years before. Marna looked equally shaken. Paula had come over armed with brandy, and Marna's glass was on its second refill.

'What is it? What's happened? ' Amanda shook the rain out of her hair.

Marna stood up and turned to face her. 'Remember Sandy? We worked with her in the Red Stairs.'

'Yeah, I know Sandy. What's she done now?'

Paula and Marna exchanged looks.

'Are you going to tell me or what?'

'She's dead!' Paula blurted out, tears threatening

to spill from the baby-blue eyes and destroy the inch of mascara that covered her false lashes. She fished out a hanky from under her bra strap and dabbed furiously at them. 'Butchered by a bleeding maniac! I heard her body was all wrapped up like a mummy, and he cut her from head to toe and took all her hair, and—'

'Paula, shut up!' Marna snapped, noticing the colour draining from Amanda's face.

'I don't believe you!' Amanda sat down heavily in one of the chairs. 'When?'

'They're not sure exactly.' Marna took another swig of brandy. 'Maybe two or three days ago.'

Amanda's mouth dropped open. She motioned to Marna to pour her a glass. 'What do you mean, they're not sure? Jesus Christ! Paula, you must know! When did this happen?'

'I don't have all the details yet.' Paula glanced at her mobile, resting on the floor by her feet, as if she couldn't believe it wasn't ringing. 'I'm waiting on calls. When I do, I'll let you know.'

'Oh my God.' Amanda accepted the glass of brandy from Marna and took a sip. It slipped down her throat and made her feel sick.

'The cops only found the poor cow last night. They broke down the door of that flat of hers – you know, the one she was working in. As far as I know, she'd been dead for at least a day or two by then. The kiddies had been over at her ma's house or something and didn't realise she hadn't come home.' Paula's voice shook.

'They found her in her flat? Oh, Jesus, poor Sandy.' Amanda closed her eyes. The sensation in her neck had crept down her arms, making all the fine hairs stand up. 'Do they know who did it? Have they caught him? How the hell do you know all this, anyway? I haven't heard a fucking thing about it on the radio or the telly. It wasn't in the paper, was it? If they found her last night, surely we would have heard something?' She looked at Marna.

Paula shrugged her shoulders. 'I was told by a good source that it should be on the six o'clock news tonight. I don't know if they have any idea who did it; they haven't even released the story.' Her huge chest heaved and she dabbed at her now-dry eyes again. 'It could be a client – who knows? Poor bitch. I knew she should never have left my place. Why wouldn't she listen to me?'

'Jesus, Marna. I can't fucking believe it.' Amanda slumped back into the chair, fishing around in her pockets, searching for her cigarettes. Her hands trembled as she lit one. 'Her poor little kids … Ah, Jesus, why would someone want to do that? Are you sure, Paula?' she asked, desperately hoping that Paula had somehow got her wires crossed.

Paula nodded. She was sure.

Amanda lowered her head and sighed. She had not been close friends with Sandy, and Marna, it had to be said, hadn't liked her at all. That didn't alter the feelings of disbelief and horror. Sandy had been one of them. They had known her, worked with her, spent shifts talking and watching TV together. Amanda knew her to be a devoted mother to her two kids – surely that had to count for something in this shitty life. Upset and shaken, she downed the last of her brandy and poured herself another.

At six o'clock, they turned on the television and waited for some mention of Sandy. It came in the form of two minutes read by a po-faced presenter who delivered his lines with professional detachment.

A woman's body had been found. A Garda spokesman said they were treating the death as suspicious. An appeal was launched for any information. A quick shot of the outside of the building that had housed Sandy's flat.

There was no mention of Sandy's profession, no mention of the circumstances surrounding her death. It would be a brief respite. The three women were fully aware of the media interest this would generate: the next day, the tabloids would be full of stories of prostitution. Nothing made a murder more interesting than the added spice of sex and intrigue. Nothing sold crummy papers faster than a hooker biting the bullet.

'Time to batten down the fucking hatches,' Paula said forlornly. She threw back the dregs of her glass. Amanda and Marna nodded. They were all genuinely upset by Sandy's death; but they knew this tragedy would spark a renewed interest in their business. There would be speculation and gossip in the guise of journalism. Old stories would be brought back from the dead and updated and re-worded to appear new and fresh. Comments from 'sources close to the victim' would be printed with ghoulish relish. The death of a mother, tragic and pitiful, would be sensationalised into a paper-selling soap opera.

'Fuck it!' Marna said, a little drunkenly. 'I'm closing up and going for a proper drink. You guys coming?'

'Never said a better word, darling!' Paula lurched out of her chair and yanked the TV plug out of the wall. The newsreader disappeared with a pop. 'Come on, I'll get in the first round.'

'I can't, I have to get home.' Amanda stood and buttoned her coat.

'What?' Marna stared at her. 'Jesus, Amanda, one fucking drink, in memory of Sandy!'

'Marna, I have to get back.'

'Why? What the fuck is so important?' Marna's voice wobbled. 'It's only one fucking drink!'

'Marna, I – I can't ...'

'Ahh, just fuck off and go, then.' Marna waved one hand in the air and yanked her coat off a chair so hard that the chair crashed to the ground. 'I know, I get it: don't ask any fucking questions.'

'Jesus, Marna, are you drunk?'

Paula righted the chair. 'Come on, Marna, love, don't be upsetting yourself.' She shot Amanda a snotty look over Marna's back. 'Go on ahead, Amanda; I'll make sure she's all right.'

Amanda felt herself bristle. 'I have to go, Marna.'

Marna pulled on her coat. 'So go! Don't let the death of one of our own fucking stop you from whatever the fuck it is you do. Jesus, Amanda, don't you get it? That could have been any one of us. Me, you—'

'But it wasn't.'

'Oh, just fuck off home.' Marna collapsed into a sobbing heap, and Paula folded her arms around her.

Stung beyond words, Amanda whirled on her heel and left the sitting room. She heard Marna's angry words ringing in her ears the whole way home.

By the time she arrived back at the apartment, it was late and she was exhausted. The news of Sandy's death had shaken her badly, more than she was willing to admit even to herself.

She leaned against the mirrored wall of the lift and squeezed her eyes shut. She had spoken to Sandy Walsh three weeks before, and now she was gone.

Her apartment was dark and quiet. Normally the silence was a welcome relief; tonight it simply felt oppressive.

Amanda's single status was self-imposed. Though she wasn't a loner by nature, the single lifestyle suited her well. In her business it was almost a necessity. How did you explain to a man what you did for a living? When did you explain?

She switched on the lamp in her sitting room and sat down heavily on the enormous suede sofa. Through the windows of the apartment, she saw a pale half moon, struggling against the clouds. She felt odd and disjointed; the silence she normally appreciated so much unnerved her. She got up and stepped out onto the balcony. It was cold out; she shivered as she stared out across the city, her mind inevitably wandering back to Sandy.

Could Sandy's killer be someone she herself knew – someone she'd looked after? Were their lives so cheap? She tried not to think of Sandy's children, orphaned – for what? What chance had Sandy had against a man? She had been tiny, for Christ's sake … Amanda went back inside, threw off her coat and lay back down on the sofa. She switched on the TV and stared vacantly at the screen.

They hadn't always got along with each other, but she had genuinely liked Sandy. They had worked together for almost two years at the Red Stairs. In a business where pretence was a way of life, Amanda had found Sandy's habit of calling a spade a spade refreshing. Sandy never pretended to like a person if she didn't, and she didn't give a shit if someone didn't like her. She was a decent woman, with no airs and graces, trying to provide for two kids. Now she was dead.

How had it happened?

That part was easy, if Amanda was honest about it. Most of the working girls she knew, including herself, were complacent about security.

If you do a job for long enough it becomes normal, almost routine. Sure, she worried about the police, the taxman, the newspapers getting a photo of her; but murder … that was never even contemplated. She'd worked for nearly five years without any serious trouble from a client. They weren't street girls; they didn't get into cars with strangers, to be driven off to God knew where. Their clients came to see them, on their own turf. Of course that didn't mean total security, and she knew many a girl had had a few digs from clients, especially from early shooters. And, sure, she herself had been threatened more than once – but murder? Why would they think about murder? They had enough to worry about.

She stood up and crossed the room to a large bookcase, her hand automatically reaching for a leather-bound photo album; this was something she often did in times of stress. She carried it back to the sofa and flicked slowly through its pages, smiling at the ones where she was a scowly, pudgy baby. The final photo was the last picture taken of her parents, eight months before they had died. Her father stood rigidly, squinting at the camera, the way he did in every photo; her mother was wearing that slightly anxious expression Amanda remembered so well. Amanda traced her finger across her father's face and held the photo up to the light. The picture captured the essence of him so completely that it was almost as though he was there next to her.

Amanda's stomach lurched, and she closed the album with a snap.

It killed her that she hadn't spoken to them before they died. It had been her own stupid fault; she and her father were too alike, both of them fiery and strong-willed. He had tried his best to mould her into something she wasn't, and she had rebelled against him in the only way she knew how: by cutting them off and running away to the city. If she had known how little time she had left with them, she would never have wasted a second of it on petty arguments. Now it was too late, and guilt was all she had left to feel. She missed them so badly it sucked the air out of her when she thought of them.

Amanda hugged the album close, kicked off her boots, pulled her legs up and curled up in a foetal position. Still thinking of Sandy and death, she drifted into a light sleep.

The telephone jarred her awake an hour and a half later. It was the land line; it had to be Marna. She groped for the phone and knocked it to the floor.

'Hello.'

'Amanda, I'm sorry for disturbing you at home—'

She sat up, trying to clear her head. The album slipped from her grasp and fell to the floor. 'Who is this?'

'It's Michael Dwyer. Detective Sergeant Michael Dwyer.'

'How did you get this number?' she snapped, now fully awake.

'I need to speak to you, Amanda.'

'I asked you how you got this number.'

'If I've caught you at a bad time, I can call you tomorrow,' he said, ignoring her question.

Amanda rubbed the heel of her hand against her eye. 'What do you want? I doubt this is a social call, so spit it out. Why are you ringing me?'

'You may not have heard yet, but a colleague of yours was killed two nights ago. We've been asked to lend a hand with the investigation.'

'*We* who?'

'Vice.'

'You've got some fucking neck ringing me.'

Michael sighed down the line. 'We are trying to build up a background of the victim. We know you knew her, Amanda; your mobile number was found next to the phone in the victim's home. We know you worked with the victim some time—'

'Her name is Sandy.'

'What?'

'Stop calling her the fucking victim. Her name is Sandy.'

'Sorry. Look, we need to gather any information that can help us with our enquiries. Anything you can contribute would be of great help. The sooner we catch the—'

'I don't have anything to contribute. I worked with her, that's it.'

'Amanda, please. There might be something you know, maybe something you don't rea—'

'I told you, I don't know anything about it.'

'We'll still need to talk to you.'

Amanda sighed and reached for her cigarettes. She lit one with a shaky hand and took a deep drag. 'You bastards. All right. When?'

'The sooner we meet up the better. Maybe I can call tomorrow—'

'Not tomorrow!' she yelled down the phone at him. 'The day after, Monday. I'll ring you and we can meet up then. If that doesn't suit you, then tough fucking luck.'

'Right, fine – Monday it is, then,' Michael said hastily. 'Any information you can give us will be treated with the strictest confi—'

'Save it, Sergeant. I've heard all that shit from you lot before, and look where that got me.'

Amanda slammed the phone down. The conversation was over.

Michael Dwyer again. She glared at the phone. The fucking cheek of him. How dare he ring her for help?

She snatched the phone to her chest and dialled Marna's number. Then she remembered the argument earlier and hung up. Marna was probably pissed as a fart with Paula, or sleeping it off. Either way, she wasn't going to call.

Amanda ground out her cigarette and stood up slowly. She was stiff and cold. She went into her bathroom and turned on the shower, stripped off, leaving her clothes where they fell, and stepped under the powerful jets of water. She washed her hair and conditioned it, running her fingers through it slowly. The jets pummelled her back, and gradually the tension left her body. When she was finished, she turned the taps off and wrapped her dressing-gown around herself as tightly as she could.

She caught sight of her reflection in the bathroom mirror and was startled to see how dreadful she looked. Her skin was blotchy and pale and she had dark rings under her eyes. She realised she hadn't eaten for almost twelve hours; no wonder she looked like shit.

Padding back to the sitting room, she ordered a pizza. Forty minutes later she was munching her food and feeling better. She finished her food and popped two of Marna's special emergency calm-down tablets into her mouth, washing them down with a bottle of beer. She watched television until, at last, she felt the tablets take hold. Why did Sandy have to have her number by the phone? The last thing she needed was another tête-à-tête with Michael Dwyer. She rubbed her eyes with the heel of her hand and sighed.

'Keep it together,' she said softly to herself. 'Keep it together.'

She went to bed and slept, a dreamless sleep, far away from the clutches of her day.

8

While Amanda slept, across town, Paul 'Tricky' McCracken was having unforeseen problems of his own. The owner of Red Hot and Blue and eight other agencies was working himself up into quite a temper. He drummed his fingers against the dashboard and tried to think.

Two of his apartments had suffered walkouts. Four girls in all had downed tools and left him in the fucking lurch. They said they wouldn't work with the Eastern European girls – said the girls were undercutting them too much. And, no matter how much Tricky threatened and cajoled, they were refusing to return to work. That meant he was losing money hand over fist, since the Eastern European chicks couldn't answer phones or direct clients to the apartments. Fuck, half of them didn't even know what fucking country they were in.

He glared at the mobile in his hand and swore softly. He knew who was behind this little standoff. That cunt Kate had been bitching about the money dropping off all last week.

He dialled her number. It went to her answering

machine. The fucking bitch had switched off her phone.

'Kate, this is your bleeding boss here. If you ever want to enjoy another day of your stupid cunting life, you better get your arse back to the fucking apartment, pronto. Don't make me call you again, you dumb snatch. Next time I won't be so fucking polite.'

He dialled another number and got a girl who had been working earlier in the day and was finished for the evening. She initially refused to come back in; she started whingeing on about being tired after her twelve-hour shift and needing to spend some time with her eight-month-old son. Tricky hadn't time for gentle persuasion. He opened his notebook and read her parents' address to her. After that the stupid bitch agreed to stop being silly and get her arse back in to work. At least that was the apartment on Mountjoy Square up and running.

He checked through his notebook for someone to cover Kate. The stupid bitches were like sheep – one got fucking notions and they all got them. He'd have to start being a little more hands-on, keep the cunts on their toes. If it wasn't for the raids, he'd be in keeping an eye on business.

He tried another number, but it was off too. 'Bollix!' This was not what he'd had in mind for tonight. He had planned to give job interviews to two English girls who'd phoned him earlier in the week. They had sounded young and pretty desperate. He had planned to have a good time, get the two bitches to show what they were made of, before he sent them packing. English! Not fucking likely. He wanted girls who'd do anything for a client. The Eastern-bloc girls were perfect. Man, could they turn a trick. None of this 'I don't do this and I don't do that' bollix. Give him an Algerian or a Russian any day.

But he still needed a few English-speakers to man the phones properly. And Kate was a looker – all blonde hair, big tits and baby-blues. She could wipe the floor with most of the girls he had. And that was the problem right there: the bitch fucking knew she was hot shit. He'd teach her a lesson she wouldn't forget. He couldn't have his staff thinking they could get one over on him.

There was a problem: the bitch was too clever for the usual stunts. She seemed to know he had the places bugged. She rarely spoke about her personal life to the other girls. If she had, he'd have known everything he needed to know by now.

'Fuck! That fucking cunt!' He slammed his hand on the steering-wheel. Who the fuck did she think she was? No one hung up on him.

But she had, and that bothered him. Did she think she could *get away* with that? Did she think he'd let that one *slide*? Did the cunt think he was going *soft*?

No sooner had the thought entered his head than it left again. Tricky knew his women. He knew what their boyfriends, husbands, parents did for a living. He knew what they thought of him, what they thought of one another. He knew which ones to talk nice to and which ones to keep in line, which ones were easy to turn and which ones always kept their mouths shut. He knew if his girls were over-charging the clients. He knew if they gave out personal numbers. He knew if they were thinking of leaving. He knew everything he needed to know to control his girls, without ever having to set foot on the premises. And so he should – he'd spent nearly two thousand quid on bugging equipment so that this kind of shit wouldn't bother him.

That fucking Kate had pushed him too far. The more he thought of her, the angrier he got. He didn't tolerate tarts trying to get one over on him. Troublemakers had to be dealt with swiftly and mercilessly.

He pulled a steel cigarette case from his pocket and flipped it open. Inside was a plastic wrap of cocaine, a hand-forged silver straw and a Gillette blade. He chopped out a long line on the dash with practised ease, hoovered it up and closed the case with a snap.

Paul 'Tricky' McCracken was the fifth and youngest son of Paudy 'Lobes' McCracken, a violent, work-shy layabout who had abandoned the family whenever the need to travel (or a younger woman) called, leaving the young Paul at the mercy of Iris McCracken, who was just as violent as her husband and far less merciful. With a ferocious drink habit and six mouths to feed, Iris often resorted to prostitution to pay for both. She regularly had 'visitors' at the family home, and, while the other McCracken children knew to make themselves scarce, Paul was reluctant to leave his ma in the hands of the rough men who called to their battered front door. Once, while he was loitering on the dog-shit-filled green behind the house, he had heard the unmistakeable screams of his mother coming from the house. Fearing for her life, the scrawny eight-year-old had raced home, his fists at the ready, ready to defend her to the death against whatever pain was being inflicted upon her. The sight he saw as he burst into the grotty bedroom was burned into the child's eyes forever. His mother knelt on all fours across the bed. Her skirt was up around her waist and her head was thrown back. She was roaring like a bull, while the white, bare arse of her caller slapped in and out with such force that her knees left the bed a little with each thrust.

Paul stopped dead in his tracks, mesmerised by the scene before him. So this was what happened. His brothers had been telling the truth. He looked at his mother's flushed face, the cords that stood out on her neck; the man's tightly screwed-up eyes, the way his mouth was pulled back in a rictus of ecstasy. The smell of sweat, the animal grunts of the man, the howls of his mother, engulfed him. A flutter of disgust, rage and something else, something he could not name, flamed through his body.

He didn't know why he did what he did next – perhaps it was because she was his mother, perhaps it was the shock – but Paul ran screaming into the room and, with all his might, planted his left foot deep into the white buttocks of his mother's rider.

The ensuing moments had been blurred by the years. He knew the man had screamed and slapped him about a little. He knew his mother had been furious with him. He vaguely remembered seeing the man throw some coins towards her. But most of all Paul remembered the look on the man's face as he rode his mother, and the look on her face as she let him.

From that day on, Paul's interests centred around the house, where he watched and eaves-dropped on his ma's visitors. She knew what he was doing, but she never prevented him. She claimed he was her little protector and laughed when he flushed. She once encouraged him to sit on a chair at the end of the bed while she serviced a man whom Paul knew to be a priest from the local Catholic church. The man offered his ma extra if the boy joined in. Seeing her eyes calculate a price, Paul slipped off the chair and fled the room.

That one occasion aside, Paul stayed around his ma more and more. Sometimes she was too drunk to remember if the caller had paid her or not, but Paul made sure no man left the house without leaving some cash behind. If he got the occasional clout on the ear when he reminded them to pay, so be it. That was the rule: if they wanted to come back, they had to pay, or he'd make sure his mother knew they had stiffed her. They could do what they liked to her, but they could not fuck with the family money. He began to understand there was a way out of the poverty trap he had been born into. Paul's calling had come.

He tested his own power over the weaker sex as soon as he could, and he learned from an early age to pick his victims carefully. Girls held no mystery for him: they were weak, especially the younger ones. If he pretended to like them and gave them sweets, they were putty in his hands; if he was mean to them, they cried. He played with them, toyed with their affections and laughed at their confused faces when he rejected them. With smooth talk, he could convince any girl to do just about anything. At the age of fourteen, he convinced a ten-year-old girl to take off all her clothes and let him have a good look at her; when the girl's father found out and called to the house that evening looking for him, Paul lied so convincingly that his elder brother was blamed. Later that evening, his brother gave him a bloody nose and called him a tricky bastard. His ma rushed to his defence, slapped the older boy across the face and pushed him out the door into the rain.

She took Paul into her arms and cooed over him until he fell asleep in her arms.

The nose healed, but the name stuck.

At seventeen, with some help from Iris, Tricky honed his ideas and opened his first knocking-shop. The one-room flat at the bottom of a mucky lane in Ranelagh was staffed with some of the ugliest women imaginable. The women – including Iris – smoked non-stop, drank like sailors, had bad teeth, wore bright eyeshadow and squeezed their misshapen bodies into cheap satin nighties. Tricky was repulsed by them; he would never have touched one of them with a barge-pole. But, as soon as he opened the place at eleven in the morning, the money came in steadily. Compared to a quick fumble in a car up a dark alley, the attraction of lying down in an actual bed was too much for the men of Ireland to pass up. By the time his mother kicked it from cancer a year later, leaving Tricky in sole charge of the business, he was already making serious money.

Tricky sighed at the memory of his first brothel. He should have been fucking retired by now. Would have been, too, if he hadn't let himself get talked into doing a bank job with his older brother Cormac. 'Foolproof,' Cormac had said. Tricky lit a cigarette and shook his head; he should have known that the only foolproof thing was that his gobshite brother couldn't organise a piss-up in a brewery. By the end of that fateful day, two security men were wounded, one fatally, and he and his fuckface brother were looking at a serious stretch in the Joy. Goodbye lucrative brothel business, hello keep-your-arse-against-the-wall.

The 80s … fuck, that was when he should have made his money – when the men weren't choosy. Tricky snorted and took a deep drag on his fag. Now you had to have shower facilities, clean towels, expensive ads every fucking week, web pages and young girls who knew how to fuck like pros. You had to have videos, costumes, equipment, girls who pissed on command, girls who did threesomes and looked like they enjoyed it, girls who didn't mind where a client stuck it as long as he paid, girls who never got tired, never forgot to shave and never, ever had periods. If you didn't have all that, you soon fell behind the fifty-odd brothels that did.

Tricky took a deep breath and reassured himself that he was not losing his touch. He was the king. He had the best-looking girls, he had nice clean places – and now, thanks to the Garda raids, half the competition had been wiped out. Fucking A-OK.

He'd even found a use for the Vice team. Fuck knew how many calls he'd made to various stations, complaining about other brothels. He got his girls to ring, claiming to work with the competition and protesting about clients. He knew the gardaí had to act on a complaint, even if it was bullshit. He wasn't sure how many places his complaints had closed down this year alone – but the competition was suffering and his profits were right up. He'd even managed to get the team to nab Amanda and her brass-mouthed snatch of a friend.

He was on top … and yet this Kate bitch had fucked up his evening. Tricky drummed his fingers on the dashboard. What did he know about her?

He had her address – he'd picked that up the same week he hired the bitch. It had taken three nights of following her to be sure, since she refused all offers of lifts. But he was a persistent and diligent spy. The bitch thought she was clever, but she was nothing compared to him.

Gunning the engine of his BMW, he pulled onto the street and drove across town, towards Portobello and the leafy street where Kate rented a flat on the second floor of a red-brick Georgian house. He parked the car under the beech trees across the road and switched off the engine.

His lips twitched in anger. The lights were on in her flat. The fucking whore was home while he was left with two places sitting idle. His hand reached for the door handle, but it stopped in mid-air.

The bitch didn't know he had her address. That could be his trump card, and there was no point in playing it now. No, he would save this for another time. He'd ask the Whale if he fancied a little fun. The Whale liked blondes.

Tricky smiled, all his anger vanishing in a single puff. He turned on the engine, put the big car into gear and threw one last glance at the window of Kate's flat.

'I'll be talking to you, bitch. Real fucking soon.'

His good humour restored, he drove back across town, whistling tunelessly. Halfway to his gaff, he grabbed his phone and dialled the Whale.

'I've got a job for you. Need you to pick up two English ones from Dun Laoghaire. They're coming in off the evening ferry.'

'You hiring?' the Whale asked.

'Nah, fuck 'em, but that doesn't mean we can't have a little fun. They're on their own. Don't know nobody. The one I spoke to didn't sound old enough to bleeding work.'

'OK.'

'I'll get them on the mobile, tell them who to look out for.'

'Right.'

Tricky hung up and put his foot down. He needed to check in with Emma before he could enjoy his evening fully. Once he knew she was all right, he could kick back and enjoy a bit of fresh meat.

9

At nine o'clock on a freezing Monday morning, Michael sat in Phoenix Perk on Dame Street, waiting for Amanda Harrington and trying desperately not to fall asleep.

Michael, operating on only three hours' sleep, was exhausted. He had considered phoning Amanda and postponing until the next day, but he hadn't. He'd figured she wouldn't be sympathetic.

He closed his eyes for a second and had to force them to re-open. The tiredness he'd been fighting on the night shift was back and creeping over him. He yawned and stared out the window. Where the hell was she?

Five minutes later, as he was beginning to wonder if she would arrive at all, he spotted her striding down the street, oblivious of everyone, talking into her mobile. He would have recognised her anywhere. Tall, long dark hair flowing down her back, huge sunglasses even though the day was cloudy – but it was the distinctive walk that marked her out. She didn't so much walk as stride, as though the street belonged to her and her alone. She carried herself with all the arrogance of a lady of the manor. To see her on the street, one would never in a million years have guessed her profession.

Michael wondered again why this particular woman was a prostitute. He wondered why anyone would work in such a profession, but he understood only too well the social problems, the drugs, the grinding poverty, that drove some women to it. But why this one? She was well spoken, obviously intelligent; everything about her hinted that she came from a good background. What the hell was she doing caught up in this racket?

Amanda stopped outside the coffee-shop window, acknowledged him with a curt nod, and carried on with her conversation. When she was finished, she snapped her phone shut and came inside. The conversation had obviously not been suitable for police ears.

She lowered herself into the chair opposite him, looking uncomfortable and cagey. She didn't take off her coat or remove her sunglasses. Her face was pinched and her mouth pulled into the defensive line Michael was beginning to recognise.

He leaned forward. 'Thanks for coming. Can I get you a tea or a coffee?'

'I'll have a cappuccino.' She placed her cigarettes on the table between them, like a barrier.

The waitress must have sensed hostility in the air; she gave both of them a nervous glance as she took Amanda's order. They waited until she returned with the cappuccino before they spoke.

'So how have you been?' Michael decided to try polite conversation. 'You look a little tired.'

'What do you want?' She yanked off her sunglasses and eyed him with open dislike. She hadn't slept much the previous night, and it showed, both in her appearance and in her mood.

'I'm pretty tired myself – just came off the night shift. Haven't had much sleep.'

If he was looking to crack the ice, he needn't have bothered. Amanda rolled her eyes and tapped the table with her index finger.

'I'm not here for a chit-chat. What is it you want, Detective?'

'All right.' Michael folded his hands on the table. 'I'm trying to see if you can fill in a few details about Sandy Walsh. I've already told you, anything you can tell us may be of some use in our investigation.' He watched Amanda's face; she continued to look at him like he had just crawled out from under a rock.

'We're trying to put together a list of men who are known to frequent brothels and who've been blacklisted.' He shrugged. 'So if you know anything that could be useful, anything at all, you can tell us. The person who killed her might strike again; the feeling is that he's—'

Amanda took a sip of her coffee and glanced at him. 'Why the concern? I thought that was what you lot wanted: fewer hookers on the streets. Sounds to me like this guy's doing you a favour.'

'That's not fair, Amanda, and you know it,'

Michael said quietly. 'We're all working very hard to find this guy.'

He jumped as she slammed her cup down on the table. Froth splashed over the side and onto her lighter.

'Don't you dare come the fucking injured party with me,' she said angrily. 'What the fuck do you know about *fair*? Did you read any of the papers yesterday? Do you think it was *fair* that Sandy was splashed all over them, written about like she was some piece of trash? Do you think it's *fair* that her kids will probably find out what their mother did because some fuckwit hack thought it would be a great way to shift Sunday papers? You lot make me sick. You hound us one week, then come whingeing and asking for our help the next. Well, screw the lot of you. You can't have it both ways.' Her voice had begun to rise, and with an effort of will she lowered it again. She glared at him, her eyes over-bright. 'Don't talk to me about fair, Detective Dwyer. I hope the word chokes you.'

'Now wait a minute—'

'I'll answer your stupid questions. But you need to understand something.' As she leaned across the table, Michael caught a hint of her perfume, soft and feminine – nothing like the woman wearing it, he thought angrily. 'When you and your operation closed places like the Red Stairs and all the other half-decent brothels, in your great fucking sweep to rid Dublin of the pimps, it was the girls who suffered the most. Women like Sandy, and God knows how many others, were forced out of the only bloody jobs they had. What the fuck did you think they were going to do? Retire? Work in shops? Now they're working with no security, no fucking back-up, afraid to work in groups because then, of course, it's a brothel. So when a few more of us get bumped off, you think about that.' She leaned back in her chair and stared out the window. 'I hope you find the bastard who killed Sandy, I really do. Just don't expect us to come running to you lot for help.'

Michael was gobsmacked by the sheer ferocity of the attack. He stared at Amanda as if she had reached out and slapped him.

'You act like we're the enemy here,' he said incredulously.

'If the cap fits ...'

'Well, we're not.' He threw up his hands. 'You act like you're doing nothing wrong, and ... I don't know, maybe that's how you see it, I don't know how it works in your head. But I've a job to do, and I'm not here to argue the finer points of Irish law with you!'

'Ah, at least you've dropped the best-friend routine, Sergeant,' Amanda fired back. 'Show your true colours – that's better. We don't want to keep pretending we're on the same fucking side, now do we?'

'What side? What is *your side*?' Michael's voice rose with exasperation. 'You were breaking the law! You may not like it that you got caught, you may not think the law is right – but stop acting like I personally hounded you into court, because I didn't! Nobody held a gun to your head. You do the job you do, and that's your business. Frankly, I don't give a shit!'

Amanda flinched, and Michael instantly regretted what he had said. 'Look, I'm sorry I—'

But the damage had been done. The temperature of Amanda's voice dropped below freezing. 'Ask me whatever the fuck you hauled me here for and let me get the hell out of here.'

Michael took a deep breath, pulled a notebook from his pocket and flipped it open. He noticed his hands shook slightly; he put it down to exhaustion. 'How well did you know Sandy Walsh?'

Amanda lit another cigarette. 'We worked together at the Red Stairs a few years ago.'

'But you were friends, you knew her well?'

'I wouldn't have called her a friend. I know lots of people, none of them well.'

'Was she seeing anyone, do you know?'

'You mean like a boyfriend?'

'Yes.'

'How should I know? I can't recall her mentioning one. As far as I can remember she was married once, but I wouldn't swear to it.'

Michael nodded. He knew about the husband. Darren Walsh lived in England with another woman and hadn't had the decency to sound upset at the news that Sandy had died. He hadn't even asked how the kids were. The only thing he'd

enquired after was Sandy's house, which would go
to him, as he was still technically her husband.
Michael had pretended they'd been cut off and
hung up on him.

'Did she ever talk to you about clients? Were
there any she wasn't comfortable with – maybe
someone trying to come on to her or giving her a
hard time?'

'I don't think so. Sandy's clients were mostly
regulars. Look, we weren't really that close. I told
you, we knew each other from way back but we
weren't exactly chatty.'

Michael tapped his pen against his teeth. He
wasn't sure if she was being deliberately uncooper-
ative or not. 'What about you?'

'What about me?'

'Have you run into any clients who … you
know, make you nervous or edgy?'

Amanda's face screwed up with scorn. 'Clients?
Not really. I mean, we have the usual crowd of
gobshites to watch for. I wouldn't call them
problem clients as such – more annoying than
anything else; fucking carpet-walkers.'

'I'm sorry, what do you mean? Carpet …'

'Walkers; you know, time-wasters. Gobshites
who call to a place, ask to see every girl on the shift
as if they're trying to decide which one to pick, ask
them a bunch of stupid questions, then suddenly
remember they have to park the car or get money
from the back. We call them carpet-walkers,
among other things.'

'I see. So, basically, there's nothing you can tell me.'

Amanda crushed out her cigarette. 'Look, I know she worked for that fucking psycho McCracken for a while. You need to talk to Grapevine Paula. Sandy worked at her place for a long time, too. She might be able to help you.'

'Grapevine Paula?' Michael repeated, passing a hand over his forehead. 'And she is?'

'I'll give her your number.'

'You could give me hers.'

Amanda cocked an eyebrow. 'Yeah, right.'

'Will she ring?'

'She'd sit on your face if you gave her enough gossip.' Amanda smiled nastily.

Michael wrote 'McCracken' in his notebook and underlined it. He was getting a headache. This whole meeting had been a complete waste of time. Either she didn't know anything, or she wasn't about to share it with him. Amanda's accusations had upset him a little. They shouldn't have, but they had.

'You mentioned McCracken. Do you know any of the girls who may have worked with her there?'

'Nope.'

'Did she ever mention any problems she may have had with him?'

'Not to me.'

'Nothing about any threats? She never said anything to you that suggested she was frightened of anybody?'

'Nope.'

'You called him a psycho. Why did you say that?'

'Everyone calls him that.'

'Did you ever work for him?'

'Nope.'

He closed his notebook and rubbed his hand over his eyes again. 'Well, if there's anything else you can think of, or if you hear something, maybe you'll give me a call.'

Amanda snorted. 'Oh, of course. Very first number I'd dial.'

Michael had taken as much sarcasm as he could for one day. He stood up to go, hesitated, and sat back down.

'Amanda, I'm sorry you feel like I'm the enemy. But let me tell you something: I wouldn't have wished that poor woman's death on anybody. And, for the record, I was disgusted at the way some of the papers reported her death. I don't know how they got half those details. I hope you can believe that.'

Amanda looked up at him. For a moment he thought she had tears in her eyes; then she blinked and they were gone, and her hard mask fell back into place.

'It doesn't matter a damn what I think, Sergeant. We're the underdogs here. And the underdogs always get kicked. So do me a favour and save your speech for someone who gives a shit.'

* * *

Half an hour later Amanda let herself into the office. She wasn't surprised to find Marna perched on the sofa in the sitting room, knitting, with the TV on but turned down low.

'I knew you'd be here,' Amanda said, shrugging off her jacket. 'You must have had to dress in the taxi to get here that fast.'

Marna raised an eyebrow. 'Well, maybe if you'd told me before this morning you were meeting Dwyer I'd have offered to go with you. Well?' Her fingers flew, clickety-clack. She always knitted when she worked, making bedspreads, jumpers, scarves, anything to keep her hands busy. 'So let's hear it.'

'What?'

'What did Judas of Iscariot have to say for himself?'

Amanda grinned. She went into the kitchen and put the kettle on. 'Not much,' she called over her shoulder. 'He asked me a few questions about Sandy.' She leaned against the sitting-room door. 'I more or less told him it was his fault she was dead.'

'You did what?'

'Not him, all of them – fucking cops. Closing places down, leaving people like Sandy with no choice but to work solo. That kind of thing.'

'Well, you were right. What did he have to say to that?'

'Nothing, really, but he was pissed off when he left. You could tell by the way his 'tache wiggled.' Amanda smoothed her hair back from her face.

'He wanted to know if I'd ever worked for McCracken.'

'What did you say?'

'I said I hadn't.'

Marna stopped knitting. 'Why?'

'I don't want to get involved with this shit, Marna. Anyway, why should I help him? That bastard is the reason I have a criminal record.'

Marna shrugged her shoulders. 'Well, fuck him and his facial hair. They couldn't care less about any of us.'

'He said he was on our side.'

'What bloody side?' Marna snapped. She threw the wool down. 'Jesus, I'm so sick of being portrayed as a victim. The papers are going on about this business as though it's the last refuge of the damned! What the hell do they know? They've never interviewed me or you or anyone else I know, so how the hell can they keep writing the same tired old shit? Do they think we're all fucking brain-dead or something? Do they think we can't work in this business without some fucking bleeding-heart reason behind it?'

'I looked at Michael Dwyer this morning, and he was all full of concern and appealing to my good side to help him, and all I could think of was him reading out the evidence against us.' Amanda shook her head. 'Then he tried to play the empathy card.'

Marna snorted. 'There's some psycho on the loose, and what have we got to protect us? The fucking Vice squad. Jesus' – she shook her head – 'lucky us.'

Amanda held up her hand dramatically. 'Marna, think about the money!'

Marna stood up, put her hands on her hips and cocked her nose imperiously in the air. 'The money,' she said in a deep growl, 'is *contaminated*!'

Amanda started to laugh, and the sound startled her. She realised she hadn't laughed properly in days, maybe even weeks. Ever since the damned raid, her life had been nothing but a series of anxious moments.

'That's it!' Marna clapped her hands. 'We're leaving this life of debauchery! Amanda, close this place up. I know we make a fortune, I know I like fur and gold and a good bottle of wine, I know we have savings and pension plans – but, dammit, it's all for nothing, I tell you! The money is *contaminated*.'

Amanda laughed harder, raised her hands to her face and felt a tear in the corner of her eye. She dashed at it quickly, before Marna could notice. She wasn't fast enough.

'Shit, Amanda,' Marna said, suddenly serious. She went to Amanda. 'What's wrong? Why are you crying?'

'It's nothing. I'm … well … these last few weeks have been pretty rough.' She wiped her eyes. 'I'm sorry about the other day. I should have gone with you.'

'I know, I know,' Marna said softly. 'But things

will get better. We're still a team, aren't we? Fuck it, fuck crying and fuck that stupid old bitch of a judge.' She put her arms around her friend. 'Look, what the hell is going on with you? I know something's up. Why won't you talk to me? I might be able to help.'

Amanda stiffened and pulled away.

'There's nothing wrong. I'm OK,' she said gruffly. 'I'd better get changed. I've got that guy who likes to dress up as a baby coming in – can't let him see me like this.' She wiped her eyes and picked up her bag.

'I'll make you a coffee,' Marna said softly, hurt.

'Yeah, great.' Amanda nodded and closed the sitting-room door behind her.

Marna stared at the space where Amanda had been and shook her head. Whatever was going on with her friend and partner, it was clear that she was neither expected nor allowed to help.

Michael fought bumper-to-bumper traffic and eventually made it to his three-bedroom semi in Lucan exactly an hour and a half after he'd left Amanda Harrington in Phoenix Perk.

Exhaustion deadened his limbs; his only thought was to cart himself up the stairs and hit the sack. He collected his mail from the mat in the porch and shuffled through it – nothing but bills and an ad for a travel agency offering 'Amazing prices!' if you booked your holiday with them 'right now!' Michael stared at the front of the brochure. A bronzed man with pecs only a gym-rat could love swung a petite blonde high in the air on some tropical beach somewhere, probably in Thailand. Thailand, where girls as young as eight or nine were sold to brothels and pimps by families desperate for money. Little kids walking the streets, lips painted red, eyes as dead as cue balls, looking for wealthy Europeans to ply their trade with. And there was no shortage of takers. There were agencies that specialised in sex tours for the 'discerning gentleman'. Everything and everyone had a price.

Michael snorted wearily. Jesus, he needed a break. The operation had corrupted his mind. Even a stupid travel mag made him think of the job.

He balled up the glossy paper and tossed it as far as he could down the hall. Then he went into the kitchen and grabbed a glass off the draining board.

As he ran water and searched through drawers for the Nurofen he seemed to be addicted to these days, Michael pondered his earlier encounter. Was Amanda Harrington right – had they done more harm than good? Who would be the judge? What good was he or any of the others against the relentless tide of sex and pornography?

Amanda had been right about one thing, anyway: it wasn't going to be easy to get help from the working girls. For the last fourteen months, the prostitutes of Dublin had watched as place after place was raided and closed down. And this time the squad had played dirty. The DPP wanted results. Girls either gave statements against employers or were threatened with prosecution. Some girls had been brought to court; the squad had never done that before. Now the same officers were asking the girls to come forward and help the very same unit investigate the murder of one of their own. No wonder the reactions ranged from indignant disbelief to downright hostility.

Michael rubbed his hand across his gritty eyes. He was getting a ferocious headache. It was there behind his lids; he could feel it building like a tidal wave, threatening to engulf him at any moment.

He swallowed two Nurofen, sipped his water and tried to think about something else. He glanced out the back window. The garden was running wild from neglect; the raised beds were thick with weeds, and the grass was rangy and overgrown. Maybe on his next day off he'd spend a few hours tackling it. But even as he thought about weeds, another part of his brain was picturing the body of Sandy Walsh, her hands blue and cold as ice. He closed his eyes, but her head, shorn and covered with crusted blood the colour of fresh clay, filled his mind.

They were not at all as he had imagined they would be, the prostitutes. There were a lot of women like Amanda Harrington and Marna Galloway working in the business – women who, rightly or wrongly, believed they were doing an honest day's work and looked upon people like him as little more than occupational hazards. But Michael Dwyer believed in his job. He believed that the law was the law; without it, there would be anarchy.

He washed out his glass and replaced it on the draining board. Then he climbed the stairs to his bedroom, ready to drop. His head had barely touched the pillow when the phone rang.

Disbelievingly, he fumbled for it. 'Dwyer.'

'Mike, it's Ed.'

'What is it?'

'You'd better come in. There's been another one.'

He didn't need to ask what Ed was talking about. 'Is it that same guy?'

'Looks like it. I don't have many of the details yet, but yeah, I think so.'

Michael rubbed his hand over his eyes. Amanda Harrington's angry words echoed in his mind. 'When?'

'They think early this morning. It's a bad scene, Mike. Stafford says you'd better come in.'

Michael sighed and sat up. 'I'll be there.'

10

It was too much of a coincidence. He looked at the pages of the blood-splattered address book and re-read the names for the third time. The same names had cropped up in each of the whores' books, with the same numbers corresponding to each name. It had to be them. Four names: Amber, Tiffany, Ebony and Aeisha. Fake names, whores' names. Names of sin. He might never have found them … but the last one had their real names in brackets. How thoughtful of her.

He closed the book and slipped it back into the plastic bag. She hadn't even put up a struggle. It was true, then: they knew already. They under-stood that he was saving them, saving the men they would have corrupted. It was a vocation.

She had called out to God to save her. And God had delivered His blow.

He closed his eyes and felt at peace with the world. It had been proven. The voice had been silenced. He was going to cleanse them all.

The sharp trill of the house phone penetrated Amanda's brain and spiked into her dreams.

She moved slowly, pulling the covers over her head, trying to shut out the noise. Thankfully she heard it stop. It immediately started again.

Amanda stuck her head out from under the covers and checked the bedside clock: nine-thirty. She tried to remember what day it was – Tuesday? Wednesday? Who the hell would want to wake her this early? She rolled over and reached for the source of the offending noise, desperate to silence it before her head exploded.

The night before came rattling back to her. Five hours drinking red wine in the bar of the Burlington Hotel with a client who was pretending to be a German spy, even though he was from Meath. The evening had culminated with Amanda dragging him to his hotel room to beat the information the Allies needed out of him with a paddle, while he lay bare-arsed across the bed screaming, '*Schnell! Schnell! Achtung!*' until he came all over the plastic revolvers he wore strapped to his ample waist.

'What?'

'You asleep?'

'You ring a second ago?'

'No. Are you still in bed?'

Amanda closed her eyes again. The pain behind her eyes was unbelievable. Maybe she was having a brain haemorrhage. 'Fuck, Marna, this better be good. You know I had a call-out with the Commander.'

'Then you should have had a fucking phone

with you.' Marna sounded pissed off. 'I thought we had an agreement about that. If you're on a call-out, you buzz me when you're finished. That way I know you're safe.'

'Marna, spare me the lecture. What do you want?'

'Paula called earlier. She wants—'

'Paula? You woke me for fucking Paula? I'll call you back in about half an hour.' Amanda hung up. She rolled across the bed and got up on unsteady feet. Her head was pounding, her tongue felt furry and her mouth was parched. And as for her stomach … She was way too hungover to deal with a case of 'Paula wants'.

She made her way to the bathroom, almost tripping over her coat, which lay where she had flung it drunkenly the night before. Opening the medicine cabinet was torture. She knocked stuff over and cursed. Finally she located what she was looking for and made her way to the kitchen. There she made the Cure: two Disprin and one Alka-Seltzer dissolved in three inches of water, a splash of tomato juice and a snifter of cranberry juice on top, stir until everything was mixed and chug it down. It tasted vile, but it was absolutely guaranteed to combat all manner of pain and suffering.

She was refilling her glass with water and making false promises never to drink again when she spotted the light flashing on her answering machine.

'Oh, what now?' She staggered out of the kitchen, dropped onto her suede sofa and reluctantly hit Play. There were three messages. The first two were from Marna, sounding snotty and worried at the same time. The third was from Paula, who had never called her at home before. Amanda hadn't even realised she had the number.

'Darling, it's me. So, I met that cop pal of yours. Although, honey, I'm not exactly thrilled you sent him my way, I forgive you. He's a cutie. Couldn't help him much – but you know, can't hurt to know another boy in blue. So, anyway, hope you were talking to Marna. Were you? I need an answer kind of sharpish. Marna's no problem with it; can't see that you would either. Marna says you've been kind of shunting the hours lately. Not that she's complaining. Well, not that it's any of my business even if she was. Hey – Sergeant Dwyer, is he married? I didn't see any wedding ring and doesn't he have that whole lonely thing going on? Not that I'm saying I'm interested – all that hair above the lip, not really my style, although some women find that very masculine. Don't you think those Clooney eyes are—'

Amanda hit Stop, then Delete. She drained the last of her water before she returned Marna's call.

'What does she want?'

'Didn't she leave you a message?'

'I couldn't listen to it, she was turning my stomach.'

Marna told her. Amanda listened and knew

that, as badly as it had started, this day was only going to get worse.

'Let me see if I have this right. You want us to take on some girl who we don't know from Adam, to work for us, at our apartment? You want us to be pimps now?' she asked disbelievingly.

'Oh, please, don't start that bullshit. This girl is looking for work and Paula thinks she'd be great for us. No kids, no boyfriend and no drugs.'

'If she's that hot, why doesn't Paula want her?'

'Paula says there's hardly enough shifts to go round as it is. Her ladies are grumbling.'

'What's that got to do with us? Marna, if we get caught with a girl working for us, we're finished.'

'As far as I can see, it doesn't make any difference if we have a girl working for us or not. It's all the same in the eyes of the law.' Marna's voice took on a distinctive steely edge that Amanda recognised. It meant she had already made up her mind and was simply going through the motions until Amanda agreed with her. 'When it's only the two of us, we're running a business. If it was twenty-two, we're still running the same business. The only difference is that we would make some serious money. I'm telling you, Amanda, I'd rather be hung for a sheep than a lamb any day of the week. Anyway, with you disappearing half the fucking time I could do with someone else to—'

'All right!' Amanda's headache had increased a notch. 'How long's she been with Paula?'

Marna paused. 'About a month.'

That pause worried Amanda. 'Where did she work before that?'

'Paula said she's really nice, no bullshit with her – comes in, does her shift, goes home.'

'That's not what I asked.'

'Look, don't go all bat-shit on me. I'm—'

'Where was she, Marna?'

'Well, she did a few shifts at the Archway, and … City Stars.'

'City fucking *Stars*!' Amanda almost dropped the phone. 'She worked for Tricky? You must be fucking *joking*! You can't hire one of his girls!'

'Stop shouting,' Marna said, raising her own voice. 'Look, how about we meet her, get a feel for her first, before we dismiss her completely?'

Amanda took a deep breath and counted to five in her head before she spoke. 'I'm not even going to dignify that with an answer. You're thinking with your damn bank balance, as usual. You don't get it, do you? If we take this girl on and Tricky gets wind of it, he'll be all over us like a rash! Imagine his reaction when he finds out we're poaching his staff as well. Talk about really rubbing his fucking nose in it.'

'We're hardly poaching his staff. She's been gone a month at least.'

'He won't see it like that.' She pressed her hand to her head, trying to ease the steadily growing thumping. 'You don't know him, Marna!'

'She's working for Paula, isn't she?'

'Paula's different! Even Tricky knows not to fuck with her. And Paula doesn't want shit either –

that's why she's trying to palm her off on us! Marna, listen to me. *No fucking way.* We don't need that kind of hassle.'

'No, you listen to me,' Marna snapped. 'Fuck Tricky; I don't give a shit about him. I'm in this business to make money, right? So I am arsed if I'm going to let that bollix dictate my life. We've got to take chances sometimes. We always said we wanted to be out of the game before we were fucking forty, right? We make good money, I'm not denying that, but we could do better. If girls come to us looking for work, the least we should do is weigh up the pros and cons, without worrying about Tricky.'

Her voice softened. 'Amanda, listen. Think about it. I know you're freaked out, but—'

'You know what he did to me,' Amanda said softly. 'You want that to happen again?'

'How can you say that?' Marna sounded hurt and offended. 'But it was years ago. Let's move fucking on! This girl sounds kosher to me; why don't we at least meet her? Huh?'

Amanda gritted her teeth. 'I said I don't want her.'

'Well, fuck that! Can you promise you're going to be in all of next week? The week after that? Are you going to be there every single day?'

'Marna, I can't—'

'Exactly. I need someone to cover when you're not there. I can't keep working alone. This isn't just up to you.'

'So do what you bloody want, then! Why the fuck did you bother ringing me in the first place?' Amanda slammed the phone down, ripped the line out of the wall and burst out crying. She ran for the bathroom, barely making it before she vomited into the toilet.

Amanda wiped her mouth with a wad of tissues, threw them into the bowl and flushed. She sat on the floor and waited for her stomach to stop heaving.

What was happening to her? She had never felt more miserable in her entire life. She didn't blame Marna for being angry. The truth was, Marna was right: they did need somebody else, especially now, with Amanda spending less and less time there. But, Jesus, not one of Tricky's girls.

Amanda hauled herself up and leaned over the sink. She ran cold water and splashed her face. How could Marna be so stupid? Didn't she remember how bad it had been when Amanda had left him? Didn't she understand how dangerous he really was? Of course, Marna had never actually worked for him; and Amanda knew that, unless she'd actually been through it, no woman, no matter how many horror stories she heard, ever really understood how soul-destroying it was to be at the mercy of a vindictive, malignant bastard like Tricky.

Sick at the sight of herself, Amanda dragged on a dressing-gown and returned to the sitting room. But the normally peaceful room did nothing to ease her suffering. She looked around at her furnishings – the oversized sofas and chairs, the oil painting over the fireplace for which she had paid a bloody fortune, the antique lamps and raw-silk cushions. These were the things she had thought she wanted – the trappings. Was it worth it? She didn't know any more. She only knew she felt miserable, claustrophobic and ready to scream.

She needed some air. Ignoring the biting cold, she opened the French doors and stepped out onto the balcony. It was a bright, clear day, and, as she gazed across the city, the fresh air revived her more than any painkillers could. Behind her, the bells of Christchurch were ringing, sending out their message, calling to the faithful.

It must be nice, she thought, to have some faith to call on in times of need. But Amanda didn't believe in praying for inspiration. She listened to their musical chimes and breathed deeply, forcing her body to relax.

She wrapped her gown more tightly around her body and watched a sleek magpie land on the apex of her roof. He didn't seem in the least troubled by her presence. He cocked his head at her; the sun bounced off his feathers, casting an almost-emerald hue on his black back.

'One for sorrow,' Amanda said to him softly. 'Isn't that the way it is?'

The magpie chattered and flew off, rising high above the canal. Seconds later he disappeared over the buildings on the opposite bank of the river, leaving Amanda alone again.

11

Detective Inspector Jim Stafford was not in a good mood. Felim Brennan was not a happy camper; and when Felim Brennan was not a happy camper, Jim Stafford felt Felim Brennan's considerable boot up his arse.

It was because of Brennan that the Special Vice Squad had been set up in the first place. After years of blind eyes and ho-hums, the gardaí had been drafted in to tackle the exploding number of pimps operating in and around the city. The main objective had been to close down as many of Dublin's main brothels as possible.

Easier said than done, thought Stafford sourly. First you had to find them; then you had to prove the place was a 'house of ill repute' before you could close it down. The fact that it took time to do all this didn't seem to impress the Commissioner in the slightest.

'But you're not closing them, Jim,' Felim Brennan barked down the phone. 'From what I hear, you're *relocating* them. Every time one shuts, another opens up.'

Stafford gripped the receiver and counted to

ten under his breath. Brennan hadn't an original thought in his head; he was no doubt repeating what the Minister for Justice had spewed at him. Relocating, indeed.

'We need to be seen to be dealing with the problem, not moving it around. We need to see convictions, Jim. Get them into the courts, get heavier fines, whatever it takes.'

'We do have seventeen convictions under our belts at the moment, sir.' Jim rubbed his back. Why did he never have a chair that supported his spine properly? 'With quite a few more pending.'

'This operation's heavy on the overtime, Jim, costing the department dearly. Now, you may want to think about that. Bring them in, Jim – high-profile guys. Give the tabloids something to really sink their teeth into. Let Joe Public know we are going to *break* these law-flouters.'

'Sir.'

'Now, I want you and the rest of the team to assist the officers investigating the murders of the two prostitutes. There's going to be huge media interest in those murders, Jim, and I want us to be as professional and as courteous as possible. That's got to be our number-one priority.'

'Sir?'

'A *united* front, a wall of justice. We need Joe Public to *feel* we can and *will* protect the streets from this madman.'

Stafford rolled his eyes. Whenever Brennan got a whiff of media pressure, he spoke in soundbites for weeks after. These calls made Stafford's ulcer sing like a canary.

'Sir, we are gathering background information on both women, and we will naturally pass this on to the murder team.'

'Good man. Robert Scully is leading the investigation. You know Bob, don't you?'

'Yes, sir, I do.' Oh, he knew *Bob* well. They had been at Templemore Training College around the same time. Stafford thought Robert Scully was a pompous, patronising, brown-nosed bastard. He suspected Scully didn't think too highly of him either.

'The murders are our *number-one* priority at the moment. I want all efforts combined to catch this man. Is that understood? I mean, Jim, my office has been fielding calls half the morning. Seems some of those reporters have got wind of the connection already. Was there anything in the papers this morning?'

'I haven't had time to read newspapers,' Stafford said, hoping Brennan would get the dig. 'But I don't think anyone has printed the word "prostitute" in connection with Tessa Byrne just yet.'

'Well, when they do, we need to be prepared. *Hysteria*, Jim – it sets in like wood-rot in a lumberyard.'

'Yes, sir.'

'Good man. Keep me posted on any further developments. As soon as we make an arrest, I want to be able to say that it was a *joint effort* between Vice and Murder. A team effort, if you will.'

'Yes, sir.'

'I want Joe Public to see that it works, having special units dealing with individual types of crime. I want this to be seen for what it is: *unification of the force*. You know what I mean, don't you, Jim?'

'Of course.' Jesus, his bloody back was killing him.

And so it went on – Brennan describing what he expected, while Stafford agreed with his every word. The Commissioner was well aware of the media and of the Irish public's view of policing. He was a man who took his job very seriously indeed, and because of this he expected results. If there were none, he wanted to know the reason why.

When Stafford got off the phone with Commissioner Felim Brennan, he kicked his bin across the tiny office. Then he stood up and walked gingerly around his desk, trying to relieve the stiffness in his back. He considered the implications of what he had been told.

He understood the need to pool resources to catch the man who had murdered the two women. In fact, he relished the opportunity to use his time for something other than the constant watching and waiting involved in the closure of sex dens. But the timing was a curse. They had been so close to catching one of the most dangerous men in the sex trade. Now, because of the murders, it looked like they would have to pull back for a while.

That sickened him. If they could close McCracken down, then at least eight of the main agencies, probably more, would be knocked out of action. It would have made Stafford's day – no, his year – if that prick had been caught. He didn't much care about the others, one way or the other. McCracken was a different matter.

Stafford had lost count of the number of girls he had interviewed over the last few months who had trembled and lost their memories at the mere mention of McCracken's name. It was no good trying to force them to talk, as far as Stafford could see. Whatever McCracken had over the women on the game, be it the threat of violence or something else, it clearly worked. Whenever he was mentioned, even the mouthiest of girls clammed up. It was only through Grapevine Paula that they knew as much as they did, and even her information was limited – a first in Stafford's experience, and probably in hers.

Over the last few months, Jim Stafford had developed a deep hatred of Paul 'Tricky' McCracken. Now it looked like the fucker was going to roam free for another while.

The phone on his desk rang. Stafford eyed it balefully and snatched it up, half-expecting another bout of Felim Brennan's headline jargon to further corrupt his thought process.

It was Michael Dwyer. 'Remember that background check you asked me to do?'

'What?'

'Emma Harris,' prompted Michael.

'Oh, her. Yeah, what about her?'

'She leased that apartment in her name three months ago, like she said. But I checked with a few other agencies, and her name has appeared on at least three other apartments I can trace, all over the past ten months. Four places in less than a year. Nobody moves that much. I think she's opening apartments for McCracken.'

Stafford eased his body back into the chair. 'How does she manage it? Don't the agencies look for some bloody proof of ID before they let places out?'

'They do, and she gives them it. The bank accounts she gives for the direct debits are genuine and set up in her own name. Last one – which, incidentally, has since been closed down – was set up four months ago. It's the work references that aren't worth the paper they're written on, of course. The letting agency found that out when they tried chasing her down for breaching the lease.'

'Aye, that's always the way.' Stafford booted the drawer of his desk closed. 'We can't arrest her for breaking a bloody lease.'

'True, but here's where she got a little sloppy. The bank where she opened the last direct-debit account also holds her own accounts, personal accounts. I think we may have something to go on.'

Stafford grabbed a pen and a piece of paper. 'Shoot.'

'She opened at least three separate accounts with this bank in the last eighteen months. She deposits money frequently, but she's clever – never more than five hundred pounds a pop, and it's spread out over the three accounts. When an account reaches seven thousand, it's cleaned out and the whole process starts again. Very neatly done, very low-key. I'd imagine that, if we checked with other banks, we'd find the same system. Now that is hardly a crime ...' Michael cleared his throat. 'Depending on where the money is coming from. Like, say it was the proceeds of prostitution.'

'We *know* where it's coming from! It's McCracken's pimp money. We need to prove it.'

'Emma Harris has a real job – well, one that pays tax. She could claim it's simply savings. Hell, she could say it's money she won on the horses.'

'She won't say that.'

'She might. She has plenty of experience with financial matters.'

This threw Stafford a little. 'Really? What does she do?'

'She's an accountant – with Acton and Pierce Ltd, no less.'

'Fuck.' Stafford scribbled down everything. He squinted at the page as if the words had suddenly changed to Chinese. 'Are you sure about this, Mike?'

'Positive, sir.'

'That one's going to be the chink in McCracken's armour. We're going to turn the heat up under the arse of Emma Harris.'

Stafford heard Michael rustling paper. 'Oh, I almost forgot – one other thing. The address she gives for her personal accounts is … oh, here it is. 27 Leeson Parade.'

Stafford whistled. 'Nice area. She own or rent?'

'She owns it. Big mortgage, taken out in October of last year. And she drives a nice little BMW.'

'They must pay well in the accounts these days. Do a little more digging. Find out how much money she's earning and do the sums. If she's in cahoots with that fucker McCracken, I want her pinned. I want McCracken! So make sure of your information this time.'

There was a long pause on the other end of the line.

'We were sure of the information the last time, sir.'

'Aye, that's why we were standing there like eejits and McCracken was nowhere to be seen.' Stafford rubbed his back again. 'Look, Mike, I don't mean to snap at you. Get your arse back here; we've got a fucking powwow with the department's fucking poster boy coming up in an hour's time. Can't be late for that, can we?'

'I suppose not.' Michael hung up.

Stafford rooted out the slim file that contained

all the information he had on Paul McCracken. He opened it and slipped the address inside. Most suits of armour, he mused, had a weak link somewhere. With any luck, they had found McCracken's.

Gerry Cullen listened to the message on his voice mail and thanked his lucky stars he'd already left his house, so Ellen couldn't see the guilty expression on his face. As if he didn't have enough shit to deal with at the moment. First he was on nights all week, causing him no amount of grief with his wife, and now this.

He ran his hands through his hair and pressed his fingers against his temples. If only he had never called into that place when his wife was pregnant. If only he had never met that blonde bird. Now he was totally fucked. He would never forget the shock he'd got when she approached him in court that day. What the hell could she want from him?

He glanced back towards the house and caught sight of his wife's pale face watching him from the living-room window. He started the car and reversed out of his driveway. She waved. Gerry pretended he didn't see her.

It was her bloody fault he was in this mess, he thought sourly. If she hadn't refused him sex for the last six months of her pregnancy, he would never have had to find relief where he had. And what a fucking mess this would turn out to be if anyone got wind of his little secret. He could kiss any chance of promotion goodbye; he'd be lucky if they let him stay on the force.

He should have known this day would come, the day when she would use her hold over him. He opened the car window to let in some fresh air, thought of his wife with her seemingly permanently swollen belly and cursed again.

'Gerry, so glad you could make it.' Stafford spotted him before he'd got through the front door of the station, and glowered at him.

'Sorry I'm late, sir.'

'Briefing room, now. We've got company.' Stafford turned his back and picked up the front-desk phone. 'And for God's sake tuck that shirt in.'

Gerry took the stairs three at a time. Typical, Stafford catching him being late again. Christ knew what Stafford wrote about him in the weekly reports. He'd be lucky if he didn't get a reprimand soon. Certainly he doubted he'd ever get another call-up for a squad.

Reaching the conference room, he was surprised to see all of the Vice team, a number of detectives from his station and some he didn't recognise. There were at least thirty men and women there; it was down to standing room only. Gerry leaned against the wall and nodded to Miriam Grogan, who was seated near the front. She nodded curtly back. He saw Ed over by the window, talking to a cute sergeant with a fine set of knockers pressed against the stiff material of her shirt. Gerry forced his gaze away. Shit, women were truly his bloody downfall.

A hush fell on the assembled gardaí as Detective Inspectors Bob Scully and Jim Stafford entered the room and made their way to the front.

'Good evening, ladies and gentlemen.' Bob Scully sounded as if he were addressing a public gathering as a guest speaker. He was about the same age as Stafford, but that was where the similarities ended.

Scully was in his early fifties; he was tall and broad-shouldered and looked like a man who could play a few sets of tennis without breaking a sweat. His face was slightly tanned, and he wore his thick grey-peppered hair in a style that most men of his age wished they could carry off. He wore an impeccable navy suit, a brilliant white shirt, a red tie and gleaming black shoes. And when he smiled, as he was doing now, the wattage was sixty-plus.

Gerry looked around the room and saw that the gaze of every female in the place, married or single, rested dreamily on the man at the head of the room. Well, every female except Miriam Grogan, whose head was buried in a pile of notes.

Fucking dyke, Gerry thought, feeling instantly better about the pass she'd turned down earlier in the year. He should have known.

'Is everybody settled?' Scully's cultured voice was that of a natural orator.

Stafford scowled at the floor. Scully probably practised in front of the mirror with a hairbrush.

'Good. Now, as you all know, we are here to investigate the murder of Sandy Walsh and the murder of Tessa Byrne. This is to be a combined effort between the Vice team and the Murder team made up from the two districts involved. You may make your introductions after this meeting.' He paused and let his eyes sweep the room, moving slowly over the assembled faces, making as much eye contact as possible. Gerry dropped his gaze to the floor.

'So what do we know so far? Sandy Walsh was brutally murdered a little under four weeks ago by an unknown assailant. Tessa Byrne was murdered last Friday night, also by an unknown assailant. We know a little about each of the women, and there is no doubt that the deaths are connected. Both women died from asphyxiation. They were smothered with plastic – cling-film, to be exact. Both women were assaulted before they were killed, although neither woman was sexually assaulted. Sandy Walsh had her hair removed, Tessa Byrne her teeth.'

Around the room, several people shivered involuntarily. Gerry noticed the cute sergeant leaning into Ed's shoulder. Fuck, why couldn't he get a hot bitch like that? He could comfort her, comfort her all night. Probably better than old Leather-Patch Cairns could, too.

'Copies of both the ballistic reports and the

post-mortem will be handed out at the end of this meeting.' Scully cleared his throat. 'Now, both women were known prostitutes, and because of this, the Vice team – headed by Detective Inspector Jim Stafford, seated behind me – has been asked to assist with the investigation. I trust we will all benefit from this … unusual arrangement.'

He looked down at the papers in front of him. 'As you know, I will be heading the murder enquiry. For those of you who don't know me, I'm Detective Inspector Robert Scully. Any questions you may have may be directed to me after this meeting.'

He rambled on for another twenty minutes about the seriousness of the situation and the positive things that would come from working as a team. Gerry Cullen could see Jim Stafford becoming more agitated by the second, and he smiled to himself. He knew Stafford hated playing second fiddle to anyone.

Eventually Scully finished his speech. 'I'm now going to turn you over to Detective Inspector Stafford, who will outline what we have at the moment. Jim, the floor is yours.'

Stafford hopped off the edge of the table he was sitting on and cast an eye over the group. 'Let's take stock of what we know. Sandy Walsh was a prostitute. She worked alone in a basement flat on Mountpleasant Street. Now, there was no sign of forced entry, which leads us to believe that she allowed her attacker to enter. Sandy was assaulted, stripped, bound head to toe in plastic. She was forced to ingest used condoms. Ultimately she died from asphyxiation due to the fact that she vomited. The assailant then posed her body in a sitting position and cut her hair off. The attack was unhurried and pre-planned. There was nothing rushed or disorganised about it. I don't need to tell you, that's troubling.

'Tessa Byrne, on the other hand, had been a part-timer and, as far as we can ascertain, had retired from prostitution. She was attacked in her own home. Her husband, a taxi driver, was lured from the house to Malahide on a nonexistent job, giving our boy plenty of time to gain entry to the house and attack Tessa. Again, the attack was unhurried and violent. This suggests that our killer has taken the time to study the victims and learn their habits. It suggests a high degree of pre-meditation.' Stafford glanced down at his notes. 'The attacker removed Tessa Byrne's teeth with pliers. This was done while she was conscious, and Tessa died as a result of choking on her own blood.'

Several of the officers in the room, hardened men and women, shuffled in their chairs.

'The neighbours, those around Sandy's flat and those around Tessa's house, have been less than useful. Nobody seems to have seen anything, but I don't buy it. They need to be canvassed again. There must be something they noticed, either on the days in question or in the days leading up to the murders. I don't care how mundane it is, I want to know about it. Got me?'

Thirty-something heads bobbed as one.

'The Vice squad will question the working girls. Sandy Walsh didn't always work alone, and we think Tessa may have worked in a few of the brothels in town at some point. My lot know many of the prostitutes already, so they might be more comfortable talking to us.'

Michael Dwyer, who had come in late and was standing by the door, almost laughed out loud. If anything, dealing with the Vice team was sure to piss the women off.

Stafford noticed him smiling and nodded his head towards him and Gerry Cullen. 'We need to talk to everyone we spoke to at the time of Sandy Walsh's murder, got me? Did the women know each other? Did they ever work together? Did anyone have a grudge against them personally? Had either woman been threatened recently?' He paused and cleared his throat. His voice didn't have the same deep timbre as Scully's, but what he lacked in depth he more than made up for in volume.

'I also want the people they worked for interviewed. Now, I expect this to be difficult, as I'm sure the brothel owners will be unwilling to come forward. Explain to them that this is a murder enquiry, not a raid; appeal to their consciences, if they have any. The more information we get, the more likely it is that we'll find our boy before he collects any more trophies. Got me?'

Robert Scully, who was busy straightening the seam of his trouser leg, visibly winced at this turn of phrase.

'If you have any questions, you address them either to me or to Detective Inspector Scully. If you find any information, you bring it directly to me or to Detective Inspector Scully. Understood? No exceptions.'

The sea of heads bobbed again.

Stafford stepped down and let Robert Scully have the floor. The brief was simple. They were to split into as many units as possible and gather information about the two women from friends, workmates, bosses, ex-bosses, family members, whoever they could find. They needed to piece together a connection between the two women as soon as possible.

'One other thing,' Scully added. 'Tessa Byrne had a red Chinese-style handbag that she used every day. Her husband has looked high and low for it, and it hasn't turned up anywhere in the house. That is a vital piece of evidence and I want it found. It may contain her mobile and various other items, such as her pass-book for the bank, her purse and her address book. As there was no forced entry, it's possible that Tessa knew whoever killed her. We need to establish who was the last person to see or speak to Tessa on the day she was killed. We're checking the mobile-phone records at the moment. If our killer contacted her on her mobile, there's a chance he contacted Sandy Walsh the same way.

'I don't need to stress how important it is to find the phone. I want to know who Tessa spoke to, who she texted, who texted her. I want a list of the numbers. I want to compare any numbers she had to any numbers Sandy Walsh had. I want to know why the killer took her phone and not Sandy's. It will also help us to eliminate genuine callers from our enquiries.' He glanced around the room. 'Now, ladies and gentlemen, if there is nothing else, then I—'

'No, there is one other thing.' Jim Stafford stood up and glared around the room. 'If I get one sniff that any of you lot are leaking information to the papers, I'll make sure that the only leaking you're doing is against the side of a wall at the dole office. Got me?'

Nobody said anything, but clearly everybody got him perfectly.

Scully's smile was a little strained. 'We will meet back in this room on Friday morning at nine o'clock, to discuss and share our information. Thank you for your time.'

'I have a bad feeling about this one,' Stafford said quietly to Scully as they watched the last of the gardaí troop out.

'Do you, Jim?' Scully smiled patronisingly. 'I'm sure that, now that we're all operating together, we shall apprehend him before he strikes again.'

'You think so?'

'Of course.' Scully straightened his tie. 'We're dealing with a disturbed mind here, Jim. These women are targets – easy ones. It's quite possible our killer is only warming up. You know, I attended a psychological assessment course last year and learned a great deal about the workings of the dysfunctional mind. It was really quite fascinating.'

Stafford didn't answer. He didn't need to attend a course to know that whoever they were chasing was one sick fuck.

'This will be a difficult one, but I think we can handle it. Of course, we appreciate whatever information the Vice team can pass our way, but I feel it will be only a matter of time before we catch this man. We have only to read the signs.'

Stafford snorted. 'Disturbed or not, the fucker's wearing gloves and he's studying them before he makes a move. I'd say he was pretty smart.'

'Yes, well.' Scully yanked down his amazingly white cuffs and smiled thinly. 'I'd better crack on. I have a meeting with a criminal profiler in half an hour. Amazing woman – really steps into the mind of a killer.'

'Hope she's got fucking wellies. She'll need them for all the shite she'll have to wade through,' Stafford said, and lumbered away to find Gerry Cullen to vent his spleen on.

12

The next morning, across town, Marna was trying to strike up a conversation with a deeply silent Amanda and failing miserably. They were in a rough-and-ready coffee house on George's Street, waiting for Kate.

'He's pretty, isn't he?' Marna held the photo of the young Italian waiter under Amanda's nose for inspection.

Amanda took the photo, gave it a brief glance and handed it back.

'Well?'

'Yeah, he's a real dish.'

'Small dick, though – and it's all over *very* quickly. No matter what I do to distract him, off he goes. Lock and load, and that's it. Can't last the pace.'

She looked fondly at the picture once more before putting it back in her bag. Daniele was only twenty, tall, very handsome and of course very Italian. She frowned slightly; he was also un-reliable, full of shit, too quick in bed and – worst crime of all in Marna's book – getting it for free.

Marna shook her head sadly. If she was going to

be with a man for pleasure, then he ought to be remarkable in the sack. If she wanted an unsatisfying quickie she could get one in work, and be paid handsomely for her time and trouble. Still, he was young and he had the body of a god. She decided she'd graciously give him another chance to impress her. If he didn't improve, well … *Ciao, bello.*

She glanced across the table at Amanda, huddled in her jacket, her head buried in the paper. Marna sighed and checked her watch again: half past nine. Where the hell was the girl? If she wanted a bloody job, the least she could do was make the effort to turn up on time. It didn't take a clairvoyant to see that Amanda's limited patience was wearing thinner as the minutes rolled by.

'So how long are you going to keep this up?'

'Keep what up?' Amanda raised her eyebrow over the top of a page.

'Don't play the innocent with me. The mood. It's really starting to get on my tits.'

'Oh, I'm not in a mood. I'm tired and fed up of waiting in this hole for some girl who a) is probably not going to show and b) I don't want to meet anyway.'

'It's only been fifteen minutes. She'll be here.'

'Whatever.' Amanda returned to her paper.

Another five minutes passed in silence before the wood chimes over the door announced the arrival of a new customer. The woman who walked in paused and looked around, sizing up each occupied table. Marna studied her carefully. She was seriously pretty – five foot five, with pale-blonde hair pinned up by a comb. She wore an old pair of jeans, a white shirt and a well-worn leather jacket. Even in this attire, Marna noticed, she had every male head in the place swivelling in her direction.

Marna prodded Amanda's foot under the table. 'Our eagle has landed.'

'So pluck it.'

The woman's eyes rested on Marna, who nodded. She crossed the room, pulled out a chair and dropped down beside Marna.

'I'm really sorry I'm late – the traffic was a nightmare.' She had a sing-song Cork accent. 'Thanks for waiting. I'm Kate.'

She offered her hand to Marna, who shook it and introduced herself, and then to Amanda, who ignored it and kept her name to herself. If Kate found that rude, it didn't show.

Marna ordered her a coffee, and they made small talk while they waited for it. Amanda never glanced in their direction.

Finally Marna could bear it no longer.

'Look, Paula told us you were looking for work, but the thing is, we're not sure if we can help you. She must have told you that we don't actually run an escort agency?'

Kate nodded. 'Yeah, she told me. But I've been at Paula's for nearly a month now, and she can only offer me three shifts a week, max – and even at that, some of the other girls are bitching.' She shrugged. 'It's not enough money. Paula said that you guys work privately but that you advertise on the web for new clients ...' She paused, looking from one face to the other. 'I've got clients on my own phone; I'd bring them with me.'

Amanda raised her head over the paper and shot Marna a look that could have soured milk. 'Yeah, and probably take half of ours when she goes.'

Kate glanced at Amanda and narrowed her eyes. 'I'm offering to bring in my own business in return for a place to work. What's wrong with that?'

Marna smiled and patted her on the arm to take the sting out of Amanda's words. 'I think what she's trying to say is, if you have your own clients, why don't you set up on your own? What do you need us for?'

Kate shifted uncomfortably in her chair. She glanced at Amanda again. Amanda stared at her coldly. 'What's wrong? Didn't understand the question?'

Kate's pale face flushed. 'First, I don't have the money to set up on my own. I'd need cash for deposits and things. Second, I don't think I *could* work on my own – not with all the shit that's going on at the moment. I heard about what happened to that woman over in Rathmines.'

'I understand,' Marna said, 'but you have to realise, we've never taken on anyone to work for us before. I'm not sure we even need someone.'

'Paula said you might be looking to expand a bit.'

'Did she, now?' Amanda said. 'Where would she get that idea?'

Kate swallowed. Paula had also warned her to expect a little hostility from Amanda, but she hadn't expected such open dislike. She decided to grab the bull – or, in this case, the cow – by the horns.

'Look,' she said angrily, 'I don't know what your fucking problem is, but I wouldn't even ask for a job if I wasn't completely desperate. With all the fucking raids, the main brothels are closing left, right and centre. The agencies are very cagey about hiring new staff, and half of them are on the fucking move every other week – I should know, I think I've tried most of them in the last week.' She leaned across the table. 'I'm just trying to get a job, OK? If you can't help, then say so and I'll be on my way.'

Amanda took a sip of coffee and eyeballed her. 'Marna tells me you worked for Tricky up until recently.'

'So?'

'So that's my main worry. I know Tricky; he doesn't give up on his girls that easily – especially not the good-looking ones like you. So either he sacked you, in which case there must be something seriously fucked up about you, or you left, in which case we don't need the shit that will come after you.'

She put down her cup and searched Kate's face, looking for any sign that this girl was not as straight up as she seemed; but she could smell the fear and desperation on Kate. No actress in the world could be that convincing.

'Tricky.' Kate's pretty face screwed into a sneer. 'Paula said you know him. Worst three months of my life. The bastard had the place bugged. Most of the girls are terrified of him, and the ones that aren't are probably sleeping with him. Did you know that he tries out each girl personally before he hires her?'

Amanda nodded. She knew all about Tricky's interview techniques.

'Tricky.' Kate wiped her mouth with the back of her hand as if the memory left a bitter taste.

'So what happened with you, then?'

Kate pulled a battered packet of Silk Cut out of her pocket and lit a cigarette. She smoked for a moment, her eyes far off and her jaw clenching and unclenching. Marna cleared her throat. Amanda waited.

Eventually Kate took a deep breath. 'He's seriously involved with some guy smuggling in Algerian and Russian workers. The Whale goes over to vet them out, picks out the best-looking ones and has them shipped over.'

Amanda shrugged. That was hardly news; everybody knew about it.

'These girls will do anything, and half of them are fucking crazy. They'd cut your throat as soon as look at you. And they work non-stop. Next thing you know, Tricky starts getting rid of the Irish and English girls. He puts eight or nine foreign workers on a shift. The ad money goes up to forty a shift, and that's per person. He's slapping fines all over the place – you leave a damp towel in a room, bang, you owe him twenty euros. In the meantime our money goes right down.' She shook her head. 'Jesus, some of those girls had barely turned eighteen, and they'd been in the business four, maybe five years already. And they were so fucking *hard.* You took your life in your hands even turning up for a shift, and if a client picked you over them … good luck. Of course, Tricky won't let the foreign girls know too much about where they are, so there has to be an Irish girl on every shift, manning the phones and keeping an eye on the others in case there's trouble.' She shook her head. 'These girls do things that we've never even heard of, and for half the money. We weren't making a penny. A few of us got together and decided we'd had enough. We walked out. I told Tricky on the phone I wasn't going back.' She took another long drag on her cigarette. 'He said that was fine – acted real nice about it. I should have known … it was so stupid of me. I thought he'd decided to let it go because I wasn't worth the trouble – you know, seeing as he had all these new girls.'

Amanda realised her own hands were shaking. She swallowed and forced her voice to sound calm. 'What happened?'

'Two days after I left, he sent the Whale round to my place.' Kate forced a smile, a wretched, tortured grimace that chilled Marna to the bone. 'I don't know how he even had my address; I was always so careful.'

Amanda snorted softly. She too had once thought that, and she too had suffered for her arrogance.

Kate passed her hand across her head and smoothed her hair. She was close to tears. 'You know he films the Whale at work now? Turns the whole thing into a little … production.' She closed her pale-blue eyes tight against the memory. 'He said he has buyers lined up who would be happy to see … see … what they did to—'

'All right, enough!' Amanda said sharply. Her stomach was doing slow flips and sweat was inching its way down her spine. At that moment she wasn't sure who she hated more – Marna for bringing her there, or Kate for dragging every memory she had so carefully repressed screeching back to the surface of her mind. 'We get the picture.'

Marna's mouth dropped open. 'He *films* it?' She shook her head. 'Jesus Christ. Why didn't you go to the cops?'

'And tell them what?' Amanda retorted. 'He'll say she agreed to be filmed, she'll say she didn't, it'll go to court and the world and its mother will know all about it. Not to mention that she—' Amanda jerked her head towards Kate. '—would have to take the stand against him, and fuck knows what the Whale would do to her before that happened.'

Kate shrugged and wiped at her eyes. 'Anyway, after that, he more or less left me alone. Rang once or twice to fucking remind me of the tape, but otherwise …' She shrugged.

'That's because you were with Paula,' Amanda said. She looked deliberately at Marna. 'When she leaves Paula's place, she loses all her protection.' She picked up her cigarettes, folded the newspaper under her arm and left. She was convinced that if she stayed another minute she would be sick.

Kate turned to Marna in surprise. 'Is that it? What about the—'

Marna held up her hand. 'I think you should leave it there. I'll talk to you in a day or so. Say hi to Paula for me.' Then she grabbed her bag and ran after her friend. By the time she got outside, Amanda was halfway down the street. Marna groaned and raced after her.

'Wait!' she called. 'Wait, dammit. I'm not built to run in high heels.'

Amanda stopped and lowered her head. Marna shifted her handbag onto her other shoulder and linked arms with her. 'You OK?'

Amanda started to walk again. 'Fine.'

'You don't look it.'

'I haven't thought about that shit for a long time.'

Marna shrugged. She waited for a few steps. 'She seemed nice enough, didn't she?'

'I don't know. It's hassle, Marna. I don't know … I don't like it.'

'You say that about everything.'

Amanda turned to face her. 'Look, if you really want her, then hire her. But you're going to have Tricky down on us. As long as you know that.'

Marna grinned. 'Don't worry about him. I'm going to put a spoke up that fucker's arse.'

Amanda stopped walking so fast Marna's arm almost bent backwards. She grabbed Marna by the shoulders and shook her.

'Owww—'

'Marna, you've got to promise me: don't mess with him.' Amanda shook her again. Her jaw was clenched and her eyes gleamed. Marna thought for a second she looked a little crazy.

'Jesus! Stop bloody rattling me, will you?' Marna tried to break free, but Amanda's grip was like steel. 'All right – all right! Jesus, Amanda, lay off the caffeine, will you?'

Amanda released her and took a deep breath. 'I'm sorry. But, Marna, if something happened to you …' She shook her head, and her bottom lip trembled. 'I don't know what I'd do.'

Marna smiled. 'Nothing's going to happen to me. C'mon, I'm sorry I freaked you out. Buy you the latest copy of the *Phoenix* to make it up to you.'

Amanda laughed and shook her head. 'You're bloody crazy.'

Marna grinned too, but in her head she was sure Paul 'Tricky' McCracken already knew they were off limits.

13

'You know you're my bitch?'

Bound and gagged, the man could only nod his head frantically. Sweat dripped down his forehead and into his eyes. He was unable to move his hands without causing incredible pain to his testicles, so he ignored the sweat and kept his eyes on the nipple-clamp leads Amanda held in her hands.

She stood directly in front of him, making sure he could see the whip snaking around her leg. It was tempting to laugh in his fat, blinking face, but she held it in; that would have ruined the level of ominous threat. She wondered if he realised how ridiculous he looked, perched there like a pink, spit-roasted pig. A rope tied his hands to his testicles, and from there she had looped it around his ankles and up behind him to the steel ring attached to the collar he wore around his neck. Amanda held the end of the rope in her left hand. Whenever she felt like his mind was wandering, she yanked the rope, triggering an alarming chain of events.

'And what do I do to bitches?'

It amused her to think that, with one gentle tug,

she could make this large man topple over onto his face. And he was paying her for the privilege.

'I own you. You're mine.' She opened one of the clamps and pinched his nipple hard with its serrated edges. 'I can do whatever I like with you, bitch, and you can't do a single thing about it.'

The damp head bobbed up and down. His eyes glazed over as the pain spread across his chest in waves.

'You think I'm joking with you?' She took up the slack on the rope.

This time the head shook furiously. Muffled groans came from behind the silver ball gag.

'Shut up!' Amanda cracked the whip in her other hand. It flicked out, snapping under his swollen balls. 'Do not speak! Do not whine like a dog.'

Silence; the eyes blinked at her. Rivers of sweat ran into his eyebrows, stinging his eyes.

'Did I ask you to speak to me? Do you think I *want* to talk with *you*?' She leaned dangerously close to him and jabbed a finger into his pudgy chest. 'Do you think I *want* to hear your pathetic, disgusting voice?'

God, she thought, he has bigger tits than I do.

The eyes blinked, and he slowly shook his head. Unbidden, his piggy little pinkie rose from a mass of wiry ginger pubes. Amanda tried hard not to kick him there. She wanted to, but that wasn't his thing.

'You are not fit to speak to me, bitch. I run the show in here! You're not even fit to look me in the eye.' She paced back and forth in front of him, trailing the whip behind her. 'Where should you look?'

The eyes dropped obediently to the floor.

'You want to get out of here alive, you need to serve me.'

The head bounced eagerly; through the wisps of a bad comb-over, his sweaty dome gleamed.

Amanda held the moment, letting him suffer, making him wait. 'I'm not even sure if you should be allowed to do that!'

Again the head bobbed. His shoulders drooped, beseeching her to force him into submission.

'I'm glad you are looking at my leather boots.'

He whimpered like a beaten dog.

'Do you know what I did in these today?' Amanda lifted one leg so that the steel heel glinted in the light. 'I *marched* in these. I *marched* in here and threw a prisoner on the ground and I *marched* all over him. I *marched* on his back, I *marched* on his front and I *marched* on his balls. And I *marched* on his face, in these shiny, leather boots.'

Her client swayed, and his eyes rolled up to her face. Amanda read his expression easily: he had reached his limit.

She wrapped the rope around her hand and, with a vicious tug, dropped him to the floor. He landed heavily on his knees and crouched there, unable to tear his eyes away from the patent shine of her boots.

She ripped the gag off, grabbed the back of his head and forced it lower.

'Make yourself useful, then, you fat piece of shit. Clean my *marching* boots. Do a thorough job, or I'll make sure that you won't be able to sit for a bloody week! I'll confine you to isolation.'

While he slobbered and licked her boots, Amanda stared at herself in the mirror that covered one wall of her room. She wore a PVC army hat, a camouflage shirt tied at her midriff and tight latex combat shorts – and, of course, the *pièce de résistance*: thigh-high patent-leather boots with eight-inch steel heels that pitched her forwards onto her toes like a dancer. Her hair was tied back in a ponytail so tight it hurt her eyes. And today, this particular client had asked her to wear a huge fake moustache, the type an army general would wear. She hummed under her breath, trying to drown out the sound of her client. His wet slobbering was making her feel a little ill.

'Put some bloody effort into it!' She brought the whip-handle down hard on his pale, spotty behind. It was a rubber whip, well greased, much more severe than a leather one. Red welts criss-crossed the faint marks already there – last week's beating had been particularly severe.

The man drooled and licked with renewed vigour. Finally, Amanda could bear it no more. She loosened the rope, allowing one of his pudgy hands access to his penis. Slobbering and pulling his dick at the same time, he worked feverishly until his breathing began to hitch and his back spasmed. With a muffled groan, he shot his load across her feet.

Amanda grimaced. She leaned over him, grabbed a box of Kleenex off the locker and waited for him to stop moaning and twitching.

'Jesus, Emmet, were you saving that up or something? Make sure you get it all up, there's a good lad.' She passed him the tissues.

'Is that an order?' Emmet quivered like a crushed strawberry jelly on the floor.

Amanda frowned. She hated it when they tried to keep up the fantasy after they came. 'Do you want to have a shower before you head back to work?'

Emmet sighed and rolled up into a sitting position. 'Oh, all right. I won't be too long, though. I've to get back to work sharpish – the regional manager's making one of his impromptu visits today. The bastard thinks I don't know about it, but I do. I got word. He's not the only one who can—'

'Mmm.' Amanda was already unlacing her boots. She couldn't wait to get them off and disinfect them.

'—make surprise visits.' Emmet knew when the session was over. 'Can I have a fresh towel?'

'Sure. Do you need a hand getting out of those ropes?'

'Nah, I can manage, thanks.' Emmet expertly untangled himself and wiped his stomach with a slowly disintegrating tissue. 'Will I book now?'

'What?'

'For next week.'

'Actually, I might not be here.' Amanda pulled off her boots, relieved. Eight-inch heels were absolute murder to walk in. They made her toes bunch into painful points.

'Well, I suppose I'll call, eh?'

He stood naked in front of her, hands on his hips. Bits of Kleenex stuck to the top of his diminishing pink knob. Amanda averted her gaze.

'Why don't you hop in the shower, and I'll pass that towel in?' She never understood why, as soon as they came, discipline clients forgot what had occurred moments earlier. And she would never understand why even the most physically unattractive men were content to stand around naked. Did they never look in a mirror? Were they really that oblivious of how they looked?

She went into the sitting room. Half an hour of humiliating Emmet had lifted her mood somewhat. She grabbed her cigarettes and glanced over at Marna, who was curled up on the sofa, her face pale as a ghost's.

'Jesus Christ, I don't know why that little shit doesn't admit he's gay and be done with it.' Amanda flung her whip into the travel crate that held all her uniforms and equipment. She had kept it in her room for a while, but too many pieces had gone missing. Now it stayed in the sitting room, where she and Marna tripped over it at least five times a day.

'He made me wear this.' Amanda pulled off the moustache and the hat and shook out her hair. 'Now he says he wants me to pierce his balls with an awl. I mean, come on—'

Marna cleared her throat. 'There's been another one.'

'Another what?'

'Another girl murdered.'

Amanda stopped stripping. 'What?'

'I don't know any of the details. It'll be on the two o'clock news.'

'Anyone we know?'

'I don't know yet. Radio said her name was Tessa Byrne. But you know names mean nothing.'

'Jesus, Marna.' Amanda yanked the latex shirt off, sending buttons popping in all directions. 'Ring Paula. If anyone knows anything, she will.'

'Stop snapping at me.' Marna picked up her mobile and dialled Paula's number. She paced back and forth, waiting for the connection. Her eyes met Amanda's across the room and she shook her head.

'Engaged. I'll try again in a few minutes.' She snapped the phone shut and pressed it against her chest.

Of course it was engaged, Amanda thought. The gossip line was probably red-hot with speculation and questions. They'd be lucky if they could get through in the next hour.

'Do they think it's the same guy?'

'I told you, I haven't a clue. I only caught the

tail end of it on the news.' Marna dropped into her armchair.

Amanda yanked off the last of her outfit and flung it across the lid of the case. She stormed across the room and grabbed her jeans from the back of her chair.

'Where are you going?' Marna said nervously.

'First I'm going to buy a fucking paper, then I'm going for a drink.' Amanda pulled on her jeans and a dark-red cashmere jumper. She sat down to put on her boots.

'What about your client?'

Amanda jumped up, opened the door and roared down the hall, 'Hey, Emmet! Get your arse in gear and get out. Madame can't fucking wait all day for you, so stop fucking about and get dressed and get out, will you!'

Marna stood up. 'Amanda—'

'What?' Amanda whirled around and glared at her. 'The fucker wants to be dominated, doesn't he? Well, today he's going to have to take the real with the imaginary.'

'What about our appointments? I've got one in ten minutes.'

'Fuck 'em. They'll call back.'

Marna closed her eyes and took a deep breath. It was a cardinal sin, and one of her own personal no-nos, to turn away money. She opened her eyes again and stared at a slightly demented-looking Amanda for a few seconds. Finally she nodded. 'OK, let's go.'

As Amanda harried a partially dressed and wholly confused client out the door, Marna tried Paula's number again. She wasn't at all surprised to find it still busy. Her second mobile rang; it was her client, calling to confirm he was in the vicinity. Regretfully she turned him and his cash down.

Fuck it, she thought savagely as she hung up on the disgruntled man. There was always something going on in this business. Never a dull moment.

It was six o'clock before they got any more information on what had happened, and by that time both Amanda and Marna were more than a little drunk. After several attempts, they had eventually contacted Paula, who had agreed to join them for a drink.

'OK,' Paula said as she squeezed her ample frame into the seat. 'This isn't gospel, but it's pretty close.'

'What?' Marna and Amanda said in unison.

'She was killed at her house.'

Both Amanda and Marna gasped. 'Her house!'

Paula glanced around. 'Yes, but from what I've heard, she was out of the business.' She leaned in, a look of smug one-upmanship plastered across her face. 'She used to work the streets, you know.'

'Ah.' Marna sat back. 'You see? A street girl.' She glanced at Amanda pointedly. 'And you made us run out of the fucking apartment for that.'

'For what?' Amanda said softly.

'She was probably a junkie or something. You

know what that lot are like.' Marna took a swig of her vodka and Red Bull and settled back into her chair, a look of relief mixed with irritation across her face.

'What do you mean?' Amanda asked.

'Oh, come on, Amanda,' Paula said. She flagged down a passing lounge boy and ordered a double brandy. 'Isn't it obvious? She was probably killed over drugs or something. I wouldn't be surprised if one of the others did it; that lot would sell their grandmothers for a bag of smack. Or maybe she owed money to the wrong person. Who the fuck knows?'

'Jesus, Paula. How can you sit there and come out with all that shit?' snapped Amanda. 'It doesn't matter a damn if she worked on the street or not. What's the difference between them and us? At the end of the day we all sell the same thing, Paula: fannies. The only difference I can see is that we charge more. If that makes us better than them, I don't know how.'

Paula's mouth smiled, but her eyes were cold and her cheeks flushed. She patted her hair and pulled her tight cardigan closed over her double-D bosom.

'God, Amanda, la-di-da,' she sniffed. 'You know, honey, it's funny, I don't remember you ever having that fucking social-worker air to you before.' She arched an eyebrow. 'When did you become so damn righteous?'

'Don't mind her,' Marna said, spilling her drink

a little as she waved it. She jabbed Amanda in the arm with her fingernail. 'You wouldn't hire a girl off the street. You wouldn't even work a shift with one.'

'So what? That doesn't mean—'

They stopped talking as the lounge boy brought Paula's drink. Paula threw it back in one go and ordered another.

'Don't fucking lie, Amanda. Marna's right: you wouldn't hire one of them. Not without checking her arms for track marks first.' Paula rummaged in her bag for her lipstick. 'Then you'd spend all night carrying your handbag around in case the little fuck rifled it. Shit, darlings, been down that fucking road before. Those bitches would rob the sight out of your eye.' She found the lipstick and applied it expertly without a mirror. 'Honey, you can do all the preaching you like. We're not the same as them. They're trash. You wait and see – it'll be about drugs. I'd bet my life on it.' She made a loud smacking sound to spread the berry-colour around her lips.

Amanda drained the last of her drink and stood up. She suddenly felt sick.

'I'm going home.'

'Jesus, it was your idea to come here,' Marna snapped. 'You made us shut up shop for the day, now you're bailing?'

'You closed up?' Paula spluttered, aghast. The Four Horsemen of the Apocalypse couldn't force Paula to shut down. She even resented closing for

Christmas Day; she claimed it was a day for the lonely, and what better place for the lonely than between the legs of a good woman? 'For a junkie you don't even know?'

'Yeah.' Marna shook her head and took another slug of vodka. 'It was either that or spend another day working alone.'

Paula shot Amanda a look of disgust, and Amanda felt a rush of guilt.

'Paula, don't fucking start with me.'

'I heard you were a cunt to poor Kate today, too.' Paula pursed her lips.

Amanda tossed her hair over her shoulder. She was damned if she was going to explain herself to Grapevine Paula. 'Marna, I'm going.'

'So go. You around tomorrow?'

Amanda stiffened. 'You know I am.'

'Do I?' Marna stared mournfully at the ice in her glass. She was more than a little drunk; she was totally smashed.

Amanda leaned her hands on the table. 'Look, are you all right? You want me to call a taxi?'

Paula's second brandy arrived. She grabbed it in both hands and ordered Marna another drink without being asked. 'I'll make sure she gets home OK,' she said sweetly. 'Don't trouble yourself.'

'Marna?' Amanda said stiffly. 'You staying here?'

'Yeah.' Marna folded her arms and stared at her blearily. 'I'm staying.'

'Suit yourself.' Amanda nodded to Paula,

turned on her heel and left as quickly as she could, pushing her way through the rapidly filling pub. Outside, she stopped and leaned against the wall. She glad to be in fresh air, glad to be alone.

What the hell was wrong with her? A few months ago she would probably have agreed with every word Paula had said. Now, the hooker hierarchy seemed ridiculous.

And yet, until recently, she had been part of it, believing the unspoken snobbery. Private workers looked down on escort girls, escort girls looked down on brothel girls and everyone looked down on the street girls. Paula was right: she would never have hired a girl from the street – not without checking her wallet every five minutes, or biting her lip if the girl spent too long in the bathroom.

Disgusted with Paula and herself, Amanda headed home, trying to clear her head a little. She hadn't felt so isolated and unhappy in years.

Head down against the cold, she crossed the street and turned towards home. She tried not to think of the hurt look on Marna's face as she left. Maybe it was time to let Marna in on what was happening. She couldn't keep her in the dark forever. It was putting too great a strain on their friendship. Maybe it was time to tell her that she could hardly bear to look at clients any more, let alone let them touch her. Maybe it was time to tell Marna that she didn't care any more if they were busy or not, if competition opened nearby, if someone closed down, if the web page needed updating, if they'd run out of tissues or oil or washing powder or dry towels. Maybe it was time to tell her that every time a mobile rang she wanted to scream and hurl it through the window. Maybe it was time to tell her that every time a client rang the doorbell she wanted to curl up and cry.

Maybe it was time to face the facts: they wanted different things. Ever since the raid she had felt differently, weary, angry. She no longer had the mental strength to continue in a job she loathed.

Lost in her thoughts, Amanda didn't notice the black BMW cruising slowly beside her in the bus lane. She almost walked into the door as it swung open in front of her. It was only when the immense dome-like head of the Whale emerged to block her path that she realised she was in trouble.

She tried to side-step around him, but it was too late. A great meaty hand gripped her by the shoulder. Amanda's eyes strayed to his swollen knuckles. Years of throwing punches and cracking heads had morphed them into one puffy mound of flesh.

'Get your fucking hand off me.' She tried to sound tough, mean, unconcerned about what was happening. 'You hear me? Move it, before I yell the place down.'

The Whale's hard mouth twitched. He wasn't fooled; people like him never were. 'He wants a word with you.'

'Yeah? Tell him to make an appointment like everyone else.'

'Shut the fuck up and get in the car.'

He yanked her off her feet and hurled her into the front seat with startling ease. Before she had a chance to take a deep breath and scream, he'd slammed the door shut and leaned his massive bulk against it to make sure she stayed put.

The car's interior reeked of cigarette smoke, cheap perfume and Chinese takeaway. Paul McCracken lounged sideways in the driver's seat. He stared at Amanda. She stared back. She hadn't seen him in almost a year, and yet he looked exactly the same as the last time she'd had the misfortune to meet him: greasy black hair cut short, shifty blue eyes, pointy teeth, pointy nose. The only difference she could see was that he had abandoned the Champion Sports tracksuits in favour of Ralph Lauren. He was still a scumbag, but better dressed.

'Long time no see, bitch.'

Amanda shuddered with revulsion at the sound of his voice. You could dress him up, but all the money in the world couldn't change the nasal inner-city whine. A flutter of fear gripped her by the base of the spine.

'Y-you must be fucking mad, grabbing me like this.'

'Easy, though, wasn't it?'

'What is it you want, Tricky?' she asked, trying to stay calm and controlled.

Tricky lit a cigarette, filling the car with more fumes. He blew smoke-rings in her face and grinned when she turned away.

'I hear you've got something that belongs to me, know what I mean?'

'I don't know what you're talking about.'

'Yeah? That right?'

'Yeah.'

He lunged across the seat so fast he caught her completely off guard. She yelped as he grabbed her face and dug his fingers into her cheeks.

'Let go of—'

'Shut the fuck up.' Veins stood out on Tricky's neck. He dragged her face closer. 'Don't fucking mess with me, you cunt.' Spittle hit Amanda's face and she grappled with his hand, trying to prise it off her face. It was like trying to loosen a steel trap. 'Next time I won't be so fucking understanding. I warned you not to fuck with me. Didn't I?'

'Let go!' She felt herself begin to panic. The cigarette was dangerously close to her eye.

'You think you can threaten me?' he snapped. 'Get some cunt to ring up and fucking warn me? No one does that to me, you bitch – *no one.* You better get back on the cunting phone and call that arsehole off. Threatening fucking *me* with the fucking *cops.*' He shook his head disbelievingly and dug his fingers in even harder. Amanda felt her teeth ache in her gums. 'I oughta take you out to the flats and leave you there with a syringe in your arm.'

'Please! I don't know what you're talking about!' All Amanda's attempts at keeping her cool were gone. Her heart hammered so loudly she was surprised Tricky couldn't hear it.

He held her for another few moments before thrusting her head away, so hard it snapped off the passenger window. Amanda bit her tongue and her vision blurred.

'You can go now,' Tricky said dismissively, turning away, as if she no longer held any interest for him. 'Go on, get out. Remember, you fucking played with the wrong man. I'm letting you know now: when this fucking shit with the squad dies down, I'm gonna be looking for you. Tell that snatch Kate what we did last time is only the bleeding warm-up. Maybe we can have a little twosome next time – you, her and a couple of boys from the 'Brack. Know what I mean?'

Amanda fumbled to get out. She was so shocked by the speed of his assault, and by what he was telling her, that she couldn't work the door handle.

'Here, bitch – before you go …' There was triumph in his voice. 'Don't forget to tell Katie how easy it was to pick you up.' He laughed and tapped the horn softly. 'Remind her she's not any harder to trace.'

The Whale shifted his bulk enough to let Amanda make an undignified, tumbling slide past him. His pale eyes rested on her, taking in the tears and red marks on her cheeks. She backed away, sweat gathering in her armpits and down her back. Tricky was frightening, but the Whale was a whole different matter. She had only to look into those emotionless eyes to become paralysed with fear. He did what he did, and he enjoyed his work. The fact that a psycho like Tricky paid him was a sheer bonus.

After what seemed like an age, the giant heaved himself back into the car. Tricky gunned the engine and the BMW screeched off down the street, leaving stinking rubber tracks inches from the curb.

Amanda backed up against the silver railings outside an office building and slid down onto her haunches, oblivious to the curious looks of passers-by. Her mind raced, trying to piece together some kind of sense from what Tricky had said. Who had threatened him? Why did he think it was her?

'Oh, no.' She closed her eyes. Marna – it had to have been Marna. How else would Tricky have connected Kate's name to her? So this was the spoke up Tricky's arse?

When she felt she could trust her legs to work again, Amanda stood up. All around her people were walking, chattering, hurrying home from their work. Had any of them noticed she had been snatched off the street? Even if they had, would they have done anything to help her?

She pulled her coat tightly around her and hurried home. Home – her sanctuary. She laughed bitterly until she cried again.

14

'It's not much to go on, is it?' Michael Dwyer scanned the report containing the forensic details of Tessa Byrne's untimely demise. 'She suffocated on her own blood.' He shook his head as he read through the report. 'Awful bloody way to go. Says here her nails were all broken. She must have fought him like a tiger.'

'Whoever's doing this has a real problem with hookers,' Gerry Cullen said.

'What makes you say that?'

'Well, it's obvious. He stuffs condoms down the first one's throat.'

'Oh,' said Michael.

'Jesus, he dragged this poor bitch through the house by her teeth. Look at the report – there was blood all the way from the back door to the bedroom. And he didn't cut her anywhere else.'

'Why do you think he went after her? She wasn't in the business any more.' Michael kept reading: Tessa had a fracture of the right cheek-bone and bruising to her face that indicated she had been struck a number of times before she had finally been asphyxiated. Poor woman; she really had fought for her life. He hoped she'd landed a few decent blows before she died; fingernail scrapings had revealed dried blood – not hers either.

Gerry shrugged. 'Who knows? I'll bet you anything he's a fucking pervert, one of those guys who like being burned with candle-wax and shit. I've seen all that stuff on Sky One. This one chick had this guy in chains, and she was—'

While Gerry rambled on, Michael read through the ballistics reports on both crime scenes and frowned. Hair and fibre were a nightmare. So many people had come in and out of Sandy's little flat that it would take ages to separate their traces, let alone compare them to anything picked up at Tessa's house. It might take weeks to sort through it all, and meanwhile there was a very dangerous man running about his city. He closed the report with a sigh and settled back to wait, oblivious to the nattering beside him.

It seemed he spent half of his life waiting for something – waiting to talk to somebody, waiting for information, waiting for a lead to turn up. It had bothered him when he was younger, when all he wanted was action. Now he enjoyed the wait; it gave him time to allow his mind to work, to soak up information, to remember details that might be important.

'And it's weird he didn't rape her,' Gerry was saying.

'No semen was found in her vagina.' Michael rubbed his eyes and sat up.

'You'd think he would, though, what with her all tied up and all.'

Michael glanced at him. 'What has that got to do with it?'

Gerry shrugged. 'Nothing. I'm just saying – she's all helpless and shit … But why her teeth? It's fucking sick, that's what it is. I'm never going to see cling-film the same way again, I can tell you. Next time the wife makes sandwiches for my lunch, she can use tin foil to wrap them.'

Michael scowled. That was disturbing him, too. There was no doubt in his mind that the killer had some reason for targeting the women the way he had. But why cover them with cling-film? In all his years on the force, he had never heard of a killer using cling-film to murder. Never had an everyday kitchen object – with the exception of the humble carving knife – been used with such devastating effect.

Michael's mobile rang. It was the call they had been waiting for.

'You can go in now; she's been informed. Don't make any fuss – ring the doorbell,' Stafford barked down the phone. 'And tell that Cullen to keep his bloody mind on the job. I'll talk to you later.'

'The boss says we can go in now. Oh, and that you're to keep your mind on the job.'

'As if I would do anything else!'

Michael grinned at Gerry's look of sheer indignation.

★ ★ ★

'Darlings, we've been expecting you!' Grapevine Paula cooed as she wound a leg around the door. 'Sergeant, you look like you could do with a bit of TLC.'

Michael grinned and took a step back. She had obviously been on the gargle; the alcohol fumes could have knocked down a horse at twenty feet. 'Good to see you, Paula.'

Paula, wearing her blonde hair piled high on top of her head and very little to cover her modesty, seemed positively ecstatic to see two gardaí at her door. It was a far cry from the usual reception they got in brothels.

Michael introduced the grinning Gerry and the two men followed Paula's swaying arse up the dingy stairs and into the shabby front room on the second floor. This was Shangri-la, one of the oldest and best-known knocking-shops in all of Dublin.

God, Michael thought, what a bloody dump.

Years of subsidence had caused the old building to slope gently to the right. The staff room was covered in peeling wood-chip wallpaper, painted a garish shade of fuchsia. Old velvet curtains, so faded and layered with thick dust that it was difficult to guess their original colour, hung over the grimy windows. The creaking floor was covered in a swirling floral carpet, and ancient tasselled lamps stood over an ugly fireplace painted in black gloss. The only other furniture in the room was a sofa, three overstuffed chairs and a wardrobe, bursting with clothes and uniforms, that dominated one wall. There were magazines and clothes strewn everywhere.

Michael wrinkled his nose at the pungent, cloying smell of air-freshener and stale perfume that barely covered an underlying stench of mildew and wood-rot. The whole building was one rotting hulk of a fire hazard; and yet this dump was one of the busiest brothels in town.

Paula settled herself rather unsteadily into a sagging armchair by a payphone bolted to the wall – Michael noticed it was off the hook – and waved at them to take a seat. Michael and Gerry moved some clothes and perched on the edge of the salmon-pink sofa.

'Jim called earlier, told me you were coming. It's about the murders, isn't it?' Paula said, all wide-eyed concern.

'Yes, it is. Thank you for taking the time to talk to us again,' Michael said, trying hard not to look at Paula's breasts. It might have been easier if there hadn't been so much of them on show.

'Think nothing of it, pet. Anything we can do to help you catch the fucker, we will.' She crossed her legs, revealing a lot of dimpled thigh under the short, see-through robe.

Michael cleared his throat and averted his gaze. 'You remember what you told me the last time we spoke …' He consulted his notebook. 'You said you thought Sandy might have known her killer.'

'That's right. Poor old Sandy – she used to

work here, you know. Lovely woman – and those poor little kiddies … It breaks my heart when I think of what happened to her. Is it true that he plucked the hair from her head using tweezers?'

'What? No … Who told you that?'

She waved a heavily jewelled wrist. 'Oh, you hear these things.'

'He cut her hair off,' Gerry said, and Michael could have kicked him in the nuts.

'Really?' Grapevine Paula almost shimmered with interest. 'Creepy. Did he take *all* of her hair, if you know what I mean?' She pointed to her crotch in case they didn't.

Michael frowned. 'We are not at liberty to reveal any information at the moment. You must understand that. Now, did you know the second woman, Tessa Byrne?' He passed her a photo. It had been taken the year before, at a party. Tessa was smiling prettily at the camera; a green-and-white party hat sat askew on her wavy hair.

'No.' Paula looked disappointed. She tapped the picture with her nails for another few seconds before passing it back. 'I don't think so. Now, don't get me wrong – I may have met her at some stage. But so many women come and go through this place …' She waved her hand around the decrepit room. 'It's hard to remember everyone. But, that said, I doubt she ever worked here. You can ask the girls if you like. They're all in next door. I rounded them up, even the ones who were off tonight, when I knew you boys were coming.'

Michael looked surprised. 'That's very good of you.'

She flashed him a wide grin. 'Well … I do want to help, but I also don't want you calling back looking to talk to ones you missed.'

Gerry grinned. Unlike Michael, he was ogling her breasts freely.

'I read your statement from the last time,' Michael went on. 'Can you tell me again why Sandy Walsh left here?'

Paula shrugged. 'Sure, it's simple. I have ten girls working here, not including myself – two on each shift. The shift changes twice a day, except on Sundays when two girls work all day. Some shifts are busier than others, so I swap girls around a bit – that way, everyone gets a crack at a good shift. But that didn't suit our Sandy, did it?'

'Why not?'

'Sandy wanted to work the same days every week, two long days, and no weekends. God, we were always at loggerheads about it. She said she'd had enough and she left. It happens all the time. I work myself, so I know it gets a bit annoying, never being on the same day – but it's a fair system, right? That way everybody gets nights off and a weekend off at least every other week. But Sandy wanted to work the same shifts every week.'

'So she left?'

'She left, all right.' Paula smiled wolfishly. 'I make no exceptions. This is my place, and if you don't want to play by my rules …'

'Do you know where she went to work next?'

The smile faded fast. 'I told Jim when he called. She went to work for that bastard Tricky.'

'Tricky?'

'Yeah – you know, Paul McCracken. Everyone calls him Tricky. How she thought he'd ever let her work the way she wanted, I'll never know. Not that she lasted long with him. Mind you, she was a bit long in the tooth for Tricky anyway. He probably only took her on to cover during a shortage. I told Jim the same thing.'

Michael made a note of that and tried not to smile at 'Jim'. He hadn't realised she and Stafford were on a first-name basis.

'Don't you mind people leaving?'

Paula's eyebrows shot up. 'Why would I, Sergeant? It happens all the time in this business. I'm well past the stage of worrying over a girl leaving.' She leaned forward, exposing more cleavage. 'Nobody's that good. The only thing I remember thinking is that she'd made a mistake going to work for that little bollix.'

'Why was that?' Gerry asked.

Paula sighed and sat back in her chair. 'He's a bad one – nasty little prick. If you lot heard half the stories I've heard over the years … well, it would make you sick. I'm not saying they're all true. I've heard plenty said about myself, you know, and not even half of those … Well, you know, if you throw enough shit some of it has to stick. Did you know he tried to get me closed down one year? Rang the papers and made up dreadful stories about this place, he did – the fucking nerve of him.'

'It didn't work, then?'

'Course not! I pay my taxes. This is a legitimate massage parlour; I don't care what some rag says about me. Tell you the truth, the free publicity wasn't half-bad. The phone here was hopping for weeks afterwards.' She looked at the unhooked phone mournfully.

'What about the other stories?' Michael asked. 'What did you hear?'

'Oh, you know.' Paula gave him a coy look and fluttered her eyelashes. 'I hear things. Course, it's all second-hand – other people's stories.'

'Why don't you tell me some of them?'

'Tell you what – why don't you ask the girls? Some of them have first-hand experience of Tricky, if you know what I mean.' She leaned further forward and tapped the side of her nose conspiratorially. Her breasts surged against the material, threatening to break free in a tsunami of pink flesh.

'We sure will.' Gerry Cullen was finding it more than a bit difficult to concentrate. And, worse, he was sure something was stirring in his pants. He moved his legs about to cover it and tried to think unsexy thoughts.

'She would have done grand for herself here, you know?' Paula said wistfully. 'The clients all adored her. Very popular girl, was our Sandy. She had a way about her.' She winked at Gerry. 'Very *open*, she was.'

Gerry leaned forwards slightly. Michael glanced at him and scowled. What the hell was wrong with the man? Why was he squirming about like that? 'Can you remember when she left?'

Paula pursed her lips. 'Hmm … it wasn't during the summer, I'm sure about that …' She hesitated. 'No, I'm right. Her kids were back in school, and that's why she was whingeing about working weekends.' She looked up at the ceiling, trying to pinpoint the time. 'I'm sure it was September – late September, early October?' She frowned at her own uncertainty. 'Tell you what: when I go home this evening, I'll look it up for you. How's that?'

'That would be great.' Michael hoped everyone would be this helpful.

Paula beamed. 'Anything to help. I used to be able to remember these things off the top of my head, but nowadays … huh, head like a sieve.'

Michael doubted that very much, but he nodded along. 'Would you mind if we had a chat with the other girls now?'

'Don't you want to ask me any more questions?' Paula managed to look relieved and disappointed all at once. 'You know I'd be happy to reveal *anything* you think might help.'

Michael blinked, and Gerry shuffled about some more. Michael wasn't a hundred per cent sure she meant what he thought she did, so he ploughed on. 'I think that will do, for the moment. We may need to get back to you at some time in the future. If we do, we'll let you know in advance.'

'Sure, darlings, give me a ring. Jim has my number, if you need me.' She stood up. 'I'll show you where the girls are, if you'll follow me.'

She sashayed past them in a cloud of perfume. Michael noticed that Gerry had given up all efforts to look at anything other than her backside. Actually, he had to admit, it *was* very hard to look at anything else; even he was drawn to its Ruben-esque magnificence.

The 'girls', all ten of them, were congregated in a smoke-filled room next door. Like Paula, they were all bursting with curiosity; they began firing questions as soon as the two gardaí walked through the door. Michael and Gerry decided to speak to them individually; it was the only way they could get a word in edgewise.

Even at that, the interviews took almost two hours, and by the end of them Michael had a headache from the constant cigarette smoke and Gerry's eyes were out on stalks. Unfortunately, they had learned very little about Sandy Walsh that they didn't already know; but one of the women had known Tessa Byrne, although she couldn't tell the officers much except that Tessa was nice, kept herself to herself and had definitely worked at one of Tricky's places. They had also gleaned infor-mation, a lot of information, about the character of one Paul 'Tricky' McCracken. If sheer hatred could kill, McCracken would have popped his clogs years before.

So the gardaí did not leave empty-handed.

Paula showed them to the door, with warnings to 'mind the stairs' and 'watch your footing' every two seconds. Downstairs at the main door, a four-inch-thick steel creation that must have weighed half a ton, Michael thanked her again for her time.

'Please, Sergeant!' She laid a flirtatious hand on his arm. 'Really, it's nothing. I only hope you catch the bastard.'

Michael hesitated and closed the door again. 'Paula, I don't want to take up too much more of your time, but I was wondering about something, and maybe you could help me.'

'What is it?' Paula leaned in, her eyes sparkling.

'How well do you know a girl called Amanda Harrington? You remember she was the one who gave me your name last time.'

Paula squealed out loud and slapped him on the arm. 'Ha! No, nice try, Sergeant.' Her green eyes flashed with delight. 'Now listen to me. I was only out with them earlier this evening. Forget about that one. Frosty as fuck, is our Amanda. And you don't strike me as the sort of man who likes to take a beating.'

Michael grinned sheepishly and rubbed his moustache. 'No, well …'

'Look, Marna's a doll. But that Amanda … she's not right in the head, in my view.'

Michael frowned. 'You think she's … what? Disturbed?'

Grapevine Paula raised one shoulder. 'She

worked for that McCracken for a long time. It's left her …' Paula touched the side of her head.

'She told me he was a psycho.'

'Well, there you are. She's taking these deaths kind of hard. Her and Sandy, they knew each other from the Red Stairs and from McCracken's place, you see.'

Michael's frown deepened. 'I didn't realise they were such friends.'

'Me neither.' Paula sniffed. 'But then, that Amanda's very bloody touchy about her privacy.' She folded her arms; again the cleavage cavern deepened. 'Very touchy.'

'Well, thank you again. If you hear anything else, be sure to give us a call. The sooner we catch this guy, the safer you'll all be.'

'Don't worry, Sergeant, if we hear anything you'll be the first to know. Give my regards to Jim.'

She stood waving goodbye, oblivious to the fact that she was practically naked, until they reached their car. Only when they opened the car door did she slip back inside.

'Phew – Jesus. No wonder Stafford told me to keep my mind on the job,' Gerry said as he started the car. 'Nice woman, though – friendly, like.'

Michael looked at the door thoughtfully. 'Yes, she certainly was. Very helpful.'

Not everybody was quite so pleased to see the Vice squad on their doorsteps, as Miriam and Ed were finding out.

'Look,' Ed bawled through the intercom, 'this is not a raid! We're here to ask you a few simple questions. Now will you open the door and let us in!'

'This is ridiculous.' Miriam stood with her hands on her hips and glared at the closed door. 'Ring the boss. Get him to call the owner of this shit-hole and get these stupid bitches to open the door.'

'They would have let us in if you hadn't shouted, "Police, open the door," when they answered the intercom,' Ed snapped. He leaned his head against the locked door.

'What the hell was I supposed to say?'

Ed ignored her and strode back to the car to ring Stafford. It was a pain in the arse working with Miriam. She never used common sense when bullying would do instead.

Miriam watched him go. It never failed to piss her off, the way they were supposed to handle these women with kid gloves. She couldn't understand why she had to mind her Ps and Qs. These were prostitutes, for Christ's sake. She waited by the door and fumed until Ed returned.

'Well?'

Ed shrugged. 'He says to wait for a few minutes and he'll call the owner again.'

'Oh, that's just great! We stand around like two spare pricks, while these bitches are laughing at us from behind this fucking door.'

Ed glared at her pale, tight face, the thin line of her angry mouth, and cursed inwardly. Why had he got stuck with her – especially when they wanted the prostitutes to open up to them a little? He leaned back against the wall, folded his arms and shut his eyes.

Eventually, after more calls and much cajoling, they gained entrance to the apartment building. Trudging up the stairs to the second floor, neither officer expected a lot of co-operation from the girls they were about to encounter. Their expectations proved correct.

'Nah, never heard of her,' the pretty brunette said when Ed asked her about Sandy Walsh.

'What about Tessa Byrne? Ever heard of her?' Ed showed her the photo and fought to keep the irritation out of his voice. This was the third and last girl in the apartment. The first two had been even less communicative. At least this one looked like she was actually listening.

'Is that the old one killed during the week?' She made eye contact with him for the first time in almost ten minutes.

Ed sighed. Old one? Tessa was barely thirty-five. 'That's her. She was killed last Sunday night. Do you know her?'

'Heard she was a street girl.' The blue eyes blinked slowly. 'Nah. How would I know her? I don't work the streets.' She went back to picking at her purple nail polish.

'How do you know she worked the streets?' Ed frowned.

'Dunno. Heard someone saying it.'

'Look … Susie, anything you may know or may have heard could be important. The man who killed those women is very dangerous. He may attack again, at any time. The next time it might be you or one of your friends …' He gave up as the young girl gave a long, exaggerated yawn.

'Are we boring you?' Miriam's hostile tone flicked through the air like a whip.

The dark head half-turned in her direction, then stopped and returned to Ed. 'Look, can I go now? I've told you all I know, which is nothing, yeah? So, if you don't mind …' She held Ed's gaze for a second, then dropped her eyes again. 'If I hear something, I'll let you know. *OK?*'

Ed stared at her. She was about eighteen years old; thin as a whippet, fragile and as hard as nails, all at once. She should have been at home with her family, or out with friends – not sitting in an apartment being interviewed by the police about murder.

Miriam stood up behind him. 'C'mon, Ed, let's go.'

He remained sitting for a few seconds more; he was aware that the young hooker was watching him from under her eyelashes when she thought he wasn't looking.

'You don't look like a cop,' she said suddenly.

'I get that a lot.' He smiled at her, and she gave him a slight smile in return.

'Ed, come on! We're wasting time.' Miriam tapped him on the shoulder.

'If you hear anything, anything at all, call us.' He handed the girl his card.

'Yeah, whatever.' Susie shrugged and turned the card over and over in her hand.

And that about sums it up, thought Ed on the way back down the stairs: *whatever.*

'Did you leave a message telling him we wanted to speak to him?' Stafford gritted his teeth and gripped the phone harder.

'Yes, I've already told you. He's unavailable tonight. I can't reach him; all his phones are turned off and I have no idea where he is,' said the female voice on the other end of the line.

'Make sure he gets the message. And make sure he understands how important it is that he gets in touch with me. Tell him I don't want to have to come looking for him, but if I have to, I will.'

'I'll make sure he gets the message, loud and clear.'

'Tell him this is a murder enquiry and we're talking to everyone. Got me?'

A long sigh. 'Yes, I get you. I told you, I'll pass the message on.'

'Make sure you do.' He hung up. 'Fucking pimps – always hiding behind the skirts of some woman.'

'Are you surprised?' Bob Scully asked mildly, and leaned back in his chair. They were in Scully's office – which, Stafford noted with some irritation, was considerably more plush than his own box-room.

'Not where this one is concerned,' Stafford

said. He rubbed his hands over his tired eyes. 'Not by a long shot. Best thing would be to drag the fucker in, attach a Taser to his balls and keep shocking him until he talks.'

Scully stared at him with open disdain. 'God, Jim, you're Neolithic in your thinking. You need to develop a *rapport* with people on the phone; you can't go in threatening them and expect success. You should try to be more subtle. A helpful technique is to imagine you're talking to someone who is mentally deficient. That way, you keep cool and never—'

Jim Stafford stalked out of the room. If he had to listen to another helpful hint from Scully, he'd strangle the stupid bastard with one of his Armani ties or bludgeon him to a pulp with one of the many glass awards the fucker displayed around his office. Christ, I must have seriously pissed someone off to get stuck with such a fucking knob, he thought as he stormed downstairs for his ninth cup of coffee in two hours.

15

'What's eating you?' Stafford glanced across his desk at Michael, who sat with his hands laced behind his head, his feet tucked under his chair and his normally placid expression replaced by a scowl. 'You've a face on you like a slapped arse.'

'I'm wondering why people tell lies. What makes them think they can get away with it?'

Stafford grunted. 'I think that's bloody obvious.'

'Not to me, it isn't.'

Stafford put down his pen and gave Michael an impatient look. 'What's brought all this on?'

'Do you remember the two women we arrested a while back – Amanda Harrington and Marna Galloway?'

Stafford tried to put faces to the familiar names. 'Them two hoity-toity ones?'

Michael nodded. 'I interviewed Harrington a few days after Sandy Walsh died. Routine stuff, nothing major. I knew they had worked together in the Red Stairs. Her name and number were in the phone book we found at Sandy's house.'

'And? What about her?'

'She claims she barely knew Sandy, and that she never worked with her anywhere other than the Red Stairs. She specifically told me she had never worked for McCracken.'

'So?'

'According to your friend last night, not only did she work for him, she got Sandy Walsh the job there.'

'I see.' Stafford rubbed his temples. 'Who told you that – Paula, was it?'

'The one and only.'

'Paula's usually spot-on with her information.'

'How do you know her so well?' Michael asked casually. 'If you don't mind my asking.'

Stafford began to laugh. 'I know Paula a good few years now – and it's not for whatever reason you're thinking.'

Michael feigned innocence. 'I don't know what you mean—'

'Don't give me that shite, Mike. I know what you're thinking, and you're way off. Paula and me go way back. When I was working down in Kevin Street, about three years ago, Paula worked in one of the first places I ever raided. We didn't really raid back then; we just went in and closed them down for a week or two. Paula's cute, though. She set up on her own and made sure she kept a clean business – no drugs or young girls, nothing that would attract attention. When she heard we'd formed a proper vice squad last year, she registered the business. Now she pays minimal tax and claims she's running a legitimate massage parlour.'

'I've been in there,' Michael said. 'It's a knocking shop.'

'Hard to prove if you can't catch them in action. Another thing: Paula doesn't advertise, so you can't say she's soliciting.' Stafford grinned. 'Did you meet the girls?'

Michael nodded. 'Talkative bunch.'

'Aye, when it suits them. Not one of those women would ever give evidence against Paula. She's too clever for that – runs a tight ship. Don't let that fluffy act fool you; that one's as sharp as a razor. I'll tell you another thing, too: if Paula says Harrington got Sandy Walsh the job, chances are she's right.'

'So why did Harrington lie about it?'

'Go ask her.' Stafford picked up his pen and started writing. 'Ask her. Give her a ring and get her to meet up with you. Don't sit around here waiting to work it out. Find out what she doesn't want you to know.'

Michael nodded. 'I don't like people lying to me.' He leafed through his notebook for her number. 'Makes me wonder what else they're trying to hide.'

'Get her to come to the station. In my experience, nothing rattles people more than having to spend time in this shit-hole,' Stafford said with the trace of a smile. 'Especially people who're hiding something.'

★ ★ ★

Gerry combed through the pile of papers on his desk, trying to catalogue them into some sort of order. He had taken nearly twenty fresh statements last night; now it was time to go through each one carefully. He groaned at the thought. It was going to take him at least an hour.

It wasn't like the statements were worth anything, either. All the women he had spoken to had offered nothing more than abuse about the gardaí in general.

Ed came into the room carrying yet more papers under his arm.

'Don't even think about adding to what I have already.' Gerry rolled his eyes to heaven. 'I'm knackered, and it's not even half-twelve yet.'

Ed grimaced. 'Don't worry. This is my lot that we collected last night. Believe me, I know what you mean about being knackered; I think I got about two hours' sleep. How are the kids?'

'Noisy.' Gerry slid out a chair for him. 'Where's the pit bull?'

Ed shrugged. 'I haven't got a clue and I couldn't care less.' He sat down, opened up the first statement, then promptly closed it again. 'I swear, Gerry, it's a wonder we got a word out of those women last night. You should have heard her – proper little Hitler.'

'Yeah?'

Ed glanced at the door. 'Have you noticed anything funny about her lately?'

'Funny? Funny how?'

'I don't know, really. Just funny.'

Gerry scratched his head with his Biro. 'Well … she's moodier than usual. Bit snappy or something – although that's not exactly unheard of with her, is it?'

'It's probably nothing.' Ed checked the door again. 'I was only wondering if you'd noticed, that's all.'

Gerry picked up a file. 'I wouldn't worry about it; you know what she's like.'

'Yeah, you're probably right. But I don't want to get fucking stuck with her again in a hurry.'

At four o'clock the same evening, Michael spotted Amanda Harrington climbing out of a taxi and running through the rain towards the station door. Not that he was lurking about waiting for her, or anything; he just happened to be at the front desk. He hurried out to meet her.

'Thanks for coming.' He held the internal door open for her.

Amanda smiled coldly and shook some raindrops from her hair. 'Your message didn't really leave me with much choice.'

'No, I suppose not.'

They went up the stairs and along a corridor on the first floor.

'If you'll wait in here …' Michael opened the door of a tiny interview room and flicked on the light. 'Take a seat.' He pointed to one of the two chairs on either side of a scarred and battered table. 'I'll be back to you in just a second.'

Amanda pushed her damp hair from her forehead and glanced around the room. It was cramped and claustrophobic and needed a good coat of paint; the walls, once a pale primrose, were scuffed and nicotine-stained and covered in scrawls and gouges. The floor was carpeted with what Amanda always thought of as Call-Centre Blue, a hard-wearing rough synthetic carpet that would scrape your knees if you fell on it. 'You want me to wait here?'

'If you don't mind.' Michael smiled and disappeared back out the door, closing it with a muffled thump.

Amanda felt warm after coming in from the cold, but she was loath to take off her coat. She didn't intend to be there long enough for the heat to bother her, anyway. She took the chair facing the door and settled down to wait.

When Michael Dwyer hadn't returned after five minutes, Amanda began to fidget. Something about police stations always made her feel anxious and guilty, even when she'd done nothing. She took off her coat, folded it on the back of her chair and waited, her patience wearing thinner by the second.

By the time Michael eventually returned another five minutes later, carrying a pad and some pens, she was starting to feel sick from the oppressive heat in the little room. 'Sorry about that; I got a little held up,' he said, ignoring her obvious discomfort. 'Would you like a cup of coffee or anything before we start?'

'No,' Amanda said quickly, terrified he would disappear again.

'Water?'

'Tell me what you wanted to talk to me about.'

Michael pulled out the other chair and sat down. 'Sandy Walsh—'

'I told you everything I know about Sandy the last time we spoke.'

'Did you indeed?' he said sceptically.

Amanda drummed her fingers on the table in front of her. 'Yes, I did. Why did I have to come here? You think I have nothing better to do with my time?'

'Better than helping in a murder enquiry?'

'You know what I mean.'

'No, I don't.'

Her grey eyes narrowed. 'What can I do for you, Sergeant?'

Michael opened his notebook, leaned back in his chair and flipped through it at a leisurely pace. He was in no hurry, and now that he had her full attention he wanted her to sweat a little.

'The last time we spoke, you said you worked with Sandy Walsh at the Red Stairs. Correct?'

'Yeah. So?'

'You said that you kept in contact with the victim purely on a professional basis, and that you didn't know her that well.'

'Yeah.' The finger-drumming stopped, and Amanda looked a little less irritated and a lot more cautious.

'You failed to mention to me, however, that you did work with her for a period of time at City Stars, an agency owned by one Paul McCracken. In fact, you claimed you hadn't worked for him at all.'

'I never—'

'You didn't mention that, in fact, it was you who got Sandy Walsh the job with McCracken's agency.'

He glanced at her over the top of the notebook and caught her look of surprise; a second later it was gone, and an expression of fierce disgust crossed her face. 'Oh, now I see. Paula. That vindictive bitch. She told you this, didn't she?'

'I'm not at liberty to say.' Michael closed the notebook. 'Why didn't you want me to know that?'

'I must have forgotten.' Amanda shook her head slowly; her hair came loose from its ribbon and flowed over one shoulder in a wave of chestnut. 'I believe I also told you half the girls in Dublin worked there.'

'You did, so why lie about working with her?'

'I told you, I forgot.'

'You forgot? A woman you know is brutally murdered, and you *forgot* to mention you got her a job with one of the most violent pimps in the city?'

'Oh, now I see: you think I've got something to hide. Is that it?' Amanda screwed up her face. 'You think I'm covering up some – what? secret plot to murder Sandy?' She laughed. 'Well, I'm sorry to disappoint you, but I didn't mention working with McCracken because it wasn't worth mentioning.'

'Why did you lie about working with her? Why didn't you tell me you got her the job?'

Amanda scraped her chair back and stood up. 'What fucking difference does it make who got her a job and where?'

'Do you know Tessa Byrne?'

She swung her coat on and walked towards the door. 'No, never heard of her.'

'You sure? She worked for McCracken for a while. Maybe you've *forgotten* her too.'

'I'm leaving. Next time you want to talk to me, call Fergus first.'

'Why are you getting so defensive?'

'I'm not.'

'Why don't you tell me why you lied about working with her?'

She reached for the door handle, her back to him. 'Do I need someone to key me out?'

Michael rose slowly. 'It doesn't look good if you leave here without talking to me. We're in the middle of a murder investigation. Two women are dead.'

'Do I need someone to key me out of this building or not?' Amanda spun to face him, and, under the harsh lights of the worst interview room ever, Michael saw raw fear in her grey eyes.

He took a step towards her and held out a hand. 'Look, if McCracken—'

'Do I need someone to key me out, Sergeant?' she repeated. This time her voice was tinged with panic.

Michael lowered his hand. She was hiding something; he knew it. The air almost crackled with her fear. But he sensed that, whatever it was, bullying her was not the way to get it out of her. 'The desk sergeant will open the main doors for you.'

'Thank you.'

'I'll need to speak to you again. You know that, don't you?'

She shrugged and left. By the time he reached the door, she was already halfway down the hall.

Michael was on his way up to the second floor, still trying to work out what exactly he had said that had freaked her out so badly, when he met Ed trotting down the stairs.

'Good, you've saved me a trip.' Ed's hair was standing on end and he was looking more like a professor than ever; he wore a striped shirt and corduroy pants in a very teacherly shade of olive-green. 'I was coming to get you.'

'What is it?'

'Stafford's looking for you. He said to tell you Paul McCracken finally surfaced. He wants to know if you'd like to go to the interview with him.'

'Tell him I'll be right there.'

Ed nodded and hurried back up the stairs. Michael followed slowly. Why had Amanda Harrington jumped out of her skin like that? Was it the mention of McCracken?

The sight of a grinning Stafford, bouncing down the corridor like a Jack Russell, stopped him in his tracks.

'There you are.' Stafford clapped his hands together and jiggled his thick eyebrows. 'That weasel McCracken called one of our lines. Claims he only got our message half an hour ago.' Stafford smirked and hitched his pants high around his waist. 'I'll bet you a week's wages he's spent the day ringing round to see if we're really talking to everyone. Aye, he's worried in case we're trying to trap him.'

'Is he coming in?'

'You must be joking. No, Mike, we're going to meet His Prickness on neutral ground. He's *helping* us with our enquiries.' Stafford checked his watch. 'Right; grab your coat and let's go. I wouldn't want to keep the little shit waiting. He might change his mind about offering his precious insights to the likes of us.'

16

Stafford drove through the darkening Dublin streets like a man possessed. He swore at traffic lights and at other drivers. He turned corners on two wheels and used the handbrake to slow his momentum. By the time they hit Dame Street Michael had begun to make strange hissing sounds, hoping he'd slow down, but to no avail. Stafford was not going to be diverted from his quarry.

'The phone records are in,' Stafford said, changing lanes without looking in any of the mirrors and almost colliding with a 19A bus.

'Who has them? Scully?'

Stafford nodded. 'Got them about an hour ago. Bugger of a job getting them.'

Michael hissed extra loud as Stafford almost mowed down a pedestrian on a clearly marked crossing. 'At least we can run a check on who called Walsh now.'

Stafford grunted.

'Where are we going, exactly?' Michael asked, as they raced over O'Connell Bridge and took an extremely sharp right on an orange light.

'North Strand. He wants to meet in a pub.'

'We're not going to get there at all if you keep this up,' Michael said. They swerved around a cyclist, and a car behind them blared its horn.

'What?' Stafford looked at the speedometer. 'Oh, shite! I see what you mean.' He slowed down a fraction. 'Remember, Mike, this prick might be able to help us more than he thinks. We're just going to ask him a few questions, that's all. I don't want to antagonise the little bastard or anything like that. Got me?'

'No problem.' They rounded Busaras doing a steady 70mph.

'When this case is all over, then we go after him for the knocking-shops. Got me?'

'Sure.' Amiens Street was a blur. They cut through orange lights by the Five Lamps pub and did a superb impression of the Dukes of Hazzard over the next bridge.

'Ah, grand – here we are.' Stafford hauled at the wheel and shot across the road through two lanes of oncoming traffic. He skidded to a halt outside the blue-and-black front of the North Strand Arms.

'Now remember: don't fucking annoy him. Let's find out what we can and get the little shit on side. With any luck, if we give him enough rope he'll hang himself. We'll have plenty of time to deal with his other business later. Got me?'

Michael didn't bother to answer. He was busy thanking the Lord he'd made it out of the car.

* ★ *

The North Strand Arms was a neat, old-fashioned pub run by a local family. They did a good trade at lunchtime, offering decent pub grub at reasonable prices. The nights were good too, with a nice crowd of locals and very few young people to upset the peace of the seasoned drinkers. At this time on a Wednesday evening it was quiet. Three old men sat at the bar, nursing pints of Guinness in silent companionship; the single barman sat reading the paper at the other end of the bar.

Jim and Michael walked across the blue carpet, weaving around little tables, towards him.

'Evening. What can I get you?' asked the barman without looking up.

'Two coffees.' Michael reached for his wallet, noticing the suspicion on the barman's face as he looked up at the strange request. After sizing them up he became a bit friendlier. Michael knew they stood out as gardaí, and when the barman said, 'Take a seat, gentlemen, I'll drop it over to you when it's ready,' it was another way of saying, 'Sit anywhere but here at the bar.'

They took a table on the far right-hand side of the lounge, where they had a good view of the door. Stafford rubbed his legs and checked his watch again. 'Actually, Mike, we're a bit early.'

'Not to worry; that gives us a chance to go over what we'll ask him.'

'Now, Mike, I don't want to rattle this fella's cage – not yet. Got me?'

Michael sighed. 'I know that, sir; you said. But I think we should make the most of this meeting – find out what this guy's all about.'

'Fine, fine, but this is a separate issue from the pimping. The more this fella thinks we're not interested in his other line, the more information we'll get out of him.'

The barman arrived with their coffee. They waited for him to leave before they spoke again.

'We know that Sandy Walsh worked for him before striking out on her own. We now know that Tessa Byrne worked for him at some point too. That's a link, Mike. I don't know what sort of link yet, but it's a link.'

Michael cocked his head. 'What are you getting at?'

'I'm saying that, after looking over some of the recent statements you and the team brought in, I think we can't rule McCracken out as a suspect. More than one finger's been pointed in his direction.'

'You think so?' Michael took a sip of his coffee. It was piping hot, freshly brewed and strong, not like the frothy, lukewarm crap he normally endured in cafés. 'Does Scully think he's a suspect?'

'Scully doesn't know his arse from his elbow. If he hasn't studied it in a course, it doesn't exist. Look, Sandy Walsh was a career hooker, in the business for the long haul; Tessa Byrne was a part-timer and a good many months out of the game.

There really isn't much to link them, except McCracken's place.'

'Apart from the fact that they both worked as prostitutes.'

'Aye, but the thing is *where* they both worked.' Stafford eyed the door. 'So let's have our chat, get a feel for him. We don't need to go bothering our great leader with this yet. Got me?'

'OK.'

The arrival of Paul McCracken ended any further discussion.

Michael nudged Stafford with his knee. McCracken hadn't spotted them yet, so Michael had a few seconds to check him out freely. He wasn't impressed with what he saw.

Paul 'Tricky' McCracken was thirty-eight. He was close on six foot, but thin as a rake and round-shouldered. He wore straight black jeans, a T-shirt and a silk bomber jacket. His black hair was cut short, and he had so much wet-look gel plastered on it that it glistened under the bar lights. His nose was ski-jumped and his eyes were off centre. A gold hoop glinted in his left ear. He looked exactly like fifty other scumbags Michael could think of, and it annoyed him that this pathetic excuse for a human had successfully evaded the Vice squad for the last few months.

As McCracken spotted them, a slow, smarmy grin crossed his face. He nodded and swaggered towards them.

'How you doing? Sorry I'm a bit late. Traffic's

shite.' He stood in front of his table with his hands in his pockets. 'Bad fucking business, this, eh? Murder.' He shook his head. 'Can't say I'm bleeding surprised. Lot of fucking nutters out there, know what I mean?' His shifty eyes scanned the cops' faces, checking for some reaction.

'Thanks for taking the time to see us.' Stafford indicated for him to sit down. Tricky took the seat farthest away from them and closest to the door.

'No problem. What do you need to know?' He licked his lips. 'Anything I can, like, you know, do to help and all that ...'

Michael nearly laughed out loud.

After brief introductions – slightly awkward, as none of the men offered to shake hands – Stafford made the opening move.

'Look, McCracken, no need to take up too much of your time,' he began. 'We know that Sandy Walsh worked for you before she went to work on her own. We know Tessa Byrne worked for you at some stage, about two years ago. I have pictures here if you need to see them to confirm.'

Michael knew why Stafford hadn't even bothered to ask whether the women had worked for McCracken, even though they only had the word of one of Paula's girls about Tessa Byrne. He was letting on that they knew more than they did.

Tricky, however, was well prepared. 'Yeah, show us the pictures.'

Stafford passed them across the table. Tricky

glanced at both of them and passed them back. He didn't even pause before he answered.

'Yeah, both of them birds worked for … at a place I owned. Long time ago now, though.'

'How long did Sandy Walsh work for you, exactly?'

'I dunno. A few months or so, thereabouts.' His eyes never stopped flicking from one face to the other.

'What about Tessa?'

'As far as I can remember, she only worked for me a couple of days. Her and a mate.'

'She had a friend working with her?'

'Yeah, she bleeding split at the same time.'

'Do you remember her name?'

'Nah, it was a long time ago.' He grinned at Stafford. 'Tell you what – I'll ask round, see if anyone remembers.'

'They only stayed a few days?' Michael said pleasantly. 'That's not very long, is it?'

Tricky shot him a cool look. 'It happens, you know what I mean?'

'Maybe they didn't like the way you ran things.'

Tricky folded his arms across his body and looked at Michael. 'Don't know what you're fucking on about. What's that supposed to mean?'

'No? I hear you like—'

'Do you know of any grudge somebody might have had against either of the women?' Stafford butted in.

'Hmmm.' Shifting in his chair, Tricky pretended

to give the question some thought. It was all Michael could do not to lean across the round table and slap the back of his head.

'The thing is,' Tricky said eventually, after much squinting at the ceiling, 'I don't know nothing about these birds. I mean, they worked for me and all that; but it's not like I'd know nothing about their personal life, know what I mean? I don't get involved with fucking personal shit. Don't have no time for that crap.'

Michael balled his hands up under the table. In his mind he re-read one of the statements Ed had shown him earlier that day. It was from a girl called Stacy. She claimed McCracken had followed her home on the first and only night she had worked for him. She had made the mistake of refusing to have sex with him. Enraged, Tricky had thrown her out and she had gone home – only he had forced his way into her flat and raped her at knifepoint. When she'd threatened to go to the police, he had laughed at her and told her to go ahead. It would be her word against his, and she was a prostitute. He'd told her that he'd tell the gardaí she'd consented, and that he could pull any number of witnesses to say she'd been flirting with him all night. She said that, after that night, he had often driven by her house, roaring abuse out the car window; that he'd called her a whore if he ran into her on the street. Eventually she had moved house to get away from him.

Ed, his antennae tingling, had recorded everything she said, word for word. When she finished talking, he had asked her to sign it. Stacy had refused to sign the statement and said she'd retract everything if he ever told anyone. She said she didn't want to press charges – what was the point? Ed had tried for almost an hour to talk her round, but she wouldn't budge. In the end, she wouldn't even confirm that she had worked for Tricky.

Michael thought of Amanda Harrington. What must she have gone through with this little fucker, if she had been with him for a long time?

'So you see, I can't really help yous much there. I mean, they never had no shit at my place.' The eyes flicked again, resting firmly on Michael. The voice was laden down with phoney indignation. 'I make sure my girls are well protected. Do a better job than yous cunts, too.'

'Very commendable,' Stafford said smoothly. 'Perhaps some of your current workers might remember the women.'

Michael tried not to grin at the amiable way Stafford was talking. He knew his boss was playing a blinder; even Tricky looked puzzled by his polite and wholly uncharacteristic way of speaking.

'Nah, man.' Tricky waved a dismissive arm. A gold bracelet as thick as a bike-chain glinted before disappearing back up the sleeve of his jacket. 'I don't have none of the same staff I had back then. I wouldn't think any of the bleeding ones I have now even know them birds.'

'We're talking to all women who are working at

the moment. Some of them may have had problem clients at other establishments. I'm sure you understand that.'

'Eh … yeah.' Tricky pulled a face. 'I dunno … The girls are kinda, you know, jumpy about talking to yous lot.'

'That's OK. We'll be very easy on them. They don't need to worry about a thing.'

'Yeah … I dunno about getting them to talk.'

'We could call to see them at their place of work, if that would make them more comfortable,' Stafford offered with a shrewd smile.

'Nah, Jaysus. I know yous lot have got your work cut out at the moment. Nah, I'll make sure they call in to yous over the next day or so. No bleeding point making more work for yourselves.'

Stafford beamed at him. 'We appreciate your concern.'

Michael rolled his eyes. Stafford was laying it on a bit thick.

'No problemo. Anything to help, eh?' Tricky smiled back, showing lots of tiny crooked teeth. He was not looking as confident as he had been earlier. Michael felt a distinct stab of pleasure at seeing him squirm.

'Well, that wraps it up for the time being.' Stafford sat back in his chair, smiled benevolently and signalled to the barman – who was pretending not to see him – for the cheque.

Of the two men staring at him, he didn't know which was more confused – Tricky, because he wasn't going to be asked any more questions, or Michael, because he was letting Tricky go.

'Thanks again for taking the time to see us.'

Suspicion flickered across Tricky's face. 'That it?'

'For now.'

Tricky twitched. 'Eh … yeah. So … I hope yous catch the fuck.'

'I'm sure it's only a matter of time.'

Tricky stood up; he was eager to bolt, but didn't want them to see it. 'I'll make sure them girls talk to yous. Tomorrow or Friday all right with yous?'

'Perfect,' Stafford said sweetly. 'You know where we're based?'

Tricky grinned. 'Yeah, I've an idea.'

'Oh – one last thing. You had no problem with these women, did you?'

'Nah. Why would I?'

'Do you remember where you were on the twenty-second, say between two and five?'

Tricky spread his arms wide. 'Not trying to hide nothing, but I couldn't tell you where I was yesterday. I'll check with me girlfriend – I've a feeling I was with her, tucked up in bed, know what I mean?'

Stafford nodded. 'Perhaps you can ask her to give us a call and confirm that?'

'Why?' Tricky's eyes narrowed. 'You think I knocked off them birds?'

'No, but it helps if we can eliminate people from our enquiries. So if you have someone who can confirm your whereabouts, so much the better.'

'No problem, Inspector. She'll tell you I was with her.' He rattled off the name and number of one of the girls who worked for him. She would say he'd been with her. She would say anything he asked her to, or she could spend the evening with the Whale.

Tricky gave the detectives one last bemused smirk, stuffed his hands in his pockets and swaggered out of the pub.

The door had hardly closed when Michael rounded on his boss. 'What the hell are you up to? We've been after that bollix for months, and you treat him like a long-lost friend? You could have found out how many places he has, how many girls are working for him – but you didn't ask anything. What the hell's wrong with you?'

Stafford ignored the insolent tone. 'Listen to me, Mike. McCracken knows we're talking to everyone about the murders, and he'll compare notes. So we treat him exactly the same way as everyone else. If we treated him differently, he'd soon cop, and the last thing I want is to put that prick on his guard. I read that statement Ed brought in last night too, and I'm telling you now, McCracken is right up there on my list of people to watch.'

Michael grunted. 'He's a piece of shit.'

'Aye, I know.' Stafford picked up the car keys. 'Let's go. We've got work to do.'

'What?'

'We're going to get what we need to start a fire.'

★   ★   ★

The black BMW raced across town, driven by the steady hand of the Whale.

'Fuckin' pigs. I don't know what I was bleeding worrying about,' Tricky said to his silent driver. 'They were asking about them two slags that were bumped off. Never even asked me about the business nor nothing. They're never gonna find out nothing this way.' He laughed, then stopped.

'The only fucking thing is, they want to talk to the girls.' He thought about it for a second. That bothered him. That would fuck him up good, murder investigation or no murder investigation. None of the foreign girls had immigration papers; they'd be held for deportation as soon as they set foot in the station. Then he'd be out their earnings and the money he'd paid their handlers – plus he'd have to replace them, and that meant shelling out more cash up front.

'Fuck, we need to rustle up a few locals for some interviews.'

'How many?' the Whale said.

'Five, maybe six. The pigs don't know how many I've got working for me. I'll send down a couple that won't fucking hang themselves. Or me.'

'Risky.'

'Got no choice; don't want the fat cunt callin' to the apartments.' Tricky glanced at the Whale's profile. 'We talk with them first, make sure they know what to say and what not to bleeding say.'

The Whale's mouth twitched.

Tricky searched through his pockets for his cigarettes. 'Fucking cops, man. No wonder this country's the way it fucking is.'

By the time Amanda reached her apartment, she had calmed down. She could have kicked herself for overreacting to Michael Dwyer's questions.

She didn't want any police attention, she didn't want to be connected to Tricky, and she didn't want Michael Dwyer breathing down her neck. She couldn't afford that. She shouldn't have gone anywhere near him. Now she'd gone and aroused his suspicions by acting like a bloody idiot again. What the hell was it about that man that made her so aggressively stupid? And how had she forgotten the first commandment: thou shalt screen thy calls? Maybe it was the lump on her head where she'd hit Tricky's car window; it had obviously dulled her senses.

She let herself into her apartment, slammed the door and flung her bag onto the hall table. *That bloody Paula, always sticking her big oar in, mouthing and bitching …*

She stormed into the sitting room and dialled the office.

'Marna, it's me.'

'Where have you been? I've been calling and calling! Look, if this is about the other day—'

'What's going on with that fucking Paula?'

'What?' Marna asked, confused. 'Paula?'

'Yeah, Paula.' Amanda clenched her fist and stared at the ceiling. 'She told Michael Dwyer I worked for McCracken. And she told him I got Sandy the job.'

'So? You did work for him.' Marna sounded edgy and defensive.

'I told him I didn't, remember? He called here today, insisted I come in and explain why I'd lied to him.'

'Why didn't you tell him to get stuffed?'

'Oh, brilliant plan. Then they'd really have gone to town on us.'

'So what! You worked there, you didn't work there – what difference does it make?'

'It makes a difference, Marna!' Amanda snapped. 'What is it with you and Paula lately? Seems like she knows more about you than I do. She's telling me I'm not doing the same hours, you're thinking about expanding ... What is all this shit?'

'Amanda—'

'No! Lately she's privy to all our business, and I'm fucking sick of it. Grapevine fucking Paula, of all people. The one person guaranteed to drop me in the shit.'

'What the hell are you talking about? What shit?'

'Don't fucking discuss me with anyone else. Thanks to that bitch, I have Dwyer watching me.'

'Jesus, Amanda, listen to yourself – you're fucking paranoid!' Marna's voice rose. 'Look, what is going on? Where were you today? You don't show up, you're missing for days on end, you think everyone's out to get you ... I mean, Jesus Christ—'

'I don't expect anything different from Paula. It's you I thought I could trust.'

'You *can* trust me!'

'I asked you not to mess with Tricky! I told you how fucking dangerous he is! But did you listen? Did you fuck! Who did you get to call him up and threaten him? That gobshite cop from the courthouse?'

Marna didn't answer.

Amanda knew then. Her head began to throb.

'So here's what we'll do, Marna. You call that Kate girl and you tell her she can have a job. She can have my fucking job. I'm done, that's it, I'm out.'

'Amanda, please – I'm sor—'

'I'll be in to collect my things.' Amanda slammed the phone down and burst into tears.

17

Night-time was coming. He opened his eyes and watched as the shadows crept across the walls of the sitting room, deepening, black fingers stretching out from the corners, skulking forwards like timid animals approaching a stranger.

He watched them advance, minutes ticking by into half an hour. It soothed him, the light of day dying like the headlights of a car when the battery runs down. It amazed him to think he had once feared the dark, when all along it had been his friend, his ally.

He rolled off the camp bed and stretched, listening to the bones of his spine pop and clunk into place. He would leave soon, after he had attended to his mother. *Mother* ... He smiled softly. She had been so happy the night before; it was the best she'd looked in ages. How her hair had shone in the soft lamp-light. It had been so good to hear her laugh again, to see her radiant smile. It had almost broken his heart. He felt tears of joy spring into his eyes. If only she knew how happy it made him to do things for her. She said not to fuss, but he didn't mind; it was a pleasure. After all the sacrifices she'd made for him, there was nothing he wouldn't do for her.

He cocked an ear and listened: nothing. He hadn't heard the voice in the last few days. Perhaps it had gone. He smiled, stood up and crept softly up the stairs to check on Mother. He inched open her door and peered into her room. The Sacred Heart of Jesus over her bed glowed red, casting a soft light over the crumpled bedclothes. She lay on her back, sound asleep, as he had known she would be. Tonight, he would be free to do as he pleased. And what he pleased to do was call on the blonde.

Michael hung up the phone, sat back in his chair and whistled. 'Phew! That is one angry woman.'

'No joy?' Stafford was perched on the corner of Michael's desk, swinging one fleshy leg backwards and forwards like a schoolgirl.

'Nope.' Michael smoothed his moustache and glanced up at his boss. Whatever Stafford was up to, he was playing the cards close to his chest.

'Did you appeal to her conscience?'

'I don't think she has one. I don't think that woman even considers the word a part of the language.'

'How did she explain renting four separate apartments over the last year – especially when she owns her own house? And especially when we can prove at least three of them were used as escort agencies?'

'She didn't. She said she didn't know anything

about any fucking agencies. Then she told me to mind my own fucking business, said if she wanted to rent the fucking Eiffel Tower she would. Oh, yes – and if I called her again, she'd fucking sue us for fucking harassment.'

'That's a lot of fucking.'

'Yes, sir, it was.'

Stafford shook his head gently. He slid off the table and hitched up his trousers. 'Aye, some people never learn. You give them the opportunity to do things the easy way, and they choose the hard.'

'What do you want to do? She's a tough cookie.'

A smile crept across Stafford's face. 'She'll come around, Mike. You'll see. They all come around in the end.'

Emma Harris snapped her mobile closed and rolled her eyes. She'd been expecting the call, and her prepared speech had been flawless; nevertheless, any dealings with the gardaí at this stage in the game made the adrenaline surge through her body like volts of electricity. Poor stupid Detective Dwyer's ears were probably ringing. She put the phone down carefully on the glass table by her side and returned to watching *Law and Order*, marvelling at how easy it was to get TV criminals to talk. On TV, all a police officer had to do was look menacing and slam his hand on a desk; next thing you knew, the crooks crumbled like puff pastry.

Emma shook her head: nonsense.

During the ad break, she thought about the call again. Maybe she had gone overboard during the raid, offended the fat one a little too much. Certainly they'd had her looked into. She considered it and quickly discarded the thought. No, she had acted appropriately.

She would have to let Tricky know about the call.

She picked up the phone, then stopped. Her fingers traced the numbers, but she did not dial. She couldn't bear the thought of having him screeching down the line at her. He was already mad enough today, what with his sudden pressing need to find Irish girls willing to walk into a cop shop and lie for him. Not that he wouldn't find them, Emma thought; there were always girls willing to do stupid things for men like Tricky.

Half an hour later the house phone rang. Emma sighed and pressed Mute just as Mariska Hargitay was offering a deal to a terrified 'perp'. She checked her caller ID screen, recognised the number and picked up.

'We have to move,' the familiar voice said.

'It's too soon.' Emma fumbled for her cigarettes. She lit one and inhaled. 'Look, stop, I'm fine ... What? ... Of course I'm stressed out, so would you be if you ...' She trailed off. 'Look, I'm fine. I've managed this long, haven't I? Stop worrying.' She shook her head as she listened. 'No, Tricky doesn't suspect a thing.' Emma tried to

keep her voice steady. 'I miss you too,' she said.
She wound the phone line around her fingers and
bit her lip. 'Be careful, OK? I couldn't bear it if
anything happened to you. Don't worry, we'll be
together soon. I love you.'

She hung up and went to the window and stood
staring out into the darkness. The night seemed
suddenly cold, and as she rubbed at her arms she
was surprised to feel tears streaking down her face.
She wiped them away furiously.

Tears were for fucking losers.

He had studied the building and knew there were
only three apartments on her floor, and none of
them directly faced her front door. The whore
liked a little discretion – and, as luck would have it,
so did he. The only snag was the security camera
in the foyer, but the cap and glasses he carried in
his sports bag should shield his identity suffi-
ciently. Of course, he could scale the gate and
come up from the car park underneath. But on the
run-through he'd performed the week before, he'd
been on his way back down in the lift when he'd
got stuck with some chatty old bitch with a blue
rinse, carrying a reeking bin-bag that looked like it
was about to split at any second. Three floors of
'nice weather' banalities and the steady drip-drip
of whatever was leaking from the bag onto the lift
carpet had been almost more than he could stand.
And when he and the old bitch had finally reached
the basement, he'd had to lurk about the car park,

pretending he'd lost his car keys, while she waited by the bins, blathering on. He knew it had been a close call. If she hadn't remembered a soap she wanted to watch and left him alone again, he would have had to get rid of her. And that was not on the mission sheet.

He stepped away from the shelter of the wall and peered up at the second-floor window. He'd been there for over an hour, but the lights remained off, the curtains open.

She wasn't there. Somehow he'd missed her. He raged silently and kicked his heel against the wall. This would not do. He had a mission.

A mangy-looking black dog trotted purposefully down the wet street, cocking its leg every few feet and sniffing at takeaway wrappers and bins in search of some tasty morsel. It wasn't a large dog, about the size of a small collie; nevertheless, he pressed himself tightly against the wall and held his breath, waiting for it to pass. He did not like dogs. Somehow they sensed he was different; whenever he had the misfortune to meet one, it growled and barked at him.

It came within a few feet of him and stopped. He cursed; either it had caught his scent, or its keen night vision had picked him out of the shadows.

'Go on now,' he said, flapping his arms madly. 'Get away.'

'That won't work,' the dog said, and sat down on the wet concrete.

He stared at it in horror. 'I didn't know you could speak,' he hissed.

'You don't know a lot of things,' the dog said, and bared an impressive set of teeth. 'Why are you here?'

'I'm not telling you,' he said. Then he frowned and pretended to look at his watch. This was probably a trick. Dogs didn't talk. Or maybe they did, but certainly not to him, not normally. But then, maybe he wasn't listening hard enough … After all, they all barked at him. Maybe that was it: they were trying to tell him something, but he hadn't been able to understand. But now he did. Was it another sign?

His head was beginning to hurt. He sighed and tapped the face of his watch. It was a dilemma. But what else had he to do tonight? She wasn't there; he might as well listen to what the dog had to say.

'Well?'

'Good choice.' The dog wagged its curved tail. 'The other one has a place in Terenure. Big place, very fancy. Lots of lights and trees.' The dog cocked its head. 'You know, it has a big garden at the back; easy to slip in there unnoticed.'

'That's very helpful of you,' he said. He tapped his watch again. 'This was not how I planned it.' He glanced up at the window, then back at the dog. 'I have a plan.'

'Sometimes things change.'

'I don't believe they do.' He stepped out of the shadows and swung his foot at the dog's head. The dog jumped up, skipped easily out of range and continued its journey without a hint of concern. He watched it go. When he was sure it was gone, he resumed his watch on the darkened window. Another hour passed: nothing.

He ground his teeth together in frustration. Had the dog been telling the truth? Did things change? Unthinkable.

Seconds later, a cab pulled up outside the building and a woman stepped out and slammed the door.

He ducked back against the wall and watched as she paid the cabbie. His heart skipped a beat as he recognised the hair under the street-light. Such wonderful hair. It was her, it was definitely her … That lying dog bastard. He would have to learn to be better at reading those that would try to deceive him. Fucking dogs … If only his foot had connected with its head.

He pressed in behind a wheelie bin as the taxi did a slow three-point turn, its lights travelling over his hiding-place. Finally it accelerated and disappeared into the night.

He smiled as lights came on in the long window. He watched her close the drapes against the night and rubbed his hands along his thighs. She would not be easy, but she would be worth the effort. Once he had her immobilised, he could—

The alarm on his digital watch beeped into life. He jumped and bit his tongue. Time to go – time to attend to Mother. He glanced back at the window and balled his fists in frustration. He had no choice but to leave. Soon Mother would wake and wonder where he was.

He picked up his bag, slung it over his shoulder and trudged down the street, disappointed but undeterred. He would call back. And if he ever saw that dog again … well, he'd simply kill it.

18

Tricky kept his word. The next day Jim Stafford got a call saying that five girls, claiming to be from City Stars and Red Hot and Blue, had trooped into the station and plonked themselves down in the foyer with about as much enthusiasm as a funeral party. One of the girls had approached the reception desk, asked to speak with Stafford and rejoined the other four. They didn't talk to one another and they all chewed their nails or smoked non-stop, despite the duty sergeant asking them twice to stop. Stafford grunted and dispatched Michael and Gerry to deal with them.

Although they were interviewed separately, the girls told identical stories, almost verbatim, to the two irritated guards.

No, they didn't know either of the victims. No, they didn't know of anyone who might. No, they couldn't recall any client who had displayed violent tendencies. Yes, they realised the seriousness of the situation. Yes, they were sorry they couldn't help more. No, they wouldn't care to speak off the record. No, Paul 'Tricky' McCracken was a model employer who didn't even raise his voice to them, let alone his hand.

It was a complete and utter waste of time.

'Like listening to a tape recording,' Gerry remarked to Michael after the last one had signed her statement and left. 'We could have saved ourselves some time and stuck five signatures on the one statement.'

'He has them well rehearsed, all right.' Michael stood at the window and watched the last girl disappear into the back of a waiting taxi. 'Makes me sick. We should be protecting girls from the likes of him, not listening to them spew his words out of their mouths. You could see they were all scared shitless.'

'What can you do?' Gerry shrugged. 'Until this murder case is solved, we can't touch him.'

'It makes my blood boil. The sooner we're back on the job, the better. I'm going to enjoy closing that bastard down for good.'

'Don't let it get to you, Mike. He's not worth worrying about. Sooner or later his luck's gonna run out.'

'I bloody well hope so.'

Gerry yawned. He was exhausted. The last few days had drained him. Working odd hours, overtime – it all added up. No wonder the usually easygoing Mike was snapping like a cranky dog. 'What time are you finished up at?'

Michael pinched the bridge of his nose between his fingers and exhaled hard. 'I don't know. Around six, if I'm lucky. Stafford has something he wants to talk to me about.'

'Me and Ed and a few of the lads are heading for a pint after work. Want to come?'

Although normally Michael would have balked at sharing any more time with Gerry than was necessary, the weariness won out. It would have cost him more energy to think of an excuse not to go. 'Yeah. That might not be a bad idea.'

'We're only going across the road.' Gerry gathered up the useless statements. 'I'll give you a shout later.'

'Thanks.'

Michael stayed at the window for a few minutes. He needed a breather. Interviewing those girls had given him a headache. They were so young and frightened. He had noticed the welt on the last girl's arm, and his memory had flashed back to Tricky's smarmy face in the bar. He knew the girls had been worked over.

His mobile vibrated inside his jacket. He pulled it out and stared at the screen. The number was withheld. He answered.

'It's me.' Amanda Harrington's clipped voice sliced through the static. 'Are you busy?'

Michael felt a sudden, inexplicable flutter in his chest at the sound of her voice. 'Not this very second.'

'I owe you an explanation about yesterday.'

'Would you like to meet? Do you want to come down here?'

Amanda laughed. 'No, thanks. How about

Hourican's at the bottom of Leeson Street, in half an hour?'

He glanced at his watch. 'I can do that.'

She'd already hung up.

She was there before him, far down the back of the small pub, tucking into a bowl of vegetable soup. Michael gave her the once-over as he approached her. She had dark rings under her eyes and her face was paler than usual, but other than that she looked lovely. She wore a dark-red polo-neck and black wool trousers, and her long dark hair, tied in a ponytail, gleamed under the lights of the bar.

'Amanda.'

She looked up, nodded a greeting and put down her spoon. 'Do you want something? The soup here is the best.'

'I'm fine. Thanks anyway.' He pulled up a stool and sat beside her.

'Don't mind if I carry on? I haven't eaten all day.'

'Work away.'

He waited. For someone who hadn't eaten, she picked at her lunch like a bird. Finally she pushed the bowl away and reached for her cigarettes.

'Not hungry?' Michael nodded towards the half-full bowl.

'Never am these days.' She lit a cigarette and eyed him through the smoke. 'I should probably say I'm sorry for yesterday's little performance.'

'Do you want to tell me what that was all about?'

Amanda gave a tiny shrug. 'You caught me off guard. I thought I was going to be asked questions about Sandy, not about that shit-hole or about Paul McCracken.'

Michael shrugged. 'You can't talk about one without the other. It was the last place Sandy worked before striking out on her own. It's the only place that Tessa Byrne and Sandy Walsh both worked in. It's only natural we'd like to know about him.'

'I hate having anything to do with that place. Even talking about my time there upsets me.'

'Why? Half the prostitutes in Dublin must have worked there at some stage.' He said it with a smile, gently reminding her of her own words.

Amanda glanced at him, and for a split second her eyes lost some of their wariness. 'That's some memory you have.'

'Thanks.' He pulled his notebook out and opened it to a fresh page. As he rummaged for his pen, he caught a trace of her perfume and wondered what it was called. 'McCracken doesn't just have a high staff turnover. I've heard things about him lately – disturbing things.'

'I'm not surprised.' She waved to a woman with short chestnut hair who'd just come in. The woman waved back and mouthed, 'Hi.' She took off her coat, slipped behind the bar and tied an apron around her slim waist. Michael glanced at the girl and back at Amanda.

'Is this your local?'

'No.'

Michael sighed. She really ran hot and cold, this one. 'How long did you work for McCracken?'

Amanda raked her fingers through her dark hair, scraping it back from her forehead. 'About a year.' She flicked him an accusing glance. 'I used to work at the Red Stairs before that, but then you lot came along and shut it down.'

'Marie's place?' Michael shook his head. 'That wasn't us. We hadn't even formed then.'

'I don't mean you personally. I mean the gardaí, the good old boys in blue.' She picked up a beer mat, flipped it a few times and began to shred it. 'Ten of us out of a job, like that.' She clicked her fingers. 'Marna took a job the same day in Cherry's, an escort agency over in Donnybrook.'

'Ah. … Cherry's.' Michael nodded. He *had* been responsible for that closure; it had been less than a year ago, and he remembered it well. The owner, an aggressive, hard-faced little bitch from Finglas, had spat in his face when he'd confiscated her takings. It had been all he could do not to slap her.

Amanda watched him, a half-smile on her lips. 'I knew that place would ring a bell with you. Marna said you guys were very heavy-handed when you raided.'

'She wasn't there.'

'She heard all about it.'

'I'll bet she did.' He rolled his eyes. 'Tell her not to believe everything she hears.'

'Anyway, when the Red Stairs closed, Paula …
You know her, right?'

Michael didn't respond. He knew she was
baiting him.

'Paula,' continued Amanda, 'offered Sandy and
me a job. Sandy took it.'

'You didn't?'

'No.'

'Why not?'

'I didn't want to work there. It's a kip, and Paula's
not the cuddly fucking saint she tries to make out
she is, either,' she said sharply. 'I rang City Stars
instead.' Michael watched her expression harden.
'Everyone kept saying how busy it was, that the girls
were pulling in a fortune … Actually, that part was
true. The problem wasn't the money; the problem
was that prick Tricky. He was only out of jail a few
months then, and he hadn't exactly – how shall I put
it? – hit his stride.' She curled her lip in disgust.
'Biggest mistake of my life – and believe me, I've
made some whoppers. I can't believe how stupid I
was. I knew from the moment I met him that he was
a bastard. Know what I mean?' She did an eerily
accurate impersonation of Paul McCracken. 'But
you get hard in this business. You think you can
handle anything, you know?'

Michael rested his arm on the table. A lock of
her hair had worked its way loose from the
ponytail, and he felt his hand twitch with the
longing to reach across and smooth it off her
shoulder. 'You found out you couldn't?'

'It took me about three weeks to figure out he has the places bugged.' She glanced at him again. 'Did you lot know that?'

Michael nodded. 'I've heard.'

'He knows everything – where a girl lives, what her family does, everything. If you try to leave, he springs it on you. And in this business that's every girl's nightmare – having your friends and family find out what you do ...' She shook her head. 'Unthinkable.'

'Did he threaten you with that?'

Her face remained inscrutable, but Michael could see the hurt in her eyes. 'He couldn't,' she said. 'I've got no one to care what I get up to.'

'What about family, friends?'

She shook her head. 'My parents are dead,' she said matter-of-factly, 'and, apart from an old aunt who probably can't remember what I look like, that's it.'

'No brothers or sisters?'

'No.' She twisted away from him and picked up her lighter. 'And you can stop giving me that look. That's the way I like it. I can do what I like when I like, and there's no one to tell me otherwise.'

Michael smiled. Ever since his wife had passed away, the life Amanda was describing had been his life too, so he knew how lonely she probably was. 'Did McCracken ever threaten you?'

She shrugged and ripped at the beer mat. Michael glanced down at her hands; they were long and fine, but her nails were bitten to the quick and, no matter how calm she pretended to be, they moved with a nervous energy of their own.

'He tried various ways to make me stay. None of them worked.'

'Like what?'

'He made things difficult. He knew where I lived, and he must have made hundreds of threatening phone calls to me, usually in the middle of the night. And no matter how many times I changed the number, he found out what it was. He blacklisted me with other brothels.' She looked up into Michael's surprised face. 'You didn't know he could do that, did you? It's not only the girls who're afraid of him; some of the other owners are too. Not because he could hurt them, but because, if he was pissed off enough, he could make life hard for them too.'

'How?' Michael said.

'He'd ring the tabloids, complain and make up some bullshit story. I know for a fact he often called your lot pretending to be an outraged neighbour or a concerned citizen. Other bosses don't need that type of hassle, especially over one girl. So believe me, when Tricky blacklisted me, I couldn't get a job this side of Christmas. Nobody would take me on.'

'What did you do?'

'What could I do?'

'You just stayed there?'

'I was paying a big mortgage; I needed the money. So I stayed until my circumstances changed,' she said quietly.

'Changed in what way? How did they change?'

She lit another cigarette and let the question float for a second. Michael couldn't read the expression in her eyes. 'Let's say he overplayed his hand.'

'How? What do you mean?' Michael was intrigued; this was not what he had expected to hear today. He was glad to learn more about McCracken. And he was glad to spend some time talking with Amanda Harrington.

'Nothing – it doesn't matter now.' Amanda picked up a fresh beer mat and twirled it.

'Amanda, what happened?' he asked softly. 'How are we supposed to nail this fucker if nobody will talk about him? We know he likes to hurt girls, there's nothing he likes better. Can't you talk to me?'

'Nothing to talk about. I left, there were problems, they got sorted out. By that stage Marna was sick of escort work, so we hooked up and went to work together. A year later you lot arrested us and dragged us to court, and now here we are.'

'That's it?'

'That's the condensed version.' She blew out a stream of smoke. 'That's all I'm willing to say about it. It's ancient history now – and I thought you wanted to know about Sandy.'

'I do.'

'Then let me tell you about Sandy.'

'Fire ahead.'

She smiled – not a real smile; the smile people

use to be polite. He blinked. There was something in her expression that reminded him of something, but he couldn't put his finger on it.

'I made another big mistake getting Sandy Walsh a job with Tricky. But she kept ringing me every bloody week, moaning about Paula's. She said she couldn't work for her any more because Paula kept changing the shifts every week. Said she wasn't making the same money as before because her clients never knew what day she was working.' She ran her fingers through her hair. 'Sandy was driving me nuts. Every bloody time I was home, she rang, whingeing – Paula this and Paula that. She pleaded with me to get her the job at City Stars, and no matter how hard I tried to put her off …' Amanda shrugged. 'I told her straight what a prick Tricky was. Sandy said she didn't care. I told her he bugged the places; Sandy said he could listen to her all day if he wanted. I told her he was planning to get rid of the Irish girls and replace them with immigrants. She said so what, she'd work until he got rid of her. All she cared about was the money. She'd heard the stories, same as me. She kept asking how much she could make, how many girls were on a shift, how many shifts she could get. It was like Tricky's was the Holy Grail, the way she went on about it.'

Michael reached for his notebook. Amanda glanced at it and shook her head, so he put it back in his pocket and motioned to her to continue. 'See, the thing is, that's the way it is in this business. Once a place gets a reputation for being seriously busy, girls will do anything to get in there. And competition to get in is fierce. So if you know someone already working there, she can put in the word.'

'Really?' Michael couldn't believe what he was hearing – girls begging to get into the brothels … 'Even if it means working for McCracken?'

'Back then, yeah, even if it meant working for that bastard.' Amanda grinned at his puzzled expression. She knew he didn't understand. He was a black-and-white man, and what she was telling him was nothing but various shades of grey. 'Sandy was no different. As long as she could make cash, she didn't give a shit about anything else. Next thing I know, she's accusing me of not wanting her there because she'd be competition. Eventually I got sick of it; I got her an interview with McCracken, and he gave her a job.'

'Why didn't you want to tell me about this?' Michael said. 'I don't understand. What's the big deal?'

Amanda shook her head. 'I knew Sandy. She was one tough cookie. I knew she wouldn't put up with Tricky's shit, and I knew there'd be trouble.' She looked up at Michael's blank face and clicked her tongue in annoyance. 'That's the real reason Saint Paula didn't want her: because Sandy Walsh rocked the boat in every place she ever worked in. She didn't give a shit if Tricky tried to blackmail her. Her family knew what she did for a living; no matter how much they might deny it now, they knew.'

Michael nodded.

'It was a disaster waiting to happen. She called his bluff after a few weeks there. Started to piss him off – little things, really. He couldn't bully her the way he did everyone else. She wouldn't work on if somebody didn't turn up for a shift. She wouldn't work the weekends. She told him to fuck off one day in front of a few of the other girls—'

'If she was that bad, why didn't McCracken fire her?'

Amanda started to laugh. 'Money, Sergeant, money. Tricky may have hated her, but she was busy, so he kept her on. He didn't want to lose somebody who could bump up a shift by as much as four clients, no matter how mouthy she was.'

She rested her chin on her hand, and her voice grew weary. 'I know it sounds like nothing to you, but I should never have got her a job there. She never knew where to draw the line. She started to fiddle the books for more and more money – not writing it down when a client came in, pocketing the house money as well as her own, that sort of thing.'

'And Tricky found out?'

'Of course he did. Girls in our business are very fucking jealous, Sergeant. Sure, they liked Sandy – she could be really funny. But she was also really busy.' Amanda smiled sadly. 'Sandy wasn't the best-looking woman, but she could wipe the floor with most of McCracken's girls back then. She had a real way with the clients; if she opened a door, nine times out of ten the man stayed with her, even if he'd called looking for someone else. That was her downfall. Girls don't like losing clients. They don't like losing money. So, of course, somebody hung her out to dry.'

Michael stroked his moustache and wondered if Amanda realised how vicious she sounded when she spoke about McCracken and his places. Whatever had happened between them, Amanda Harrington, for all her poise, was still hurting.

'Then what?'

'The bastard trapped her. Sent in a friend who offered Sandy a cut price if she could do him fast and not take the house money,' Amanda said angrily. 'That was always Sandy's weakness: if someone offered her cash, she couldn't turn it down. The second the client left, Tricky went in, grabbed Sandy by the hair and dragged her into another room. He was so fucking angry he was practically foaming at the mouth. I'd never seen him like that before. He threw her into the room and she fell against one of the lockers. He ordered another girl to pack up all Sandy's things into a bin-liner. The he went back into the room and closed the door.' Amanda sighed and closed her eyes. When she opened them again, Michael saw the strain in her face. She was telling the truth: talking about McCracken was agony for her.

'It was crazy. I was in another room, but I could

hear them screaming at each other. He threatened Sandy, and she laughed in his face. Jesus, she never knew when to shut her mouth. I heard her warn him not to fuck with her if he knew what was good for him. Tricky lost it; he slapped her across the face, split her lip open. He came bursting back into the staff room dragging her by the hair, and she was screaming … Her lip was bleeding; there was blood all over her face.' Amanda shivered. 'Nobody said a word; we were all terrified. He gathered up all her things, grabbed her by the hair again, threw her out on the street and chucked all her clothes after her.'

Michael shook his head. The bastard could have been had up for assault, actual bodily harm. If only women reported pricks like McCracken. 'What then?'

'It was terrible. The paranoid shit said we were all in on it, accused us all of trying to rob him. Said we had screwed ourselves, if we thought we could get away with that we were wrong. He raised the house money, but wouldn't let us charge the clients any extra. He said we could pay back whatever Sandy had taken, with interest. Two days later he hired the Whale.'

Michael glanced down at her hands again and saw they were shaking. 'Who?'

'I'm not surprised you don't know him.' Amanda looked down at her hands and forced them to stop trembling by laying them flat on the table. 'Girls don't mention him. He's Tricky's right-hand man. Big fat ignorant bastard.'

'What do you mean? What does he do?'

'Tricky calls him his security.' She smiled at some private joke. 'Fucking security – can you believe that?'

'Who is he?'

'Dunno. He turned up that night with Tricky and started throwing his weight around.' She checked her watch. 'Look, I've got to go. I only came to explain about yesterday.'

Michael wanted to hear more. He scrambled for something that might stop her leaving. 'How's Marna these days?'

'Oh, same old Marna.' Amanda wound a scarf around her neck. 'I'll tell her you were asking for her when I see her.' She picked up her cigarettes and put them in her bag.

'If we need—'

Amanda clicked her tongue in annoyance. Her grey eyes searched his for some sign of comprehension.

'Do I have to spell it out for you?' she snapped impatiently. 'Nobody talks about Tricky if they can avoid it. He finds out when people go shooting their mouths off.' She shook her head. 'I've done my time with him; I don't need any more trouble.'

'Nobody is going to know about this conversation,' Michael said, stung.

Amanda pulled a face. 'I can't take that risk.'

'I can assure you, anything you tell me is confidential.'

'Yeah, right.' She smiled sadly at him and shook her head. 'And I thought I was the naïve one here.'

Michael scowled. He didn't like the tone or the implication. 'What are you suggesting?'

'I'm not suggesting anything.' She stood, grabbed her coat and swung it on.

'What did Sandy threaten McCracken with?'

Amanda stopped buttoning her coat. Her face went slack. 'What?'

'You said, "He threatened her, she warned him not to fuck with her if she knew what was good for him." What was it she threatened him with?'

Amanda frowned and pursed her lips together. She was clearly desperate to leave, but he could see she was considering his question. 'I don't know,' she said eventually. 'But I did hear her yelling something about tapes.'

'Tapes?'

'Some shit about tapes. Maybe she was going to report him for bugging the places – not that it would have done any good, since you lot can't catch him anyway.'

Michael flushed with irritation and closed his notebook with a loud snap. 'We'll catch him, you can be sure of that.'

Amanda raised an eyebrow. She turned up the collar of her coat and folded her hair under it. 'No, you won't. He's well ahead of the game. Everybody's heard about the great raid where you scared some poor cow half to death in her own apartment.'

Michael jerked in his chair. 'How did—'

'Everyone knows about that!' She grinned slightly at the look on his face and relented. 'Let's face it: he's blessed with cunning when it comes to the cops. People like Marna and me are easy targets for you lot – all you have to do is turn up and, idiots that we are, we'll go quietly – but Tricky? That's a whole other ball game.' She glanced towards the door again.

'Do you think Paul McCracken is capable of murder?'

Amanda dropped her gaze, and it was a few seconds before she answered. 'I've got scars, Sergeant,' she said finally. 'Not physical ones; in here.' She tapped the side of her head. 'Nobody ever gets off scot-free in this business, and believe me when I tell you this: McCracken is capable of anything. I've known him do terrible things for no other reason than his own sadistic pleasure.' She raised her head and looked at him coolly. 'Behind it all, he's a coward, but that doesn't stop him being dangerous. If anything, it makes him worse.' She held out her hand, signalling that she really was leaving this time.

Michael didn't know why he did it, but he grabbed her hand and gripped it tightly in both his own. 'If you ever need to talk to me again, call me. Doesn't matter what time. I'll give you my home number, too.'

'I don't want it.' Amanda stared at him. She snatched her hand back and shook her head. 'For what? Why in the name of God would I call you?'

Michael flushed. He had been too forward, and now he felt humiliated. 'I don't know. If you need to talk, if McCracken's giving you problems—'

'You think I need a shoulder to cry on?' Amanda smiled coldly, and Michael saw a flash of pure anger in her eyes. 'I don't. I've done all the talking I'm going to do, Sergeant.' She leaned closer to him. 'Listen to me very carefully. I've told you everything I know about Sandy Walsh, and now I want to be left alone. Stop calling my house. I don't need any heart-to-hearts. As someone once told me, nobody held a gun to my head and forced me to enter my profession. This is my life, Sergeant; I chose it, and I don't need any sympathy from you.'

'Amanda, I'm not trying to—'

'Good. Let's leave it at that.'

Her eyes skittered away from him, moving in the direction of the door. Escape, he noticed: she always aimed for escape.

'It's been an experience, Sergeant.' She nodded and walked away.

Michael watched her leave the pub and wondered what the hell had happened to her to make her so resistant to any offer of help. Surely she understood he wasn't trying to patronise her. He genuinely liked her; she had to know that. He *knew* she knew that.

He leaned his arms on the table and felt the lingering sense of familiarity that crept over him every time he talked to her. Amanda Harrington bothered him, her hot-and-cold style confused him; and yet, on some deeper level, he understood her single-mindedness, her fierce rejection of his offer of a friendly ear, her refusal to thaw. He recognised all the symptoms of a life spent alone.

Michael knew all about being alone.

He rubbed his hand over his eyes and stood up, feeling a great weariness descend on him. He needed to find Stafford. His boss would be very interested to hear that Sandy Walsh had threatened McCracken and that there had been bad blood between them. He found the keys of his car and wondered what Sandy had had on Tricky.

By the time he got back to the station, Stafford had been and gone again. Michael closed his office door and went down to the main squad room, where he found Gerry hunched at a computer.

'I'm looking for the boss. You seen him?'

'He was here earlier,' Gerry said gloomily. 'The fucker's making me type out all my statements. Claims he can't read my handwriting.'

'Any idea what time he'll be back?' Michael asked. 'I need to speak to him.'

'Try him on the mobile.' Gerry was concentrating on the computer screen. He walloped a few keys with his index finger. 'Shit.'

'What's wrong with you?'

Gerry wiped his hand across his brow. 'It's this fucking typing. I hate it, Mike. I'm never going to get any better at it.' He jabbed the keyboard hard again. 'This is going to take ages.'

Michael left him to it. He glanced at his watch; it was twenty past three. He grabbed the phone on his desk and called Stafford's mobile. It rang for an age before Stafford answered.

'Mike, I'm over at the drop-in centre on Haddington Row. I'm checking if any of the women who use the place reported anything unusual to the staff here.'

Michael winced; Stafford had a habit of shouting into mobiles.

'I met Amanda Harrington. She gave me some interesting information regarding McCracken. He definitely had a problem with Sandy Walsh. I thought you might like to hear it.'

'Aye, I'll be back over that way in about an hour,' Stafford roared down the line. 'Can it wait?'

'Yes.' Michael held the phone at arm's length. He saw Gerry watching him.

'Right! Talk to you soon,' Stafford bawled, and hung up.

Michael shook his head, sat down at his desk and took out his notebook.

'Amanda Harrington – she one of the girls we brought to court a while back?' Gerry asked.

'You remember her?' Michael lifted his head, surprised. 'I didn't think you were with us the night we raided them.'

'I wasn't.' Gerry shrugged, and his eyes went back to the screen. 'I remember her from the courthouse. Good-looking chick, tall, dark hair. She in some kind of trouble?'

'I didn't realise you cared so much.'

'Wouldn't mind her slapping my bare arse for a while.'

Michael checked around his desk for a pen. He thought that if he looked up and saw Gerry grinning, he might get up, go over there and punch him in the face.

'Wonder why they're hooking? They don't exactly seem the type.'

Michael located a Biro and thought of Amanda's troubled grey eyes. 'Who knows?' he said after a few seconds. 'They may not seem the type, but they're damaged, all right; they've just covered over the cracks better than most.'

19

'So Amanda Harrington lied about working for McCracken,' Stafford said.

'I think a lot of girls lie when it comes to McCracken,' Michael said carefully.

'Tell me something I don't know.' Stafford, perched on the desk, folded his arms across his barrel chest.

'He assaulted Sandy Walsh. Split her lip open in front of witnesses.'

'Did he now.' Stafford's eyes glinted.

'That's what Amanda Harrington says.' Michael took a bite of his sandwich and handed Stafford the statements from Tricky's girls.

Stafford put them down on the desk without looking at them. 'You don't believe her?'

'I believe her about the blackmail, and I believe her when she says Sandy Walsh got a bit of a hiding. Doesn't mean I trust every word out of her mouth.'

'What makes you say that?'

'There's something she's not telling me, I know it.'

'Anything interesting in these?' Stafford poked the papers hopefully.

'Nope.'

'Didn't think there would be. Another fuckin' clam-up job.'

'Five separate statements, nearly word-for-word identical.'

'At least we've got the phone records for Tessa Byrne's mobile now. Lot of numbers, Mike; lot of numbers.'

Michael laughed and threw his sandwich wrapper in the bin. 'There's going to be a few married men sweating over the next few days.'

'Scully's convinced he has this case sewn up.' Stafford thumbed idly through the statements. 'What do you reckon about Walsh and McCracken?'

'Amanda Harrington said McCracken is capable of anything. And he didn't like Sandy.'

'That's not exactly grounds for murder, is it? I wonder what she had on him. Tapes, eh? Maybe she was going to pull the plug on his little eavesdropping set-up.'

'I don't know,' Michael said. 'But why would he bother to kill her after all this time? If she was going to report him, she'd have done it before now.'

'True,' Stafford said, and hopped off the desk. 'Nobody saw anything. Nobody knows of any reason why anyone would want to kill either woman. It's a bloody mystery.' He pulled a sour face. 'Scully's not interested in the McCracken angle. He's convinced it's a client.'

'That's the most probable scenario,' Michael said evenly.

'Aye, but McCracken wouldn't be too far off

my radar either.' Stafford grunted and threw down the useless statements. 'What's the deal with this security man?'

'Amanda said he just arrived one night with McCracken. She called him the Whale.'

'Amanda, is it?' Stafford took a seat, leaned back in his chair and grinned.

Michael flushed like a schoolboy. 'Look, sir, I only meant—'

'It's all right, Mike. She's a good-looking girl; only natural she'd catch your eye.' Stafford's brows jiggled up and down.

'She hasn't caught my anything,' Michael said stiffly.

'Aye, well, none of my business one way or the other … But you know, Mike, try not to get too close to that one.'

'I told you, I'm not.'

Stafford snapped back up in his seat and slapped his hand down on the desk. 'The Whale. I've heard that name mentioned before some-where. Get Ed to look into it. He sat on one of McCracken's apartments at the beginning of the operation. He's got photographs of everyone who went in and out of the place – for all the bloody good they did us.'

Michael glanced at him. Stafford was still furious about the botched raids. It was bad enough to mess up one, but they had raided McCracken's places three separate times and never found a single working girl. Michael rose to go.

'Did you get a description of this fella?' Stafford said.

'She called him a big fat fuck.'

Stafford raised his eyes to heaven. 'Jaysus, that narrows it down. I'll call Paula, see if she knows who he is. Actually, I should get you to call her; seems she took a bit of a shine to you.'

'That's OK, you can call.' Michael stuffed his hands in his pockets and headed for the door.

'Mike?'

He turned back. 'Yeah?'

'There's nothing wrong with finding another woman attractive, you know.' Stafford's expression was kind. 'It's been a good many years now. Life moves on.'

Michael nodded and fled. He couldn't face the pity in Stafford's eyes.

An hour and a half later, Ed dropped two photos on Michael's desk. 'That's your guy, the one you were asking about.'

Michael picked the photos up and studied them carefully. He understood why Amanda Harrington didn't want a visit from this man.

The first photo was a full-colour head-and-shoulders shot of a man who looked like the product of generations of careful breeding for thuggery. The second photo was a full-body shot of him coming out of an apartment building. The Whale certainly lived up to his name. He was a giant of a man, big and mean-looking as a hungry grizzly. A shaved, bullet-shaped head sat on his meaty shoulders; there was no neck as far as Michael could see. A thin silver scar – probably made by a knife, or maybe a bottle – ran the length of the right side of his face; Michael guessed he was very proud of it. He wore the uniform of a hard man: bomber jacket and combats, both black. His massive arms hung by his sides like two slabs of beef.

'He only went in at night – not every night, mind you. And he never came back out the same night, so I figured he was a resident of the complex.'

'Did he have a key or did he ring a bell?'

'Both.'

'Could you not see which doorbell he was ringing?'

'Not in that place. The doorbells are sunk into the wall. And this guy' – Ed tapped the head shot – 'always stood blocking them.'

'Why didn't you tell us about him at the time?' Mike said irritably. 'We should have been told.'

'Because I thought he lived there. He went in most nights, but he never came back out, and we were looking for guys who were out within half an hour. I thought he was someone who came home late. The only reason I even have these photos is that I didn't like the look of him.'

'Do we know who he is?'

'We're running his picture at the moment.'

Michael gazed at the photos again. 'Let me know when we have a name.'

★ ★ ★

It took them less than half an hour to find the identity of the man the prostitutes knew as the Whale. It came as no great shock to Michael that he had a record dating back almost twenty of his forty years.

Michael tapped on the door of Stafford's office and held up the record sheet. 'I know who our man is.'

Stafford waved him into a seat. 'Anthony O'Connor.'

Michael stared at him. 'How did you know? I only got the records this minute.'

Stafford leaned back in his chair and grinned at Michael's disappointed face. 'Paula couldn't wait to volunteer his name.'

'Jesus, she's fast.'

'She's a fount of information, that one, but only when it suits her.'

Michael dropped the sheet on Stafford's desk. 'This O'Connor is a nasty piece of work. Armed robbery, assault with intent, grievous bodily harm, assault and battery, sexual assault … It goes on and on.'

'Violent man,' Stafford said quietly. 'And working for McCracken.'

Michael nodded. 'This man here is the reason none of the women will talk to us properly. Even girls who left McCracken's place over a year ago won't talk for fear of him.'

Stafford laced his fingers in front of his face. 'That girl we found in the raid on McCracken's last place … what do you think? Time we paid her a visit?'

'Who?'

'Why, little Miss Harris, of course.' Stafford smiled nastily. 'You've got her work address, right?'

Michael nodded. 'You're thinking of going to her job?'

'Aye, put a little pressure on her.'

'What about Scully?'

Stafford's face darkened and his eyebrows knotted together in a single line. 'What about him? This is a follow-up to a raid. Not something to trouble him with, Mike. Got me?'

'But won't he—'

There was a knock on the door. Gerry stuck his head in.

'Sir, Bob Scully's on the phone for you. He says it's important.'

Michael gave a little start. With all the talk of bugs, he was getting paranoid.

'I'll be right with you,' Stafford said. As Gerry left, he turned to Michael. 'We leave Scully out of this. It's nothing to do with the murder enquiry, right? I have a gut feeling about that Harris. She needs to know we haven't forgotten about her.'

'When?'

'No time like the present.'

Michael sighed. He could kiss his chances of going for a drink goodbye. But then, maybe that wasn't such a bad thing.

20

Heavy rain lashed the two men as they made their way across Lower Baggot Street and up the steps of the beautiful Georgian building owned by Acton and Pierce Ltd. Flustered and red-faced, Stafford shook water off his coat in annoyance. 'How come there's never any parking to be had anywhere around these areas? You'd think there'd be at least one space.'

Michael looked at the black sky. 'There's never a space when you need one.'

Stafford said, 'Aye.' He yanked open a heavy glass door and they stepped inside.

They drip-walked across a luxurious burgundy carpet to a vast oak reception desk, behind which an elegant woman in her forties was eyeing them with barely disguised distaste. Her hair, prematurely grey, was cropped close to her head. She wore tiny bifocals on a silver chain, a black silk shirt and a pearl necklace that had probably cost more than Michael earned in a month.

'May I help you gentlemen?' she asked.

Stafford leaned a wet arm on the desk. 'You

have a woman called Emma Harris working here. We want to speak to her.'

A single jet-black eyebrow arched. 'Do you have an appointment?' She laid her hands on the keyboard in front of her. Michael noticed her nails. They were about two inches long and painted a strange milky white. They looked like a porn star's hands.

'Give her a ring and tell her Jim Stafford is downstairs.'

The receptionist glanced over his shoulder, studying Michael's windswept appearance coolly. Returning to Stafford, she appeared to have made up her mind. A steely smile appeared, as if it had been waiting in the wings for its time on stage.

'Unless you have an appointment, I doubt Miss Harris would appreciate being disturbed. She is *extremely* busy. Perhaps, while you are here, you can make an appointment to see her later in the week.'

Stafford leaned further across the beautiful desk. Michael shuffled his feet and glanced away.

'I realise Harris may be busy,' Stafford said, 'but so am I. Call her and tell her that Detective Inspector Jim Stafford and Detective Sergeant Michael Dwyer are standing downstairs like two fucking drowned rats. I'm sure she'll free up some of her valuable time.'

The receptionist never batted an eyelid. 'Of course. You should have said it was a police matter, Inspector. Perhaps you and your sergeant would like to take a seat while I inform Miss Harris of your presence.'

She waved a talon in the direction of two velvet sofas.

'Thank you *so* much for your help.' Stafford winked at her.

The receptionist waited until the men had taken their seats before she lifted the phone. She was out of earshot, which was probably the reason the sofas were positioned so far away from the main desk.

After a brief conversation, she hung up. 'Miss Harris will be with you in one minute,' she called over. Michael nodded to her and Stafford gave her an exaggerated bow of gratitude. She curled her lip at him and returned to her work. Michael guessed she was used to dealing with surly buffoons and their sidekicks.

As the steam began to rise from his coat, Michael took in the opulence that surrounded them. The high ceiling gave the reception area the airy feeling of a cathedral. Tasteful paintings hung in elaborate frames, lit from underneath by cleverly concealed spotlights. A curved staircase, covered by the same deep carpet, wound its way up to the next floor. An enormous chandelier hung over the foyer, its thousands of glass droplets twinkling like stars. The place reeked of money.

In less than a minute, a pair of long legs appeared on the bend of the grand stairs. Stafford felt Michael sit up and take notice. The woman coming towards them was completely transformed from the spitting hellcat of the raid.

Stafford whistled softly. 'Well, well, lookie here.'

Emma Harris wore a fitted, pinstriped navy suit with a skirt that barely reached her knees, and high-heeled court shoes. Under the jacket a bright pink shirt was open at her throat. She wore very little make-up, and her jewellery was expensive and understated. Her blonde hair was pulled neatly up into a fancy topknot. If it hadn't been for the incredulous expression on her face, they would never have recognised her.

'Miss Harris, I'm sorry for disturbing you,' the receptionist said, injecting more weary annoyance than was necessary, 'but these gentlemen insisted on seeing you.'

Emma smiled tightly. 'That's fine. Thank you, Flora.' She glared at Stafford. 'Would you gentlemen follow me, please?'

'You clean up well.' Stafford made sure the receptionist heard him.

Emma's face hardened. 'This way, please.' She stalked off down a corridor.

The two detectives followed her to a large, airy conference room. The long room contained a highly polished oak table, twelve high-backed chairs and a well-stocked hostess trolley. One wall held a massive picture that Michael couldn't make head nor tail of, although he suspected it came under the heading of 'art' and was probably worth more than his car.

Emma closed the door and motioned to them to sit down. The two men settled into two chairs. It was all very civilised.

'You fucking bastards.' Emma stood pressed against the door. 'Who the fuck do you people think you are? How dare you come here? This is my job!'

'Well, we thought a little personal visit might jog your memory about McCracken,' Stafford said nastily. 'Maybe you'll recognise the name this time.'

'You … This is *harassment*.'

'Miss Harris, calm down.' Michael took out his notebook. 'Look, try and be sensible about this. You may as well talk to us; we aren't going away.'

'You can't do this.'

'Don't try to be nice, Mike. She thinks she has us all sussed out. Tell me this: how come your name is on so many apartment leases?' Stafford waved his hand to a chair directly opposite his. 'Still, you'll need to be able to rent when that nice house of yours is seized.'

Emma paled slightly under her make-up. 'What?'

Stafford smiled so evilly that Michael felt the hair on his arms rise. 'I'm saying I have a friend down at CAB who would be only too happy to have a little look through your finances. Now I know, seeing as this is your job, you might think you're good at hiding money, but let me tell you something – this guy could sniff out a crooked note from across the sea.'

'The CAB?' Emma rubbed her hands together. 'What the hell would they want with me? I'm not a criminal.'

'No?' Stafford shrugged. 'Well, call me stupid, but it looks to me like you're a major player in the vice world. And that, girlie, makes you just the sort of person CAB likes to look at.' Stafford ran his finger over the desk. 'Maybe it would be worth checking out this operation, too, just to make sure everything's kosher.' He raised his head, and now the smile was gone. 'Your bosses … understanding sort of crowd, are they?'

Emma suddenly looked very sick indeed. 'You wouldn't!'

'Try me.'

She stepped away from the door, and her anger vanished as quickly as it had surfaced. 'All right, Detective, you win. What is it you want?'

'Information. The sooner you talk to us, the sooner we're out of your hair.' Stafford beamed at her.

Emma approached the table slowly. 'Look, I realise I probably should have been more helpful last week.' Her voice was soft and reasonable. Michael was amazed by her ability to switch the charm on and off like a light. 'But you scared me so much that … I was in shock.' She tilted her head and offered them a disarming smile. 'Of course, the more I think about it, the more I understand how it must have seemed to you. You were doing your job – and I respect that.' She pulled out a chair and sat down. 'Afterwards I was appalled at the way I had treated you all. I really was ... ashamed. I mean, people make mistakes, right?'

'Aye, that's often the way.' Stafford grinned. He was enjoying this sudden burst of repentance.

'The thing is,' she continued, smoothing her short skirt over her shapely thighs, 'I may be able to help you with your ... enquiries after all.'

'Really?'

Emma nodded and leaned forwards, breathy and wide-eyed. 'Absolutely. But not here. I mean, you understand I can't have my boss asking me about this chat.'

'Would you like us to call to ... What was the address again, Mike? I swear, my memory these days ...'

'27 Leeson Parade.' Michael knew that Stafford's memory was as sharp as a blade.

'We could call there. At your convenience, of course.'

Emma stared at them, and her face paled even more. Michael knew her mind was working overtime. She had to be worried. They had found her place of work and her home address. They had information that could bury her.

'No, Inspector, there's really no need to call to my home. I would be more than willing to come to the station.'

Michael was impressed by her self-control. He was even more impressed by Stafford's casual pretence of indifference.

'That's grand. Saves us a trip back here. Isn't that right, Mike? Mike here was complaining about the parking.'

The hazel eyes widened. 'So … when would you like me to call in? Tomorrow?'

Stafford scratched his chin. Eventually, after careful deliberation, he shook his head. 'I can't fit you in tomorrow; we're busy for the next few days. How about next Monday – say six o'clock?'

'Next Monday?' She fiddled with her silver rings. 'You don't want me in sooner?'

'Monday's fine.' Stafford smiled again. 'We can have someone pick you up, if you like – give you a lift to the station.'

Emma recoiled. 'No – that's very kind of you, but it's no trouble. I'll make my own way there.'

'Aye, grand job. Ask for me or Mike. The desk sergeant will let us know you've arrived.' Stafford looked over at Michael. 'I'd say that's about it. Did you have anything to ask while we're here?'

'I think we've taken up enough of Miss Harris's time, for the moment.'

'Aye,' agreed Stafford. He stood up to leave. Emma Harris was up and at the door before they had even pushed their chairs back.

'One more thing, Miss Harris. Do you have a mobile phone?'

She looked puzzled. 'Of course I do. Why?'

'May I have the number?'

She gave him a long hard look. 'May I ask what for?'

'In case I need to change the time for Monday. Is it a problem?'

She hesitated. 'Of course not.' She recited the number in short, staccato bursts. Michael jotted it down.

On their way back to the reception area, Stafford allowed himself time to have a good look around. 'It's a nice place you work in,' he said.

'Yes, it is.' Emma walked faster.

'Pays well, does it?' The question seemed innocuous enough, but again Michael saw the pinstriped shoulders stiffen.

'Yes, it does.'

Finally they reached the main foyer. Emma turned to face them. 'Well, thank you for calling to see me.' She spoke loudly for the benefit of the receptionist.

'Thank you for taking the time to see us,' replied Stafford, equally loudly.

The corners of Emma's mouth twitched. 'Goodbye.'

'Bye, for now.' Stafford held out his hand. A brief look of distaste crossed her face, but she gripped his hand and gave it a shake. Michael forced himself not to laugh.

Emma nodded to Michael and, without another word, turned and walked back towards the stairs, leaving them to exit on their own.

After another dash through the elements, the two men reached the car and dived inside. Michael wiped the rain from his face and glanced at Stafford.

'Why did you leave it until Monday? I thought you would want to speak to her as soon as possible.'

'I do.' Stafford grinned. 'But I want her to sweat a little bit first. And I want a better background check on her. If she's working in a respectable job, what's she doing involved with the likes of McCracken?' He put on his seat-belt and started the car. 'I want to know a lot more about our accountant friend before we interview her. This gives us a few days to dig up something we can use. Got me?'

'Sure.' Michael wondered how much of this keen interest was related to the night of the raid.

'The first thing you do is check back over the apartments she rented in the last year. Check the references she gave. I want to know how deeply she's involved with McCracken, and why.'

'Do you think she'll roll on him?'

Stafford shrugged, started the car and pulled out. 'No harm checking.'

Michael gripped the door handle and tried not to think about Stafford's driving. 'I'll go over the apartments and the references. I can check with some of the girls we've interviewed and see if they know her. She doesn't strike me as the sort of person who makes friends easily.'

'I'll ask Paula.' Stafford shot round St Stephen's Green at nearly sixty miles an hour, swapping lanes as if there were no other cars on the road. 'Maybe she's heard of our Emma.'

'The grapevine,' Michael said with a smile.

'Aye,' Stafford nodded. 'God bless the grapevine.'

It was too damn quick.

Emma's hand shook as she dialled Tricky's mobile number. She couldn't believe they had called to her workplace. She felt sick, dizzy. She focused on her breathing, trying hard to steady herself.

'What?'

'It's me. We've got to talk.'

'For fuck's sake, not now! I'm in the middle of something. I'll call you later.'

Emma gripped the phone hard. 'I've had a visit from the gardaí. Here at work.'

There was silence on the other end of the line as Tricky digested this piece of news.

Emma banged her hand down on her desk. 'Are you still there?'

'What did they want?'

'They want me to go see them next Monday.'

'Yeah? What did you say?'

'I told them I'd go, of course!'

'Bollix! What did you say that for? Fuck 'em. I hope you didn't tell them anything.'

'Of course not. Don't be so stupid. I'm not going to hang myself. And the only reason I agreed was to get them the hell out of here before anybody started wondering why two cops wanted to speak to me.'

'OK, OK. Keep the head!' She could practically hear Tricky's brain ticking. 'Right – meet me later, when you leave work, and we'll work out what you'll say. Don't fucking panic; half the time these bastards know nothing. They only let on they do so you'll trip yourself up, know what I mean? Sure, I saw the fuckers myself the other day. Shower of cunts, asking fucking bullshit questions.'

Emma pressed her fingers between her eyes to relieve the pressure building there. 'OK. I have to go.'

'Listen, don't go getting your bleeding knickers in a twist. It's this murder shite. It'll all blow over in a few weeks or so. What's the story with the money? It got through all right?'

'The money's safe. They can't trace it; nobody can, except me. That's the last thing I'm worried about.'

Tricky let out a long sigh of relief. 'You're a good girl, Emma. Keep your chin up and let the fucking bastards swing.'

'Easy for you to say.'

'I told you I'd look after you, didn't I?'

'Yes.'

'You're my girl, Emma. Don't lose the head. Fuck 'em. They got nothing.'

'You're probably right.' Emma laughed lightly. 'I suppose it was the fright of seeing them downstairs.'

'We still on for tonight?' Tricky asked slyly. 'I got a cure for tension right here for you. Wear that red G-string, the one with the funny fur.'

Emma rolled her eyes. 'Jesus, how can you think of sex at a time like this?'

''Cause you're a sexy bitch when you're scared,' Tricky said. 'Just fucking wear it.'

'OK, I'll wear it.'

'Right. Try and relax – don't worry about nothing.'

Emma hung up and rested her forehead in her hands. A mountain of paperwork lay strewn across her desk. She had two meetings in less than half an hour, one with a big client who would demand her undivided attention.

She pulled a little silver pillbox out of a drawer and spilled two Xanax out onto the palm of her hand. She scooped the tablets into her mouth and crunched them up. They tasted vile, bitter and chalky at the same time. She chewed them slowly, methodically, allowing her mind to probe the complexities of her problems.

Two minutes later, Emma smiled. Sometimes the best solution to one's problems was the easiest option of all.

Tricky turned off his phone and lay back on the bed. It was no use: for all his bravado, his nerves were getting the better of him.

'Here!' He raised himself up on his elbows and scowled at the young girl who was sucking desperately on his shrivelled penis. 'Give it up, will you, for fuck's sake!'

She glanced up at him nervously. 'I'm really sorry. I nearly had it … then the phone—'

'Shut up!'

He sat up and hauled on his trousers. While he dressed, the girl watched him from the bed, unsure what to do next. She should have been in double geography with Mr Donaghue, not lying between Paul McCracken's legs.

Tricky strode over to the window, pulled back the curtains and checked the street outside. The evening had darkened and he was beginning to get a feeling that something was not as it should have been. That old sensation of self-pity was flaring up, ready to cripple him for the night.

'Em …' said the soft voice behind him. 'Did I get the job?'

Tricky went to the bedroom door and flung it open. He cast his eye over the fifteen-year-old, staring at her naked, slightly chubby body. She blushed and tried to cover her breasts with the sheet.

'Take the fucking sheet down.'

She immediately did as she was told. Her skin was milky white and her pubic hair was natural and wild. Her breasts were large and already starting to sag from too many summers wearing cheap halternecks without a bra.

Tricky shook his head. 'You didn't get no job. You're too bleeding fat, for one thing, and you're fucking shite in bed. No wonder I couldn't keep it hard. Look at the bleeding state of you, you fat bitch.'

The girl's face reddened and her bottom lip wobbled. 'But you said—'

'Get your fucking clothes on and get the fuck out of my flat, you dozy bitch! You're useless. Serves me right. Next time I'll get me a real woman.'

The girl made a funny keening sound and burst out crying. She scrambled off the bed and stumbled around awkwardly in search of her school uniform.

Tricky liked to watch them as they tried to get dressed. Tears excited him – young girls crying, mortified, begging for another chance at a job in his fictional modelling agency. He liked them like that. Sometimes he would grab them and say he was sorry, stroke them, bring them around and fuck them all over again. Then he'd promise to call, before throwing them out. It never ceased to amaze him how pathetically grateful these dumb bitches were for a scrap of affection.

Today, however, he had more pressing matters to attend to, and he wanted the teenager out of there.

As soon as she was half-dressed, he grabbed her arm, frog-marched her down the stairs and flung her out onto the street. He slammed the door behind her so he wouldn't have to waste any time listening to her sobbing and asking what she had done wrong.

As soon as he had the place to himself again, he picked up his phone. He would soon find out what all this police shit was about. The bastards, calling to Emma's work … She was the only woman Paul McCracken trusted completely. And that was as close to love as he could get.

21

The alarm beeped and beeped, until eventually Amanda rolled over and whacked it so hard that it slid off the bedside locker and hit the ground with a satisfying thump.

She lay in bed for another few minutes, savouring the warmth and enjoying the tail end of the dream she'd been having before that infernal racket had destroyed it.

She dragged herself out of bed, threw on her dressing-gown and padded up the hall towards the kitchen. She might as well go in to work. She had regulars whom she had no way of contacting to reschedule – and Marna … she really had to talk to Marna.

She sighed. As always, no sooner were her eyes open than she began to worry again.

She thought about Michael Dwyer. She knew he was interested in her, and not in a purely professional way. She had caught a whisper of the look at the courthouse; in Hourican's, she had read it on his face as easily as she could read large print. He had offered friendship, and she had thrown it back in his face. She hoped she'd thrown it hard enough. She hoped he had received the message loud and clear. Did he really think she would be open to him, especially after the way he had spoken about her in court? Amanda shook her head. Romance, the luxury of women, had lost all its appeal for her.

She lit a cigarette and made coffee. As she stirred milk into it, she practised her speech, went over the words she would need to tell Marna about her decision.

Poor Marna. It would be terrible, breaking their pact, their business, possibly their very friendship; and yet Amanda felt a new lightness in her soul, a sense of rightness. Maybe she could have worked for another few months – but why put off the inevitable?

Sure that she was doing the right thing and terrified that she was about to make the biggest mistake of her life, Amanda sipped her coffee and thought about how fickle life was. If circumstances were different, she and Marna would have been friends forever. But Amanda knew that when girls left the business, they left the life and all the people behind. It hurt her badly to think of a life without her caustic, charming friend. But she had no choice. None at all.

'So that's it, then.' Marna buttered toast in the office kitchen. She wore a scarlet kimono, and her blonde hair hung freely down her back. Around her left ankle, a thin chain hung with tiny gold Chinese symbols tinkled faintly when she moved.

Amanda leaned against the kitchen door and searched Marna's taut face for any sign that she understood her decision. 'Look, it's not just Paula, it's not Tricky, it's …' She splayed her hands wide. 'It's everything.'

'I see.' Marna piled blackcurrant jam on her toast.

'Marna.'

Marna sighed and put down her knife. 'What do you need me to say? You've already made up your mind, so what do you want from me? My blessing? Fine, you have it.' She wiped her hands on a tea-towel and picked up her toast. 'When were you thinking of going?'

'I don't know exactly. Maybe on Monday.'

'That soon, eh?'

Amanda scowled; Marna's pretended indifference irritated her. 'Well, why not?' she said angrily. 'You've got Kate to fill in. It's not like you need me here. You're always whingeing that I'm not here half the time anyway. This way you'll be better off; the business will be yours – and we've built up a good one, Marna, it's not like I'm leaving to open up somewhere on my own. You'll do fine.'

'Are you trying to convince me or are you trying to convince yourself?'

'I need this. I need to leave.' Amanda felt tears at the back of her throat. There was so much tension between them, and she couldn't find a way to bridge it. 'Can you understand that?'

'No, I don't understand anything, because you won't tell me what's wrong,' Marna retorted. 'But you're right about one thing: maybe I would be better off with Kate. At least she can be here. At least she wants the money. What the fuck's wrong with you? You've been like a cat on a hot tin roof for months. Why won't you tell me what's really bugging you?'

'God, don't make this out to be more than it is.'

Marna arched a perfectly plucked eyebrow. 'OK, so I'm wrong, you're happy and everything's fine. My fucking mistake!'

'Marna, I can't do this any more!'

'So go! It's not a problem. Get yourself sorted, take some time out.'

Amanda shook her head. 'Marna, I won't be coming back.'

'Right. You're going to do – what? Live on your savings? And when they run out, what?' Marna snorted and slapped the uneaten toast back down with such force that she knocked the plate off the table. 'Go be poor – you'll soon find out it's not for the faint-hearted.'

'Don't you fucking lecture me,' Amanda snapped. 'Me, of all people. Not for the faint-hearted! Jesus Christ, what a stupid thing to say.'

'Girl, if I said half the things you need to hear right now, me and you would be talking for a year!' Marna yelled. 'You need a good kick up the arse!'

Amanda stared at her for a long second, then whirled on her heel and left. Marna heard the front door slam behind her.

Marna leaned against the worktop, breathing hard. She checked her watch and switched on the three mobiles charging on the counter. What the hell was going on with Amanda? They never spoke to each other this way. Marna knew Amanda was angry about her call to the cop, but at least it had shown Tricky they weren't going to put up with any shit. What were they supposed to do – roll over and lie down every time they had a crisis? Maybe Amanda was right: some distance between them might not be such a bad thing.

Distracted and upset, she washed the plates, clattering them almost hard enough to break them. She hoped Kate was still available. She couldn't keep working alone, not with some fucking nut-job on the loose. And it was so boring – no one to talk to, only the TV for company. It was not an option. She needed someone she could depend on. If Amanda didn't want to be there, that was her choice, but she was acting like a selfish bitch.

Marna sighed heavily. They weren't joined at the hip. She'd manage fine without Amanda.

Something woke him. He rubbed his eyes and stared at the carriage clock on the grey mantelpiece. It was still early. He listened intently to the surrounding silence, mistrustful of it. Even as he lay there, the chatter in his head began again, taunting him.

He'd spent another futile night staring at a darkened window. He couldn't believe that she hadn't been there, again. He had been so angry, so utterly furious, that he had almost gone across the street and kicked the door down to search for her. Something wasn't right. They were acting against him. Perhaps they knew. Was it possible she had spotted him the first night?

He didn't think that was possible.

He rolled over onto his shoulder and stared, unblinking, at the wall. This was nothing, he told himself; it was a challenge, a test of his persistence, his commitment to his mission. He would not be swayed.

Tonight he would return to the place. He would not be distracted; there would be no errors—

'Son!' The cry was anguished.

He threw back the sleeping-bag, leaped up and raced across the room. 'I'm coming, Mother!'

'Son … help me …'

'Mother!' He hit the first step so fast that his ankle twisted under him, sending him pitching forwards, and he bashed his knee hard off the next step. He grunted and his eyes watered.

'Son! Where are you, son? Don't leave me alone.'

Despite the pain in his leg, he tore up the stairs and along the landing. He burst into her room and practically threw himself across the faded rose satin bedspread. She was sitting bolt upright in the bed and had obviously been in that position for a while.

'Oh, Mother, I'm sorry …' He felt sick with

guilt. He should have come up and turned her over when he got home, but he had been too angry and disappointed.

'There, there … I'm here. I'm here.' He moved up along the bed and stroked her soft hair. He leaned in and kissed it. It smelled of her, her perfume. It was soft and springy; he'd washed it for her the day before.

'Son. You left me here alone.'

'No, Mother. Shhh. Shhh.' He wrapped his arms around her frail shoulders and rocked her gently. God, she was so thin beneath her house-coat; he could almost feel her bones grinding together. 'I'm here now. I'll never leave you. Shhh.'

He sat and nursed his mother until she was peaceful again. After an hour his neck ached and his joints cried out to change position, but he did not move and he did not complain.

He thought of the blonde. She always got back late, always alone. She would not open her door to him that late. He would need to rethink his strategy.

He formed a plan. It was risky; it left him with a certain amount of exposure. But things had changed. He was on a mission now. Because of that, he would be protected.

He glanced up at the Sacred Heart. The blond, blue-eyed Christ stared back, watching over him, protecting him, telling him that he should not falter.

He was still.

22

Bob Scully read through the last of the twenty-six statements filed neatly on his desk. It had been taken from a young heroin addict by the name of Barbara Sinnott, four months before the first murder.

Barbara had been picked up during a raid on Shelly's massage parlour, a cheap downmarket hovel on Amiens Street. Because of doubts over her age, she had been brought to the station and questioned for some time. Initially she had given the gardaí more abuse than information. After they'd held her for a few hours, however, her need to get out and score had far outweighed her need to be belligerent.

Her statement made for interesting reading. It was tragic, in a way – a social disaster. She had left home at fourteen to get away from an abusive father, winding up on smack before her seventeenth birthday, resorting to prostitution to feed an increasingly expensive habit.

But, three pages into her rambling and barely coherent statement, a name jumped out at Scully – a name that Jim Stafford had been trying to ram down his throat for weeks. Paul McCracken. Scully read on.

According to her statement, Barbara and a friend had been touting for business on the corner of Benburb Street, a well-known pick-up area, late one Wednesday night. A car had pulled up across the street and honked at them. The weather was freezing and business slow, so they were delighted that somebody had come looking. It meant they'd have some money for the night. It had been Barbara's turn, so she had jumped into the car. The man had driven Barbara deep into Phoenix Park, where he had beaten her, choked her, raped her and left her for dead.

Her description of her attacker was excellent. He was big, very strong, with a shaved head and a scar down his face. He drove a BMW; she remembered because she had mistakenly thought a guy driving such an expensive car had to be 'kosher'. But, better than that, she had recognised the same car a few weeks later, when she had been back out on the streets and working on the corner of Fitzwilliam Square. She had asked around and some of the older women had told her the car belonged to Paul 'Tricky' McCracken, a well-known pimp.

Scully made a quick note to speak to Ed and Miriam, who had interviewed the girl. He wanted to speak to Barbara Sinnott. And to Amanda Harrington, whoever she was. Stafford had sent him a note mentioning her story about the assault on Sandy Walsh. And, while Scully firmly believed that the man they were looking for had been one of her clients, it wouldn't do to disregard other possibilities. That was what separated him from tunnel-visioned gardaí like Stafford.

The office was deserted. The only light came from a single lamp illuminating the desk where Miriam worked alone. She had reports to type up, and she was determined not to leave until they were done. Stafford had already bawled her out once that day, for turning up late; she wasn't about to add any fuel to his fire.

Head down, shoulders hunched, she worked in total concentration. She was so engrossed that, when the phone rang, she jumped and walloped her knee off the underside of her desk. Wincing and cursing, she snatched up the phone.

'Vice.'

'Ah, glad I caught somebody. Who am I speaking to?'

'Miriam Grogan, sir.' She recognised the deep, booming voice immediately. Thank God she had decided to work late. Thank God she hadn't gone to the pub with the others. Scully was someone with serious clout; if she could help him out in some way, he might remember her in his final reports. 'How can I help you?'

'Miriam! The very woman I wanted to speak to.'

Miriam felt a small tremor in her leg. 'How can I help, sir?' she repeated.

'Do you remember a girl you and Ed Cairns interviewed – oh, I'd say about five months ago? Her name was Sinnott, Barbara Sinnott. I believe you brought her in for questioning – some query about her age.'

Miriam frowned and racked her brains. They had interviewed so many prostitutes in the last few months that the name meant nothing to her. True, they hadn't brought that many to the station; but they'd brought enough to make them forgettable. 'Sorry, sir, I can't place her at the moment.'

Scully sighed heavily. 'I read her statement earlier. She was attacked while working on the streets and by all accounts suffered a rather brutal assault – semi-strangled, left for dead.'

'I can come up if you like, take a look at it for you.'

Scully laughed. 'No, thank you – I'm actually at home. I appreciate your offer, though. Perhaps tomorrow, if you have a spare minute.'

'Absolutely – first thing in the morning.'

'Excellent. Good night.'

Miriam hung up and went back to work, trying to concentrate. After a few minutes she gave up; her train of thought had been completely broken by the unexpected call.

She massaged the back of her neck and tried to think which interview could have warranted a late-night call from the man himself. She leaned back in her chair and stared at the ceiling. Barbara Sinnott … the name was familiar, but that was about all.

She decided to call it a night. She tidied up her papers and switched off the computer, wondering whether to tell Michael about the call. She knew she should; he was, after all, her immediate boss and as such should be informed. But why shouldn't she just find out what Bob Scully wanted first? Why get Michael involved yet? It might be nothing. Anyway, Scully had said he was looking for her. And Michael seemed to have a lot on his plate at the moment. He and Stafford were always running about like fucking Starsky and Hutch. No, this would keep until she knew what the score was.

She waved goodbye to the garda on duty at the gate. The young man waved back in surprise. In all his time there, he didn't think he'd ever seen Miriam Grogan smile before.

He moved quickly, skirting the camera's reach and edging towards the stairs. He carried the bag in his left hand, and as he trotted up the stairs he chanted his new mantra under his breath.

'I'm on a mission. I'm on a mission. I'm on a mission.'

He made it to the second floor without meeting a single person. He reached up and, protected by his mother's old gardening gloves, smashed the overhead light. The hall was plunged into darkness. He waited, hoping no one had heard the glass break and decided to investigate.

When nobody came, he moved again. Outside the blonde's door he unzipped the bag, peeled off the gardening gloves and replaced them with surgical ones.

He slipped back into the shadows and waited. She was on her way up. He had broken the front-door lock earlier that night; as soon as her taxi pulled up outside, he had crossed the street and simply walked in the door ahead of her. She had never even noticed him as he passed her. It was as if he was invisible.

He listened. Her footsteps on the stairs, her soft curse when she tried the lights. He held his breath. She came down the corridor and fumbled with the lock. He inhaled her perfume and recognised it as nothing more than the stench of dying, decaying flowers. They wore death on them, these whores. Wore it and wielded it.

She finally opened the door. He moved out of the shadows and hit her as hard as he could, with the poker he'd brought from home. He'd learned a lesson the last time. The last one hadn't fallen when he struck her with his fist; in fact, she had almost managed to get the door closed. He had had to hit her repeatedly, and his hand had ached for a week afterwards.

The blonde made a strange grunting noise and pitched forwards, her bag spilling onto the hall floor.

He hissed, pushed open her door with his foot and hauled her inside. While she lay moaning on her floor, he ran back into the hall, searched around for the contents of her bag and kicked them into the apartment.

He slammed the door and turned back to the woman. She was trying to crawl towards the sitting room. He watched her legs scrabble for purchase on the wood floor. He raised the poker once over his head and brought it down hard on her crown.

She collapsed and did not move again. In the silence, he rejoiced. The mission would continue.

23

'Thanks for taking the time to see this.' Robert Scully gave Miriam a firm handshake and a hundred-watt smile. He was wearing a single-breasted black suit and a yellow tie. Miriam wore jeans and a grey jacket that had once been black.

It was very early on Friday morning, coming up to the shift change. The station below bustled with people coming and going.

'Sorry to have kept you waiting.' He motioned her to the soft leather chair on the other side of his desk. 'I was on a call. With the commissioner.'

'No problem.' Miriam couldn't force herself to sound impressed. She hadn't slept a wink all night. She ached all over and was almost trembling with fatigue.

'Can I get you anything – tea?' Scully settled himself behind the desk and folded his neatly manicured hands in front of him.

'No, thank you; I'm fine.' Miriam stared at his awards and wondered if he polished them every day.

'Ed not with you?'

'No, sir. Detective Stafford needed him.'

Scully grunted in annoyance. He slid a file across to Miriam. 'Have a read of that and see if you can remember her.'

Miriam picked up the slim file and scanned it quickly. It was a report on a raid, one of their earliest, right at the beginning of the operation. Barbara Sinnott ... She stared at the paper, knitting her brows in concentration as she tried to put a face to the name. Ah, yes: skinny little thing with a foul mouth. She had dragged the little bitch in for questioning because of her youthful looks. Turned out she was young, but not young enough for them to hold her. A heroin addict. Another of life's rejects.

'I've checked through some of the other statements you and your team have accumulated over the last few months. There are plenty of bad clients out there, but nothing to equal the ferocity of our killer.' Scully steepled his hands in front of him. 'Jim Stafford may have been right all along.'

'About what?'

'Maybe it's time I took a good hard look at this McCracken.'

'Really?'

'Yes. Amanda Harrington – do you know her?'

Miriam shrugged. 'She's another prostitute.'

'Well, she spoke to Michael Dwyer yesterday. She claims that this pimp, McCracken, beat Sandy Walsh – quite badly, I believe – when she worked for him.'

'I see.' A mass of conflicting emotions surged

through Miriam as she read the girl's statement. 'Did she give a statement to that effect?'

'No, that's the problem. From what Stafford tells me, everyone despises this man McCracken yet no one is willing to put pen to paper and make a formal complaint.'

Miriam looked up. 'Not even Harrington?'

'No, but I think we can get her to amend that.'

Miriam forced a smile. How could she have been so stupid as not to remember Barbara Sinnott before? 'Sir, this description – it's definitely not Paul McCracken.'

Scully nodded and straightened the cuffs of his shirt. He looked a little uncomfortable, as if reciting information sourced by Stafford was not something he relished. 'According to Detective Stafford, the man described there matches the description of a thug called Anthony O'Connor. Jim tells me that this O'Connor works for McCracken. Now, Miriam, if you and Ed could find this girl and get her to make a formal complaint against O'Connor, we might have a chance of looking further at these two. We can at least insist that O'Connor give us a DNA sample. What do you say?'

'You want me to do it?' Miriam stared at him.

'Well, Vice should handle the working girls. I'd imagine that you have already developed a rapport with many of the women.'

Miriam didn't laugh; this was too good an opportunity to pass up by admitting that she despised the working girls and they weren't too keen on her either. 'I can bring her in. But, sir, you have to remember one thing.' She waved the statement. 'This girl is a junkie, and they change their stories every time you talk to them. Chances are she won't be able to remember what her mother looks like, let alone a man who she claims attacked her months ago.'

Scully smiled broadly. 'Be that as it may, Sergeant, McCracken has been named as a possible suspect, and O'Connor as one of his associates, so we need to verify this statement. I must say Stafford seems convinced McCracken is behind the murders – very insistent, he is. And if this girl can offer us any evidence that one of McCracken's associates is as dangerous as Stafford says, then we must speak with her. Don't you agree?'

'Yes, sir.' Miriam tucked the file under her arm. 'I'll go over it and see if I can track her down.'

The moment Miriam left Scully's office, she ran out to the car park and sat in her car. She lit a cigarette with a shaking hand and glanced at the slim file on her passenger seat as if it were a fresh shit.

Fucking goddamned junkie! How had she missed her? Thank God she hadn't told Ed about the call. At least that bought her some time to think. She rested her head on the steering-wheel and groaned out loud. What the fuck was she going to do?

She looked at her watch. It was probably too early to reach him … She chewed her lip, switched her mobile on and hit a number. Unusually, he answered on the very first ring.

'Yeah?'

'You've got trouble.'

'Where the bleeding fuck have you been? I've been trying to get you for the last two fucking days!' Tricky screamed down the phone.

'I know, I was b—'

'Don't talk to me about fucking trouble! I *know* all about trouble! I've had two of your fucking muppets hassling Emma – asking questions at her bleeding work!'

Miriam's heart shuddered in her chest. Suddenly panic and lack of sleep threatened to overwhelm her. She felt dizzy and close to fainting. 'What?'

'Between that, and that fucker ringing me up and telling me to steer clear of them cunts – what the fuck am I paying you for? You trying to stitch me up, or what?' He was near-hysterical.

'Who? Who rang you? Who called in to Emma? Who?'

'Who? Who?' Tricky mimicked. 'How the fuck should I know? You're the so-called fuckinh detective!'

She pressed her hand to her forehead. 'I need names, McCracken. I'm not psychic.'

'I got fucking names! I got names coming out of my arse. Stafford and Dwyer – the same pricks

I met – they're the ones were giving Emma hassle. Dunno who the other joker was, but his number came up on my phone. He told me he was a fucking cop. Told me he'd be watching me and to back off that Harrington bitch.'

Oh, no … shit, shit, shit, Miriam thought. Why hadn't she known about any of this? Maybe they suspected her. Maybe everyone was in on it but her …

'Who was it?'

'Dunno, didn't give a name.'

'Give me the number.'

Tricky read the number and she scribbled it down. 'Are you sure this guy is one of us?'

'Yeah, I'm sure. Culchie fuck. I'm not worried about him. It's them two arseholes I'm bleeding worried about. Fuck, Grogan, I pay you enough fucking money to know about these things, don't I? You're supposed to be on the ball. Now you're going on as if you haven't a fucking idea what the story is.'

'You pay me to warn you about raids. That's all.' She squeezed the steering-wheel until her knuckles went white.

'Yeah? Well, you better hope to fuck I don't get no more unexpected hassle.'

'If it wasn't for me, you would have been pulled in a long time ago.'

'Shut up, you stupid bitch. Don't go acting the bleeding martyr with me.'

Miriam closed her eyes, and in her mind she

saw herself, for the rest of her days, playing lackey to this bastard of a man. Gambling – her addiction, her passion – had led her to the abyss; and McCracken had been more than willing to help her in. 'You're about to be pulled in, in connection with the murders.'

'That's a load of my bollix.'

'I'm telling you what I know. Your fucking henchman attacked and raped some junkie a few months ago in the park. Goddamn it, Paul, he drove your car to do it.'

'What?'

Miriam allowed herself a tiny smile. At least the bastard sounded shocked. 'Stafford knows Anthony works for you. All I'm saying is, be prepared to be pulled in for questioning. Now, I've offered to bring Sinnott in, so you've got a few days' grace. And I'll make sure she doesn't mention you when she's questioned. She'll change her story.'

'Don't give me that shite. Grace, my arse.' He was silent for a second; then: 'Get me an address. I'll take care of the junkie bitch good and proper.'

Miriam closed her eyes tight. She knew what he was asking.

'I don't want her talking to no cunt. Not now, not ever.'

'But—'

'Get it. I'm only gonna talk to her. Know what I mean?'

Miriam grimaced. 'I can't do that.'

'How much you in hock to Big Joe?'

Miriam swallowed. 'Ten.'

'You lying cunt. He clocked you at thirty-six. You think he won't collect because you're a pig? Fuck, he'd enjoy it all the more, if you ask me. Tell you what: you get me that address, and I'll sort something with him.' Tricky laughed nastily. 'Cut that lump down to size for you before you choke on it.'

'And all you want is to talk to her?'

'Keep me informed about this other investigation shite. I don't want some cunt upsetting Emma. I want her left the fuck alone.'

He hung up.

Miriam stared at the scrap of paper in her hand. The number looked familiar. She scrolled through the numbers on her phone and realised why.

Dumbstruck, she stared at the screen. Why would Gerry Cullen be warning Tricky off?

24

From an upstairs window, Michael watched Miriam climb out of her car and slam the door. He was curious about the file she was holding; he recognised it by the green tag on the cover, as one of the files they had earlier given Robert Scully, and he wondered why Miriam would have it now.

He was still pondering that one when Stafford came up the hall. 'What are you doing gawking out the window?'

'Nothing.'

'Exactly. If you have time to do nothing, I'd love to know why.' Stafford passed on by.

Michael sighed. Back to reading statements. Anyone who said police work was interesting had obviously never investigated a thing.

Later that evening, Tricky McCracken and Anthony O'Connor sat in a wrecked, shit-brown Toyota Celica and waited outside a run-down house that had as many boarded-up windows as glass ones. The house was divided into more than twenty cheap, dingy bedsits. Number 1, in the basement, was the last known address of one Barbara Sinnott.

They had already been inside, but the stink of rotten food and mildew had driven them back out to the car.

'Wouldn't have to do this, man, if you fucking kept away from them cunts.' Tricky shook his head and smoked for a moment. Lecturing Anthony O'Connor was not easy. The Whale could snap him in half if the notion took him. It was like lecturing a bull elephant. 'I mean, what is it with you? You want pussy, I'll *give* you pussy, as much pussy as any man can handle. Clean pussy, not that fucking street scum, Anto. They're crawling.'

'You think I need you to get women for me?' The Whale kept his eyes on the street. He didn't raise his voice and he didn't sound angry, but Tricky felt a tremor of unease.

He shook his head. 'No. But, fuck, Anto … I mean, the worst fucking timing, this is. Cops are looking for a reason to snag me, and you go and—'

'She's here.'

The sight of Barbara Sinnott staggering up the road ended the conversation, much to Tricky's relief. He waited until she was almost at her door before he sprang out of the car. Girls sometimes ran when they saw him coming, and he didn't want to have to chase her.

He needn't have worried.

'Hey, Barbie doll, how you doing?'

The young woman lifted her head and stared at

him through glazed black eyes. Limp hair hung down over her face and her cheap parka was filthy, stained with God knows what and torn in several places. Chunks of her hair were matted so badly that it would have taken shears to sort it out. Her skin was blotchy and covered in spots; her bottom lip was split and scabby. She was eighteen years old.

'Who wants to know?' She squinted. 'Oh, it's you.'

'I want a word with you. Inside.'

'Ah, fuck, what now?' She swayed defiantly. Her hand wiped at her mouth; to Tricky's disgust, a piece of the scab broke away and her lip began to bleed. 'Why can't yous leave me alone? I didn't do nothing.'

'Yeah, I know.' Tricky grabbed her upper arm. 'Come on, Barbie. You're not in any trouble; I only want to talk.' He pulled her towards the steps. Barbara stumbled against him. Whatever resistance she might have put up obviously didn't seem worth the effort to her.

She wiped her mouth with her sleeve. 'Will you give me a lift into town afterwards?'

Tricky led her down the steps towards the basement. 'Sure.'

Barbara stared at her front door. 'It's broken,' she said thickly. 'It's broken.'

'Yeah, I broke it,' the Whale said from the top of the steps. 'Sorry.'

Barbara stiffened. She turned unsteadily and stared at the vast apparition descending the steps towards her.

The Whale smiled when he saw she had recognised him. 'What happened to your face?'

Barbara opened her mouth to scream, but the Whale moved with surprising speed for a man of his bulk. He trotted the last few steps, drew back a foot and kicked her in the chest. Barbara fell backwards, cracking her head off the concrete wall and crumpling into a heap at Tricky's feet.

'Get her in.' Tricky pulled out a syringe and a three-gram bag of the purest heroin money could buy. 'Make sure she don't make a sound.'

The Whale dragged the groaning girl into the bedsit and pinned her to the greasy lino of her tiny kitchenette. Someone, maybe even Barbara, had tried to make it a little less like the hovel it was by painting it bright yellow. But the Whale didn't notice these things. He leaned one massive knee on her chest, gripped her chin and forced her to look at him.

'If you hold still, it won't hurt as much.'

Barbara Sinnott began to cry. She wet herself. Disgusted, the Whale slapped her across the face, so hard that he knocked her out.

Tricky set to work. He flicked open his Zippo, emptied the heroin onto a much-used metal dish and waited for it to cook. In less than two minutes the acrid smell and faint hiss of the pale-brown liquid filled the silent room. Tricky nodded to the Whale. The Whale grabbed Barbara's left arm, pulled it out of her coat and rolled the sleeve of her tattered jumper up to her bicep.

'Fuck.' Tricky shook his head. Barbara's slim, pale arm was a mess of bruises, new and old, and needle wounds, some open, others dry and healing. 'This cunt's on the way out anyway.' He looked at the Whale. 'Man, hope you didn't stick your dick in this one.'

The Whale's massive head turned in his direction, and for a moment Tricky wished he had kept that particular sentiment to himself.

He filled the syringe, tied off Barbara's arm with the belt of her jacket and pulled it tight. Nothing much happened.

'Her vein's shot. Close her hand.'

The Whale grabbed her small, delicate hand and balled it into a fist. Barbara groaned and licked the blood from her lips, but she did not regain consciousness.

Eventually the vein surfaced. Tricky emptied the syringe into it. Then they stood and waited.

Barbara's weakened body couldn't cope with the purity of the heroin. In less than a minute she began to convulse. Her heels kicked against the filthy floor, her eyes rolled white in her battered face and thin streams of pale-yellow foam trailed from the corners of her mouth. It took almost twenty minutes for her heart to stop.

Tricky and the Whale watched. Then they tidied everything away, making sure they left no trace to show they had ever been there.

25

Scully and Stafford were arguing outside the interview room when Michael and Ed came around the corner. Miriam was there too, leaning against the wall, looking like she was made of stone. Her face was marble-white and her eyes were surrounded by faintly blue skin. If Michael hadn't known her better, he'd have thought something had upset her.

The animosity between Scully and Stafford was almost palpable. For once, Scully didn't exude his characteristic smooth charm; in fact, he looked irritated and, Michael noted, faintly queasy. Stafford, on the other hand, looked demented, his fists balled by his sides as if he was about to punch Scully square in the nose.

Tessa Byrne's friend Abby Gaffney was still weeping into tissues inside the interview room. Half an hour of describing her and Tessa's time working for McCracken had completely devastated her. She was only twenty-two and wasn't in the business any more – she'd left almost as soon as she fled McCracken's place after deciding being a prostitute was nothing like *Pretty Woman*; she was in college now, and she had a boyfriend and he was really nice, and could they please not tell her parents ... Then she'd burst into tears and bless herself. After the fifth crying jag Scully had conceded she'd had quite enough for one day and excused himself, leaving his female sergeant to console her.

He had barely made it out of the interview-room door when Stafford, who had been waiting in the hall, had pounced.

'Bring McCracken in.'

'For what? What have we got to go on?' Scully had demanded. 'We have nothing to charge him with.'

'Tessa Byrne worked for McCracken. Sandy Walsh worked for McCracken. How many more women who worked for McCracken have to die before we haul that little bollix in and squeeze the fucking truth out of him? I just want to talk to him!'

Scully had loosened his tie. 'Look, I know you're angry, but yelling won't help the situation.'

'I'm fucking beyond angry!' Stafford's face had turned stroke-purple. 'I told you from the start to look into that bastard.'

It was at this point that Michael and Ed came around the corner.

'I am looking into it.' Scully glanced over at Miriam, who was staring at the carpet. 'Miriam, have you and Ed made any progress on finding Barbara Sinnott?'

Ed looked confused. 'Who?'

'Barbara Sinnott,' Scully snapped.

'Who's she?' Ed, Michael and – loudest of all – Stafford said in unison.

'The girl attacked in the park.'

Stafford rounded on Miriam. 'You didn't tell me you and Ed were looking for her.'

'Excuse me,' Ed Cairns said angrily. He jabbed a finger in Miriam's direction. 'She didn't tell me I was supposed to be looking for her, either.'

'I only got the brief yesterday.'

'So?' Ed demanded. 'When were you going to inform me?'

'Never mind that,' Stafford said. 'We can deal with that later. Did you find her?'

'She's a heroin addict, for Christ's sake,' Miriam snapped. 'They're not exactly easy to find.'

Stafford shot her a look so poisonous she actually flinched. 'Aye, I'm aware of that, Sergeant. I don't need reminding from you.'

Miriam bowed her head. 'I'm sorry.'

'Look,' Scully said eventually, after a moment of awkward silence, 'this is getting us nowhere.' He smoothed his perfect hair. 'Anthony O'Connor. Bring him in and ask him a few questions about this attack. I suppose we can try to get him to give evidence against McCracken.'

'What about McCracken?' Stafford demanded.

'McCracken? I don't mean to be rude, Jim, but she didn't say McCracken attacked her.'

'O'Connor works for him.'

Scully shook his head. 'We can't touch him for this. We'll get O'Connor and ask him about her, but, until we've something concrete, we have no reason to pursue McCracken.'

'You're chasing the monkey when we need the organ-grinder,' Stafford said.

'I don't have time to discuss this.' Scully sighed and began to walk away. 'I'll bring O'Connor in,' he called over his shoulder. 'Perhaps you'll be so good as to get our witness.'

Stafford watched him until he was out of sight. Then he turned and poked Miriam in the shoulder. 'You – my office. Wait for me there.'

'Sir, I—'

'I said my office.'

Miriam nodded and walked away, her head low, her feet dragging as though she had a wrecking ball tied to her neck. Stafford watched her go, and his lip curled slightly. 'Ed, you didn't know anything about bringing that girl in?'

'No, nothing.'

'OK, then. You go back to the squad room, see if you can find me an address for Barbara Sinnott. I want it ASAP, got me?'

'Yes, sir.' Ed nodded and walked away.

'Mike …' Stafford rubbed his hand over his eyes. The purple had drained from his face, leaving him grey and washed-out. 'I need you to come with me. Tessa Byrne's mother is downstairs.'

'How is she?'

'She's not good, Mike. Not good.'

* * *

Tessa Byrne's mother was not dabbing at her eyes, she was not sniffling, she was not hysterical. She sat on a plastic chair in the foyer, her head bowed, her hands lying still on her lap. She wore a long black coat, and her dark-brown hair, streaked with grey, was tied back into a loose ponytail. Grief covered her like a shroud.

Stafford placed a hand on her shoulder. She lifted her head, and Michael was startled by her face. He had never seen such pain, such total and utter grief and disbelief. Unsure of what to say, he nodded to her; any words of comfort he might have uttered were of no use here. He nodded to her and she nodded back.

Stafford said, 'I'm sorry, Rose, but we don't really have anything new to go on.'

'She was a devoted mother,' Rose said, and her voice trembled with the effort of holding back her pain. 'The little one – she keeps asking where her mummy is. I don't know what to say to her.'

Stafford nodded. 'I know, Rose.'

'My angel,' Rose said softly. 'She was such a nice girl.' Her bottom lip trembled. 'A good girl. She's left it all behind …'

Stafford put his arm around her shoulders and, despite the curious looks from passing gardaí, held on while she cried.

Michael moved away to give them a little privacy. He stared at his shoes and made a decision: if it was the last thing he did, he would catch the person responsible for all this grief.

Someone tapped him on the shoulder. Michael turned around. It was Ed. 'What?'

Ed held up a piece of paper and nodded at Stafford. 'The address he wanted. For Barbara Sinnott.'

Michael looked at Stafford's broad back. 'Come with me; we'll go check it out for him.'

Ed pulled a face. 'You sure? It's eleven o'clock at night.'

'Best time to catch people at home.'

'What about Stafford?'

'I think he's got plenty to occupy him for the moment.'

'Everyone's talking about Stafford and Scully's blow-up.' Ed shrugged and ran his fingers through his already wild hair. 'What the fuck is going on, Mike?'

'I don't know,' Mike said truthfully. 'I really don't.' He took the paper from Ed's hand and headed for the door. 'But it's about time we started making some serious headway. So let's start with finding this girl.'

And so they found Barbara Sinnott. People claim the dead are only sleeping, waiting for the next life. But if Barbara Sinnott was sleeping, Michael thought, looking at her tiny rigid body, her clenched hands and her staring eyes, then she was having the worst nightmare of her short and brutal life.

He shook his head and pulled out his mobile, ready to break the news to Stafford that the fragile threads linking the murders to McCracken were steadily unravelling.

26

Amanda gave up trying to sleep after 6.00 a.m. She opened her eyes and stared at the patch of light on her bedroom wall. She hadn't slept a wink since Marna had called her, four hours earlier, to let her know about Barbara. Both she and Marna had known her, albeit briefly, in the Red Stairs. She had been one of the girls who'd left with Paula.

The telephone conversation had been strained and uncomfortable. Amanda had offered to meet Marna, had even offered to call over right away, regardless of the time. Her offer had been declined.

'I thought you'd want to know, that's all,' Marna had said before she hung up.

Amanda got out of bed, went into the kitchen and poured herself a bowl of cornflakes. She ate two spoonfuls and pushed the bowl away again.

Her eyes drifted to the windows. There were tears on her cheeks. So much for escape; so much for change. She should have known better. The business never let you go.

* * *

Later that morning, Anthony 'the Whale' O'Connor arrived at the station. A very subdued Stafford joined Scully to question him.

The Whale showed no nervousness when questioned about Barbara Sinnott. In fact, he positively beamed when Scully brought her up.

'That little junkie? Yeah, I know the one you're talking about.'

Stafford hid his surprise. He had expected O'Connor to deny all knowledge of the girl. 'How do you know her?'

O'Connor shrugged and scratched his stubbly chin with a swollen hand. He was dressed in grey tracksuit bottoms and a T-shirt stretched to capacity over his massive frame. He must be immune to the cold, thought Scully. He could have been dressed for a run, except for the huge, unlaced steel-capped boots. 'I make it my business to remember the troublemakers,' he said finally. 'It's my job to remember trouble.'

'Why do you call her a troublemaker? What kind of trouble was she?'

The Whale fixed Stafford with a cool gaze. 'Want to tell me what this shit is all about first? You lot rang my house and asked me here, so I'd like to know what I'm supposed to have done.'

'What kind of car do you drive, Mr O'Connor?' Scully cut in quickly.

'I don't.'

'You don't what?'

'I don't have a car.' The Whale laughed and

cracked his knuckles loudly. 'You dragged me out of bed for bullshit like this?'

Scully leaned across the desk. 'I asked what kind of car you drive.'

The Whale's eyes narrowed. 'BMW,' he grunted.

'Colour?'

'Black.'

'Are you the registered owner of the car?'

'The car belongs to my boss.' The Whale smiled, letting his pale eyes roll from one face to the other.

'That would be Paul McCracken. Right?'

'You already knew that, didn't you?'

'He's a pimp, Mr O'Connor. You don't mind working for a pimp?'

'Is he?' The Whale yawned. 'Well, there you go – learn something new every day.'

'What is it you do for McCracken, exactly?'

'I'm his driver.' He folded his arms across his chest. A tattoo of a naked woman riding a dragon covered the bulging muscles of his left arm.

'Why would a man like McCracken need a driver?'

The Whale shrugged.

'Is that all you do for him?' Scully said.

O'Connor smiled, and Stafford yearned to drive his fist into his face. 'Yeah, that's all I do.'

'Tell us about him. What's he like?'

'He's a fucking saint.'

'Would it surprise you to know that Tessa Byrne and Sandy Walsh worked for him at some point?'

'Did they?' the Whale said, looking more bored by the second.

Scully frowned. 'Have you ever seen him be violent to any of the women who work for him?'

'Never.'

'Why did you refer to Barbara Sinnott as a troublemaker?' Stafford asked.

O'Connor rolled his eyes. 'She's a smack-head. I hate all that shit.'

'How do you know that?'

'She tried to work at a place my boss owns, about six months ago. I knew she was a fucking junkie straight away. Her job was terminated.'

That surprised Stafford. In her statement, Barbara had vehemently denied ever working for McCracken. She'd claimed she didn't even know what he looked like.

'She worked for McCracken?' he said. In his mind he was adding up the numbers. Three women dead, three women who had worked for McCracken.

'I said she tried to,' the Whale corrected him. 'I put a stop to it.' Suddenly he laughed. He shook his head and looked slowly from one detective to the other. 'That's what this shit is about?' He let out a long, thin whistle. 'Little bitch! She always said she'd get me back.'

'Get you back?' Scully enquired.

'Yeah. For turfing her out on her fucking ear. Junkies … I should have fucking sussed it from the off. What's she say I did? Raped her, robbed her? What?'

Stafford shot Scully a quick look. He knew Scully was losing interest.

'So you deny assaulting Barbara Sinnott?' Stafford snapped.

'Of course I fucking do,' the Whale roared. 'Am I under arrest here, or what?'

'No, you're not.'

'Right!' The Whale stared at Stafford. 'Now you fucking listen to me. You asked me to come down, and here I am. Now, are we done, or am I gonna need to phone my solicitor?'

Stafford leaned across the desk and jabbed a pudgy finger into the Whale's face. 'Keep the act up, O'Connor. But I know you fucking hurt that kid, and I know you know she's dead and can't point the finger. Keep it fucking up! I'll—'

'Detective Stafford! Sit down!' Scully said, aghast.

The Whale smirked. 'You want to ask me about that, too? Maybe I murdered her? What'd she die of?'

'You fucking know, I know you do.'

The Whale shook his head. 'Do I need to be here any longer? Look, either charge me and let me make a call, or let me go fucking home.'

'There's no need for calls,' Scully said sharply. 'If we need to speak to you again, we know where to find you.'

The Whale stood up, dwarfing Stafford. 'Don't think you can drag me in for this sort of shit too often. This is fucking harassment.'

Stafford spun away and went crashing out the door. The Whale glanced at Scully.

'See that guy – he's losing it.' He sniggered. 'Fucking losing the plot big-time.'

Scully tried not to look like he agreed. 'Please wait here. I'll get someone to show you out.'

As the Whale left the station, Scully went up to Stafford's office, where he found Michael checking through old statements from girls who might have worked for McCracken in the past. Scully nodded to him, slipped a slimline Nokia from his pocket and hit a button.

'Andy,' he snapped down the line. 'Have you checked on the rest of those numbers yet?'

Michael glanced up. The normally cool voice was beginning to sound more than a little strained.

'I don't care,' Scully was saying. 'How hard can it be? Get on with it, man. I want every number from Tessa Byrne's phone traced … I don't care; do it.' Scully snapped the phone shut and sighed. 'How long is it going to take to get the labs back on Sinnott?'

'Coroner says sometime tomorrow evening. How did the interview with O'Connor go? Did he say he knew her?'

Scully leaned against the wall and stuck his hands in his pockets. 'According to him, she worked for McCracken, but he had to get rid of her for drug use.'

'Funny, him remembering her so easily.'

'Oh, don't you start too, Sergeant. What is it with you people?' Scully raised an eyebrow. 'Look, I know Vice has it in for—'

Stafford came in, spotted Scully and scowled. 'What do you want?'

'I was telling Michael here that O'Connor said he knew that girl.'

'O'Connor remembers a girl who worked for McCracken for one weekend.' Stafford barged past Scully and sank into his seat. 'Way too convenient for my liking. Why would he remember her so well, after all this time?'

'That's what I said.' Michael shrugged.

Scully sighed. 'Because she was trouble, that's why. She was on drugs.'

'That's crap. I don't buy that. How convenient, too, that's she's dead.'

'She died of an overdose! Your own team found her lying in a puddle of her own vomit!'

'She did have a lot of bruising on her face,' Michael said to Stafford. 'We're waiting on the lab reports, but I'll bet you she was assaulted before she died.'

'What if somehow McCracken—'

'Jesus, Jim, enough!' Scully exploded. 'My God, McCracken again … You've had a bee in your bonnet about McCracken from the word go. You *want* to believe that girl was assaulted by O'Connor, because it gives you an excuse to have another crack at McCracken.'

Stafford's face darkened. 'I believe it,' he said

viciously, 'because, unlike you, I have experience of that pimp and his like. I believed the girl because this kind of thing is right up McCracken's street. Hurting defenceless women is what that prick does best. Anthony O'Connor was too fucking smug when we spoke to him. Paul McCracken is the man we should be putting pressure on.'

Scully raised his eyebrows. 'I haven't heard anything yet about him assaulting anyone. A lot of hearsay and gossip, but nothing solid – no statements, no proof, no evidence that would even get us a warrant.'

'And you're not likely to hear anything if you ignore any girl with the balls to complain. Why would they bother coming to us if they think we're going to accept the word of a dirtbird like O'Connor over theirs?'

'You've had plenty of chances to garner evidence against McCracken. I will not let you turn my murder case into your personal vendetta.'

'We may as well look at him. Your lot haven't turned up any other suspects, have you?'

Scully's voice was ice-cold. 'Now you listen to me. I'm investigating murder, not the bully-boy antics of a pimp. 'Let me say it again so you understand: there is nothing, no physical evidence, to link McCracken to the murders, and I've checked his alibis for the nights in question. So what else would you like me to do, Jim? I need more to go on than the word of a clearly distressed teenager who was probably out of her head on drugs and who clearly had an axe to grind. What do you want me to do – demand girls come in here and tell us what we want to hear? Is that the way you work, Jim? Is that your solution? We have nothing to connect McCracken to the murders, nothing even to suggest he was involved. And the fact that every working girl in the city dislikes him doesn't make him a killer.' Scully took a breath and forced himself to calm down. 'I understand your frustration, Jim, I really do. But we can't pin this on him because it suits you.'

'Those two,' Stafford said doggedly, 'are in this up to their fucking necks, you mark my words. While you're fucking around trying to find a connection, they're covering their tracks.'

'Then find something for me to look into!' Scully snapped. 'With respect, Jim, we can't go blundering after someone on your personal hunch. We need something to go on. And I mean something more than your hurt pride.'

Stafford's face flushed. 'My team are trying to assist you with your investigation, you pompous fucker. My team have taken statements from hundreds of women in the last few weeks, and one name keeps cropping up – McCracken! So how much more do you need?' He was standing, leaning across his desk. 'But if you don't want to work with me, if you don't want our help or our experience, take it up with Felim Brennan!'

Scully glared at him. 'I appreciate what you're

trying to do. But you're letting your dislike of McCracken cloud your judgement.'

Stafford shook his head in disgust and walked out, slamming the door behind him.

Scully glared at the door for a few seconds, as if waiting for Stafford to come bursting back in. Finally he turned to Michael. 'Sergeant.'

'Sir?' Michael's ears were still ringing.

'I've been informed *he* has you working on something other than this investigation at the moment.'

'Sir, it is connected to—'

Scully held up his hand. 'Listen to me, Sergeant. Your orders are to work with my team for the duration of this investigation – and that means reporting to me, do you understand? This is my show, and I need to know my officers are working to find the killer, not operating on their own crazy agenda.'

Michael flushed. 'Sir.'

'Stafford takes things too personally. I know he's been after McCracken for a while now, but really – trying to create evidence where none exists … His judgement's certainly not what it used to be.'

Michael stared at him. He had been working with Stafford for the best part of a year, and, while he knew his boss was sometimes a little over-tenacious, he had always found his judgement to be sound. 'You don't think it's a bit odd that this girl is dead?'

Scully's face might have been hewn from granite. 'I'll let you get on with your work,' he said. Then he left, closing the door gently behind him.

'I can't believe Anto would bang some bird in my car,' Tricky said to Emma in a café on Dame Street, later that day.

'He's a fucking liability! I told you, you should get rid of him.'

'Nah, man. He's fucking sound. Useful, too. But ...' Tricky shook his head again. 'Doing that? Now, of all times? Fucking crazy, man.'

Emma clucked soothingly; she had been listening to this for the last ten minutes. 'Honestly, Paul, let him go. Christ knows what he'll do next.'

'Here, I'll give you a laugh.' Tricky changed the topic of conversation. He knew Emma hated the Whale, but getting rid of him was not an option. The truth was, he wasn't sure whether he could, even if he'd wanted to. The man worked for him and everything, but there was something ... something wrong with him. Something that made even Tricky nervous. 'That bitch Miriam rang last night, crying over that fucking junkie.' He gave a sly smile. 'You should've heard her. She was shitting herself when I told her she was a bleeding accessory.'

Emma put her cup down and stared at him. 'Accessory to what?'

'The bitch that Anto rolled with.' Tricky scowled at her. 'She ODd, I told you.'

'The one that made the complaint?'

'Yeah. She won't be doing any more complaining.'

Emma didn't ask. She had watched him fling a syringe into a plastic bag and bury it at the bottom of the skip across the road from her house. He had warned her to say he had been with her all night. She didn't need to ask any more questions.

'About this little Q&A the cops have planned for me—'

Tricky shook his head and dropped ash on the table. 'I know you'll be all right. I trust you. I'd bleeding want to, after all the money I've given you.'

Emma lit a cigarette. 'What is it, then? Clearly something's troubling you.'

Tricky's face darkened. 'That fat fuck Stafford. He's got a bleeding line on me, I can feel it.'

'He knows nothing.' Emma shrugged. 'They can't pin anything on you, so fuck them. The only thing you ever had to worry about was the Criminal Assets Bureau – and, thanks to me, they're never going to find a single penny of your money.' Emma laughed. 'My God, it's so well hidden I'd be hard pressed to find it myself at the moment.'

'I know that. Jaysus, that's well sussed.' Tricky smirked. Emma could see him beginning to relax. 'Yeah, you're right. I don't know what the fuck's wrong with me.'

'Nothing. You're careful, and that's what keeps

you one step ahead of the rest of the pack.' Emma grinned suddenly. 'I know the best way of throwing them off the scent. But you have to keep that other fucking dog on a tighter leash. Jesus, it's not like he hasn't enough women he can poke for free.'

Tricky perked up and leaned across the table. 'What are you going to say? Say you was renting them apartments for someone else?'

'I've been giving it some thought, yes.'

'Who?'

'I was thinking about the Harrington bitch.'

'Fucking brilliant.' Tricky's face almost split in two with the smile. 'Fucking bitch. I made her what she is. I gave the cunt a job – and she made serious fucking money at my place. Then she went and robbed half my clients when she left. Cunt thinks she can rob my girls, too … Yeah, say it was for her.'

'Don't worry about her,' Emma said coldly. 'You wait and see, Paul. I told you before: revenge is a dish best served cold.'

'Like them sayings, don't you?' Tricky laughed, leaned across the table and ruffled her two-hundred-euro haircut. 'That's what I always liked about you, Emma. The moment I met you, I knew you were different from all the other cunts. You're special.'

He grabbed the back of her head, pulled her towards him and shoved his tongue into her mouth.

'Now. Don't you worry about a thing – leave it

all to me,' Emma said breathlessly, when Tricky came up for air. 'You concentrate on staying low and keeping out of trouble.'

Tricky settled back in his chair and winked. 'I never doubted you, know what I mean? Anto – now, he worried about you in the beginning, but not me. Harrington, huh? I've scores I want settled with that one, and I can't get near the bitch myself at the moment.'

Emma smiled and drained the last of her coffee. 'I'll settle the score, don't worry. I'll settle it once and for all.'

27

Glorious was he. He stared at his reflection in the cracked mirror, admiring the new look. His hair, the straggly brown hair that had bothered him so, was shorn. He would model it for Mother when she woke. He hoped she would not be too upset. He suspected she would understand: between caring for her and the mission, he hadn't the time for such vanities as hair. When she recovered, he would grow it back.

He rubbed his hand over his head, feeling the alien bristles. Tonight he would hunt again. His time was precious. Already he could feel the difference. He knew he would not always have the luxury of time.

He looked into the sink. Dried blood from where he had washed his hands lined the basin. He picked at it idly with his fingernail while he stroked his head with his other hand. The bristles were causing static. Little crackles of electricity fired against his palm. It was tickly. He giggled.

Tonight he would tackle the dark one. She would be there, with her whips and her chains. He trembled slightly. She was evil, truly evil; she liked to inflict pain, to humiliate and torture.

Well, he would show her what it was like to be punished. She would bow before him and be punished for her filth.

Ed put down the phone and shook his head. 'Poor old devil. I nearly feel sorry for some of them.'

'Why?' Scully was not in the humour for sympathy.

'You can tell some of them are lonely. They're not doing any real harm, are they?' Ed put a tick beside the number on the sheet in front of him. 'That old fella was telling me how much he missed her. He was nearly crying.'

Scully snorted in disgust. 'I didn't see any of them rushing to us with any information about how Sandy Walsh died. We have to go chasing them.'

'They wouldn't, would they, sir? They're embarrassed. Most of this lot are married.'

'They could still have called us,' snapped Scully. 'Don't go wasting your sympathy on them, Ed. If they were that fond of her, they could try helping us catch whoever it was who killed her. Don't be so bloody naïve.'

'Yes, sir.' Ed let the subject drop. Scully had been in a foul mood all day, and he didn't want to be on the receiving end of one of his legendary lectures on civic duty. But at least he was here, not stuck with the seriously fucked Miriam. Gerry had told him that the whole station had heard the dressing-down Stafford had given her.

'Why did he leave Sandy's phone behind and not Tessa's?' Scully said suddenly.

'I don't know,' Ed said.

'How many callers are left unaccounted for from Sandy's?'

Ed consulted his paper. 'Five, sir.'

'Five? Why the hell are there so many?'

'Sir, three are pre-paid mobiles. The owners didn't register them with the phone companies, they're not answering the phones, and there are no names on the voice-mail messages. The other two are phone boxes.'

'Damn it to hell.' Scully scowled. 'Get the exact times those calls were made from the phone boxes.'

'Yes, sir.'

Scully stood up and headed for his office. 'And, Ed …'

'Sir?'

'I want them today.'

It was a bad night, wet and stormy; Marna figured that only the most dogged client would venture out. Even the phones were dead. Marna sat on the couch, knitting, one eye on the television and the other on Kate.

Kate was plucking her eyebrows and sighing every few seconds. She was bored. Marna thought that, if a client didn't appear soon, she was going to toss Kate out the window face first.

She'd forgotten what it was like to work with someone new, forgotten that you had to adapt to another person's habits, that a person could get on your nerves simply by looking at you. With Amanda, it had been easy; they had been in synch. They had liked a lot of the same things – foreign films in the afternoon, Thai food, white wine on Friday nights if they were both working. Kate liked chips, she liked Oprah, Montel and Sally Jessy Whatever, she liked beer and popcorn, and she had never watched a foreign film in her life – she said she liked Jim Carrey films. Marna shuddered.

She hated to admit it, but she missed Amanda. They had fit – at least, until Amanda had gone all weird and abandoned Marna to a girl who couldn't sit still for two seconds.

'They're like buses, aren't they? Nothing for ages, then three come at once.'

'Wishful thinking,' Marna said. But she didn't really mean it. The truth was that she didn't want to work – but, as Paula had said to her earlier when she said she was thinking of taking a few days off, what was safe? She was better off working with another girl than going home alone. At the moment, no working girl wanted to be alone.

'Did you hear that the guy killing is actually a priest?' Kate said suddenly. She put down her tweezers and mirror. 'That's why he goes for us.'

'That's the stupidest thing I've ever heard.' Marna looked up in surprise. 'Priests, Kate … Jesus. Where the hell did you hear that?'

Kate shrugged. 'That's what they're saying.'

Marna grabbed the TV remote; she didn't want to have this discussion right now. 'They say whatever they want to say. That doesn't make it true.'

Kate wouldn't let it drop. She pulled up a chair near the sofa. 'Well, Paula has this client, right? And he knows this other guy who knows someone in the morgue, and he said that the bodies had crosses burnt onto their foreheads.'

'That's crap. Don't believe everything you hear.' Marna turned the television up slightly and hoped Kate would get the message.

'Poor bitches. I heard that Tessa Byrne was really nice. Girl I know had a few shifts with her, said she was as sound as a pound – real easy to get along with. Not like some. Jesus, did I ever tell you about this one girl I worked with? What was her name – Shalimar, Sallimar … no, wait, was it Charlimar? Shit, I thought I had it there …'

The doorbell rang. Marna sprang off the couch and rushed to buzz the client in. She was grateful for whoever it was. If she had to listen to another of Kate's long-winded stories she would scream.

At eleven o'clock on Saturday night, Ed received a call at his desk. He listened and jotted down every word. Then he shot off in search of Jim Stafford.

'Stafford around?' he asked Gerry, in the hall.

'He's gone home.'

'What about Mike?'

'Mike's still here. He's down in the interview room going over statements again. What's going on?'

'I've got a phone call, anonymous. A woman claims she saw a black BMW parked on Mount-pleasant Street on the day of Sandy Walsh's murder.'

'Yeah? Why didn't she come forward before?'

'She says she's just back from holiday.' Ed grinned. 'It gets better. She says she only noticed it because it was blocking her in, and she was going to have it towed. She even remembers the plate.'

'Is it who we think it is?'

'It could be. I need to find Mike.' Ed hurried down the hall. He had heard about the heated exchange between Stafford and Scully. And, although he wasn't a man to take sides, it pleased him to think that maybe the old boy had been right all along.

'She wouldn't leave a name?' Michael looked sceptical.

Ed shrugged. 'She said she'd prefer to remain anonymous.'

Michael put down the file he was reading. 'That's the trouble with people these days. No-body wants to get involved.' He read through the message again. 'How did she sound to you?'

'Hard to say. Well-spoken – thirties, forties … I don't know, Mike; it's hard to tell.'

Michael stared at the paper. He didn't want to get his hopes up. It would have been different if the woman had left her name. They could have paid her a visit, confirmed the report before they called Stafford.

'What do you want to do, Mike? The plates almost match.'

Michael stroked his moustache and studied the paper. It was a good plate match, only two numbers out. It could be McCracken's car.

'So what do you want to do?' Ed repeated impatiently.

Michael picked up the phone. 'I'd better ring Stafford.'

'He's in bed, Mike,' Mrs Stafford protested.

'You might want to wake him, Claire.'

'That poor man never gets a minute's peace and quiet.'

'I wouldn't call if it wasn't important.'

A few minutes later, a thoroughly grouchy Stafford came on the line. 'What?'

'It's me. I'm sorry to disturb you at home. I thought you might want to hear this.'

'Go on.'

'Ed got a call about twenty minutes ago, anonymous. A woman said she remembers a black car parked on Mountpleasant Street the day Sandy Walsh was murdered.'

'Make?'

'BMW, black. The thing is, she remembers the plate number – well, a partial. It was blocking her car in and she was about to ring and have it towed, but when she went inside she heard it start up and drive off.'

'Do the plates match McCracken's car?' Stafford sounded fully awake now.

'Not exactly. Two digits out.'

Stafford was quiet for a few seconds. 'Mike,' he said finally, 'do me a favour?'

'Sure.'

'Sit on this.'

'What?'

'Sit on this. At least until we have a chance to check it out.'

'Why?'

'I don't want Scully hearing this until we find out a little more.' Stafford whistled softly. 'I knew that fucker was involved in this somewhere. I could feel it.'

'Sir,' Michael said quietly, 'it's not going to look good if we keep this to ourselves.' Across the table Ed was shaking his head.

'We'll see. Sit on it till Monday anyway. Got me?'

'Yes, sir.'

'Thanks for ringing.' Stafford hung up.

Michael replaced the receiver and studied the plate number again.

'What did he say?' Ed asked.

'To sit on it till Monday.'

'What? Why?' Ed frowned. 'It proves he was right about McCracken.'

Michael turned to him. 'Don't worry, he'll make sure Scully knows it was you who took the call.'

'That's not what this is about. Why is he going to keep it until Monday?'

'I think he doesn't want Scully thinking he has a one-track mind.'

'Fair enough. But, if it is him, I want Scully to know I took the call.'

Michael laughed, stood up and patted Ed's shoulder. 'We'll tell him, I promise. You'll get your praise. Here's a pat on the back to tide you over.'

Ed grinned. 'Fuck off.'

Michael yawned and rubbed a hand over his chin; to his surprise, there was a fair amount of stubble there. It had been at least three days since he'd had time to shave. 'You want to nip across the road for a pint?'

Ed looked at his watch, and the grin spread a little wider. 'You're on.'

'I'm here for Amanda.'

The man carrying the sports bag didn't look like one of Amanda's usual clients, but nevertheless Marna plastered on her friendly smile, fluttered her eyelashes and gave him the once-over. He was slightly scruffy; his suit looked like it could do with a good ironing, and his hair left a lot to be desired. 'Come in, why don't you? Don't let all the heat out.'

'I'm here for Amanda,' the man repeated, his gaze dropping.

Marna frowned. Then it clicked: he was probably a discipline client. 'Sorry, she's not here.'

'Oh?' He looked disappointed. 'I have a mission.' He moved away from the door, then turned back and regarded Marna intently. 'Do you punish?'

Marna was about to shake her head, but then she thought again. It was a slow night, and all of Amanda's equipment was still there. How hard could it be? And it wasn't like Amanda wouldn't have done exactly the same thing if the roles had been reversed.

'What's your name, ducky?'

'John.'

She pushed the door open and moved back to let him in. As he passed her, she wrinkled her nose at the smell of stale sweat. 'You'll be wanting a shower, I take it?' she said sweetly.

He waited for her to close the door. 'Where do I go?'

'I haven't seen you before.' Marna frowned.

'I met her in the Red Stairs.'

'No way! I used to work there.' Marna smiled. 'Great memories.'

He held up his hand. 'I am married.'

God, Marna thought, these discipline clients are such sad freaks. 'Well, that's nice.'

He lifted his head, and a slow grin spread across his face. 'I'm on a mission.'

Marna smiled, a little puzzled. 'Yes, you said.'

'Yes, I said. Sometimes things change; I get it now.' He hoisted his bag higher on his shoulder. 'I like your breasts.'

28

Emma climbed out of bed and tiptoed across the floor. Tricky snorted, muttered something and rolled over onto his back. His naked body shivered from her absence, and Emma carefully tucked the duvet around him.

She found her clothes and tiptoed down the stairs. It was early, too early for normal people to be up and about – but then, she thought with a grim laugh, what constituted normal anyway? She dressed at the kitchen table and expertly rolled a joint, borrowing heavily from the bag of grass Tricky kept in a shoebox under the hot press – all the better to dry it with, my dear.

Ten minutes later she was on the road, blowing lungfuls of sweet smoke out through the car window. Emma liked Dublin in the mornings, before people cluttered it up and the traffic made your head ache and your temper rise. She zoomed through the near-empty streets in her BMW, enjoying the speed of the little car. It was raining and the roads were slippery, so she used the brakes a little early, letting the back wheels slide on the bends before spinning the wheel and straightening out again. It was fun.

She stopped at a Spar and bought a fresh baguette, a litre of milk and four packets of M&Ms for a sudden attack of the munchies. Two streets later she parked in front of her house and hopped out, whistling as she locked the car.

Behind her she heard a car door slam, and immediately she was on her guard.

'Miss Harris.'

She whipped around. 'What the fuck?'

'Can you come with us, please?' Gerry Cullen's hair was standing up and his clothes were crumpled; he looked as if he'd been in his car all night.

Emma looked him up and down. She grinned. 'Were you waiting here all night for me?'

Gerry glowered at her. After a night of surveillance, he was in no mood for banter.

'Who'd you piss off?'

'Please, let's go.'

Emma held up her hand. 'Look, I'll come with you, OK? Just let me go inside and put my milk in the fridge.'

'Don't try anything funny,' Gerry snapped.

Emma looked at him, bemused and a little stoned. 'Man, the fat one must really hate you.'

Amanda tossed clothes into her suitcase with vicious, jerky movements, closed the lid and threw her full weight on it. The damn thing wouldn't close. She took everything back out and tried again. Different system, same result. The lid stayed firmly half an inch away from the lock.

'Arrrgh!'

Amanda kicked the bed. She was exhausted, but she couldn't sleep, no matter how hard she tried. And, God, had she tried; she'd downed two sleeping pills and half a bottle of wine a few hours before, and still her nerves jangled and snapped.

It was lashing outside; heavy grey clouds rolled across the sky as far as the eye could see. A sudden gust of wind splattered raindrops against the penthouse windows like a handful of pebbles. She went to the window and rested her forehead against the cool glass. Every time she tried to focus, her thoughts shifted to Marna. She had never thought leaving the business would be anything other than a relief, but it wasn't that simple. She was leaving a whole way of life. True, now she was free to do something else, to make something of her life. Maybe that was what was so scary: maybe now she would finally have to rely solely on herself and accept that her life and future were finally resting in the palm of her hand.

The apartment phone rang for the second time that morning and again she ignored it, letting the answering machine pick up. Nobody knew she was home.

She pulled a second suitcase out from under her bed and resumed packing. She pulled her Prada coat out of the wardrobe, hurled it onto the bed and watched as it hit the nightstand, knocking one of her favourite Kilkenny lamps to the ground, where of course it smashed.

Amanda yanked the suitcase to the ground in a rage. Then she threw herself on the bed and wrapped the duvet over her body. In five minutes she was so deeply asleep it would have taken Lucifer himself to wake her.

Kate slammed the phone down. She had rung twice already, left messages on both the mobile and the house phone, and still there was no word from Amanda.

Exhausted, she leaned back against the wall and watched the nurses bustle about. She hated hospitals, hated the smell, the sounds, the sticky warmth.

The initial adrenaline of last night had long since left her body. Now she was tired, irritable and starving. She rubbed the back of her neck and glanced at her watch: ten twenty-five. Should she wait around for—

'Hey, there – Kate, is it?' A nurse poked her head around the corner. 'Your friend is asking for you.'

Kate nodded wearily. 'I'll be right there.'

29

Emma took off her coat, folded it neatly over the back of the chair and relaxed. She was still a little stoned.

After a few minutes the door opened and Stafford came in, followed by Michael Dwyer.

'You're an early birdie,' Stafford said pleasantly.

'Inspector.'

Michael glanced at her. She was dressed in jeans and a white T-shirt; her hair was loose, tumbling over her shoulders in soft waves. She wore no make-up except for a dark-plum lipstick. She caught him looking at her and smiled broadly, flashing perfect teeth. She was a picture of smug confidence.

The confident smile irritated Michael, and he sat down and opened a fresh statement sheet with a sinking feeling that this was going to be another waste of time. Other than sub-letting the apartments, they had found very little to press her on.

After she gave her name and address, Stafford fired the first question. 'Why were you renting apartments for Paul McCracken?'

Emma tilted her head. 'I wasn't.'

Michael groaned inwardly. Just as he'd thought: she was going to brazen it out.

'We have in our possession three separate lease agreements for three apartments in the Dublin 4 area, all bearing your signature and all from the last year.'

'Do you?' She raised her eyebrows in mock surprise.

'You know damn well we have.' Stafford pushed the copies across the table. 'That's your handwriting, your bank-account numbers and your employment references. They weren't that difficult to find.'

She made a great show of studying the papers, reading each page slowly, taking her time. When she had finished, she pushed them back across the table to Stafford. 'You're right: they're mine.'

'Can you tell us why you rented these apartments for Paul McCracken?'

'They weren't for him.'

'So who were they for?'

'I don't recall.' She didn't even try to mask the fact that she was lying.

'Did you ever live in any of these rented apartments?' Stafford asked, with as much patience as he could muster.

'The last one. I was having some work done on my home and I needed a place to stay. But a gang of idiots burst in one night and started to accuse me of all sorts of things.' She winked at Michael. 'That sort of ruined it for me, so I moved out soon after.'

'You didn't live in the other two, then?' Michael asked.

'You're not listening, Sergeant. I've already told you: I lived in the last one, not the other two.'

'What did you do with the other two?'

'I sub-let them.'

'You sub-let them to whom?'

She shrugged. 'To some girls, acquaintances I made. Why? That's hardly a crime.'

'Can you give us their names?' Stafford was dangerously close to blowing a fuse. Her whole attitude was rubbing him up the wrong way.

'I don't remember. I'm terrible with names.'

'Drop the act, Miss Harris,' Michael said sharply. 'We know who used those apartments and for what purpose.'

'Really? Then you know more than I do. Did you catch someone doing something illegal, then?' She leaned towards them, smiling. 'I mean, actually *catch* someone?'

The emphasis wasn't lost on either detective. She was well coached, and she obviously knew they had nothing. Michael realised they were fighting a losing battle.

'Do you know a man by the name of Anthony O'Connor?' Stafford demanded.

Her hazel eyes twinkled with mischief. 'Can't say that I do.'

'If I told you that he worked for Paul McCracken, would that help jog your memory?'

'Who's Paul McCracken again?'

Stafford dug his fingers into the palm of his hand. It was bad enough that she could sit there and lie to them, but the fact that she seemed to be enjoying it was too much to bear.

'Do you think we have time for this crap?' Michael snapped. 'You said you could help us with our—'

'I wanted you out of my office. Poor form, calling into a girl's work like that, by the way.' She winked at him again.

Stafford had had enough. He threw his pen down and pushed back his chair. 'This is a waste of time. I hope for your sake, Harris, that you have nothing to hide, because I swear—'

'Sit your arse back down,' Emma said, softly but clearly.

Michael stared at her.

'What did you just say?' Stafford spluttered.

'I said sit down.' Emma Harris sighed. 'You know, I could have kept singing that song forever, and then where would you be?'

Stafford frowned. 'Look, if you're trying to—'

'You think you can push me around, don't you, Fatty? Think threatening me with CAB is going to make me quake? You don't scare me one bit.' She sat forward in her chair. 'I wanted you to know that without me you have nothing. So if you really want the truth, you'd better be on your best behaviour.

If you're not, you can bet your last paycheck I won't say another word.'

Stafford sat down.

'Everything I told you is a pile of shit. You know it, and I know it.' Emma stretched out, crossed her ankles under the table and regarded the two detectives with amusement. 'But if you want to know the truth, that's a different matter.'

'Is it McCracken?' Stafford leaned forward across the table. 'Did he threaten you to make you keep quiet? Or was it O'Connor?'

'That fat fuck? You must be joking. I don't take threats from anyone, you included.' She laughed. 'I work for Mr McCracken, of course – know what I mean?'

A warm tingle spread across Stafford's scalp. Michael pushed the statement sheet across the table towards Emma, but she shook her head.

'I won't be writing anything down. If you want McCracken, I'll give you McCracken; but I won't sign anything and I won't repeat anything. No court, no statements. I don't want any of this coming back on me. Do we have a deal, or do I leave now?'

Slowly Stafford nodded, although he had no idea what he was agreeing to.

'Great. As long as we understand each other. Now, I should start at the beginning.'

30

'I met Tricky almost two years ago. I can't remember where, exactly – it was one night out on the town. He doesn't remember it, of course; he was so drunk and coked up, he could barely stand.' Emma smiled. 'There he was, propped up against a bar, bragging about how much he was worth, how he could have any woman in the place, how women were all whores, all that bullshit.'

Michael and Stafford exchanged glances. 'How very appealing,' Michael said.

Emma either didn't hear him or didn't care what he thought. 'Anyway, one way or another we got talking. We realised we had lots in common. I like money and he has money – that sort of thing.' She grinned at the men. 'I know what you're thinking. I'm not the sort of woman to get involved with someone like him, right?'

'You strike me as exactly the sort,' Michael said.

Emma shrugged. 'My point is, I didn't know what type of business he was in until later. A lot later. For the record, I don't give a shit how he earns his money. If girls are dumb enough to work for him, that's their own lookout.'

'Very noble of you,' Michael said. He thought of his conversation with Amanda in the pub, and he wondered if Emma Harris realised how much McCracken frightened his women.

'Sorry if I offend your sensibilities, Sergeant. Do you want to hear this or not?'

'We do. Carry on.' Stafford nudged Michael's foot under the table.

'Where was I?' She frowned. 'Oh, right … So, anyway, romance blossomed. He's really into blondes, you know.'

Stafford smiled and stored that in his head for future reference.

'But occasionally I did a little work for him too. I got paid, of course – well paid. If he needed an apartment rented, I got it for him. If he needed someone to pick money up, I offered—'

'You realise what you're saying?' Michael interrupted. He was disliking her more with every word.

'Be quiet, Mike,' Stafford snapped.

'Of course I realise what I'm saying.' She eyed Mike with irritation. 'I'm not fucking stupid, you know. Now do you want to hear this or not? I don't have to keep talking if you're not interested.'

Stafford motioned her to go on.

'The arrangement suited me fine. I got cash and he got my unwavering loyalty. Everything was fine, until you lot showed up that night and cocked it all up. Well, actually, things went downhill when he hired that fat fuck; but mainly it was the raid that screwed me. You see, being snared by the police was not part of my plan – and it gave Tricky something to use against me. Well, why else was I there?'

'You're saying that as if he set you up to get caught,' Stafford said.

'Of course he did. It was bloody obvious. Let's face it – he knew exactly when you were coming.'

Michael and Stafford exchanged uneasy glances. 'How could he know that?' Stafford asked.

'Ah-ah-ah, Inspector Stafford.' She wagged a finger at him. 'All will be revealed in good time. A girl's got to have some insurance.'

Michael shifted in his seat. He didn't like the sound of this. How could McCracken have known they were coming? 'If everything was so great, why are you telling us all this?' he asked.

'Because things change, Sergeant. The stupid fucker got greedy. He didn't want to pay for my help any more. He thought it would be a better idea if I worked for free, unless I wanted my boss to hear about your visit.'

'So he tried to blackmail you?'

Emma rolled her eyes. 'Oh, for fuck's sake, he blackmails everyone. That's what he does – and that's not the problem. The problem is that now I'm really scared of him – well, not of him, exactly; of his fucking henchman.'

'Anthony O'Connor?'

'Him?' She looked genuinely surprised. 'That creep? No, the Whale I can handle. But this new guy …'

Stafford sat up straight. 'What new guy?'

'I don't know him myself, but I've heard Tricky bragging about him. He's some sort of nutter, so of course Tricky's delighted. It's like he has a new toy. That's why all the girls are running scared at the moment.'

'Miss Harris, are you saying McCracken has hired someone specifically to hurt the girls?'

'You don't think he would? Well, tell me – what do you know about Tricky? Take whatever you've heard about him and keep multiplying, and still I doubt you'd know the half of it, Sergeant.'

Her tone annoyed Michael more than ever. 'If you were that concerned about him, why were you working for him in the first place?'

'I have only one weakness, Sergeant: I like money. But I don't see why you're being so fucking nasty. I'm trying to help.'

'We all like money. Not everyone pimps desperate people to get it.'

'Oh, please!' she hissed. 'Thanks for the sermon, but people in glass houses really shouldn't throw stones. How do you think Tricky knew about the raids? What do you think happened to that junkie – Sinnott, wasn't it?'

Stafford and Michael exchanged a long look.

'What's that supposed to mean?' Stafford said carefully. 'How do you know about Barbara Sinnott?'

'Never you bloody mind. Do you want my help or not? I came here to help you and all I'm getting is fucking grief.' She folded her arms and glared at him. 'Anyone would think I was the one going around topping the whores myself.'

Michael took a deep breath. 'Miss Harris, I'm sure you understand how pressed we are for time. Why don't you get to the point?'

Emma tucked a strand of hair behind her ear. 'What I'm trying to tell you, Inspector, is that Tricky thinks he has the upper hand. Even with your lot. But he's wrong, and I'm here to even the score.' She smiled at Stafford's puzzled face. 'Redress the balance, if you like.'

'Aye, well, so far all you've done is talk. We need proof.'

'I know that, Inspector, and that's why I'm here. I may be able to throw a bright light on that subject.'

Keeping his voice neutral, Stafford pressed on. 'Are you trying to suggest McCracken is involved in the murders of Sandy Walsh and Tessa Byrne?'

'I'm not suggesting anything. I'm telling you he is.'

'How? In what way?'

'In every way. It's what he calls "tying up loose ends". Let's try a hypothetical here. If, say, somebody like Tricky had a hold over someone, what do you bright boys think he'd do with it?'

'Blackmail them?'

'Exactly. But what if someone tried to turn the tables on him? What do you think he'd do then?'

Michael slammed his hand down on the table.

'We don't have time for riddles. What are you trying to tell us?'

She ignored him. 'Inspector, do you have a video recorder in this dump?'

'Aye. Of course we do.'

Emma hesitated for a moment. Then she pulled a cassette out of her bag and tossed it across the table. 'You may want to have a look at that, then.'

'What is it?' Stafford picked it up gingerly, as though it might bite him.

'If I'm not mistaken – and I rarely am – it's Tricky's new toy in action.' She made no attempt to mask the triumph in her voice.

Jesus, Michael thought as he glanced at her hard face, I'd hate to cross this bitch.

His phone vibrated in his pocket. He pulled it out, pressed 'Read' and stared at the text message.

'Inspector, I need to see you outside.'

Stafford glanced at him, sensing the change in his voice. 'Sure. I need to get Scully anyway.' He turned back to Emma. 'You don't mind waiting, do you?'

'Nope, take all the time you need.' Emma lit a cigarette and grinned at him.

They went out into the hall, and Stafford closed the door. 'What? What's wrong?'

'It's Marna Galloway. She's in hospital. She's been attacked.'

Stafford stiffened. 'She hurt bad?'

'I don't know.'

'Which hospital?'

'The Mater.'

'How come this went direct to you?' Stafford frowned.

'Probably Amanda Harrington – I gave her my mobile number. What if it's our guy?'

'Then she wouldn't be alive.' Stafford sighed and rubbed his lower back. 'Look, you go; I'll finish up with Madam here.'

Michael didn't need to be told twice.

31

Amanda ran down the corridor, her hair wild and her clothes in disarray. She found Marna lying on a trolley, half-hidden behind a large water cooler. She lay on her side, and someone had covered her with a lemon-coloured sheet.

'Marna!' Amanda cried.

'Mmm …'

'Marna, wake up.' Amanda put a hand on her shoulder. 'I'm sorry I was asleep – I was so tired … I should have checked the fucking answering machine—'

Marna groaned and rolled over.

Amanda gasped and took a half-step backwards. 'Oh, Marna …'

The left side of Marna's face was black and blue; her left eye was deep red, shiny and swollen shut. She had angry red marks around her neck.

'Amanda?' Her voice was hoarse and strained.

Amanda's hand fluttered to her face. She had woken up, two hours after falling asleep, to the sound of the phone ringing again. This time she had checked the messages. Her heart had almost leaped out of her chest when she heard Kate's rambling, panicked call.

Marna grunted and pushed herself up on the trolley. She was still wearing her red silk kimono. 'Where were you?' she hissed accusingly. 'Kate tried to reach—' Her voice failed. She pulled a bottle of water from under her pillow and sipped it. The doctor on call had said her throat would hurt for a few days. Getting angry probably wasn't helping.

'I'm sorry,' Amanda whispered.

Marna fixed her with a glassy, one-eyed stare. 'Do you … see … my face? Where—' She began to cough. Amanda reached for the bottle, but Marna knocked her hand away.

'I don't blame you for being mad.' Amanda withdrew her hand and sat next to her on the trolley. 'I didn't get the message until half an hour ago. I came straight here.' She stared at the bruise on her friend's cheek. 'Is it sore?'

'What the fuck do you think?' Marna snapped. 'It's fractured.'

'Jesus.' Amanda swallowed and lowered her head. 'What happened?'

Marna sipped more water and glared at the top of Amanda's bent head, her good eye glittering with fury. 'Some man … attacked me. Did this …' She mimed pressing her fingers into her damaged throat. 'Last thing I remember … Kate's screaming blue murder and … spraying Mace all over the place.'

Amanda raised her head. 'Did you recognise him? Was it a regular? What did he look like?'

Marna snorted and took another sip of water. 'He looked like a client. That's what he looked like.'

'Oh, Jesus … Oh, Marna.' Amanda put her hand on Marna's arm. 'You were so lucky. Lucky Kate was there, lucky—'

'Lucky?' Marna spluttered. 'You … stupid bitch …' She coughed so violently the water spilled over the sheets. This time Amanda grabbed the bottle out of her hand.

'Marna, please, I'm trying to—'

'I wasn't lucky!' Marna croaked. '*You* were lucky. It was you he was looking for … He asked for you by name.'

'What?' All the breath went out of Amanda's body.

Tears squeezed through the slit of Marna's swollen eye and rolled down her bruised cheek. Her voice had almost disappeared. 'I could have been killed, for all you fucking care.'

'Don't say that! I do care!'

'You left me to … work alone.' Marna dashed at her tears. 'You fucking ran out on me. You swore you wouldn't … but you did.'

Amanda felt as though she'd been slapped. 'I'm sorry,' she said quietly. 'I'm really sorry.'

Marna nodded and turned her head away. 'I don't know what's going on with you, but Michael Dwyer is on his way, so maybe it would be best if you cleared off. After all, none of this concerns you any more.'

'Marna, please – I said I'm sorry—'

'Yeah, well, sorry's not fucking good enough.' Marna lay back down and pulled the sheet up over her shoulder.

'Marna,' Amanda said tentatively, 'please don't mention me to the police.'

'Why not?' said Marna.

'Please, I can't … please. I can't have them looking into me, I can't have any more meetings with Michael Dwyer. Please don't say he was looking for me, don't even mention my name.'

Marna's eyes strayed away to the wall. 'All right,' she said, 'all right.'

Amanda's shoulders slumped with relief. 'Thank you.'

Marna just closed her eyes and turned her head.

'What about clothes and stuff?' said Amanda. 'Do you want me to go to your place and pick up—'

Marna cut her off abruptly. 'I already called Paula. She's on her way in.'

'Marna, I'm so sorry—' Amanda began to cry.

'Go on, fuck off.' Marna shook her head; her blonde hair was streaked with dirt and blood. 'Go. You're not one of us any more.'

Sobbing hard, Amanda grabbed her handbag and fled.

It took Michael almost forty-five minutes to get to the Mater Hospital. He arrived just in time to catch the end of a loud and bellicose argument between Marna Galloway and a harassed-looking young doctor. Grapevine Paula was standing on the sidelines, looking slightly less made-up than usual. She nodded to Michael.

'Marna, I'm going to bring the car round to the front, OK?'

Marna swayed. 'I'll be there as soon as this eejit gets my release form.'

'Go easy on her; she's very upset,' Paula said softly as she passed Michael.

Michael nodded. He leaned against the wall and looked on with interest. It probably wasn't the first row of the day.

'I'm not staying here,' Marna said to the young doctor, who was holding his clipboard across his chest like a shield.

'If you leave now, I want you to know that it's against my advice. You have a concussion and you need to be kept under observation.'

'I don't give a shit about your advice. Go get me whatever needs to be signed.' Marna was trying to wiggle into her coat. Her movements were clumsy; the doctor had shot her full of a painkiller that should have knocked her on her ass.

'If you'd simply let me—'

'Are you going to get the papers, or will I get them myself?'

'As you wish.' The doctor stalked off, barely noticing Michael as he swept by.

Marna, now that victory was hers, crumpled

and sat back down on the trolley. Michael grinned and walked towards her.

'Oh, great, the cavalry – too late, as usual.' She had a huge white bandage around her head, but Michael could see the damage to her face.

'That's some shiner you've got.'

Marna lifted her hand to her face. 'I bet you say that to all the girls. So Kate got you, then.'

'Kate?' He shook his head. 'Who's Kate?'

'She's working with me.'

'Where's Amanda? I thought she'd be here.'

Marna's face went slack. 'She's away.'

'Away?'

'Away.'

'So what happened?' His concerned eyes swept over her bandages, her swollen face. 'Broken?'

'Fractured.' She closed her eyes, all the fight suddenly draining out of her. Her skin was so pale it looked like marble.

'When did this happen, Marna?'

'Last night.'

'Are you OK?'

'Do you know you're the first person to actually ask me that?' Marna's voice shook. After a few seconds, she opened her eyes and looked at him. 'No, I'm not bloody OK. I'm as far from OK as I'll ever be.'

Michael placed his hand over hers. Her hands were icy. 'Tell me what happened, Marna. I can't help if you don't talk to me. Who did this to you?'

She tried to smile, but her bottom lip gave way.

In an instant her strong front crumbled, and Marna began to cry.

Without even realising what he was doing, Michael leaned forward and gently pushed her blonde hair off her face.

'I'm sorry ...' she gasped.

'Shhh – it's all right,' he said gently. 'You've had a bad fright. It's OK. You can talk to me. For God's sake, what is it with you women? I'm not the enemy; I'm here to help.' He patted her back. 'Why don't you start at the beginning?'

Marna nodded, trying desperately to regain her composure. Michael found a tissue in his shirt pocket, and Marna dabbed at her nose. Even with the painkillers, touching her face was almost unbearably painful.

'Before I tell you what happened ...' she sniffed. 'Kate, the girl who called you – she was in earlier ...'

'What about her?'

'It's ... she says if you need to talk to her ...' Marna began crying again.

'What? If I need to talk to her, what?'

She sniffed and blew her nose. 'She says she won't go to the station.'

'Oh.' He smiled and shook his head. 'I'm getting used to that.'

Michael listened patiently to Marna's wavering, furious, weepy account. It troubled him to learn that McCracken had grabbed Amanda off the street a few weeks earlier. He wondered why she hadn't mentioned it when he spoke to her in the pub. He wondered why she hadn't mentioned she was going away. He wondered why he was listening to Marna and thinking only of Amanda.

Finally Marna fell silent. She looked at him from under the wet lashes of her good eye.

'Where is Amanda?' Michael asked.

'She's gone on holiday.' Marna's voice was threatening to give out. The effort of telling the story had exhausted her.

'Why didn't she tell me about McCracken threatening her?'

She shrugged. 'Amanda's not one for outside help.'

'She doesn't know what's happened to you yet?'

Marna shook her head and dabbed at her eyes.

Michael leaned closer so he could hear her. 'So what do you think might have made this man target you?'

'I don't know. I think he thought I was alone. He could have been watching the place for weeks.'

'But you weren't alone.'

'I might as well be. Amanda's never around any more.' She shook her head and frowned. 'I don't know why he targeted me, but I do know one thing: he was interested to hear I'd worked in the Red Stairs.'

'What makes you think that?'

'I don't know … his face sort of lit up when I mentioned I'd worked there.'

'Why did you mention it?'

'Small talk, usual sort of shit.' Marna suddenly leaned forward and coughed until her face turned purple. Alarmed, Michael passed her the water and patted her on the back. Slowly she regained control.

'All right?' he asked gently. 'Look, don't worry about it now. Try and get some rest.'

'I'm discharging myself from this place,' Marna said. 'I hate hospitals.'

Michael smiled at her. 'Me too.'

Marna shook her head. 'He kept saying something. He kept telling me ...' She squinted her good eye shut. 'What the fuck was it?'

'Don't worry about it; it'll come back to you.' Michael was itching to leave; he wanted Stafford to hear all of this.

'A mission. He kept saying he was on a mission.' She re-folded the tissue and dabbed at her eye again.

'A mission? Right.' Michael wrote that down and closed his notebook. 'OK, Marna, I'm sorry, but I have to go.'

'That's all right. I'm getting out of here too.'

'Oh, yes – about this Kate.'

Marna stopped dabbing. 'What?'

'The Mace she used ...'

'It was mine.' She raised her chin and glared at him through her good eye, challenging him.

'You know it's illegal, don't you?'

Marna stared at him and began to laugh, a

silent, shoulder-shaking laugh. 'Oh, Jesus, Sergeant, is it?' she croaked. 'Oh, well, if I had known … I'd hate to do anything illegal.'

32

Tricky swore under his breath. He couldn't believe his ears. That stupid bitch was giving her number to a client.

He was only ten minutes from City Stars. He could wait until the end of her shift before confronting her, or he could go in now and surprise her – maybe sample the merchandise, then kick her out on her arse. She'd have to be taught a lesson; he wasn't going to have some foreign cunt stealing his business out from under his nose.

'Did you fucking hear her?' he asked the Whale, who sat silently behind the wheel. 'She's in the place two days, and already she's handing out fucking numbers. I told you she would, didn't I? You can't trust them foreign birds.'

The Whale nodded.

Tricky lit a cigarette and picked up the headphones again. 'Listen to the cunt … You'd swear butter wouldn't melt in her fucking mouth.' He closed his eyes and listened. 'She's back in the sitting room now, yakking away.'

He yanked off the headphones and threw them down. 'That's how the fucking rot starts, Anto.

Once one thinks she can get away with it, they all bleeding do. Next thing you know, half the business is out the fucking door. We're going to talk to that bitch.'

The Whale grunted. 'I don't like that fucking cop knowing my business. She knows we got rid of the junkie.'

Tricky glanced at him. 'Grogan? She's over, man – fucking flake. Joe's gonna pull the rug on her real soon. But till then, we don't touch her.'

The Whale shrugged. 'If you say so.'

'After all this shite blows over, we can start clearing up a few things good and proper.' Tricky picked up the headphones again. 'Ah, will you listen to the way that stupid bitch Keisha answers the phone? It's a fucking joke. No wonder it's bleeding quiet; that bitch can't fucking speak proper.'

Stafford and Emma watched the tape on the TV upstairs in the conference room.

'Where did you get this?' Stafford asked quietly, as the tape began.

Emma ignored him. 'Fast-forward it. The bit you should watch—'

'Where did you get it?' he demanded more forcefully. On the screen, a scantily clad Asian girl with waist-length hair led a fat, balding man of about sixty into a dimly lit room. The angle of the shot showed that the camera was high up, in a corner.

Emma glared at him. 'Where do you think?'

He watched as the girl stripped off and helped the fat client out of his clothes, until he stood naked but for his socks. The sound quality was poor, but Stafford understood as much as he needed to.

'That's not the section I think you should see,' Emma said. 'If you fast-forward it—'

'Shut up.'

She shrugged and sat down on a table.

Stafford watched with growing revulsion as the girl sat astride the client's chest and performed oral sex for almost twenty minutes. The client groaned and squeezed the girl's buttocks so hard he left red marks on them. Before he came, he pushed her off and ordered her to lie down on the bed and play with herself. The client stood over her and pumped his dick. Finally he shot his load across her small breasts and face. Stafford watched as she tried to move out of range. She tilted her head back off the bed, giving him his first clear look at her face. Sickened, he realised she could barely be eighteen.

'Where did you get this?' he asked again, turning his head away from the screen. Emma realised this was not the time for smart answers.

'I borrowed it from Tricky's collection.' She kept her eyes steadily on his. 'His private collection.'

'What do you mean, his private collection?'

Emma hesitated. The last thing she wanted to do was give away too much information. The gardaí had to value her. They had to need her.

'I'd like to tell you more, but I don't want repercussions. I could help you a great deal, but first I need an assurance from you that I won't be held accountable in any way for what I may tell you.'

'What is it you want?' Stafford pressed Pause and looked at her suspiciously.

Emma raised an eyebrow. 'Immunity, of course. I don't want any of this affecting me in any way. I have a career to think of. Acton and Pierce would not be happy about this.'

'You must be joking!' Stafford exploded. 'By your own admission, you've assisted a known pimp in the running of his business. You've withheld vital evidence in a murder enquiry, and God knows what else you've been up to. Now you waltz in here, throw us this tape and expect us to turn a blind eye to all that?'

Emma shrugged. 'Either you want my help or you don't. I've done nothing wrong – well, apart from sub-letting a few apartments. As far as I can tell, I've been more help to you in half an hour than anyone else has been in your whole investigation. I don't claim to be lily-white, Sergeant, but I'm not responsible for Tricky's sick mind.'

'You must have known what he was doing.'

'I didn't.'

'You knew we were on to you. You're helping us because you had to.'

She laughed and shook her head. 'On to me? Bullshit, Detective; don't fucking kid yourself. Without what I'm about to tell you, you have nothing. Now, I'm willing to put my neck on the line to help you, and I want something in return. I want to be able to go back to my job, live my life and forget all about this shit.'

'And get off scot-free? Do you think—'

'Take it or leave it. Believe me, I've got more cards to play.'

'That's not up to us to decide,' Stafford said after a moment. 'That's up to the DPP. If he wants to press charges against you, there's nothing I can do about it.'

'Tell you what.' Emma nodded at the monitor. 'Play the tape first, and then see if we can't strike a deal.'

Stafford straddled a chair and pressed Play. The screen flickered back into life; the room was the same one, but the scene was different.

'This is it here.' Emma pointed to the screen with her chin. 'Watch.'

He watched.

He saw a blonde, busty woman in her early twenties enter the room, leading a sandy-haired man in his thirties. The man carried a dark-green sports bag with two white stripes. Stafford frowned. Even on the screen, this man looked suspect. He was too jumpy. The girl was laughing and showing him around, trying to make him relax; he kept glancing back at the door.

'This gentleman is, I think, the man you've all been looking for.'

Stafford heard the triumph in her voice and

glanced over at her. Emma was watching the screen, motionless, inscrutable; her eyes never wavered, though she knew what was coming next.

The assault was swift and brutal. The client had been in the room barely two minutes when he pounced, grabbing the girl by the throat and shaking her violently. Before she could scream for help, he drew back his fist and struck her a crushing blow in the face. The girl collapsed.

Stafford watched in horror as the man grabbed the unconscious woman by the hair and hauled her backwards onto the bed. Stafford could see he was excited; he was panting and his eyes were wild. He reached for the sports bag, pulling frantically at the zips. Eventually he managed to get it open and pulled out a long, slim knife.

Stafford thought of Tessa Byrne's blood-soaked stairs and felt a chill run down his spine.

Suddenly, on screen, the door burst open and a giant frame filled the doorway. There was no mistaking the shape. The Whale rushed into the room, moving with surprising speed and agility for a man of his size, and, in a blur of flailing fists, halted the client's attack.

Stafford was afraid to blink. From the moment the Whale burst in, the tape appeared to move in double time. The Whale beat the client savagely to the floor, then picked up the cowering man and dropped him on his knees. Blows rained down on the man's head and body. The client was scream-ing, trying to defend himself, crossing his hands over his face, but the Whale effortlessly hoisted him up and punched him in the stomach. The man collapsed; as he lay slumped on the floor at the foot of the bed, the Whale lifted a heavy-duty work boot and brought it down heavily on the man's outstretched hand, grinding his fingers into the carpet.

'You see what I mean now?' Emma said softly. 'The woman on there – her name's Carla, I think – she disappeared soon after that. But the guy … that's a different story. After O'Connor was finished with him, he never showed his face near the place again; but Tricky watched this tape, and he figured he could use this man and his natural talent to clear up a few problems. If the guy had refused, Tricky would have made sure you lot got this tape.'

'Where's the girl now?' Stafford asked. 'How can we contact her?'

'Couldn't tell you. Tricky got shot of her after this happened – she was only a part-timer anyway.'

'Where did she go?'

'I told you, I don't know. Why would I?'

Stafford stared at her. Emma met his gaze coolly, pulled a cigarette out of a silver case and lit it, blowing a stream of smoke in his direction.

'I've given you what you need. Can I go now?'

Stafford got up and went to the door. 'I don't think another few minutes will make that much of a difference. I've got someone who needs to see this, so stay put, got me?' he said over his shoulder.

Emma cursed under her breath and dropped back into her seat. She should have known better than to expect the cops to stick to their word. Well, there was nothing for it; she had opened the can, and now it was time to set the worms free.

33

Scully watched the attack in shocked silence. When it was over he pressed Pause, but his eyes remained on the screen. The image was frozen on the Whale's look of pure satisfaction as he ground the fallen man's hand into pulp. It was not an expression easy to forget.

'Where did you get this?' Scully asked softly.

'Emma Harris brought it in,' Stafford replied.

'Who is she?'

'I'm Emma,' Emma said from her seat at the table, where she was watching Scully with interest. This man was not happy; she had known that from the look on his face when he walked through the door. And she had picked up the hostility between him and Stafford.

'Where did you get this from?'

'I already told Fatty here.' She pointed at Stafford, who scowled. 'From Paul McCracken's private collection.'

'I see.' Scully continued to stare at her, running his eyes over her as if she were some new species. 'I see.'

'That's great. You see, he sees. Can I go now?'

'Not until you tell me about this collection.'

'For fuck's sake!' Emma whirled on Stafford. 'Look, I came in, I helped you out. Now you want to fuck me around? I told you everything I know.'

'You didn't tell me, and I'm the man leading this investigation,' Scully snapped. 'I asked you a question. What is this collection you're talking about?'

'Give me strength! Do I have to spell it out for you? Tricky tapes the working girls with the clients, right?' She looked at her watch and groaned. 'Damn it! I'm going to be late for work.'

Stafford snorted. 'That's the least of your worries.'

Emma ran her hands through her hair. Finally she sighed.

'All fucking right, then! Tricky started small first – rigged up the rooms in a place called Adam and Eve with tiny video cameras mounted in the fire alarms. It was mainly to check he wasn't being ripped off – that and he's a complete perv. But after he watched the tapes he came up with his master plan.'

'Master plan?' Scully asked.

'His money-making scheme. Unlimited porn, with no outlay. He reckons that, if he's going to have women screwing twenty-four-seven, he may as well make some real money from it, as well as the obvious. So he tapes the action and sells the best tapes abroad. The rest he keeps for himself.'

Stafford nodded. 'How long has he been taping them?'

'About a year and a half or so.'

'Do the women know this?' Scully asked incredulously. 'Are they in on it?'

Emma stared at him in amazement. 'Are you for real? He's hardly going to tell them. Anyway, he likes them to look natural. Gets more money that way.'

'And what's the deal with this man you have on tape here?'

'Look, I don't know exactly, right? Tricky trusts me, but he doesn't tell me everything. All I know is that Sandy Walsh twigged Tricky's porn racket somehow, but instead of reporting him to you lot, she tried to blackmail him. The stupid cow thought Tricky would pay her to keep quiet.'

Scully still looked confused. 'What has that got to do with this man here?'

'The man on the tape is Tricky's newest recruit. When O'Connor pulled him off Carla, Tricky watched the tape, and he knew he was on to something. He was under pressure from Walsh to come up with hush money, and this guy here' – she pointed at the screen – 'was a way out. For Tricky, it was the best possible timing, this guy falling into his lap like that. Why have a fucking dog and bark himself? It's one of his favourite sayings.'

'You're saying Sandy Walsh was killed over videotapes?'

'Yeah, only it wasn't over tapes; it was over money – a lot of money. Do you guys have any idea how much cash Tricky's pulling in for that much regular porn? He marketed it as "genuine brothel action".'

'Are you saying this man here,' Scully said slowly, 'this man was willing to murder women for McCracken, even though they had had no prior dealings?'

'From what I hear,' Emma said, 'this guy is already a few cards short of a full deck. I don't think it took much to persuade him.'

Stafford glowered at her. The flippant way she told the story infuriated him. 'And when did you figure it out, Harris? You could have come to us with this information a lot sooner.'

'No, I couldn't have. Do you have any idea how hard it was to get that tape? Do you understand the risks I've taken even to talk to you? Fuck you if you think this is easy.'

'I'm sure it wasn't that difficult for someone like you.'

'Oh, please, you're going to hurt my feelings now.' Emma put a hand to her chest in mock distress. 'Let me make something clear to you, Inspector: if Tricky finds out I've said any of this, well … I'll probably be the next corpse you'll have to investigate.'

Scully looked at the screen again. 'This is … this is unbelievable.'

Emma stood up. 'I have to go.'

'You can't leave now.'

'Why not?' She threw Stafford a sour look. 'You know where I work.'

'What's your relationship with McCracken?' Scully asked quickly.

'Girlfriend, confidante, user and patsy. I'll let Fatty here explain it.' She headed for the door. 'Oh, and don't forget, try to keep my name out of it. Tricky will hear about the tape soon anyway, but at least keep me out of it for now .'

'You think he won't know you're the one that gave us the tape?'

'He'll know, but then he knows everything. Remember the raids? He knew.'

'What does she mean by that?' Scully looked at Stafford.

Stafford's face scrunched into a tight wad of anger. 'She's hinting that someone in this department is passing McCracken information.'

'What?' Scully snapped. 'Miss Harris! Stop right there!'

Emma's shoulders stiffened, but she stopped and turned slowly.

'McCracken has someone in here giving him information?' Scully demanded.

'That's what he says. But, before you start grilling me, I don't actually have a name; I don't know if it's a man or a woman, I don't know if it's young or old. The only thing I do know is that I should have called a solicitor the first day I clapped eyes on him.' She pointed over Scully's shoulder at the furious Stafford. 'Now I'm going to go home and get changed for work. Either arrest me or stop bothering me.'

'Don't even think of going anywhere,' Scully said. 'We need to check this out, and we'll need you to be a witness.'

'I won't be a witness,' Emma replied. 'Ask Fatty: we had a deal.'

'There are no deals!'

'Yeah? Ask him.' She waved and hurried out the door.

Scully turned on Stafford. 'What *deal*? I never OK'd any deal. And who the hell is giving McCracken information?'

'I don't know!' Stafford snapped. 'She's trying to back-pedal.'

But Scully was already off and pacing. 'You should have told me about this. You should have told me why you thought McCracken was involved.'

'Aye. But I didn't know about the tape until now.' Stafford sighed. 'There's something else.'

'What?'

'Ed took a call, late the other night, from an unknown caller claiming to have seen a car resembling McCracken's on Sandy Walsh's road on the day she died.'

'I didn't hear that.' Scully frowned. 'When did he get the call?'

'Night before last.'

The frown deepened, and Scully grew very still. 'Why didn't he tell me sooner?'

'It's not the lad's fault. He would have done. I asked him to wait.'

'Why?' Scully demanded. 'That's vital information. I should have been told as soon as the call came through. What the hell were you thinking?'

'Aye, I know, but I didn't want you thinking I was just pushing you towards McCracken – not until I was sure.' He tapped the television. 'When I saw this, I called you in.'

'I should have been informed from the word go.'

'Aye, maybe so,' Stafford agreed. 'But I didn't want you thinking I was using *poor judgement*.'

Scully glared at him. 'Is there anything else that may have slipped your mind, Jim?'

'No.' Stafford rubbed his hand over tired eyes. 'We need to watch this tape again. We need to find out who this guy is. We need to find proof he's involved with McCracken.'

'That girl told you he's using this man to kill the women.'

'Harris says a lot of things,' Stafford said quietly. He looked troubled. 'You can't trust that woman. We need to find this bastard and get him to testify that McCracken knew about the murders.'

'If McCracken set this up,' Scully said, 'how is it that—'

'Fuck,' Stafford said. 'I almost forgot. Marna Galloway. She was assaulted last night.'

'Who?'

'Works with Amanda Harrington – you know, the girl who told Mike about McCracken beating Sandy Walsh?'

Scully took a step towards Stafford. 'You mean to tell me another woman was assaulted and you didn't inform me?'

'I didn't know myself until about an hour ago.' Stafford went to the window, his face screwed up in concentration. 'Amanda Harrington told Mike that Sandy threatened McCracken with tapes – I thought they were audio tapes. And we heard he likes to bug his places … Maybe Harris is telling the—'

'I want you off this case,' Scully said coldly.

'What?' Stafford turned around and stared.

'I'm telling you now, I'm going to lodge a complaint with Brennan about you. You've withheld information, withheld witnesses, ordered other officers to withhold information that could be pertinent to my case … I've had it. I want you off!' Scully pressed Eject on the video recorder and snatched the tape.

'You can't do that!' Stafford snapped.

'Watch me!' Scully slammed the door on his way out.

Half-running down the street, Emma found her mobile and dialled Tricky's number. She grinned as she remembered the look on Stafford's face when he saw the tape. That man was determined to pin Tricky down, whatever it took; he would have believed her if she'd said Tricky was the Devil himself. But now that the game had been set in motion, she'd have to be extra-careful.

Tricky answered his phone. 'Paul! Thank God,' she cried. Then she turned the hysteria down a little; Tricky would sniff out overkill.

'No, I'm not OK!' She went with angry. 'I was ambushed when I went home this morning; the fucking cops were waiting for me ... No, of course not. But they were asking me all about some girl called Sinnott, asking me about you, did I know you knew all the victims – my God, they practically suggested you were the murderer!' Emma stopped and lit a cigarette. 'No, I can't meet now; I have to get into work. I'm late as it is.'

She took a deep drag and listened as Tricky grew steadily angrier. 'Paul, listen to me. I don't know what's going on, but someone is talking – someone close. So I'd watch the fucking Whale, and I'd watch that cop bitch too.' She took another drag and smiled; she had sown seeds of doubt. 'Yeah, couldn't believe it ... No, don't panic; they're sniffing around in the dark, they have nothing to connect you to anything. But if I were you I'd stay away from your house and the apartments. Lie low – and, Paul, keep away from that bitch Grogan. I think she's in some sort of trouble in there, and you know she's the sort that changes sides ... Don't worry, this shit will all blow over; you know it and I know it. But be careful – extra-careful ... Yeah, I will. Talk later.'

She cut him off and dialled another number.

'It's me. We're all go ... No, I'm wired, totally fucking wired ... Yeah, I know – all over soon.'

★ ★ ★

He lay on his mother's bed, grinding his teeth in frustration. He had failed in his mission – failed her again. Why had this one been saved? Had the black dog been warning him?

Was it a test? Mother said people were tested in their faith; was this his test? If it was, he had failed miserably. He closed his eyes and moaned softly.

He'd thought this one was a gift, but she had been a distraction. He would not be swayed by temptation again.

He rolled over, scooped up another handful of pills and dry-swallowed them. His eyes stung, even after all the times he'd washed them out. The pungent smell of chemicals still clung to his skin.

He still had the book. He would follow the book. Do it by the book.

He ran a filthy nail down the numbers to one name, underlined many times. This one was the cornerstone, the queen bee, the leader. This would be his new mission.

No more mistakes. He would strike off the head and watch as the body died. He would cleanse. No more underlings; he would prove his worth. She would be his redemption.

34

The following morning Amanda got out of bed early and practised her speech. She had a soft spot for her maid, and she didn't want to upset him any more than she had to. She went into the kitchen and brewed coffee. While she drank it she paced up and down her sitting room.

At eight o'clock, he rang the doorbell. She stopped pacing and let him in. This was not going to be easy.

'Madame, good morning,' Colin said breezily, sailing into the hall. 'I hope you are well? It's a bit chilly out there today, but at least it's not raining. I know how you hate the rain.'

'Hello, Colin. I'm fine, thanks.'

'Wonderful. And don't you look it? Now I'll go and get changed. Have you eaten?' He eyed the coffee cup in her hand. 'Would you like me to rustle up some—'

Amanda closed the door. 'Wait, Colin. There's something I want to talk to you about. I think it's best if I tell you now.'

Her tone stopped the little man in his tracks. His face became wary.

'What is it, Madame? Is something the matter? You know you can tell me anything. I'm the soul of discretion.'

'I know.' She avoided his concerned eyes. 'I may as well come straight out with it. The thing is … I won't need you any more after today.'

Colin stared at her, open-mouthed.

'What do you mean?' he whispered. He covered his mouth in dismay. 'What have I done?'

'Nothing. I can't have you coming here any more.' He looked like he was about to cry. 'Colin, I'm pulling out of the business.'

'But … who's going to look after you?' He glanced wildly around him. 'Who's going to do your … clothes?' His voice wobbled and tears sprang to his eyes. 'Madame, do you … do you have somebody else?'

'Do you honestly think I'd let anybody else up here? Don't be so dramatic,' Amanda said gently. She had known he'd be upset, but she hadn't realised it would affect him this badly. 'Nobody could do the job like you. It's not about you, Colin; it's about me. OK?'

Colin nodded miserably.

'If you don't want to stay today, I'll understand.' She reached out and squeezed his hand.

Colin straightened his shoulders and drew himself up to his full five foot six. 'No, Madame.' He dabbed at his eyes. 'I'll stay, if you don't mind. If this is to be my last day, I'd rather work.'

'Well, I won't charge you.'

He looked even more upset at this. Amanda realised she had insulted him, on top of everything else. 'Certainly not, Madame. I wouldn't do it then.'

Amanda pulled herself together. 'Then stop nattering and go and get ready.'

Colin turned and walked towards the spare room. All his bounce and sparkle had been trounced out of him. Amanda watched him go and felt like a shit. She had grown to like having Colin as her maid. He was a sweet man, and she didn't like hurting him this way.

He stopped outside the door of the spare bedroom. 'Madame? Is everything really all right? If there is anything I can do, you only have to ask.'

'Fine,' she said. 'Everything's fine.'

'I see.' He bowed his head. 'Well, I'll get changed.'

Stafford had been expecting the call, but when it came he still felt betrayed. He stood in his hall, wearing the blue-and-red terrycloth dressing-gown his daughter had bought him on his last birthday. He could smell the Superquinn rashers his wife was grilling especially for him. He preferred them fried, but she said his heart would thank her for it.

Two minutes earlier he'd been starving. Now his appetite had deserted him.

Commissioner Felim Brennan had received a complaint. He was not happy. Ergo, he was threatening to make Stafford's life a living hell if Stafford wouldn't play ball with Detective Inspector Robert Scully.

Stafford inhaled the aroma of bacon and picked fluff off his robe while Brennan read him the riot act. Under normal circumstances he would have been defensive, arguing his case, turning the tables on Scully, pointing out that, if it hadn't been for him, Scully would never have clapped eyes on the tape in the first place. This morning, though, he waited until Brennan had vented his displeasure; then he offered a reasonably sincere apology, admitted he had been wrong to withhold information and expressed great remorse at upsetting Scully. And a very surprised Brennan let him stay on the case. Sometimes even gardaí have to prostitute themselves to get what they want.

The moment he hung up, Stafford dialled Michael Dwyer's home and asked him to make a few calls.

Michael sat at his kitchen table and half-heartedly picked at a bowl of cereal. He had left a message for a friend of his in the traffic division and was waiting for a response. Stafford had ordered him to find out more about Emma Harris. No matter what she said, Stafford wasn't swallowing her sudden U-turn.

Michael understood completely. There was something about her that he, too, found deeply troubling; but every time he tried to grasp it, the thought drifted away.

His mobile rang.

'Hey, Mike, got your message. Jesus, you're an early bird.' David Kelly was a friend of Michael's. They played squash together sometimes.

'What've you got for me?'

'Well, which address did you want? There are two.'

'What do you mean?'

'She has a BMW registered at an address in Leeson Parade. Number 27.'

'And the other?'

'Old Datsun, registered a few years ago. Car's in her name, all right, but not at any of the addresses you gave me.'

'No? So what's the address?' He listened and scribbled. 'Are you sure about this?'

'That's what comes up on screen. Beyond that, I can't be sure of anything these days. She can't have sold it; there's been no change of ownership.'

'Right. Thanks, Dave; I owe you one.'

'You can give me a three-point lead in our next match,' David laughed. 'That's if you're ever over this way again. It must be eight months since we've played.'

'Ten – and no way. I'm grateful, but not that grateful.'

David laughed and hung up.

Michael put the piece of paper in his pocket. Why would Emma Harris have a car registered to her at that address?

He checked the time and swore softly. Scully

had called another briefing for this morning, and if he didn't get a move on he would be late. He grabbed his jacket and slung the bowl into the sink. He could check out the address later.

35

At the briefing, Scully was forceful and upbeat.

'Ladies and gentlemen, we have a breakthrough!'

Every garda in the small room leaned forward. A photo was passed around the room. Scully had lifted a still from the video and made copies.

'This may be our man. He was involved in an assault on a prostitute named Carla Bannion.' Stafford had shown a still of the girl to Grapevine Paula, who, of course, had immediately recognised her, although it had taken her a full hour to come up with a surname. 'I want him found and questioned. I want this shown to all the working girls; see if anybody recognises him. I want to be kept informed. No matter how trivial anything seems, I want to know about it.'

Stafford scowled. That was the second dig directed at him in less than ten minutes. Of course, he knew Scully was smarting to see him there; he'd have to put up with the odd snide comment.

'In the meantime, we carry on with our other lines of enquiry. Talk to everybody again if necessary. Somebody out there knows this man. And

I still need to know what happened to Tessa Byrne's phone. I want to know where Carla Bannion has vanished to, I want to know where McCracken's gone, I want Anthony O'Connor questioned again.' He stared at the assembled officers. 'I want a result, ladies and gentlemen. Let's put this madman away.'

Scully stepped down from the podium and walked out. Stafford hurried after him. 'Can I have a word?'

'Not here, Jim. My office.'

'Mine's closer,' Stafford said, to annoy him.

'As you wish.'

As soon as they had closed the door, Stafford demanded answers.

'Why didn't you mention where the tape came from? And what about the information on the car?'

Scully leaned against the door and regarded him with impatience. 'I should have thought that was obvious. I don't want McCracken to know who spoke with us. And if someone from your team may have been – how shall I put it – in contact with him …'

'Now you wait a damn second. I hand-picked those people myself.'

Scully sidestepped him and sank into a chair. 'Tell me something, Jim. How many times did you raid him?'

'Three times,' Stafford admitted. 'But so what? He's a slippery bastard.'

'Didn't it ever occur to you he might have been warned about your visits?'

'That's bollocks,' Stafford said, incredulous. 'I'm telling you, no one on my team would do that. What the hell gives you the right to even suggest it?'

Scully shrugged. 'You wondered why that junkie died just when we were about to bring her in.'

'She was a junkie. She overdosed.'

'How convenient. You no longer think that was odd?'

Stafford hitched his stubby fingers into his belt and yanked his pants up. 'No one on my team would give out information,' he said doggedly.

'Look, Jim, I'm not saying they did—'

'That's exactly what you're saying! Dress it up any way you like, but that's what you're saying.'

'This is a murder case – my murder case. I call the shots here. And if I think, or even suspect, that someone is leaking information—'

'You're way off the mark. Harris is just trying to cause trouble.'

'I hope that's all it is.' Scully paused and tried to defuse the situation. 'I'm having search warrants drawn up for the homes of McCracken and O'Connor this second. I can't risk them hearing about it. We can get them on withholding evidence, and possibly in connection with the murders. But McCracken knew about the raids, right? So

I'm making sure nothing out of the ordinary occurs this time.'

'I told you, I wouldn't take too much of what Harris says as gospel.' Stafford pulled up a chair and sat down heavily. That wasn't true; he believed her about McCracken. And if she was right about that, then maybe … 'When? When do you plan to hit them?'

'Tomorrow morning, early.'

'I want to be there,' Stafford said. 'I want to be a part of the crew for that.'

Scully smiled. 'I thought you would,' he said dryly.

'Am I in, or what?'

'Sure. Michael Dwyer too. He was there when Harris came in – no point leaving him out.'

'I'll let Michael know,' Stafford said. 'You're wrong about my team, Bob. I can vouch for every one of the officers working for me.'

'I hope you're right,' Scully said softly. 'I don't ever want to be in a position to prove you wrong.'

The rain grew heavier as the day went on. Thick, black clouds hung low in the sky, smothering the city. Amanda stood at her window and looked out across the skyline with a heavy heart. Her earlier resolve had diminished considerably. She felt lonely and depressed and scared, disconnected from everything she knew.

She had tried to call Marna again and again,

but her phone was off. She tried the office; no answer there either.

She had waited years for this moment – the moment when she could quit, when she could finally take the chance and walk away from it all. She couldn't keep up the pretence any longer, no matter how hard she tried; her life was unravelling fast, and she had to move on.

She lit a cigarette and straightened her shoulders. Marna was going to have to accept it. The time for Amanda to worry about what other people thought was well and truly over.

The Modern Green bar on Wexford Street was half empty – or half full, depending on which way you looked at it. Marna accepted the gin and tonic gratefully. It was her fourth, and she was starting to feel a little better.

'I don't know if I can keep going,' she said again. 'I keep thinking of Sandy – that could so easily have been me …' She raised a hand to her swollen eye. 'At least when I had Amanda – you know, we had each other. Now …'

'I know, I know. It's terrible – especially now, when you need her most. Selfish cow.' Grapevine Paula lit a cigarette. Marna had called her and said she needed to talk, and Paula, scenting gossip like a bloodhound on a trail, had offered to have a drink with her. She was still shocked that Marna had been attacked, but her place was open. Business had to be done. 'What are you going to do?'

'Keep going, I guess. What else can I do?'

'That's the spirit, pet. You know you don't need that one anyway. The business will always be there. As long as men have dicks, you'll never be out of pocket.' Paula elbowed her in the ribs. 'You know, you could always come work with me; I could do with a classy chick like you.'

Marna nodded half-heartedly. 'Thanks, Paula, but I'm used to being my own boss.'

'Or not. You know, now you can do things the way you want.' Paula shrugged, not in the least offended. 'I know you like Amanda; we all do. But she was never the best bet when it came to business – didn't want to hire anyone, never wanted to stick her neck out too much … You can't run a business like that, Marna. You've got to take chances. Now you can hire girls in, take a back seat, rest that old fanny of yours. Your place has a good name; it'd be a shame to let it go to waste.'

'I can't believe it,' Marna said wretchedly. 'We were supposed to be a partnership, you know? All the shit we've been through in the last two years, and she decides to go without even talking to me about it first.'

'I know, pet. We all have things come at us from out of the blue.' Paula's hair wobbled as she shook her head. 'I wouldn't mind, but the worst of it was over. You've both been in court and paid your fines, and the cops are off your back, so why is she bolting now?'

'I can't believe it,' Marna repeated. 'Even when

I was hurt, she was so – she didn't even seem to care.'

Paula took a long swig of her drink. This could be a long evening. It was time to change the subject to something a lot more interesting than snotty Amanda Harrington.

'Why don't you tell me about that detective again? Did he really brush your hair off your face?' Paula nudged Marna and wiggled her eyebrows. 'Come on, give us the low-down.'

Marna managed a smile. 'Oh, Paula, how can you even think of that?'

'I'm fucking serious. If this whole shitty business has taught me one thing, it's that life's short, love; gotta grab a bit of fun where you can.' Paula patted her hair. 'I'm never going to settle for second-best again. Shit, Marna, if you don't like him I might just chance my arm with him myself. Jim Stafford told me he's a widower. Owns his own house – he can probably cook and everything ...' Paula sighed and rolled her eyes. Her mascara was as thick as treacle. 'I like a man with a bit of hair, too. Would you say that rug of his covers, you know, all of that lanky body?'

'Mike? Can I talk to you for a minute?' Stafford poked his nose around the door of the squad room.

'Sure,' Michael said. 'Ed, I'll talk to you later.' He gave Ed a pat on the back and followed Stafford to his office.

'Close the door.'

Puzzled, Michael did as he was told. 'Is everything OK?'

'Yeah.' Stafford rubbed his hands over his eyes. This cloak-and-dagger shit was starting to get on his nerves; but Scully's words were ringing in his head, and he didn't want to take any chances. 'What I'm about to tell you, Mike, stays between us. Got me?'

Michael sat down. 'Of course. What is it? What's wrong?'

'We're going on a dawn raid tomorrow. Nobody on the team knows, and I want it kept that way.'

'I see.'

'That's the way Scully wants it. It's his call.'

'This wouldn't have anything to do with yesterday, would it?'

'It's his case, Mike. We have to let him run it as he sees fit.'

Michael raised an eyebrow. 'It suited Harris to make those insinuations yesterday – just like it suited her to come forward when she did. I'd bet you a week's wages she knew about the tapes when we raided the last apartment.'

'She was spot on about Barbara Sinnott, though, wasn't she?' Stafford shook his head slowly. 'I don't know what to think any more.'

'What time are we going in?'

'I don't know yet. I'll give you a shout later; keep your phone on.' Stafford rested his chin on his hand and waved Michael away.

★ ★ ★

Tricky yelped and dropped the phone as one of his brother's little bastards kicked him square in the shin. While Tricky rubbed furiously at his leg, another of the monsters ran past, screaming, and snagged its jumper on the end of the coffee table. Tricky aimed a kick at the child's back, but it giggled and danced out of reach. Uncle Paul was funny.

The coffee table crashed over onto its side, and Tricky's skins and grass slid onto the thick pile carpet.

'Shite!'

'Shite!' two of the monsters yelled, and ran out the door, giggling and slapping seven shades of shite out of each other.

Tricky limped to the hatch in the sitting-room wall, yanked it open and stuck his head through to his brother's kitchen. 'Jay, can't you keep these fucking kids out of here? I'm trying to conduct a bit of business.'

'All right.' Jay, an older, heavier, milder version of Tricky, got wearily to his feet. 'John Paul! Steven! Stop running around! Where did you put your sister? I hear her crying.' He went off after them.

Jay's wife, Samantha, glared at her husband's departing back. She hated Tricky, hated the fact that he was in her house, hated the fact that her husband hadn't the spine to refuse to hide him. What had Tricky ever done for them except pass lewd remarks and snide comments? And here she was, cooking the bastard breakfast while he stank up their house with grass fumes and frightened her children. It was all she could do not to stab him with the fork, him and her useless lump of a husband.

'Any move with that food, Sammy? I'm fucking wasting away here.'

'Pity about you,' Samantha said under her breath, and stabbed a sausage viciously.

Tricky pulled his head back through the hatch. He would never understand why his brother didn't belt the smart mouth off of that bitch.

He picked up his phone again. 'Sorry, Emma – fucking kids. So you reckon I should stay clear of the gaff? … Right. Yeah, well, I can stop here for a while.' Tricky sighed. 'Yeah, all right – do your best … Nah, fuck it; if it's only for a day or so, I don't give a shite.'

He hung up and slumped back on the sofa. This was the biggest pain in the arse. Here he was – him, Paul McCracken, fucking king of the vice world – hiding out in a fucking dump he wouldn't put a dog in.

Tricky rolled a fresh joint and tried to think. Was Grogan setting him up? He had threatened her recently; maybe the bitch was planning on getting him sent down.

What about Anto? The fat fuck – Emma had never liked him. And Anto had been getting to be more and more of a handful lately; look at that junkie – and he'd used Tricky's own car to pick up the dirty bitch in. Was Anto planning to muscle in and take over the business?

Then there was that bitch Harrington. He had threatened her lately, too, and she was obviously tight with some fucking cop – the one who had called him and ordered him to back off. Grogan had been supposed to look into that, but she'd never got back to him with a name. Of course, Harrington was tight with that fat bitch Paula – and she knew every fucking cop in Dublin, the savvy bitch. Shit, it could be anyone trying to set him up.

In a burst of paranoia, Tricky jumped up and began to pace. He had never been very good at waiting. There had to be some reason they were asking about him. He must have done something to make them look at him. But what? He'd been careful about the junkie, hadn't left anything to chance.

Maybe the best thing would be to skip town for a few days, take some of his hard-earned cash and go on a holiday; bring Emma somewhere hot, get her to wear that little red bikini. He could get a few loose ends tied up while he was out of the country. Maybe that cop could have herself a little one-on-one with Big Joe. She was months behind on her repayments; only Tricky's handouts had kept that particular wolf from her door.

And maybe it was time to re-think his staff. The Whale was a useful man for enforcing order, and with him by his side his reputation was fearsome. But, shit, he didn't need any more reputation than he already had. He was Paul McCracken, he was the biggest motherfucking pimp Dublin had ever seen; he had the best girls money could buy; he had the tape business earning him cash even while he slept.

He did not need shit like this. He needed people he could trust. He had Emma, of course. Maybe when all the shit died down he'd slip a ring on her finger, make her more than a fuck-buddy. Shit, that girl was almost as crooked as he was.

But for now he would take her advice: he would lie low and see what the cops tried next. He'd ring that bitch Grogan and see if she really was trying to pin something on him. If she was, fuck her – fuck all of them. As Emma said, they had nothing on him.

36

The rain of the day before had cleared, but a cold, damp fog lay on the ground. The small group of gardaí huddled together around the corner from McCracken's house, stamping their feet in a futile effort to keep warm.

Scully eyed each of the other four men in turn. 'Does everybody know what to do?'

The men nodded in silence. He had already bawled them out for being too noisy.

'As soon as that door's open, Donal heads for the back of the house.'

Donal Higgins, one of the youngest members of the Murder team, nodded. He had been told all this in the van on the way here and didn't see why it needed to be repeated.

'Mike, I want you straight up the stairs with Oliver, right?' Oliver Redmond was a twenty-year veteran of Store Street – a big man, hard as nails. Michael knew him by reputation. He was said to crack the odd head if he needed information. Michael wondered at Scully's choice. Young Donal was built like a brick shithouse too, and Stafford had already commented on his fine rugby playing.

'Jim and I will take downstairs – that OK with you, Jim? Or would you rather stay here in the van?'

'I'm going in.' Stafford dug his hands into his coat pockets and tried not to look pissed off. Scully might be in charge, but he didn't appreciate being spoken to like a child. Scully had been barking orders all the way here, and he was sick of it. If he didn't stop trying to put him down, Stafford was going to kick him in the back.

'OK, then; let's go.'

Donal, all six foot four of him, stepped forward and rapped loudly on the door. They waited; nothing.

'Go again, Donal.'

Donal banged louder this time. Scully glanced at the upstairs windows. The blinds were drawn. The house felt empty to him.

'What do you want to do?' Donal asked hesitantly.

'Open it!' Scully snapped. He'd had enough messing around.

Higgins trotted back to the car and fetched Big Bertha, a heavy metal cylinder used to force doors open. Two swings at the lock and they were in.

'Right, go on. Move it!'

Michael sprinted up the stairs, shouting at the top of his lungs. 'Gardaí! Rise and shine, McCracken!' Oliver stamped up behind him, making as much noise as possible.

'Bobby boy.' Stafford waved an arm. 'After you.'

Scully pulled a face and strode down the hall. There were three rooms downstairs. The first was a very masculine sitting room with a black leather sofa, a wide-screen TV, and very little else – no books or ornaments, nothing of a personal nature. The kitchen looked like it was hardly ever used – the cooker was pristine; whatever Tricky ate, it obviously came out of cartons. There was a small bathroom, also clean and tidy, at the back of the house. A single damp towel hung over the bath.

Donal came out of the bathroom door and shook his head.

'Take a good look round, Donal. Start with the kitchen and take your time.' Scully listened to the men moving upstairs. 'Let's go and see if our friend is up yet.'

Michael and Oliver were on the landing, outside the door of the main bedroom. They had already checked the smaller bedroom across the hall.

'Well?'

'He's not here. Bed's been slept in, though – and take a look at this.' Oliver pointed to the bed, and Scully saw a dark stain on one of the white pillows.

'What is it?'

Oliver shrugged. 'It looks like blood, sir. I can't be sure, but that's what it looks like. I'd say it's fairly fresh.'

Stafford looked around the neat room for any sign of something dramatic, a struggle, mayhem of some kind. What the hell was going on here? It was six in the morning. Where the hell was Tricky? Stafford felt a knot in the pit of his stomach. *Missed him again.*

'Sir! Come and have a look at this.'

Michael was on the landing, looking at a huge mirror hanging on the wall.

'What is it?'

'Watch.' Michael grabbed the mirror and pushed. It slid to the left with surprising ease. 'It's on castors.'

'How did you—'

'I noticed the wear in the carpet.'

Stafford looked down. The carpet was worn in two small strips. The mirror had obviously been moved a lot. Even so, he didn't think he would have noticed it.

Behind the mirror was a narrow door. Stafford and Scully grinned simultaneously. Whatever was behind that door, McCracken had wanted it to remain hidden.

'Did you try the door, Mike?'

It was locked.

'Donal! Come here for a minute!' Scully shouted. 'And bring Bertha.'

Donal lumbered up the stairs, and the other men stepped back into the bedroom to give him room on the tiny landing. After studying the lock for a second, Donal grinned and gave it one sharp blow. It sprang open.

The room had originally been a walk-in wardrobe or a closet of some kind. It was tiny, about six feet by eight, with no windows. Donal pulled the light-cord beside the door.

'Holy shit.'

There were only two pieces of furniture in the room: a folding chair and a table. On the table sat a television and two video recorders. Almost every inch of wall space, from the floor to the ceiling, was covered by neatly stacked video cassettes.

'Look at this shit. It's like Xtravision in here,' Donal said in awe. 'Jesus.'

Scully elbowed him out of the way. 'The private collection Harris was talking about.' He selected a video and read the title: '*Mandy/Saffron/Eve. Oct. '98.*'

He turned back to the others. 'Right, lads, we've got a warrant. Go over this house from top to bottom. Donal, take Oliver with you and go downstairs. We'll start with this lot. We're going to need plenty of evidence bags. Mike, head down to the car and grab a few more. And bring the camera up with you.' He looked back into the video room. 'This could take a while, so let's get cracking.'

He took a deep breath. 'Looks like your witness was right, Jim.'

Stafford grunted and rubbed the back of his head. 'No sign of McCracken, though.'

'Nope. But something happened here. That's blood on that pillow – not much, mind you, but even so … Something happened here last night, and I'd sure as hell like to know what.'

* * *

Halfway down Thomas Street, Tricky stopped at the lights and checked his reflection in the rear-view mirror. His eyes were bloodshot, and he had a ferocious pain in his back from tossing and turning on the uncomfortable camp-bed his cheap bastard of a brother had offered him. When he'd finally got to sleep, it seemed like only two seconds had passed before one of those fucking evil kids had burst in and turned the television on full blast. *Bear in the Big Blue House*, first thing in the morning … Tricky decided he would never, ever have any kids.

Behind him a horn blared; the lights had changed to green. He flipped the driver a finger and drove off, muttering and cursing.

As soon as he got home, he was going to take a couple – no, a lot – of painkillers and climb into bed. He had been too paranoid yesterday, letting Emma put the wind up him like that. If the cops tried to pin the murders on him – fuck, he had a solicitor who could eat cops for breakfast.

He was about to pull into his driveway when he saw his front door opening.

'What the fuck?' He jammed on the brakes.

A man came out, went to a silver Nissan Almera and opened the boot. Tricky recognised Michael Dwyer immediately. He watched as the cop took out a camera bag and a handful of brown evidence bags and walked back towards the house.

'Motherfucker!' Tricky gasped, ducking down

behind the steering-wheel. They'd obviously found the tapes. That was not fucking good.

Quietly he reversed the BMW.

Miriam Grogan – it had to be. She had fucking spewed her guts. The lousy bitch had turned him in. They were crawling all over his house. Desperately, he tried to remember what he had there. He thought he had coke – or had he already moved it? Shit, he couldn't remember.

Tricky panicked. He stepped on the accelerator hard, but he'd forgotten that the car was in reverse. It spun backwards, smashing into a parked car behind him. The alarm shattered the early-morning quiet and brought Michael Dwyer running back out of the house. Tricky threw the car into gear, and this time he got it right. He floored it, his back tyres screeching as he roared out of the street.

Driving blindly, Tricky tried to think. What the hell was he going to do? He grabbed his mobile in one hand and frantically tried to steer with the other while he speed-dialled the Whale's number.

It started to ring. 'Thank fuck,' Tricky whispered, clasping the phone to his cheek. 'Come on, come on – what the fuck's taking so—'

'Hello?'

Tricky nearly crashed the car. That wasn't Anto.

'Who is this?' He felt sweat trickling down his back.

'Who is this?' the voice enquired calmly.

Pig. It had to be. Tricky hung up and threw the phone down. The cops were at Anto's gaff. They had been set up. Grogan had squealed. What other reason could the cops have for a dawn raid?

He took a left, swerving so hard that the back wheels spun out and he almost lost control of the car. He slowed down a little; the last thing he needed was a crash.

Tearing towards the North Circular Road, Tricky began to think. He'd had a lucky break: he hadn't been home when the cops called. And he knew Anto could look after himself. The Whale was one tough bastard, and he knew what to say to the cops.

First things first. He needed to get rid of the car. Then he'd get hold of Emma; she'd know what to do.

37

Back at the station, Scully stared at the haul of tapes stacked in brown evidence bags. They had selected one to watch, to check what exactly was on it; now he wished he hadn't.

A married man with two grown-up children of his own, he was no prude. But the graphic nature of the tape, combined with the assorted implements used, embarrassed and disgusted him. And Stafford's grinning face wasn't helping matters.

'This is unbelievable.'

'It's pretty gruesome, all right.' Stafford was clearly enjoying Scully's discomfort.

'Do people really get off on this? Do men really pay for this?'

'Aye, I guess they do.'

Scully watched as the girl on the screen rammed an oversized dildo into a dark-haired man strapped to a bed. 'Jesus Christ!' He crossed his legs in sympathy. 'They all look so normal. Doesn't he look normal to you?'

Stafford laughed. 'They are normal. That guy's probably a bank manager or a teacher. Clients are normal working men like you or me. I wouldn't be too surprised if we find a few of our more upstanding citizens in this lot, either.'

Screwing up his face, Scully glanced away from the screen. 'Don't tell me it's normal, Jim. Did you see the size of that thing she shoved up his ... ?' He shuddered. 'I didn't even know that was possible.'

Stafford laughed again. He had been working in Vice for so long that it would have taken more than that to shock him.

'Ah, Jesus ... Look what she's doing now.' Scully flushed and glanced up at the ceiling. 'I'm telling you, Jim, that's not normal – I don't care what you say.'

Even Stafford had to admit that what the girl was doing now was new to him. It looked excruciating. He watched as she threaded in the hose. Where did the water go?

'I think we've seen enough for the moment,' Scully said. 'We have O'Connor in custody, and he's had plenty of time to cool his heels. Let's go and talk to him again.'

'He won't talk,' Stafford grunted. 'Not unless you've something to turn the screws with.'

'Don't worry, my officers are combing his house. I'll find something.'

Since his arrest, the Whale had said precisely nothing. He hadn't asked for a solicitor. He hadn't spoken a word. He sat staring at the wall of Interview Room 3, ignoring the officers and humming contentedly under his breath.

'I'd give him another hour or two. Let him sweat a bit longer.'

'He's been here two hours, Jim.'

Stafford stood up and hitched his trousers higher across his belly. 'Trust me, two hours is nothing to him.'

'We need to locate McCracken and the man on the tape. And we need his assistance to do that.'

'Aye, I know. Don't let him know that,' Stafford warned. 'If that bastard thinks he has one up on you, he'll play it for all he's worth.'

Scully frowned, thinking. 'What about the girl, Harris? Get her in again and see if she can give us something more to use as leverage. And she might have some idea where McCracken would go.'

'I'll give her a call.' Stafford smiled. 'She's not going to like it, mind.'

'You don't seem too worried.'

'I'm with Mike on this one: I don't like her. I think she could have brought us this information a long time ago. She waited to see the lie of the land before she decided to help. And I think that, while she was waiting, at least two of the women could have been saved.' Stafford shook his head. 'That makes her as bad as McCracken, in my book.'

Hunched over his desk with a steaming cup of bitter coffee, Michael yawned. He was exhausted. He needed a decent kip and a shave. Blearily, he picked up the paper and flicked through it, his eyes skimming the print but seeing nothing.

Miriam came in, banging her hands together to warm them up. 'Hey, Mike, what's going on? Why's everyone buzzing about like blue-arsed flies?'

'Didn't you hear? We were on a dawn run this morning. McCracken and O'Connor.'

Miriam stopped in her tracks. 'Are you serious?'

'Yeah. The video we got the other day came from McCracken's home. You should see the place. He's got a room set up with videos from the floor to the ceiling.'

'Oh my God.' She leaned against the doorjamb. 'I thought it was a client attacking the girls? Why were you raiding McCracken?'

'According to our star witness, McCracken knew who was attacking the girls all along,' Michael said. 'He had him on tape. He could have saved those women.'

'Oh my God.'

'What's the big shock? What can you expect from someone like him?'

'Have you brought him in?'

'No. We missed the bastard – can you believe it? He arrived as I was getting the evidence bags out of the car. Legged it as soon as he clapped eyes on me.' Michael's jaw bunched; he didn't notice the relief on Miriam's face. 'If he'd only got there two fucking minutes earlier, I'd have had him … We got O'Connor, though, so it won't take us long to get McCracken. You know what that lot are like – no honour among thieves; he'll be spilling his guts before lunchtime.'

'That's great,' Miriam said feebly. 'I hope so.'

'Oh, don't worry,' Michael said, 'McCracken's not going to wiggle out of this one. They have him for withholding evidence and obstruction, not to mention the actual tapes and the prostitution charges. And we found over a kilo of what I assume is cocaine in his bloody hot press, of all places. Course, we won't know for sure until after the toxicology report, but I'd say McCracken's days are well and truly numbered.'

'Great.' Miriam forced a smile. 'Well, I'd better get on – I've got a ton of paperwork to do. And I'm not exactly in Stafford's good books at the moment.'

'Don't worry about that.' Michael smiled at her. It was true: ever since she had kept Barbara Sinnott to herself, Stafford had been treating her like shit. 'If we get McCracken, he'll forgive just about anything.'

'Yeah, that's great.' Miriam fled. She had to find McCracken. If he was brought in, he'd hang her out to dry.

'What do you mean, she's not bleeding there? Where the fuck is she, then?'

'As I've already told you, sir, Miss Harris wasn't in yesterday and she won't be coming in today,' Flora said coldly. This man was either very stupid or plain rude, or both. 'She is unwell.'

'She's not un-fucking-anything! So where the fuck is she?'

Flora sighed heavily and considered slamming the phone down. This was the second time this moron had called – and it was only half-nine. For some reason he seemed to think she was lying.

'If you would like to leave a message, I would be delighted to pass it on.'

'Tell her it's Paul. She'll talk to me. Go and get her.'

'You don't seem to understand, sir. Miss Harris is not here. By "She hasn't come in today," I mean she's not in the building.'

'Don't you get fucking lippy with me, you cunt!' Tricky screeched.'I'll come down there and slit your fucking—'

Flora hung up. If Emma Harris did show up, Flora would have a word with her about the scum she kept company with.

The phone rang again. Warily she snatched it up. 'Acton and Pierce Limited,' she said, holding it away from her ear in case of another outburst. 'How may I help you?'

'Hello. I need to speak to Emma Harris, please,' said a much calmer voice.

'Did you call a minute ago?' Flora asked suspiciously.

'No, I didn't.'

'Miss Harris hasn't arrived yet. May I take a message?'

'What time does she normally get in?'

'Who is this?'

'Detective Inspector Jim Stafford.'

Flora grimaced. 'Detective. Emma should have been here at nine, but as yet there's no sign of her. Nor was she here yesterday.'

'I'm not the only one looking for her this morning, eh?'

Flora ignored that; it was none of his business who rang. 'Can I give her a message, Detective?'

'Get her to give me a call as soon as she gets in. She knows the number. It's important I speak to her ASAP. Got me?'

'Of course, Detective.'

Flora jotted down the message and wondered what sort of trouble Emma was in. She couldn't decide which of the two phone calls she had found more disconcerting – the lout, or that wretched policeman.

Stafford hung up. 'She's not in work. And she didn't turn up yesterday, either. I'll try her at her house – no, better still, I'll send someone round there.'

'Do that. I'm going to get a cup of tea; do you want one?' Scully was still trying to get his head around some of the things he had seen that morning. Perhaps Stafford had a point: perhaps attending courses was no substitute for seeing the reality. He was beginning to see that perhaps Stafford had a use after all.

'Sure. Milk, two sugars.'

Stafford hurried off to find Michael, who he knew would jump at the chance to drag Harris in. As he strolled down the hall, he whistled tunelessly. It was amazing what ruining a pimp's day could do for a man's humour.

Tricky tried to stretch his legs in the driver's seat and groaned at the cramp in his calf muscles. He was waiting across the street from Emma's house behind the wheel of a clapped-out Fiesta, the only car he'd been able to borrow from his brother at such short notice. It was risky, but he couldn't think of anywhere else to go. His head throbbed and he thought longingly of the painkillers back at his house.

His mobile phone rang, and he checked the number before answering. The cops had been calling him all morning, even leaving messages telling him to turn himself in, the cheeky bastards. How had they got that warrant?

It was Miriam.

'Paul?'

He was glad she sounded scared. Someday he was going to hang this bitch out to dry.

'Some fucking use you turned out to be.'

'What?'

'You should've warned me they were going to hit my gaff.'

'I didn't know,' Miriam snapped. 'They told me nothing about it.'

'Oh, sure. You think I'm fucking stupid? I know

you're trying to dig yourself out of the shite, but you can't. I'm telling you, if I go down I'm taking you with me.'

'I don't know anything about the raid,' Miriam said. 'They're after you because of the video. *You* should have warned *me* about that.'

'Which bleeding video?' Tricky rolled his eyes. 'They've got nearly five hundred belonging to me. And that's not why they came – they didn't know about the tapes before they went inside. Don't bother trying to fucking wriggle out of this.'

'They knew after your friend showed them! You should have told me that fucking bitch had—'

'What are you on about, you stupid bitch?' he growled, bewildered. 'What friend?'

'Harris! You said we could trust her – and now look what's happened! She brought in the video, the one showing the attack on the girl. They're looking for Carla Bannion right fucking now!'

Tricky forgot about the pain in his head. For a moment he forgot about breathing. He forgot about the business, he forgot about the gardaí, he forgot everything but Emma's face.

'Paul? Paul! Are you there, damn it?'

Tricky rested his head against the ripped steering-wheel and tried to control the shake in his hands. 'Yeah,' he said slowly. 'I'm here.'

'Look, I have to go. You're on your own with this one. Half the station is looking for you. They think you knew who the killer was all along. She told them you knew him. This is fucking serious shit.'

'I'll call you later.' He stared across the street at his lover's house. There was a rushing sound in his ears.

Emma had brought in a video? Why would she do that?

'No, don't call me later,' Miriam whispered furiously. 'Don't call me ever again. This—'

He switched the phone off and stared at Emma's door, expecting her to come out any minute.

She had brought a video to the cops.

'You fucking back-stabbing cunt.'

His hands shook as he fumbled for his cigarettes. He lit one and tried to breathe normally. His left eye twitched uncontrollably. Inhaling deeply, he sat staring at the dashboard, trying to make sense of what Miriam had told him.

Why wasn't Emma in work?

Where was she?

Where was his money?

38

Stafford, Scully and Michael were huddled around Stafford's desk in his cramped, cluttered office, deciding what to do about Emma Harris.

'It's a good job you found that address,' Stafford said. 'We need her to tell us where McCracken is – and, from what I can tell, she's cleared out.'

'I told you I didn't trust her.' Michael shook his head. 'I knew she'd be nowhere to be found. Emma Harris is more involved in this case than she's letting on. We should have held her when we had the chance.'

'With what?' Scully asked. 'She didn't have to come to us at all.' Scully laced his hands behind his head and leaned back in the chair. 'Where is this house, Mike?'

Michael dug in his pocket and pulled out the slip of paper. 'It's in Carlow. Here's the address.'

Scully glanced at Stafford. 'What do you think, Jim?'

Stafford shrugged. 'Try it. She hasn't turned up for work, and there's no sign of her at the house here in Dublin. She's hiding out somewhere.'

'I can take a car and be there in an hour,' Michael offered.

'Do it,' said Scully. 'I'm going to have another word with O'Connor. He might feel like getting some things off his chest by now. And I've received a call from one of our men. Seems they found a syringe wrapped in a towel in his house – a syringe with traces of blood on it, no less. The lab has it now.'

Stafford frowned. 'Didn't he tell us he hated junkies?'

'That he did.' Scully nodded. 'Mike, you head for Carlow. Find Harris and bring her in.'

'Take somebody with you,' Stafford said. 'And be careful; for all we know, McCracken could be with her.'

'I'll take Gerry Cullen.'

'Let us know how you get on.'

'Yes, sir.'

'Smart fellow,' Scully remarked when Michael had left. 'Good to see someone working on his own initiative – getting her address like that. Shows he's thinking on his feet.'

Stafford didn't mention that it had been his idea. Scully probably wouldn't have liked that so much. 'He's a good man – sharp, doesn't miss much. People trip up around him because he looks so bloody laid-back. But I'm telling you, very little slips past him.'

Tricky's bladder finally forced him into action. As soon as the cop car pulled away from Emma's house, he eased himself out of the Fiesta and scurried across the street. Hopping over the side gate, he crept stealthily around to the back of the townhouse.

All of the blinds were down. He tried the back door; locked. He slipped off his jacket and wrapped it around his arm. Ears strained to catch any sound, he quickly smashed a glass panel in the door and let himself into the house. He tensed, waiting for the alarm to wail, exhaling deeply when it didn't.

He stood in Emma's kitchen and listened. The house felt empty.

He checked the rooms downstairs first, then climbed the stairs. He went into the bathroom, took a long piss and checked his watch. He was astonished to see it was twelve-fifteen. He'd been stuck in that shit-heap of a car for almost three hours, waiting for the bitch to show.

Tricky stared at his face in the bathroom mirror. He looked like shit, and he felt as bad as he looked. His skin was grey from lack of sleep and his eyes were bloodshot. He felt like he was going to have a stroke. His money; she had access to his money. What had she said – leave it to her? He pushed that thought back down and opened the medicine cabinet to find some painkillers.

'What the fuck—'

The cabinet was empty.

Tricky raced into the bedroom. The bed was made, all the furniture where it was supposed to be. He flung open the wardrobe. Only a few discarded items of clothing remained. Frantically he yanked open the drawers beside the bed. Gone – everything was gone.

Tricky backed away and sat down heavily on the bed. He moaned and dropped his head in his hands. He fought not to vomit.

She could be anywhere. He closed his eyes and thought back to the last conversation he'd had with her. He couldn't remember anything unusual. She'd been the same devious bitch as always.

Where was she? Where would she have gone?

It was one o'clock by the time Michael found the house. It was two miles outside Carlow town, up a long and muddy lane, slap bang in the middle of nowhere. The nearest neighbours were over a mile away. This was the last place he would expect to find Emma Harris.

The car juddered over another pothole, spraying muck across the bonnet. A line of rooks flew overhead, screaming into the cold air.

'Bloody hell, how can anyone live like this?' Gerry complained, as the car skidded from one side of the lane to the other. 'Welcome to rural bloody Ireland.'

At the top of the lane, a squat whitewashed farmhouse sat in a cobbled yard. Opposite the sagging front porch was a large pond, surrounded by barns and sheds. It was a typical farmhouse, nothing fancy, but someone had planted window-boxes and raised flowerbeds outside the front door. A brand-new satellite dish gleamed on the roof, and the curtains were snow-white. A black-and-white collie barked furiously at their arrival; a dark-green Land Rover indicated someone was home.

Michael unbuckled his seat-belt. 'Let's knock and see who's in.'

'What about the dog?' Gerry eyed the collie nervously. He didn't like dogs and they didn't like him.

'I don't mind the ones who bark; it's the silent ones that worry me.'

'They all worry me.' Gerry got out of the car and fell in slightly behind Michael. The collie bared his teeth between barks and lowered his head; Gerry saw his hackles rising.

'I don't know about this, Mike. He looks damn serious to me.'

'Easy, lad! Lie down.' The shout came from across the yard. Gerry turned his head slowly and was relieved to see a tall, sandy-haired man in his late thirties watching them. The man stood next to the open bonnet of a large John Deere tractor, wiping his hands on an oily rag.

'Good guard dog,' Michael called over. 'Does he bite?'

'Dunno. Never tried him.' The man shrugged. 'He might, though – if he was pushed, like.'

He threw the rag into an open toolbox and strode across the yard with an easy lope. 'What can I do for you?' He was taller than Michael and his arms were roped with muscle. He had a gentle face, intelligent and good-humoured.

'I'm Detective Sergeant Michael Dwyer. This is Sergeant Gerry Cullen.'

'From Dublin, are you?' The tall man frowned slightly. 'I'm Seamus Doherty. What can I do for you fellas? What brings you down this way?'

'Is this your farm, Mr Doherty?' Michael asked.

'It is.'

'Mr Doherty, we're trying to trace a woman who's been helping us with an ongoing investigation,' Michael said carefully. 'Her car is registered at this address.'

'At this address?'

'Yes. Are you the sole occupant?'

Seamus Doherty broke into a grin. 'Well now, there's the missus and three kids, but I doubt Moira's been helping you out.'

Michael sighed. He should have known this would be a complete waste of time.

'Come on into the house,' Seamus called over his shoulder, 'you can have a word with the missus. She might be able to help you out on this one.' The collie wagged his tail at his master's approach, but kept a sharp eye on the interlopers. Michael and Gerry exchanged glances and followed Seamus to the door, edging past the dog.

Seamus pulled off his boots in the porch. 'The missus will make you a cup of tea.'

'There's no need—' Michael began, but Seamus had decided they were staying, and that was that.

Moira Doherty was almost as tall as her husband. She was slim and pretty, with a mop of bouncy dark hair and a smattering of freckles across her nose. She greeted the two gardaí as if she'd known them all her life. She fussed and apologised for the mess of her spotless kitchen, ignored their apologies and made them tea.

Michael and Gerry, growing more uncomfortable about intruding, sat meekly at the kitchen table. A solid little boy about nine months old lay in a bouncer in front of the cooker, chewing on a string of plastic blocks. He had dark hair like his mother and his huge eyes followed their every move.

'They're trying to find a girl whose car is registered here,' Seamus said.

'A car?' Moira said, passing Gerry a cup. Michael was about to apologise again for the intrusion when her face froze.

'Oh, no … is it Emma? Has something happened to her?' Her hand fluttered up to her face and she sat down next to her husband. 'Is she all right?'

Michael put his cup down and kept his voice neutral. 'You know Emma?'

'Of course I do,' Moira said, her voice full of concern. 'Don't say something's happened to her! It has, hasn't it?'

'What's your relationship with Emma?' Michael asked carefully. He didn't want to say too much. It was obvious this couple had no idea why the police would be interested in Emma Harris.

Seamus shook his head, puzzled. 'Relationship? We don't have a relationship with her, exactly. We know her, like, both her and the sister.' He lifted his arm and waved it around the room. 'Sure, we bought this place from them over a year ago.'

Michael was surprised. 'You bought this place? From her?'

'Well, from both of them. After their parents died, God rest their souls. What else would two young ones do with a big place like this? It was sitting on the market for a year before that. They could hardly run it themselves. That's probably why the car is registered here. She mustn't have got round to changing it.'

'It's a Datsun.'

'Ah.' Moira and Seamus nodded in sudden understanding. 'Sure, that old thing's still up the back,' Seamus said. 'I must get someone to get rid of it. Sure, you couldn't drive it; it's been off the road years. Probably an old banger their dad bought to teach the girls how to drive.'

Michael took out his notebook. 'I didn't realise Emma had a sister,' he said. 'That's probably where she's gone. I don't suppose you'd have an address for her?'

'Is there something wrong?' Moira asked again in confusion. 'If something happened to Emma … oh, God, poor Amanda would be devastated. Those girls have suffered enough – losing both their parents at once like that … it was terrible. Please, Detective, will you not tell us what's happened?'

Michael raised his head, and the manic look on his face made Gerry nervous. Moira edged closer to her husband.

'Emma Harris has a sister called Amanda?' he asked.

Moira reached for her husband's hand. 'I ... I thought – well—'

'I think you've got your wires crossed there somewhere, Detective,' Seamus said mildly. 'We don't know any Emma Harris. The girl we're talking about is called Emma, all right, but her name's Harrington – Emma Harrington.'

Tricky lay flat on Emma's bed and stared at the ceiling. The gardaí were looking for him. The Whale was with the cops. The only girl he'd ever trusted had sold him out and was nowhere to be found. And without her, he couldn't get access to his own money. Without money, he couldn't get away. So what the fuck was he going to do?

He needed to find Emma. Whatever she was up to, he needed to find her right now. He would deal with the gardaí later.

Gingerly holding his head, he crawled off the bed and checked every room again. Most of her stuff was still there, so she couldn't have gone far. Maybe she was lying low in a hotel somewhere. Maybe this was all a horrible mistake. Grogan was probably making shit up, trying to push shit onto Emma. It had to be something like that.

He picked up the phone in the sitting room and

scanned through Emma's call list, hoping to find a clue to where she might have gone. Maybe she'd made a reservation in the Shelbourne; it was her favourite hotel in Dublin.

The last number flashed up, and Tricky broke out in a cold sweat. He pulled out his mobile, switched it on and scrolled down through his contact list until he found the number he was looking for. He had listed it under 'cunt'. He checked it against the number on Emma's phone.

His legs failed him, and he collapsed onto her sofa. He stared at the phone and thought of the tape she'd brought to the police. Without realising what he was doing, he picked up the phone and hurled it across the room. It bounced off the far wall with such force that a chunk of plaster cracked and crumbled to the floor.

The fucking bitch.

He'd have to make one more trip to his brother's house.

39

Scully walked down the hall towards the interview room where Anthony O'Connor was patiently waiting to be released. He met an irritable Ed Cairns outside the door.

'Has he asked for a solicitor yet?'

'No, sir. He hasn't said a word.'

Scully waved a sheet of paper. 'Let's see if he feels like talking now. Does he know his rights?'

Ed nodded. 'He's going with his right to remain silent.'

'We'll see about that.'

Scully opened the door and stepped inside.

'Anthony!' he said jovially, pulling out a chair. 'Well, I never; we meet again.'

The Whale ignored him. He was wearing black combats and a skin-tight T-shirt, and he didn't look even slightly bothered about being in the station.

'This is some predicament you've got yourself in to.' Scully glanced through the papers he had brought with him. 'Blackmail, living off immoral earnings, assault … quite the list, on top of your old convictions. Doesn't look good, Anthony.' He shook his head sadly. 'Doesn't look good.'

The Whale fixed his eyes somewhere over Scully's head.

'Of course, it's not you we're interested in – you know that. But we can't help you if you won't help yourself.'

O'Connor yawned, scratched his balls and refolded his arms.

'I can see you're not too interested at the moment.' Scully smiled nastily. 'I'll come back in a while, and maybe we'll make some progress then.' He rose to leave. 'One other thing. The night Barbara Sinnott died – I can't remember, did you have an alibi for that night?'

O'Connor didn't move a muscle, but his eyes flickered.

'You see, it's strange. You told us how much you hate junkies, and yet we found a syringe at your house. Wrapped in a towel, partially buried in amongst your rubbish.'

The eyes flickered rapidly. The Whale scratched at his scar.

'Not to worry; we should be able to identify whose blood it is any minute now. Labs are very quick these days. I mean, we already know that it contained heroin – high-grade stuff, too.' Scully grinned and waved the report in his hand. 'Can you not remember where you were, Anthony?'

A muscle twitched high up in O'Connor's jaw, and his pale eyes snapped towards Scully.

'What's the matter, Anthony? Cat got your tongue?'

'I want to see my solicitor,' O'Connor said through clenched teeth. 'I'm saying nothing until he's here. I've been set up.'

Scully's grin widened. 'Of course you have. We'll call him straight away.'

Stafford wasn't interested. 'We don't need her, Mike. O'Connor's talking his mouth off now that Scully has him on the ropes. With the syringe, we have a lot of leverage. He's a rat on a sinking ship, dying to pin everything on the other fucker.' The phone crackled with static. 'Mike? You there?'

Michael shot past a lorry full of cattle and hurtled down the road towards the motorway. 'Sir, didn't you hear me? Amanda Harrington and Emma Harris are sisters! They deliberately lied to us all along, both of them. Harrington told me she had no family at all. Now why would she lie about something like that? I'm telling you, there's something strange going on.'

'Of course it's strange!' Stafford roared. 'But what do you want me to do? Arrest them for being related?'

'Something's not right,' Michael said, exasperated. 'One claims to hate McCracken more with a passion, and the other works with him. Why would Emma Harris work for the man who, by all accounts, blackmailed and pimped her own sister? We're missing something.'

'Emma Harris – or whatever the hell her name is – brought us the tape, Mike. If it wasn't for her, we wouldn't have the evidence to arrest McCracken in the first place.'

'But why? Why did she bring it to us?'

'To screw McCracken because he pimped her sister!'

'So why didn't she come forward sooner? She must have known he was taping the girls before now; she could have handed him to us any time. Why wait? Why wait until we had her backed into a corner?'

'To save her own hide? I don't know, and right this minute I don't give a shit. Let it go, Mike. We've got other things to worry about — like finding the man on the video. That's our priority now, got me? We can look into the sisters afterwards if you want. For now, we concentrate on finding McCracken and the man on the tape. And we can start by interviewing Carla Bannion, the first victim. We got an address on her at last.'

Behind Stafford, Miriam sat frozen at her desk. While Stafford was still talking, she grabbed her coat and slipped out unnoticed.

Michael floored the accelerator. 'He doesn't want to bloody know,' he snapped.

Gerry shrugged uneasily. 'Well, Mike ... I mean, what have we got? Two sisters — they might not even get along.'

Michael shook his head vehemently. 'She dropped McCracken into our laps too easily. Dammit to hell!' He slammed his hand on the steering-wheel. 'I knew there was something familiar about her. I can't believe I didn't twig it before now. Jesus, and I call myself a detective.'

Gerry kept quiet. He didn't want to find Amanda Harrington. He was afraid she might mention his name.

Two hours later, under advice from his solicitor, Anthony 'the Whale' O'Connor gave a revised statement. Finally, Scully had something concrete to go on.

No, O'Connor had had no idea McCracken was taping the girls and the clients. He was only the driver and security man, for the protection of the girls. He couldn't be held responsible for a perverted fuck like McCracken. No, he'd had no idea the man on the tape was the killer everyone was looking for. But the man had 'fallen' when O'Connor evicted him from the apartment that night; and, as a result, he had 'forgotten' his bag and his wallet. The sports bag 'might' be in among the evidence the gardaí had collected from O'Connor's home that morning. O'Connor claimed he had been holding on to it in case the man ever tried to press false charges against him.

Of course, if he had ever suspected the man was the murderer, he would have informed the police immediately. The thought had never crossed his mind. He claimed he knew nothing about any murders or blackmail, but he readily agreed that McCracken was indeed the type of man who might get someone to do his dirty work for him. O'Connor also agreed that McCracken was a man who would think nothing of having someone – say, someone like Barbara Sinnott – killed to protect his interests, and then putting the needle in Anthony O'Connor's rubbish to frame him.

When pressed about his involvement in the death of Barbara Sinnott, O'Connor admitted he had been at her flat that night. He insisted he had been meant to wait outside while McCracken went in, but had rushed into the flat, against McCracken's wishes, when he realised his boss intended to harm the girl. He also claimed that McCracken had been 'coked off his head' and that he, O'Connor, had wanted to bring the girl to a hospital, but that McCracken had warned him, with threats, not to try it. He said he had gone back later that same evening, only to find her dead on the floor. He said he felt terrible about it.

Stafford burst out laughing when Scully came into his office and told him the Whale's story.

'He says McCracken threatened him? That little prick wouldn't be alive today if he'd so much as raised his voice to Anthony O'Connor.'

'I know that,' Scully said. 'Let him say what he wants. When we catch McCracken, we can compare stories. Meanwhile, we need to see this bag O'Connor had – see if there's anything in it that might help identify the man on the tape.'

'I wonder why O'Connor isn't giving us a name, especially when he's in this much shit.'

'O'Connor's claiming he knew nothing about this, it must have been something McCracken set up alone,' Scully said. 'He can't admit to knowing the man's name if he wants us to believe he never had any involvement with the murders.'

'I can check out the sports bag if you like,' Stafford offered.

Scully paused on his way out. 'I realise you helped with Harris,' he said stiffly. 'But don't think I've forgotten that you ordered an officer to withhold information. Frankly, you have jeopardised this investigation quite enough, thank you. I won't need your help from here.'

Stafford was stunned. 'What do you mean, jeopardised—'

'I mean exactly what I say,' Scully snapped. 'Believe me, this will not look good in my report.'

'You two-faced, conceited bastard!' Stafford jumped to his feet. 'Without my help you wouldn't have a pot to piss in, and you know it. I brought you Emma Harris, I told you about McCracken – now you want to fuck me over a phone call?'

Scully shrugged. 'It's nothing personal, Jim, but you hindered my investigation and I can't ignore it. You were given express orders to defer to me, and you couldn't stand that, could you?'

'After all the help I've given you.'

'Don't worry, I'll mention that too. You see, I don't just offer whatever information suits me.' Scully smiled coldly. 'You know what I think? I think you had hopes of catching this killer yourself

– capitalising on your vice connections. I think it bothered you that I was brought in to head this investigation. Am I right?'

'Get out of my fucking office,' Stafford said in a low voice.

'I realise Brennan expects us to work together,' Scully snapped, 'so tell you what. You go talk to Carla Bannion – I'd appreciate it if you could do that today – and leave the actual detective work to me.' He walked out and closed the door.

Stafford stared at the glass door and slumped back in his chair. He felt the dull ache in his back kick in. Scully was going to betray him after all, the arrogant bastard. Stafford picked up a pencil and snapped it in half.

The doorbell buzzed. Amanda checked through the spy-hole, then flung the door open. 'What the hell took you so long? I've been worried sick.'

Emma scowled. 'Grab one of these fucking bags and don't stand there like an eejit.'

Amanda glanced at the assortment of bags at Emma's feet. 'I told you to bring essentials!'

'These are essentials!'

Amanda grabbed the handle of the nearest suitcase and hauled it inside. It weighed a tonne.

'I like what you've done to the place,' Emma said, looking around. 'Very minimalist.' The apartment was empty. The furniture had been expertly packed up by a removals firm and sent abroad the day before; the only things left were the phone and some empty cardboard boxes. 'What the fuck are we supposed to sit on? Or sleep on?'

'I don't think we should stay here anyway – it's not safe. We can go to a hotel,' Amanda snapped. 'Don't start, Emma; my nerves are bad enough as it is, without you complaining.'

'Sorry.' Suddenly Emma hugged her sister hard. 'We're nearly home free, Amanda, so stop looking so fucking serious!'

Amanda pulled away from her. 'I am serious. I want to know what you said to the cops.'

'Amanda, let it go, it doesn't matter. All I can say is, that fucker Tricky is going to be pretty busy for a while.'

Amanda frowned. 'Did you give them the second flat in Red Hot and Blue? The name of the guy Tricky's getting the European girls from? What?'

Emma's face darkened. 'All right! Let's just say we had a tête-à-tête about how Tricky was the genius behind the murder.'

Amanda stepped back. 'What are you talking about? Why would they think that?'

Emma gave her a sideways grin. 'Tricky showed me a tape a while ago. That gave me an idea.'

'What tape?' Amanda felt a tremor begin in the pit of her stomach. 'Emma, what tape are you talking about?'

'Never mind – it doesn't matter now.'

'But—'

'Amanda, just stop. Look, we needed him out of the way while we got the hell out of Dodge, and now he's out of the way. So get off my fucking back.'

'What about O'Connor?'

'If they searched properly, he won't be going anywhere either,' Emma said, grinning. She had dug out the syringe Tricky had buried in the skip and replanted it in the Whale's wheelie bin the day before. It had been risky and stupid, but worth it.

'Emma, I need to know what you said to the c—' Amanda stopped. Her sister looked exhausted and she hadn't the heart to demand details and explanations. All that could wait; there would be plenty of time.

'Come here,' she said, and put her arms around her sister.

Scully discarded his yellow tie, donned surgical gloves and, with Ed's help, searched through the evidence bags they had brought from Anthony O'Connor's house. As is often the case, the last bag they checked held what they were looking for.

'Sir?' Ed held up the sports bag. It was made of plain, heavy canvas, with two short white handles and a white strip on the side. Scully checked it against a video still; it matched the bag on the tape.

'That's the one. Let's have a look.'

Ed placed the bag gently on the table, and Scully unzipped it and peered inside.

'Bingo,' he muttered.

'What?'

Scully pulled out a dark-green headscarf trimmed with a gold Celtic design. He sniffed it. 'Mothballs,' he said softly.

'Sir?'

But Scully had dropped the headscarf and was rummaging through the rest of the bag. 'Take a look at this,' he said excitedly.

He upended the bag onto the table, and Ed caught his breath as rolls of cling-film spilled out. From the bottom of the bag, a worn yellow scrap of paper fluttered to the floor. Ed picked it up and held it to the light.

'What is it?' Scully asked.

'I think it's a prescription form, sir.'

'For what? For whom?'

'I can't read the handwriting.' Ed squinted at it, shrugged and handed it to Scully, who studied it carefully.

'I can't read it either, but look – the doctor's letterhead is on the top of the page.' The print was faded, but still just readable. 'Dr D. Lynch, 120 Lower Dorset Street.'

He stared at the paper and offered a silent prayer of thanks.

'Ed, those unidentified calls to Sandy Walsh – where did they come from?'

Ed began to grin. 'A phone box on Dorset Street.'

'I knew the bastard would make a mistake. Get

me a car and let's find out if the good doctor can read his own bloody handwriting.'

Stafford knocked on the door and waited. This was definitely the right address; he knocked again, louder this time. Imagine that fucker Scully claiming he'd jeopardised the investigation – after the big friendly act earlier, too …

'She's not there.'

Stafford stared at the blue-haired woman in front of him. She was about seventy if she was a day. She was gazing up at him through eyes magnified a thousand times by milk-bottle glasses. 'Miss Bannion?'

'Yes – she's not there. Her cat's been crying for days now.' The old woman shook her head. 'I told the caretaker. Terrible, leaving dumb animals. I would have looked after it if she'd asked me; I wouldn't have minded.'

Stafford sighed. 'I see.' Another fucking waste of his time. And now Scully would no doubt dream up more pointless errands for him. 'Well, I'll leave her a card.'

'I told the caretaker about the cat. I found it. I told the caretaker that, too; but, you know' – she leaned in closer, and Stafford got a whiff of Oil of Olay and talc – 'he doesn't want to do anything except smoke cigarettes in the lobby. I told him the light here was broken, too, but he wasn't inter-ested. Very dangerous, it is. Not that I go out at night. No, I don't.'

Stafford took out his Garda Síochána card and filled in the time he'd called and his number. He bent down to slide it under the door and caught the odour, the faint, unmistakeable odour of death.

He straightened up. 'Excuse me, what is your name?'

The old lady smiled, delighted he was taking such an interest. 'I'm Mrs Finch. I live down the hall. Number 11.'

'Mrs Finch, how long has the occupant's cat been crying?'

'Oh, a few days now.' She frowned and the millions of lines on her forehead shifted. 'I did tell the caretaker, you know. I'm not cruel.'

'No, Mrs Finch, you're not.' Stafford pulled out his mobile and called for backup. He asked for an ambulance, too, but he already knew Carla Bannion would never be a living witness for the gardaí.

40

Dr Lynch, who was busy but friendly, did indeed understand his own handwriting – and, better still, he remembered the patient for whom he had written the prescription, even though he had written it more than a year before. He remembered because he had thought it strange that Mrs Eileen White, who was dying of leukaemia, should have ceased to attend his surgery and refused all attempts to secure her a hospital bed.

'She was a deeply religious woman, Inspector. She told me once that God would cure her – that her cancer was a simply a sin of the flesh and if she prayed hard enough He would take it away.'

'She sounds like a nut-job,' Ed said softly.

'Did you not try to convince her otherwise?' Scully asked, throwing a dirty look Ed's way.

'Of course.' Dr Lynch scratched his grey head with the end of a well-chewed Biro. 'But I'm a GP. I can't force her to go to hospital. She was perfectly aware of her diagnosis.'

'As my colleague says, she doesn't sound very *compos mentis*.'

'Being religious hardly constitutes being mentally

unfit, Detective,' Dr Lynch said coldly. He didn't like the implication that he hadn't cared about his patient.

'What about family? Did she have family? Oh, and we'll need her address, please.'

'I believe she had a son.' Dr Lynch tapped Eileen White's name into the iMac on his desk. 'Strange young chap,' he said. 'Very quiet, and very devoted to her. He used to sit outside in the waiting room every time she came here. Eileen called him her little gift from heaven.'

'What age was he?'

'Allen? Oh, in his thirties, I would think … Ah, here we are. Mrs Eileen White, 3 Culogh Road. That's only around the corner from here, actually.'

'Thank you.' Scully rose to go. 'One other thing – is there a Mr White?'

Dr Lynch shook his head. 'I don't remember her ever mentioning a husband, but she's down here as "Mrs".'

Scully nodded his thanks and left.

It took them only five minutes to reach Culogh Road. Ed parked the car and checked the address. The house was a dump; there were slates missing from the roof, the gutters were falling off, and the garden was overgrown and strewn with litter. Although it was half-three in the afternoon, all the curtains were drawn.

'This is it, sir. They don't keep it very well, do they?'

Scully gazed at the little house. It stuck out like

a scabby thumb beside the neat homes on either side of it.

'Let's go.'

Scully banged on the peeling front door with his fist. Nothing.

'What now, sir?'

Scully glanced quickly around and turned back to Ed with a gleam in his eye. 'Ed, I think that door's open.'

Ed rattled the handle. 'No, sir, it's—'

'You're not listening. It's open. Try it again. Give it a bit of welly; I think it's sticking.' Scully cleared his throat and looked away.

Ed nodded. In less than a minute, they were inside the grubby hall of Allen and Eileen White's home.

'Jesus!' Ed gasped. 'What's that smell?'

'Don't know – air-freshener or something.' Scully glanced around. On the hall table, bills were piled up behind a huge plaster statue of the Virgin Mary. He picked up one, a final reminder notice; it was dated five months previously.

'Ed, you head down the back and check if anyone's at home. I'm going to have a look upstairs.'

This was his mission. He would recreate her, and God would make her whole again. He pushed his way down the busy street, ignoring the angry comments of passers-by as he shoved them out of his way. A few shouted half-heartedly after him, but he took no notice. He was a strange sight, blundering along the street, his hair shorn in patches, mumbling and clutching a sports bag tightly to his chest.

He didn't see the stares. He was on a mission. There would be no distractions – not this time. He wouldn't allow it.

The stench of rot and decay became overpowering as Scully made his way slowly up the creaking stairs.

'Mrs White? Mrs Eileen White?' Maybe she was too sick to come to the door, too weak to answer. He didn't want to scare the wits out of her by bursting into her bedroom unannounced.

Upstairs on the landing, the smell was stronger. The windows at the back of the house also had their curtains drawn, and Scully found the gloom and silence disturbing. He tried to pull one back, only to discover that the material was nailed to the window-frame.

He rapped on the first door and called out again; when he got no answer, he pushed the door open.

It took a few moments for his eyes to become accustomed to the gloom. It was obviously a child's room. The walls were covered with old-fashioned Disney-character wallpaper, a type Scully hadn't seen in almost twenty years. A small cot was pushed against the far wall, its grubby sheets trailing on the ground; beside it was a cheap 70s dressing-table, covered in a thick film of dust. Scully quietly crossed the floor and pulled open the top drawer. Bundles of Mass cards and more religious statues lay inside.

He was about to check the next drawer when something caught his eye. He bent down and pulled at the object sticking out from under the bed. It was a heavy-duty toolbox, out of place in this childlike room. Scully flipped the lid open. The top tray was like a pharmacy; it was full of tablets, plasters, masking tape and empty prescription sheets matching the one he and Ed had found earlier. Now he knew why Eileen White had had no need to return to Dr Lynch's surgery. She could write out her own prescriptions for the next year or so if she wanted to.

Scully lifted the top tray off and felt adrenaline shoot through his veins. If he wasn't mistaken, he was looking at Sandy Walsh's notebook and Tessa Byrne's handbag.

'Holy shit.'

Scully dropped the tray and jumped back so quickly he cracked his hip against the dresser. 'Ed, for God's sake! Are you trying to give me a heart attack?'

'Sorry, sir, but the fucking smell up here ...' Ed covered his mouth with his hand and coughed. 'Find anything?'

Scully nodded. 'This is it; this is definitely our boy. What about downstairs? Any sign of the mother?'

'Nothing. You should see the state of the place. The electricity's off, and the food – what little they had in the fridge – stinks to high heaven. They haven't put the bins out in weeks, either; the rubbish is all piled up in the back hall. Place is crawling with maggots and rats. They've been putting newspaper around the doors to seal the stink in.'

Scully went back out onto the landing and into the room opposite, the bathroom. Like the rest of the house, it was filthy. There were strange dark marks dried into the enamel of the bath, and the drain was obviously blocked; thin wisps of hair floated in half an inch of blackish water. The smell was horrendous.

'What's that gunk in the bath?' Ed asked nervously. 'Jesus, it's ripe, whatever it is.' He peered over the edge of the bath and lowered his fingers towards the water.

'Leave it, Ed,' Scully said, and snatched his hand away. 'There's another room down the hall.'

'Sir, I don't mean to be questioning you or anything, but we shouldn't be in here without some kind of warrant,' Ed said softly as they moved towards the door.

'Too late for that now, lad,' Scully replied. He pushed the door open.

The stench hit them straight away, and Ed gagged. 'What the fuck?' he coughed, covering his mouth with his hand again.

It took Scully a second or two to realise what he was looking at. She sat under the picture of the Sacred Heart as though resting, the satin covers pulled neatly across her lap, a Bible under her hands.

'Jesus … Christ.'

Scully felt Ed back out of the room, and he let him go; this was no sight for any man. He stared at Eileen White, at the black sockets where her eyes should have been, the gaping dead smile of her mouth. She had passed the first stages of decomposition a long time ago; and yet the thick blonde hair under her headscarf looked clean and fresh. A horrible thought occurred to him. This was Sandy Walsh's hair.

Scully approached the bed slowly. The body was arranged with its hands folded neatly over the covers. Black leather driving gloves had been placed over them. Scully could see where her wrist bones had been wired to the tops of the gloves so they would not slip.

Allen White was a devoted son. He had tried to gather for his mother the things she needed most. Scully moved closer and shone his torch onto the corpse. The skin stretched taut across the skull was beginning to rot, but it was fresh skin, and Scully could see where White had stapled it to the sides of his mother's skull. The staples were rusting and the skin had begun to tear. The face had slipped down slightly; in another few hours it would pull free of the staples and fold away. Scully fought the urge to vomit, swallowing hard and breathing in short bursts. He stared at the blonde eyebrows. They were thin; their previous owner had obviously pencilled them in.

He had to get out of there.

'Ed,' he said softly over his shoulder. The bathroom next door, with the thick scum in the bath. He gagged at the thought of Allen White washing his dead mother and re-dressing her – not only dressing her, but recreating a body, one designed especially for her. 'Get on the phone and get the scene technicians here. We can't waste any more time. We need to find this man.'

41

Tricky waited across the street from Amanda Harrington's apartment building. He waited and watched as people came and went. In the boot of the Fiesta, a sawn-off shotgun waited with him.

'I'll ring us a taxi.' Amanda looked around the bare sitting room that had once been her pride and joy. It meant nothing to her now; she had already closed it out of her mind.

Emma, who was sitting on the kitchen counter, checked her watch. 'Maybe we'd be better off walking. We'll never get a cab at this hour.'

'Too much stuff to carry.' Amanda looked at the pile of suitcases and shook her head. 'I can't believe you brought so much stuff.'

'I left most of my stuff at the house.'

'That's your problem. You had plenty of time to move it. Half of your shit is rented anyway.' Amanda pulled out her mobile and dialled the number of the taxi company she and Marna always used for call-outs. It was engaged. 'What hotel do you want to go to?'

Emma shrugged. 'I don't care.'

'Shelbourne?'

'First place anyone would think of if they were looking for me.'

'What about the Morrison? It's only across the bridge. We could walk there.'

'The Morrison, huh? I suppose … yeah, I can slum it for a night.'

Amanda grinned. 'OK, I'll go over and make us a reservation. I feel like some air.'

'Do it over the phone.'

'Emma, it's like five minutes away.'

'Do it over the phone anyway.'

'Nobody's looking for me.'

'Do it over the phone.'

'But it won't—'

'Do it over the phone.'

Amanda stared at her sister. This was exactly what had always happened when they were kids: Emma would simply keep repeating the same thing over and over until she got her way. It had been infuriating then, and it was equally infuriating now.

'OK. I'll do it over the phone.'

While Amanda took care of the reservations, Emma rummaged through one of her bags and found her mobile. She checked her messages and let out a sigh of relief when there were none. Resting her back against the wall, she glanced around the bare room, still amazed that Amanda had managed to clear the whole apartment in less than two days.

Emma had been there exactly twice, in over two years. They couldn't take the risk of being seen together – everything had depended on there being no connection between them – and in the early days Tricky had followed her everywhere. The enforced separation had been hard, sometimes nearly unbearable. After their parents had died, they had had nothing left but each other.

'OK, we're in.' Amanda grabbed a suitcase and hauled it down the hall to the front door. 'We're going to have to share a room, but I knew you wouldn't mind.'

'Leave the bags for a few minutes. There's no rush.'

'I'll feel better when we're out of here,' Amanda called back, opening the apartment door to put the bag in the hall.

'Let's wait till it gets dark,' Emma said. Amanda didn't answer.

'Amanda?' She followed her into the hall. 'Did you—'

Amanda was walking slowly back up the hall, her head tilted back at an awkward angle, with Tricky behind her. He had her hair wrapped around his hand. Emma saw the stock of a shotgun poking out from behind her sister's jacket.

'Paul! I – how …?' The words dried in her throat.

'Shut your dirty lying mouth, you cunt!' Tricky yanked Amanda's head further back on each word. 'I worked it all out. You needed me out of the way, didn't you? *Didn't you?*'

He gave Amanda a shove and she shot forward, crashing into Emma. 'I'm sorry,' she whispered. 'I didn't see him – he … he … was waiting.'

Emma grabbed her hands and squeezed. 'It's OK. It's not your fault.'

'How fucking touching!' Tricky sneered. 'Fucking sisters. Who'd have guessed?'

'Paul, it's not what you think,' Emma said calmly, stepping towards him.

'What do I think, then? Come on!' he roared. 'Tell me – what do I fucking think?' He lunged forward, brought the gun up and smashed the stock into Emma's cheek. She cried out and crumpled to the floor.

'No! Don't you hurt her, you bastard!' Amanda leaped forward and dropped to her knees, reaching for her sister. 'Leave her alone!'

Tricky grabbed Amanda by the hair again and hauled her to her feet. 'Shut up yelling, or I'll put a bullet in her fucking head.' He kicked Emma in the side, then again in the back. 'Where's my fucking money? Don't mess me about, or I'll kill the both of you. Try me.'

'I'm looking for Paula.'

'What's your name, love?' Big Maggie looked at the wild-eyed man at the door and wondered why they always got the weirdos.

'It's John – John.'

'Come in, then, and don't be letting the warmth out.'

He darted past her. 'Thanks very much. Are you the only one working today? Is Paula here? Are there many others?'

Maggie led the way up the stairs, wiggling her arse in his face. 'Not today, love; there's only herself and myself on. But don't worry, we'll look after you.' She walked slowly, giving him a good view. The day had been slow; so far she had only made twenty-five quid for a hand-job.

'I'm on a mission.'

'Whatever you say. Are you coming from the gym?' She led him into a small, dimly lit room at the top of the stairs.

'What?'

'The bag. Are you coming from the gym or what? You look a bit out of breath.'

His eyes scanned the room quickly. There were no windows – that was good. There was a massage bench, covered with faded beach towels, and a table holding oil, talc and tissues. A big mirror had been screwed to the ceiling over the bench, for extra viewing. The room was painted red – another sign that he was on the right path.

'I have to see Paula.' He squeezed the bag close to his chest. 'She's the one I need.'

Maggie pouted and stepped closer. He noticed her sagging breasts under the revealing top and looked away.

'Relax, chicken, I won't bite,' she purred. 'I'll get her for you now. It's a quiet day, John, love –

why don't you go for a two-girl special? We'll do you a good deal.'

He backed away from her. Anger burned through him and he imagined he could smell her very skin. What was she saying – he should do both? Maybe it was another sign. Was she offering herself to him? Would two be the final sacrifice he needed? If only he wasn't so confused …

'Maybe I will.' He smoothed his hair down across his damp skull. He could feel her eyes crawling across his body and it was making him sick. 'Sometimes things change.'

'Eh … yeah. I'll get Paula and you can discuss it with her. And don't worry about anything; she'll give you a good rate.' Maggie winked and stroked his trembling arm. 'We like a bit of young blood here, and I can see you're nervous.'

42

Michael parked the car out on the street and ran into the station. Gerry, following at a more leisurely pace, watched him run up the steps three at a time. He had never seen Michael so angry. I'd hate to be in Amanda Harrington's shoes if he gets hold of her, he thought.

Michael found Stafford heading for his office with a large mug of coffee.

'There you are! I want to know why the hell you're not interested in—' Michael stopped. Something was very wrong.

'Sir, are you OK?'

'I found Carla Bannion.' Stafford raised his head and looked at Mike, his small eyes almost lost beneath his eyebrows. He leaned against the wall. 'The bastard came back and finished her off.'

'What?' Michael swallowed. 'When?'

'Few nights ago.'

'Jesus. Did you—'

'He cut off her face, Mike.' Stafford looked grey. 'The fucking bastard cut off her face and left her to bleed to death.'

Michael put out a hand and rubbed his boss's

shoulder. He'd never seen Stafford look so trauma-
tised. The lines in his face had deepened and his
eyes had lost their sparkle, as though the image
had been burned into them forever.

'Sir?'

'What?'

'Would you like to go for a proper drink?'

After a moment Stafford nodded. 'You know,
Sergeant, I'd like that very much.'

He sat on the edge of the massage bench and
waited. What the hell was keeping her? His hands
were beginning to sweat, and he didn't think he
could contain himself much longer. He needed to
get back; he had to get back to Mother. She would
wake soon, he knew it. He never left her alone
during the day.

He heard footsteps. This would have to be
quick – get the first one out of the way. He could
take his time with the second. He must stick to the
mission.

'Hi, baby. What can I do for you?' Grapevine
Paula leaned against the door-frame and stuck her
breasts out as far as she could in her skin-tight dress.

'I'm here for you.'

'Yeah? You haven't been here before, have you,
love?'

'This is my first time here.'

Paula laughed and smoothed her hands along
her body. 'And you thought you'd come to the
best? Good man – that's what I like to hear.'

'Will you help me?'

'Sure, pet, sure. You get yourself out of those clothes and I'll be back to you in a minute.' Paula held out her hand.

'How much is it?'

'Sixty quid.'

He nodded and went through the ritual of searching for the money and handing it to Paula, keeping as far from her as he could. He didn't like this one; she looked strong, and he could feel her sharp eyes burning through him.

Paula counted the money quickly. 'Are you sure this is your first time, pet? You look familiar. I'm great with faces, and I'm pretty sure I've seen you somewhere before.'

'No, it's my first time here. Please – I'm in a hurry.'

'Are you sure?' Paula stepped closer. 'I never forget a face.'

He backed up. 'I'm sure.'

'Doesn't matter, love. Get undressed and lie on the bench on your stomach; I'll be back to give you a massage in a minute.'

'Thank you.' He tried to smile. Sweat was trickling down his back.

Paula gave him one last look and backed out of the room. She went into the staff room next door, still trying to remember where she had met him before.

'What's up?' Big Maggie asked from her chair by the phone. 'Carpet-walker?'

Paula reached for her bag. 'Don't think so; he gave me the cash. I'm sure I've done him before somewhere, but he says it's his first time.' She sprayed perfume down her bra, making sure it went all over her nipples. When you had a rack like hers, everyone wanted to suck them, and nothing put a man off quicker than the taste of perfume. 'Did he seem kind of jumpy to you?'

Big Maggie shrugged and picked up a magazine. 'They all seem jumpy to me, love, specially the young 'uns. Better jumpy than cocky little bastards.'

Paula pulled off her comfy Marks & Spencers knickers, wriggled into a black thong that disappeared between the cheeks of her ample backside, popped a condom into her stocking-top and pushed up her chest.

'How do I look?'

'Like a whore,' Maggie said.

'Perfect.' Paula wriggled out the door. 'Sure, isn't that all any man wants?'

She thought she must have blacked out for a moment. The pain in her cheek was excruciating. She could hear Tricky shouting, somewhere above her. She kept her eyes closed.

'You thought you were so fucking smart, the two of you.' Tricky slapped Amanda back against the wall and spat in her face. 'Thought I'd never figure it out. Well, you thought wrong, you bitch. Nobody messes with me. Do you hear me? *No one!*'

He slapped her across the face again. Amanda's head rocked from the force of the blow and she slid down the wall, clutching at her face. Tricky yanked his mobile out of his pocket and dialled a number.

'Miriam, it's me. Yeah, you were right … What? … Listen, I'm at Harrington's place, yeah? I'll need you here … 'Cause you have to watch one of them.'

He paced back and forth across the floor. Amanda tasted blood and watched as the barrel of the gun bobbed and dipped with each step.

'Don't fucking give me that shit!' Tricky screamed. 'Get here, or, by Jaysus, you're gonna need a new fucking career, right? … I don't give a fuck! Make sure you get here, fast!'

He hung up and kept pacing. 'Fucking bitches! You're all the same – trying to screw me!'

'What are you going to do to us?' Amanda asked softly.

Tricky stopped and lifted his hand to his forehead. In his temper he had almost forgotten she was there. 'I'm going to put you fuckers in the ground,' he said. 'Only I'm gonna do it slow.' He kicked Emma again. 'Teach her a bleeding lesson, as well.'

'Always knew you were a stupid shit.' Amanda wiped her mouth with her sleeve and pushed herself unsteadily to her feet.

'Shut the fuck up.'

Amanda attempted a laugh. 'You think you're going to get away with this, Tricky? I don't—'

Tricky punched her in the stomach. Amanda doubled over and dropped to her knees as the air whooshed out of her.

'I told you to shut up, you stupid bitch,' Tricky said calmly, and punched her in the back of the head. 'Yak-fucking-yak!'

Emma slowed her breathing down and kept her eyes closed. Miriam Grogan was on her way. She heard her sister retching and made up her mind.

She was going to kill the bastard.

43

Big Maggie whispered, 'Goodbye,' hung up the phone quietly and crossed herself. She stood up on shaky legs and hurried out of the room. The call from Detective Scully had raised the hairs on her arms, but she tried to make her voice sound normal as she knocked on the door. Paula had only been in there a minute or so; she prayed she wasn't too late.

'Paula?' She knocked again, harder this time. 'Paula, you're wanted on the phone, love. It's … it's your ma. She needs to speak to you, *now*.'

She leaned her ear against the door and heard the murmur of voices; after a few seconds, the bolt was pulled back and Paula's blue eyes peeped around the door.

'Did you say my mother wants to talk to me?'

Big Maggie nodded furiously and beckoned her out. 'Yeah, she sounds really upset; she wants to talk to you right away. Right this minute, OK?'

Paula's eyes narrowed. Her mother would never ring her at work, no matter what happened.

She called over her shoulder, 'John, sweetheart, why don't you get out of those clothes? Go on, make yourself comfortable there; I'll be back to you in a second.' She slipped out of the room and closed the door.

Big Maggie grabbed her arm and dragged her to the staff room.

'Hey!' Paula tried to yank her arm back. 'Maggie, what the—'

Maggie slammed the door shut and clamped her hand over Paula's mouth. 'It's him! That's the fucker who killed Sandy! The gardaí called. They're ringing places with a description. Paula, the description – it's fucking him. I know it is. The gardaí are on their way ...' Her eyes were almost out on stalks.

Paula leaned back against the door, and the colour drained out of her face. She prised Maggie's hand off her mouth. 'Holy shit! What are we going to do?'

'Lock this door, for a start, before he gets any bleeding ideas,' Maggie whispered.

Paula shook her head. 'He'll know something's wrong. He's in there with all his clothes on, acting like butter wouldn't melt in his mouth – the prick. Fuck, Maggie, what are we going to do?'

Maggie took a step one way and then a step the other. 'Fucking hide, that's what we'll do. Lock this door; he could be in on top of us any second.'

'No, wait,' Paula snapped. 'Get me the iron bar we use to pull the shutters down.'

'What? Are you fucking nuts?' Maggie's eyes were wild with fear. 'Lock the fucking door, or I will.'

'Get the fucking bar! I've got an idea.'

Maggie backed away and reached behind the sofa for the bar. 'What are you going to do?' she whispered.

Paula snatched the bar out of her hand, gulped and blessed herself. 'I'm going to stick this through the handle of the room next door.'

'No! Don't be stupid. Let him go.' Maggie grabbed Paula by the arm, but Paula shook her hand off.

'Maggie, that guy killed Sandy, and if he gets out of there he'll kill us too. We have to keep him in next door until the cops arrive. I'll push this through; then we can lock ourselves in here.'

'No, Paula, wait – don't be—'

Paula opened the door and slipped out into the hall. She tiptoed across the dark landing to the next room, slid the bar through the handle and wedged it firmly against the doorjamb. She was moving quietly away when she saw the door jiggle and heard a roar of sheer fury from inside. Big Maggie screamed, and Paula bolted into the staff room and locked the door.

'Oh, Jaysus save us,' Maggie said softly, and slid down the wall. Paula grabbed her hand and joined her on the floor. They cowered there, listening to the client kicking the door and screaming; they could feel the vibrations as he threw himself against the door. Paula reached for her fags, lit two with a shaky hand and passed one to Maggie.

'As soon as you see the cops on the monitor, run down and let them in,' she said quietly.

'Me? Why, what'll you be doing?' Maggie stared at her suspiciously.

'Maggie, I couldn't stand up again if I tried.'

Maggie glanced down and saw that Paula's legs were shaking so hard it looked like they were attached to a motor.

Scully hit the lights and the siren and drove as fast as the heavy evening traffic would allow. He had radioed ahead, telling his men to head to all three brothels underlined in the notebook he had found at White's house. He tried Paula's phone again, but it rang out.

'Damn.'

Ed, in the passenger seat, was as white as a sheet. Scully glanced at him and felt a certain amount of pity. Ed had thrown up when Scully told him what he suspected White had done with his mother – they were sure to receive a bollocking from the crime-scene specialists about the vomit in the bathroom sink, but Scully wasn't worrying about that now. He had to find White before anyone else was hurt.

'Roll that window down if you want,' he said.

Ed did as he was told and gulped the fresh air gratefully. 'I'm sorry I was sick, sir,' he said. 'It was her head – the way he had it held on with wire … I didn't …' He closed his eyes and looked like he might throw up again.

'I know, lad, I know,' Scully said, as he turned

onto Wexford Street and mounted the path opposite Paula's place. He scanned the street for any sign of a squad car and cursed when he didn't see one. Harcourt Street was around the corner; the other gardaí could have walked down in two minutes. Typical.

'Paula, they're here.' Big Maggie jerked her head towards the monitor, and at the same moment they heard the bell ring again and again.

Maggie hauled herself to her feet and gently unlocked the door. She hesitated, terrified to step out of the room; the client was silent now, and Maggie was convinced he had freed himself and was waiting for her.

'Go on! Let them in, for Christ's sake!' Paula snapped. Big Maggie took a huge breath and ran down the stairs, expecting to feel a hand on her back any second. She opened the front door and fell into Scully's arms, gibbering with relief.

'Where is he?' Scully demanded, grabbing her by the shoulders. 'Where?'

Maggie pointed up the stairs. 'Paula – she locked him in.'

'You stay put,' Scully ordered, moving Maggie to one side. He took the stairs three at a time, with Ed behind him. Maggie considered running out onto the street; but, seeing as she was dressed in stockings, suspenders and a skirt that barely covered her arse, she decided against it and warily followed the two men back up the stairs.

'He's in there.' Paula poked her head around the staff-room door and pointed across the landing. Maggie sprinted for the staff room, and she and Paula clung to each other as Scully slid the bar out of the door-handle.

'Allen White!' Scully hammered on the door with his fist. 'This is Detective Inspector Robert Scully. I'm going to open this door now, and if you know what's good for you you'll make sure you don't give me any trouble.'

There was no response.

'Ed, stand on the other side of this door, in case he tries to make a run for it.'

Ed nodded and spread himself along the wall.

'Allen, I'm opening the door. Don't try anything funny. It's not worth it, son.' Scully slowly turned the handle, pushed the door open and peered into the gloomy room.

The young man was sitting on the bench tucked into the far corner of the room. His feet were curled under him and he was rocking back and forth, his head bent. Scully saw he had a bag clutched tightly to his chest.

He stepped into the room. 'Allen White? I'm Inspector—'

'Did they call you? Did the whores ring you?' Allen White asked. His voice was soft and childlike.

Scully moved closer. 'Why don't you drop the bag and stand up?'

'I'll never fix her now, will I?' He whimpered softly. 'How am I supposed to fix her without them?'

'Stand up and drop the bag.'

'It's my fault, you know. Sins of the flesh are visited on the weak. She said I was weak, and I … I'd been fornicating with whores. She said I made her sick. I did. I made her sick.' He looked up and offered Scully a disarming, shy smile. His left eye rolled. 'I did and the whores did – they always know. She told me it was God's way of testing her, but it wasn't. He was testing *me*. And I failed.'

Scully jumped a little as there was a loud hand-clap behind him, and Paula's excited voice said, 'That's it! That's where I remember the little prick from. The Red Stairs. We barred the weirdo a few years ago 'cause he kept hassling us to dress up in smelly old clothes and shit. Always going on about God. I told you I knew his face, Maggie, didn't—'

Paula's voice triggered something in Allen White. His face contorted into a mask of rage, and he roared, 'Whore, shut your diseased mouth!' He leaped off the bench, swung the bag and hit a surprised Scully under the chin with it. 'I will make her whole!' he screamed, and made a run for the door.

Though the bag wasn't heavy, Scully saw stars. He lunged at White and caught his right arm, but White wrestled him to one side and shoved him across the massage bench.

'*Whores! The sins of the flesh shall be upon your heads, and she will be made whole again!*' Maggie and Paula screamed and raced for the staff room.

'Ed!' Scully gasped, scrambling to his feet.

'Grab him!' He lunged over the bench and caught White by the collar, but White twisted around and punched him in the face. His strength was incredible.

Ed stood by the door, paralysed. He watched as White mashed the heel of his hand into Scully's nose, as Scully fought grimly to hold on, and still he couldn't move away from the security of the wall. It was only when Scully lost his footing and slipped that Ed managed to launch himself forward into White's path.

'I have a mission! Whores! You will not—' White was thrown backwards as Ed swept his legs from under him. Together they crashed over, but somehow White managed to bring up his leg and flip Ed over his head, onto the nightstand. A bottle of talc burst open, spraying thick white dust, and in the confusion White scrambled free. He crawled towards the door, coughing and choking; he was almost on his feet when Scully leapt on him and pinned his legs to the floor.

'Got you, you bastard!' Scully tried to claw his way up along White's legs, but White twisted one of his legs free and aimed a kick at Scully's face. Scully ducked his head, took the blow on his shoulder and held on grimly. White screamed in anger and tried to drag himself away, but Scully twisted an arm up and grabbed his wrist. White bucked and writhed beneath him like a crazed eel.

'Stop struggling!' Scully panted. 'You're only – aaahh! You dirty fucker—' Scully snatched his arm away. White had bitten him so hard he had ripped through his jacket.

'Ed, get over here!' Scully roared. Ed, finally disentangling himself from the broken table, scrambled across the floor and sprawled on White's back, digging his knee into the screaming man's spine as hard as he could.

'Sir, are you hurt?' he gasped.

'He bit me! The dirty bastard bit me!' Scully hissed. He dragged White's arm behind his back and wrenched it viciously upwards. 'Here, cuff the fucker! Merciful Jesus, that hurts—'

White's eyes rolled up in his head; he twisted around and tried to spit in Scully's face. 'Now you will see!' he roared. '*Your blood is my blood!* You will feel the sins—'

Ed jerked his head back as Bob Scully, a man who rarely even raised his voice, punched White squarely in the side of the head. White stiffened, slumped and was still.

'Dirty little shit.' Scully rolled up his sleeve and checked his arm. 'Oh, fuck … He's broken the skin. Do you see this?' He stuck his arm under Ed's nose. 'I'm bleeding!'

Ed saw the marks of White's teeth in Scully's arm, but all he could do was nod his head feebly.

'Who knows what this fucking nutcase has?' Scully panted. He scrambled to his feet, holding his arm away from his body. 'I've got to get this cleaned out.' He staggered out into the hall and hammered on the staff-room door. 'Open the door

– Paula, isn't it? Open the door! We have him under control. You can come out. I need some running water.'

'How do we know you're you?' Paula yelled.

'I'm Detective Inspector Robert Scully! I need you to—'

'You could be tricking us.'

Scully kicked the door, and both women shrieked.

'If you don't open this door,' Scully roared, 'I'm going to break it down and have the two of you fucking arrested! Then we'll see who's fucking who!'

44

The buzzer was loud in the near-empty apartment. Tricky stalked down the hall; he was back in an instant, training the gun on Emma, who was starting to move.

Miriam followed him into the room and gasped when she saw the blood on Amanda's face and Emma sprawled on the ground.

'Sweet Jesus! What have you done?'

'Here's the fucking long arm of the law.' Emma coughed and sat up. Her cheek was split open, and blood coated her face and neck. 'Tricky's little police pet. Isn't that right, Miriam?'

Miriam's dark eyes glittered. 'I knew you were trouble from the moment I clapped eyes on you. I never trusted you.'

'Where's my fucking money?' Tricky demanded.

'It's in offshore accounts, you know that.'

'I know that's what you told me, you cunt.'

'I have the books for it in a safety deposit box.'

'Get the books. You' – he pointed the gun at Emma – 'you're going with her.' He swung the gun at Miriam, who instinctively backed away. 'You're going to get the fucking books and sign whatever you need to so I can get my money back from wherever you have it stashed. She' – he motioned to Amanda – 'stays here until you get back.'

Miriam stared at Emma's bloody face and shook her head. 'I can't go anywhere with her. Look at the state of her.'

Tricky frowned. She was right. He'd fucked up the wrong one. He was so tired he'd made a mistake.

'Get her cleaned up. I don't give a fuck how you do it, but I want my fucking money and she's the only cunt that can get it.'

'This wasn't part of the deal, McCracken,' Miriam said. 'Everybody's looking for you. They're saying you knew the killer all—'

'I don't give a fuck – and stop saying that! I know nothing about any fucking killer, right? I want my money, and if you still want to have a job tomorrow you better help me. I'm warning you, don't fucking push me.'

Miriam held his gaze for a moment, then looked away. He could be bluffing, but she couldn't take the chance. She grabbed Emma by the arm and dragged her to her feet. 'Come on,' she said. 'Get up. Where's the bathroom?'

'Don't touch her,' Amanda gasped. She turned towards Tricky. 'Haven't you done enough?'

He jammed the gun in her face. 'I only need one to find the cash. So keep your trap shut.'

Emma nodded to her sister and hobbled to the bathroom, with Miriam supporting her. Tricky had kicked her in the kidneys and she could barely stand up, let alone walk.

Miriam turned on the taps. 'Wash the blood off.' She leaned back against the cool tiles and closed her eyes. This was a nightmare. How was she ever going to untangle herself from this?

Emma ran the cold tap over her wrists and dabbed at her mouth. 'This is some bad shit you're in,' she said softly to Miriam in the mirror.

'Hurry up.'

'Do you think this is the end of it for you?' Emma tried to laugh, but it hurt too much. 'Don't be so naïve. He's going to have you by the balls for the rest of your life.'

'Shut up,' Miriam hissed. She looked around for towels; there were none. She grabbed a roll of toilet paper and handed it to Emma.

Emma dabbed the tissue gently around her swollen eye. 'He's going to kill us,' she said to Miriam's reflection. 'You'll be involved in murder, on top of everything else. Although, from what I hear, it won't be the first time.'

Miriam stared at Emma, her bloodless lips forming a perfect O.

'Yeah, he told me about the junkie,' Emma said. 'That's some bargaining chip – and he can use it again and again. If he's caught, he'll blame it all on you. How do you think it's going to look? Vice cop involved with a pimp, giving him information … They'll throw the fucking book at you.'

'I said shut up.' Miriam slapped Emma across

the back of the head. 'You think I don't know all this?' she whispered. 'Do you not think I regret ever laying eyes on the fucker?'

'Then do something about it!' Emma snapped. She coughed, gripping the sides of the sink to steady herself, and lowered her voice. 'Jesus Christ, woman, you're the fucking police. If something happens here, who do you think they'll believe?'

'Like what?' Miriam hesitated, then leaned in closer. 'What are you getting at?'

Emma splashed cold water over her face. 'I'm not going to let him fuck with me or my family again,' she said coldly. 'Ever. Now, you can either help me or stay the hell out of my way.'

Miriam stuck her head out the door and checked the hall, in case Tricky was listening. 'What are you planning to do?' she said, and stepped closer to the sink.

Emma picked up Amanda's make-up bag. 'Shut up and listen.'

45

A thin, sly smile played on Tricky's lips as he watched Amanda watching him. This one had crossed him for the last time. He hated her, and yet she turned him on, in a way that Emma never quite had.

'You nearly did it,' he taunted her. 'So close, but so fucking far.'

Amanda closed her eyes to shut out his gloating face. Her head was throbbing and she was trying not to gag.

'You thought you were so bleeding clever, trying to fuck me over …' He grinned, grabbed her by the hair and forced her head up. 'What would your ma and da say, if they knew they'd two whores in the family instead of the one? Oh, yeah, that's right – they won't say nothing. I forgot they were six feet under. Best place for them, if you ask me.'

Amanda's eyes snapped open, and her voice was icy. 'That's fucking rich, coming from the son of a whore. What about your ma?' She smiled. 'Is it true? I heard she died taking it up the arse for a bottle of gin.'

The words were out before she could stop

herself. Every dog on the street knew Tricky's mother had been a prostitute, but it was the one thing he hated to be reminded of.

He was on her before she had time to draw breath. He swung the shotgun by the barrel and hit her a sickening thump in the side of her head, and she fell onto her side. She knew he would have shot her there and then if he hadn't needed Emma's cooperation.

'Don't you fucking dare speak about my ma, you cunt!' His voice cracked with fury and he towered over her, eyes blazing. 'Don't even think about her! You think you're any better? *Do you?*'

Amanda threw up her hands across her face to ward off his fist, but he stepped back and kicked her in the chest. Pain exploded across her body. She couldn't breathe. She tried to curl into a ball as he rained kicks anywhere he could connect.

Miriam came running, Emma behind her, at the sound of Tricky's shouts. 'Paul, stop!'

'Amanda!' Emma screamed. She threw herself forward and dropped to her knees to shield her sister, getting a second kick in the back. 'Leave her alone! Please leave her alone!'

'Stop it! Stop! What are you doing?' Miriam grabbed Tricky by the shoulders and pulled him back, getting between him and the sisters. 'Have you lost your fucking mind? Stop it. You'll kill her!'

'I want my fucking money – right?' He pointed a finger at Emma over Miriam's shoulder. 'You better fucking get it *now!*'

Amanda rolled her head to the side and spat out blood. Sobbing, Emma tried to help her up, but she couldn't sit. Outside, the day had darkened and black clouds rolled across the sky; rain splattered heavily against the windows, plunging the penthouse into semi-darkness.

Emma glanced up at Tricky with tears in her eyes. 'Please stop. You've done enough. I'll get your money. I'll get the books.'

Tricky narrowed his eyes. 'You'd fucking better. If you don't, I'm going to kill her first, then you.' He shoved Miriam away from him and lifted the gun. 'I mean it, Emma: you'd better not fuck with me.'

Emma nodded, brushing Amanda's hair off her battered face. 'Then you let us go, right?' she said softly.

'All I want is my money. You get me my money and I'll let you go. No hard feelings or nothing. Me and you go back a long way, Emma. I just want my money.'

'Promise me you'll let us go?'

'Yeah. I'll get out of your face as soon as I've got it.'

'I don't know if I can trust you, Paul. I mean, you've done a lot of damage here.' She sniffed. 'How do I know I can trust you?'

'Give him his money, you stupid bitch!' Miriam snapped. 'Then we can all get out of here. He's not going to hurt anyone. I'm a garda, for Christ's sake.'

'Emma? What are you doing?' Amanda whispered. She lifted her head from the ground and clutched at her sister's arm. 'Don't … give him a … fucking thing. I don't care … what he does … don't let this be for nothing.'

Miriam gave her a dirty look. 'Why don't you shut your mouth? Your sister knows what she's doing. Let her get on with it.'

'This is a load of bollix!' Tricky pulled at his own hair in frustration. 'Get my fucking money or I'll shoot this cunt in the head.' He pointed the shotgun straight at Amanda's face. 'No more messing around.' His finger tightened on the trigger.

'OK, OK,' Emma said quickly. 'I'll get it.' She pushed herself up and walked slowly towards him. 'I lied about the deposit box. I have the books here, all right?'

'Here?' Tricky said suspiciously. 'What the fuck do you mean, here?'

'Why would I leave them in a bank?' Emma smiled. It was a grotesque smile; her cheek was bleeding again and one eye was bloodshot. 'Come on, Paul, you know me better than that.'

'If you have them here …' Tricky lowered the gun slightly. 'Where are they?'

'My suitcase.' She took another step. 'I'll get it for you – then you'll let us go?'

He raised the gun again, pointing it at her chest. 'Get it.'

She nodded and moved slowly towards the

door. Behind Tricky, Miriam moved quietly into position.

Tricky followed Emma to the door, keeping the gun on her back. Emma stopped and looked back. 'Amanda, where did you put my tote bag?'

Tricky turned his head slightly towards Amanda. Miriam shifted to his right.

'*Now!*' Emma screamed.

Miriam leapt forward and tackled Tricky from behind. She twisted her fingers into his hair, wrenched his head backwards and sprayed the perfume Emma had given her into his eyes, blinding him momentarily. Emma lunged for the gun.

Tricky roared in anger and twisted away from Miriam, trying to yank the gun out of Emma's hands. 'You fucking bitch – I'll kill you!' He lashed out with his foot, and the toe of his boot cracked into Emma's shin. She screamed, but held on.

Miriam flung her arm around his neck, trying to topple him by sweeping his legs out from under him. Tricky threw a wild head-butt and connected with the underside of her jaw; her teeth clashed together on her tongue, and blood gushed from her mouth. Stunned, Miriam reeled backwards. McCracken straightened and swung Emma around, trying to prise the gun from her fingers.

Amanda could see that Emma was losing her grip on the gun. She pushed herself off the wall and crawled over to help. Every inch was agony; her chest heaved with pain.

'Miriam!' Emma screamed. 'Come on! Get—'

Tricky kneed her in the stomach. There was a dull cracking sound and Emma gurgled and slipped to her knees, the gun sliding away from her fingers. Tricky roared triumphantly and raised the gun to bring it down on her head. Amanda punched him squarely in the balls.

Tricky wheezed. He grabbed a fistful of Amanda's hair, hissed and doubled over, still holding the gun. Miriam threw her weight on his back, but she landed awkwardly, and they toppled over in a mass of grasping hands and kicking legs.

The shot was loud, and the stench of gunpowder and burning flesh filled the room. Dazed and disoriented, Amanda fell flat on her back and stared at the ceiling of her apartment. Her ears were ringing and for a moment she didn't know what had happened.

She lifted her head slowly and saw Emma lying in a curled heap, half-under Tricky's legs.

'Oh, God, no ...' She crawled over to them and pulled at her sister's shoulder. 'Emma? Are you hit?'

Emma moaned and tried to raise her head. 'I don't ... think so.'

'Oh, thank God ... thank God,' Amanda sobbed. She dragged at Emma's arm. 'Come on, Emma, please ... We have to get out of here.'

Emma pushed her away and tried to sit up. 'Get ... the ... gun,' she whispered. 'I can't reach ... Think ... my ribs ... broken.'

Amanda scrabbled across the floor and pulled

the gun from under Tricky's arm. He was curled up tightly, moaning softly and clutching at his balls; even so, he made a grab at Amanda's ankle as she crawled back to her sister. Amanda knew it wouldn't be long before he regained his strength.

'We've got to get out of here, Emma,' she panted, her eyes wild and terrified. 'Please, oh please, let's go.'

She tugged at Emma's sleeve, but Emma shook her head. 'Give me … a second … catch my breath,' she whispered. 'And get Miriam … cuff him.'

Amanda was sobbing, but she crawled over to where Miriam lay crumpled on the floor beside Tricky. That was when she saw the blood streaming from under her.

'Oh, fuck!' Amanda froze. 'Emma, she's been hit!'

'What?' Emma propped herself up on one elbow.

'She's bleeding … look.' Amanda pointed. 'She's bleeding. The mad bastard shot her. Oh, my God – sh-shit, Emma, I think she's d-dead.'

Emma dragged herself out from under Tricky's legs and half-crawled, half-slid over to Miriam. She rested her ear on the detective's back and listened.

'She's not dead, you idiot,' she said shakily.

Between them, they pulled Miriam over onto her back. She had been shot through the top of her right shoulder, at close range. Her shirt was scorched, and blood seeped from the hole where her flesh had been turned to ragged mush.

She moaned and opened her eyes. 'What happened?' she asked, in a remarkably calm voice.

'You've been shot,' Emma said.

'Why?'

Emma understood shock. She grinned wildly. 'I don't know why. Because you're an awkward bitch.'

Beside them, Tricky groaned and swore. Emma looked over Miriam's shoulder at him. 'You've fucking broke my balls,' he said. 'Ahhhh …'

Emma grimaced and slid backwards. 'Are you OK?' she asked Amanda.

Amanda's eyes were glassy, and her teeth were chattering with shock. 'W-w-we have to get out of h-h-here.'

'I know. Help me up.'

They leaned against each other and dragged themselves up. Emma was dizzy with pain. She knew she wouldn't be able to stand for long.

'W-what about them?' Amanda pointed a shaking finger at the two prone bodies.

'Fuck them!' Emma whispered savagely. 'Fuck them both. They deserve each other.'

Miriam coughed and rolled over. She pushed herself onto her knees and unsteadily stood up. Her injured arm dangled uselessly by her side and she swayed on her feet, but her voice was crystal-clear.

'Give me the gun.' She held out her good arm.

Amanda hesitated. She didn't trust Miriam any more than Tricky.

Emma laid her hand on Amanda's shoulder. 'Give it to me,' she said softly.

Amanda handed it over.

Miriam sighed softly. 'Look, Emma, I'll call this in. He won't be able to wiggle out of this one.'

Emma ignored her and made her way over to Tricky. 'Get up,' she said.

Tricky stopped rolling and stared up at her. He looked terrible; he was grey with pain and fatigue, and there was saliva on his chin and deep scratches on his forehead. But his eyes were alert and watchful.

'Get up,' Emma repeated in the same flat, dead voice. Her cheek throbbed as she spoke.

Tricky's lip curled. 'Fuck you.' He looked past her. 'Hey, Grogan, you're fucking finished, yeah? Unless you wake up and sort this. You know I didn't mean to shoot you – it was an accident.'

Miriam shook her head. 'Emma, give me the gun.'

Amanda looked at her sister. 'Emma?'

'He'll never stop, Amanda, you know that. His kind never do.' Emma raised the gun. 'Get up, Tricky. I won't say it again.'

Tricky muttered under his breath and gingerly pushed himself off the ground. His eyes were still sore and streaming, but he was beginning to recover.

'Miriam,' he said, 'we can work this shit out. I'll talk to Big Joe for you, sort this problem out – clean slate, yeah? We can sort something out.'

'Hear that, Miriam?' Amanda laughed. 'The pimp's offering you a deal. Oh, this is just perfect. Emma, come on, let's go. I'm sure someone heard that shot. We've got to get out of here.' She grabbed Emma's shoulder. Emma shrugged her off.

'I told you, he'll keep after us.'

Tricky's top lip curled into a sneer. 'You're a fucking bitch. I treated you like a queen, you cunt. You better believe you won't get away with this. The world ain't fucking big enough. You think I won't track you down?' He laughed. 'If it takes me the rest of my bleeding life, I'll make sure your life won't be worth—'

'Shut up.' Emma raised the gun.

'What the fuck?' Tricky shook his head in disgust. He stepped towards her. 'Yeah, right. What are you going to do? Shoot me? Stop acting the bollix and give me the gun. No more fucking around—'

The blast was at point-blank range, and it knocked him halfway across the room.

Amanda was too stunned to move. 'Oh my God.' She stared at Tricky's slumped body in amazement. 'You shot him.'

'Yeah.' Emma lowered the smoking gun. Miriam shuffled forward and prised it from her fingers. 'What the fuck have you done?' she asked.

Amanda pushed Miriam aside and grabbed Emma. 'Jesus Christ, Emma! Come on, we've got to get out of here!' She tugged Emma towards the door, but her sister wouldn't budge.

'You can't leave!' Miriam shuffled around and pointed the gun at her. 'You're staying put.'

Amanda stared at Miriam's pale, blood-splattered face. 'We're leaving,' she said firmly.

Miriam shrugged her good shoulder. 'I was thinking about what your sister said – you know, about him blackmailing me for the rest of my life.' She grinned and swayed dangerously on her feet. 'Now he can't.'

Amanda peered over her shoulder at Tricky, who lay twisted in an unnatural slump by the French doors. He had landed with his head twisted to the left, his body to the right; if the shot hadn't killed him, the fall certainly had. 'Whatever. We have to go.'

'She shot him,' Miriam snapped. 'I can't just let you walk out of here.'

Amanda ran her fingers wildly through her hair. 'Goddammit, you saw him! He was going to kill us! If you don't get the fuck out of our way, I swear to God I'll—'

'Amanda! Get a bloody grip on yourself! That screaming's getting on my nerves.' Emma patted her sister on the back. 'Take a few deep breaths and relax; we're leaving in a few minutes.' She glared at Miriam and straightened up as much as she could. 'We don't have time for this shit.'

'You're not going anywhere.' Miriam aimed the gun at her.

'Miriam.' Emma smiled coldly. 'I hate to point this out, but that's a double-barrelled shotgun, and I just used the last shot to turn your employer into Shredded Wheat.' Her left eye was now almost totally closed, and her voice rasped when she spoke. They needed to get the hell out of there before the neighbours called half the police force to the door.

'I can't let you leave,' Miriam said. Her voice was growing fainter. Amanda looked down. She could see she was losing a lot of blood – it was pooling around her ankle. 'I'm not going to be left here alone with this … this mess.'

'You can't stop us,' Emma said coolly. 'If you try, I'm going to make sure your colleagues know all about your little arrangement with McCracken. How do you think that will look? The man you were being paid to inform winds up dead. Covering your own ass – that's what they'll think. We'll tell them it was your idea.'

'We'll hang you out to d-dry,' Amanda said.

Miriam sighed and dropped the gun. She hadn't the strength to hold it up any more.

'What am I supposed to say?' she asked wearily. She wiped her face with her good arm, smearing blood everywhere.

'You'll think of something.' Emma glanced at her watch. The face had been smashed, but it was still working. 'Amanda, can you grab my bag?'

'Wait – take his mobile phone. They'll trace his calls if you leave it here.'

'Always thinking of yourself,' Amanda said sourly. 'Where is it?'

'Probably in his pocket.'

'Ah, Jesus.' Amanda blanched and looked over at the body. 'I'm not f-fishing around that.' She shook her head and took a quick step backwards.

'Get it,' Emma said. 'I'll get the bags.'

'Emma, I'm not t-t-touching him.'

'Amanda, please, not now.' Emma turned to face her, and Amanda saw the sweat on her pale forehead and the faint tremble in her shoulders. She looked like she was going to collapse.

Cursing softly, Amanda limped past Miriam and leaned over Tricky's crumpled body. Touching him as little as possible, she found the phone and extracted it from the inside pocket of his jacket. She held it between her finger and thumb; it was slick with warm blood.

'Throw it away somewhere,' Miriam said feebly. 'Make sure it never gets found.'

Amanda dropped it into one of her bags and wiped her hands on her trousers.

'Let's go, quickly, before somebody else turns up,' Emma said softly. 'I think I'm going to faint.'

'W-wait – one last thing,' Amanda whispered.

'What?'

Amanda spun round and, with the last of her strength, punched Miriam in the mouth. Miriam's legs folded and she toppled over, cracking her head on the floor.

'Fucking hell.' Amanda doubled over and stuck her hand under her arm. 'Jesus, that hurt.'

'What did you do that for?' Emma stared at her in amazement.

'If she's going to tell them she tried to stop us, it has to look like she put up a fight.'

'She's been shot. How much evidence do you think they need?'

Amanda laughed and helped Emma into her coat. 'Anyway,' she said, throwing a filthy look at the unconscious Miriam, 'I never liked the two-faced bitch.' She picked up two of the bags and staggered towards the door. 'Let's get out of here before something else happens.'

46

Michael inched open the unlocked door of the penthouse and crept down the hall, followed by Stafford. They had come looking for Amanda, speeding up when they heard the call of 'shots fired' on the scanner; amazingly, they were the first officers on the scene. On the way in, they had spotted Miriam Grogan's car parked on the street outside.

At the end of the hall, Michael pushed the living-room door open and gasped.

There was blood everywhere. One body was slumped by the French doors; even from the doorway, Michael knew this one would never get up again. Then he saw Miriam Grogan, sprawled in the middle of the floor, with a sawn-off shotgun by her side.

'Is she breathing?' Stafford asked quietly.

Michael pressed his fingers against her neck. 'She's got a pulse, sir, but it's weak.'

'Jesus, there's so much blood …' Stafford shook his head. 'Call an ambulance.'

'Yes, sir.'

Stafford moved towards the French doors and

stood over the body of Paul McCracken. He reached down to check for a pulse, then stopped and withdrew his hand. Who was he kidding? He could see the angle of the neck.

He leaned against the French doors. 'Mike.'

'Yes?' Michael placed his hand across the mouthpiece.

'As soon as the ambulance gets here, I want this room secured. I don't want anybody coming in or out until the crime-scene boys get here.' He sidestepped a sticky pool of blood. 'Nobody comes into this room. Got me? And as soon as you ring the ambulance, I want you to make sure every fucking officer in the city is on the lookout for the Harringtons.'

Michael nodded.

While he made the calls, Stafford looked out across the night sky. The view was spectacular. He watched car lights disappear along the Liffey, reflecting off the rain-sodden streets. He should have listened to his sergeant sooner. Sharp man, Mike; didn't miss much. While they had sat in that pub, one of his officers had been savagely assaulted. The weight of responsibility felt heavy on his shoulders.

Michael knelt down and pushed Miriam's dark hair back from her pale, blood-smeared forehead. 'Miriam,' he said softly. 'Hang in there, love. Help's on its way.' He took off his jacket, rolled it up and placed it under her head. 'You'll be all right. We're here now.'

Through his concern, Michael wondered what she had been doing here. What the hell had happened? Why hadn't she called for backup? He glanced around the room, noticing the bloody handprints on the wall.

'McCracken must have come looking for Emma.'

'Aye.' Stafford gazed at Miriam mournfully. 'Poor young one. She took an awful risk trying to stop them.'

The papers had a field day. Female detective shot by vicious pimp while investigating double murder, demented killer caught while trying to kill again … The tabloids were spoilt for choice in headlines.

Miriam Grogan was hailed as a hero, a prime example of a dedicated police force. When the journalists found out she had been protecting the lives of two women, the same women who had callously left her for dead, her hero status increased. For a whole week the papers were full of speculation and praise.

The Commissioner was delighted. Never in his wildest dreams could he have imagined better publicity. The Minister for Justice had called him at home to congratulate him on the success of his force. He held a press conference, the day after Miriam was shot, in which he spoke for a good hour about the dedication of the gardaí. He posed for every photographer and gave a comment to every journalist he came across.

Scully got a special commendation for his bravery. He accepted the award with an anxious look on his face; his hand still hurt where White had bitten him, and he was waiting for the results of White's tests. In this day and age, a bite from a human could be very bad news indeed.

Stafford and the Vice team were also commended, with Felim Brennan laying the praise on thick. As Stafford muttered to Michael, it was like getting humped by a particularly ugly Labrador.

The public loved it. No more questions were asked. The Garda press office had done its work well.

According to the papers, the gun had gone off in the struggle as Miriam, already injured, tried to stop McCracken from shooting Amanda and Emma Harrington, two alleged prostitutes who had crossed him. This selfless act of courage in the line of duty had prevented a bloodbath. Photographs of Miriam, smiling, wan and bandaged in her hospital bed, appeared in every newspaper across the country.

Photographs of McCracken, looking shifty and sullen, also appeared. Working girls gave interviews for ridiculous sums of money, all telling the same tale: McCracken was an evil scumbag, a manipulator of women, a pimp, a violent sociopath and an all-round bad man.

More carefully released information about the murders of Sandy Walsh, Tessa Byrne and Carla Bannion was also laid at McCracken's door.

Numerous articles suggested that Allen White, a disturbed and mentally unstable young man, had been the unwitting pawn used by Paul McCracken to eliminate anyone who threatened his prostitution and porn empire. Miriam Grogan was able to confirm this theory from her hospital bed: before their violent struggle, she said, McCracken had gloated about his part in the murders.

Nobody questioned how McCracken could have controlled White.

Allen White was remanded to St Augustine's Hospital for the criminally insane, for psychological evaluation. White claimed he had never heard of Paul McCracken. He said he had killed women who had worked in the Red Stairs, because that was where he had caught some disease, and that was why his mother had died. Nobody took any notice, as he also claimed that he was on a mission from God and that he intended to cure his dead mother by ridding Dublin of sin. Doctors increased his medication, and he stopped yelling. It was considered unlikely that he would ever be fit to stand trial.

Amanda Harrington and Emma Harris were nowhere to be found.

Paul 'Tricky' McCracken wasn't around to give his side of the story – not that anyone would have believed him.

Everything fell neatly into place.

The only one who had his doubts was Michael Dwyer.

★　★　★

'What about the money, sir? The Criminal Assets Bureau think McCracken was worth millions. All they've turned up is twenty thousand in a current account and five thousand in a Cashsave. Where's the rest of the money gone?'

'It's gone, Mike,' Stafford said, exasperated. 'Why are you still ranting on about this? McCracken's dead, we have the killer – so why won't you let the bloody thing drop?'

'We won't find it, that's for sure. Emma Harrington was an accountant. She probably had that money well hidden long before we turned up at that apartment.'

'Which apartment?'

'The apartment on Aungier Street. The botched raid. It was too easy, getting her that night. Why was she there? I'm convinced the whole thing was staged. Emma Harris – Harrington – wanted us to know she was linked to Tricky. That way she could feed us any old crap, whatever she wanted us to know, and we'd swallow it, hook, line and sinker.' Michael scowled. It wasn't often someone fooled him, and it left a bad taste in his mouth.

'Ah, God, not this again,' Stafford said impatiently. He leaned forward over his desk. 'We know McCracken was involved, Mike. Goddammit, he had White on tape.'

'I know that. That doesn't prove he was using White to kill those girls. White says he never knew McCracken.'

'White's insane. He was a time bomb waiting to

go off. The amount of morphine and hallucino-
genics they found in his blood, it's a wonder he
didn't think he was flying most of the time. For
Christ's sake, Mike, Miriam told us McCracken
admitted his part in the murders!'

Michael's mouth twitched. 'And I should have
realised the two of them were related. There was
something about them that always bothered me.
Exact same accent, same way of speaking – same
bloody mannerisms, even.' He shook his head in
annoyance. 'The difference in colouring threw me
completely.'

'I doubt that blonde is Emma's real colour,'
Stafford said absently.

'I wonder where they are now.'

'Who knows? They could be anywhere.'

'Well away from here, I'll bet. They wouldn't
have hung around. It looks like they were planning
to go anyway; Amanda Harrington hadn't got a
stick of furniture left in the apartment. It had all
been packed and sent to God knows where, long
before Miriam stumbled across them.'

'Miriam's lucky not to have been killed. She
was bloody stupid to go in after McCracken like
that. What the hell was she thinking? She should
have called for backup.'

'Mmm …' Michael stood up and headed for
the door. He couldn't bear the pride in Stafford's
voice.

'If it hadn't been for her, McCracken would
probably have killed those two. Then the fuckers

go and leave her like that … So much for common decency.'

'Decency?' Michael whirled round and stared. 'If Emma Harris had given us that tape sooner, we might have caught Allen White before the second murder. That one didn't give a shit. She waited and waited, and then threw us McCracken when she felt the time was right. Decency? Don't make me laugh.'

Stafford rubbed his forehead and sighed. Mike had been saying the same thing for weeks now, and it was starting to get on his nerves. Why couldn't he accept they had a result and leave it at that?

'I wonder how McCracken found out about the two of them being sisters,' Michael said suddenly. 'I only discovered it by chance; and Emma Harris – shit, Harrington – had some excellent false ID. You saw the driving licence we found at her house. It's better than the real thing.'

'Who knows, Mike?' Stafford was bored with the conversation. As far as he was concerned, the case was closed. 'Who knows? They were clever – maybe too clever. People trip themselves up somewhere, no matter how smart they think they are.'

Michael wasn't so sure. With a couple of million quid under their belts, he doubted the sisters Harrington would trip over anything.

He let the subject drop. 'Where are we watching tonight?'

Stafford grunted and rolled his eyes. 'Remember that dump we closed down a few months ago – Midnight Cowboys, it was called then?'

'What about them? I thought we brought the owner to court.'

'We did.' Stafford reached for his jacket. 'The old bitch running the place got a five-hundred-euro fine. Next day she opens it back up under a different name, with some dimwitted girl fronting it; but it's her, all right.'

'How do you know?'

'She's in there answering the bloody phones. She doesn't trust the girls not to rob her, so she's there day and night. Miserable old bitch hasn't even the brains to try and disguise her voice.'

Michael smiled. 'Jesus. Will they never learn?'

Stafford put his jacket on and eyed Michael with amusement. 'Five hundred quid? It's not exactly an expensive lesson. What's five hundred quid to someone who's making that and more a day? We're pissing against the breeze, Mike. Pissing against the breeze.'

'Not for long, though,' Michael said. 'I hear we're going back to normal duties in another month or so.'

'Not before time,' Stafford replied grimly. 'Biggest fucking waste of police time and money I've ever had the misfortune to be caught up in.'

Marna walked up the steps to her apartment with a heavy heart. She had interviewed three girls that day, all ex-employees of Tricky's. Not one of them had been suitable. Fucked up, she called them; Paula, slightly more diplomatically, called them 'damaged goods'. But not even Paula was willing to try them out, and she needed another girl now that Big Maggie had retired. Two weeks since the shooting, and there was still unexpected fallout.

Marna let herself in and picked up her mail in the hall. A slim brown envelope at the bottom of the pile of junk mail caught her eye. She recognised the untidy handwriting across the front. For a second she almost ripped the envelope in half.

She took off her coat, sat down at the dining-room table and opened the envelope carefully.

Two things slipped out: a white card with a small flower on the front and an airline ticket. She turned the card over. On the back, in the same handwriting, was one sentence. 'Living *la vida loca*.'

Marna rested her chin on her hand and closed her eyes.

47

The following Friday morning, Marna landed in Barcelona.

She made her way through Arrivals, picked up her bag, walked past the smoking security guards and stood looking around. Throngs of people moved about, greeting and hugging each other; she watched them and wondered what the hell she was doing there.

'I wasn't sure if you'd come,' said a voice to her right.

Marna whirled around, clutching her chest in fright. 'Jesus, Amanda, you scared the shit out of me.'

'Hi yourself.' Amanda took her hand. 'Good flight?'

'Let me have a look at you.' Marna stood back and stared. The woman before her was wearing white linen trousers and a long-sleeved white shirt; her long hair had been cut to a short, sleek bob and she was wearing huge Jackie O sunglasses. She seemed thinner, and under her light tan Marna could see the faint outline of a bruise around one eye. 'What happened to your face?'

Amanda smiled and picked up her bag. 'I'll tell you all about it later. Let's get out of here first.'

They walked out into the warm Spanish air. Amanda opened the door of a yellow-and-black taxi and ushered Marna in.

They drove the first few miles in silence. Marna had hundreds of questions, but now she was there she didn't know where to start.

Amanda glanced over at her. 'How's everything back in Dublin?'

'Different.' Marna shrugged. 'There's been a lot of shit since you left. The cops have interviewed me twice. The papers are all over the business, so the clients are running scared.' Marna glanced at the back of the driver's head and leaned closer to Amanda. 'That Grogan woman,' she whispered. 'They say she saved your lives, and you left her there to die.'

Amanda smiled coldly. 'Die of what? She has a thick fucking neck, that one.' She tucked her hair behind her ears, remembered the swollen, cauli-flowered damage and shook it loose again.

'You should have told me what was going on.'

'We'll talk about it later.' The dark orbs swung away. Marna leaned back in her seat and watched as the road swept by and the outskirts of the city closed in around them.

The taxi stopped on Passeig de Gracia, in the heart of Barcelona. Marna retrieved her bag from the boot and stood gazing around in the bright sunlight. It was a beautiful city. If only she could enjoy it.

'Where are we going?' She felt awkward, nervous, as though she barely knew the woman standing beside her any more.

'You'll see. Come on, this way.'

They crossed a huge circle filled with slow-moving pigeons and wove their way up one street and down another. Amanda moved fast, and at times Marna struggled to keep up. Sweat trickled down her back and her ankles hurt; but, to her relief, Amanda stopped halfway down a wide tree-lined street, outside a huge, ornate wooden door. She glanced around, unlocked the door and slipped inside.

Marna stepped into the vast entrance and gasped at the sudden change of temperature. Tiles of pale blue and crisp white stretched out before her. The foyer was airy and high-ceilinged; beautiful paintings hung from the walls, and an elaborate carved staircase with well-worn marble steps rose up from the middle of the foyer and curved into a wide, snaking bend.

Amanda crossed the hall and opened the door of an old chain elevator. 'Close your mouth. You're catching flies.'

'Do you live here?'

'Yep. Top floor.'

The apartment was huge. Tall double doors opened into a hall of marble floors and white walls. Marna stepped inside and smiled despite herself.

'Drop your bag. I'll show you to your room later. First, I want you to meet someone.'

'Is this the famous sister?' Marna was unable to conceal the hurt in her voice. 'I didn't even know you had one – isn't that crazy? Michael Dwyer told me about her.'

'I'm sorry, Marna.' Amanda took off her sunglasses. 'Try not to let her intimidate you.'

Marna caught her breath as she saw the full extent of the damage to Amanda's face. One eye was bloodshot, and a yellowing bruise spread down one side of her face, from her eye to the corner of her mouth.

'Jesus Christ. What the fuck happened to you?'

'This?' Amanda touched the side of her face. 'This is nothing. This is the price we paid for not staying in a bloody hotel.'

'What do you mean?'

'I'll explain it all later, OK?' She walked off down the hall, her heels clacking on the tiles, and Marna followed. Suddenly she felt very out of her depth.

'Emma?' Amanda called. 'We're back.'

'I'm in here.'

The voice came from behind them. A door opened and Emma stepped out into the hall, naked and dripping wet. She was trying to wrap a bandage around her ribs with one hand; the other was on her hair, which was covered in plastic and appeared to be purple.

'Thank fuck! What the hell kept you? Give me a hand with this, would you?'

'Emma, this is Marna.' Amanda stepped forward to help her. 'Marna, my sister Emma.'

'Nice to meet you, I'm sure.' Emma rolled an unfriendly eye in Marna's direction. 'Ow, shit! Not so bloody hard, Amanda! I see you have a bit of a shiner too, Marna. Welcome to the Walking Wounded club.'

Marna muttered a hello and tried not to stare.

'What did you try to do?' Amanda asked irritably, as she wound the bandage around her sister and fastened it at the back. 'I told you to wait until I got back.'

'I'm trying to dye this blonde crap out of my fucking hair. What does it look like?' Emma snapped. She leaned against the wall to steady herself, her breath ragged and painful. 'Help me inside. I need to sit down.'

Amanda grabbed her under the arm, helped her into a large, sunny sitting room and deposited her, none-too-gently, on the suede sofa that had arrived from Dublin two days before.

Emma groaned and clutched her side. Her face was grey with pain. Marna stood awkwardly at the door, watching her. 'Are you OK?' she asked.

'Sure. Never felt better,' Emma said sarcastically. She shifted her body to one side, which seemed to ease the pain slightly. 'Come in and sit down. That bastard McCracken broke my ribs. They're healing, apparently.'

She looked like Amanda; the eyes were different, but it was obvious they were sisters. Marna found it very disconcerting. She caught Emma watching her, so she moved away from the door and sat down in a plump old armchair.

'What happened to you? Both of you?' She looked from Amanda's battered face to Emma's bruised and bandaged body. 'I was told you got clean away.'

'Who told you that?' Emma asked. A little colour was coming back into her cheeks.

'Michael Dwyer. He said Miriam Grogan saved your lives.'

'He's an idiot.'

Marna said nothing. It annoyed her to hear Emma talk about Michael Dwyer that way; he had been very good to her over the last few weeks, even going so far as to keep her name out of the papers. She didn't know this woman from Adam. The last thing she wanted to do was start a row with her.

'Shut up, Emma,' Amanda said. 'You asked who told her, so don't bite her head off when she gives you the answer.'

'I'm sorry,' Emma said, not sounding it. 'Don't mind me. I'm sore and I'm fucked off with being cooped up inside all day.'

Marna shrugged. 'That's OK.'

Amanda shot her a grateful look. 'Come on, let me show you your room. Then you can freshen up and come back out for a drink.'

'What about me? You can't bloody leave me like this,' Emma snapped, catching her arm.

Amanda's face tightened and she wrenched her arm free. 'I'll come back and give you a hand washing that crap out of your hair in a minute. I need to show Marna to her room.'

'Don't be long.'

* * *

Further down the long, cool hall, Amanda showed Marna to a large room painted pale lavender and full of heavy antique furniture. Muslin curtains were draped around the bed, and the windows opened onto a courtyard at the back of the building.

'Ta-da!' Amanda opened the door wide and stepped back. 'What do you think? It's my room, actually, but you can have it for the weekend.'

'It's lovely,' Marna said. 'Where will you sleep?'

'I can bunk in with Emma for a night or two. We have three bedrooms, but we don't have furniture for the third one yet.' She hovered by the door.

Marna knew Amanda wanted to say something but couldn't find the words, but she didn't feel any need to make it easier for her. She stood and waited. Finally Amanda cleared her throat. 'I'll leave you to it. Come out whenever you're ready. Then we'll talk. I know you've got a lot of questions.'

'Is she all right?' Marna asked, tilting her head towards the sitting room. She sat on the end of the bed and slipped her shoes off her tired feet. 'Only she seems … well, she doesn't look too happy.'

Amanda shrugged. 'She'll be fine. She was always a stroppy cow anyway; now she has an excuse to act like a bitch. Try not to take any notice of her.' She started to leave, then stopped. 'Marna,' she said softly, 'I'm really glad you came.' Then she smiled and went out.

Marna lay back on the bed. 'What the hell am I doing here?' she asked herself.

48

An hour and a long shower later, Marna sat in the living room across from the newly brunette Emma, who was reclining on the sofa with Amanda perched nervously by her feet. Marna listened with growing disbelief as they recounted their version of events.

As she listened to them speak, she noticed more and more similarities between them. It was uncanny how alike they were. And yet she didn't like Emma. She was surly and rude, and her temper flared every few minutes. It could have been the pain, but Marna doubted it. Some people are naturally unpleasant, and she was pretty sure Emma was one of them.

'When did you get to see each other?'

'We didn't, really.' Amanda took a swig from her bottle of beer. 'We were afraid somebody might see us together. We phoned each other occasionally, but that's about all.'

'Is that why you didn't want Kate working for us? Were you afraid she'd guess you were Emma's sister?'

'Well, sort of. I didn't think anyone would make

the connection, but why take the risk? Plus I knew hiring her would get Tricky breathing down our necks. I wanted him to forget I'd ever existed.'

Marna glanced around the room. 'What about this place? How long have you had it? It must have cost a fortune.'

'It did.' Emma smirked proudly. She looked a lot better than she had earlier; she was still pale, but the dark hair suited her. She wore a long cream tunic and soft leather sandals. 'But we can afford it, thanks to the great Pimp Lord and Master.' She raised her wine in a mock toast. 'We've had it for six months now, ready and waiting.'

Marna was stunned. She glanced at Amanda, but her friend refused to look at her. 'Six months? Then you must have been planning to go since—'

'Since you idiots got arrested,' Emma said.

'She's been moving money over here for the last year,' Amanda said softly. 'Once Tricky heard that the Criminal Assets Bureau was investigating property and money belonging to anyone convicted for prostitution, he panicked. Emma convinced him to set up some kind of offshore account where he could hide the bulk of his money. That way, if the CAB did come after him, he could pack up and leave at the first sign of trouble.'

'And he gave you his money?' Marna said incredulously. 'Why?'

'Why not? It was my job. Everything he does is in cash, see,' Emma said. 'That way there's no paper trail. I set up some bogus account, and every two weeks or so I typed up returns on my computer in work, in case he ever wanted to see how much money he had. He trusted me. He had to; I was his only hope of avoiding the taxman.' She sniggered. 'The thing was, Tricky was easier to fool than I'd ever imagined he would be. Oh, God, was he stupid when it came to any kind of official-looking paperwork. He'd pretend to read my balance sheets, acting as if he understood every word, too fucking proud to say he hadn't a clue what was on the paper in front of his nose. It's like he needed somebody to tell him what to do.'

She sat up a little, and the smile vanished from her face as easily as it had appeared. 'I could have ripped the little prick off for another twenty years, but no – he had to start listening to that fat pig O'Connor, some moron who had barely made it out of primary school. Can you imagine? There I was, working my arse off trying to keep Tricky happy, and this fucking slob comes along and starts telling him he doesn't need me.'

'But it was getting too risky to keep fobbing Tricky off with paper,' Amanda said. 'At some stage he would have wanted to see some of his money.'

'But we didn't have the fucking money in Dublin,' Emma cut in. 'Most weekends I'd fly out of the country with cash strapped to my body, praying I wasn't stopped in Customs. I'd meet her in London, and she'd fly to Barcelona from there.'

'It was so risky,' Amanda said softly.

'I was damned if I was going to fly out and bring some of it back, just to placate the likes of O'Connor. Stupid bastard, always sticking his spoke in—'

'Emma,' Amanda said, 'stop.'

'You flew out here? When? How could you have found time to … Oh.' Marna stopped abruptly. 'Sundays. That's why nobody could ever contact you on … well, so often.'

Amanda nodded. 'I was away.'

'I still don't understand. What about Grogan – where does she fit into all this?'

'She worked for Tricky. She tipped him off about the raids – when they were going to happen, who to watch out for. Actually, she was my idea,' Emma said coolly. 'Bit of a gambling problem, has our Miriam – owes money on everything, has a second mortgage on her house, the works. I'm surprised she owns the shirt on her hairy back. That was a stroke of good luck, too: Miriam confirmed everything I ever told Tricky about the CAB. She had him paranoid as fuck.'

Marna looked at Emma. There was something about the smug way she said it, as if she knew something about everyone … 'How did you find that out?'

'I know someone from Visa credit control. When Amanda sent me the list of cops who'd busted you guys last year, I ran the names by him, and up she popped, like a fucking toadstool.' She smiled, and her hazel eyes met Marna's directly. 'It was easy to find out the rest. I can find out any-thing I want, if I put my mind to it.'

'I'm sure you can,' Marna said coldly. She got the distinct impression that Emma was warning her.

'Grogan didn't have much choice after the first call,' Amanda said. She lit a cigarette and blew out her match. 'After she had taken money from him once, Tricky threatened to hang her out to dry if she didn't keep helping him. He had her back to the wall from the word go. She's in serious debt to a guy called Big Joe Colgan – owes him about a year's wages, plus interest.'

Marna sat back in her chair and closed her eyes. This was all too much to take in. 'What about the murders? Did you know who was behind them?'

Amanda's face darkened, and she suddenly seemed very interested in her beer label.

'We didn't know,' Emma said, her voice hard. 'But I knew Tricky did.'

Marna stared at her. It was obvious this wasn't something she wanted to discuss. 'The gardaí said Tricky was using Allen White to target certain women.'

'Yeah?'

'Did you know that?'

'I already told you, we didn't know who the killer was.' Emma's voice rose slightly.

'Because, if you had known about this man, you would have gone to the police when Sandy was killed, wouldn't you?' Marna said evenly.

Emma glared at her. 'Which part of "we didn't know" don't you understand?'

'They got the right man, Marna.' Amanda lifted her head and gazed at her. 'They found Sandy's notebook at his place, didn't they? They found Tessa's bag. We saw it in the papers.'

'And neither of you was certain Tricky was using him? Right?'

Amanda frowned. She sat up and rested her hand on Emma's foot. 'You know about the tape, don't you?' she said angrily. 'How do you know about it? It wasn't in the papers.'

Marna shrugged and bit her lip. She didn't want to say too much, especially in front of Emma, who was watching her with keen dislike.

'How do you know about the tape, Marna?' Amanda said, more insistently.

'Michael Dwyer told me,' Marna said softly. 'He's not convinced about Tricky's involvement with the murders.'

Amanda smiled and picked up her beer. 'Oh, isn't he? And what does everybody else say?'

'Everybody else thinks he was involved. My question is, if Tricky was behind it, how come you' – she nodded at Emma – 'didn't know about White sooner? I mean, let's face it: if Tricky trusted you enough to give you all his money—'

'How fucking dare you!' Emma shouted. 'Didn't you hear what my sister said? We didn't have a fucking clue who was killing those women. The cops caught the right man, Tricky's dead, so why don't you leave well enough alone? Who are you to fucking question us? Miss bloody High and Mighty! Fuck you!'

Marna reddened. She glanced at Amanda, who returned her gaze with a grim smile. 'What's done is done, Marna.'

Emma yanked the cigarette out of Amanda's hand and took a deep drag. 'What I'd like to know is how Grogan copped we were sisters in the first place.'

'She heard it from Michael Dwyer. He traced your car to your parents' old house,' Marna said softly. Suddenly she wanted, more than anything, to be back in Dublin, as far away from these two as she could possibly be.

'Fuck. No wonder McCracken was hopping.' Emma laughed suddenly. 'I'll bet that bitch nearly creamed herself when she found out who I was.'

Marna sighed. 'Everyone thinks Grogan saved you. She gave the papers some story about following Tricky into your building and confronting him when she saw you were in danger.'

'Let her say what she likes. I don't give a fuck what anyone thinks any more. We got out. We took the money and we ran. People—' Emma sneered and flicked Marna a sly look. '—can think what they like. That bitch would have framed us to save her own skin if she could have. She's no better than Tricky or any of the other bastards.'

Marna looked away, startled by her anger, her

energy. 'They're not all bad. Michael Dwyer was genuinely worried about you, Amanda.'

'Don't fucking kid yourself,' Emma snapped, suddenly furious. She pushed herself up into a sitting position and pointed a shaky finger at Marna. 'You look out for number one in this life. Dwyer's no different from the rest of the scumbags. He's probably hoping you'll fall for his bullshit and let something slip about us. He must have known Amanda would try to contact you at some stage. Now you sit here and try to fucking pretend he's some kind of social worker …' She jerked forwards on the sofa and held her hand tightly against her side. 'Well, he's not some caring fucking little saviour or whatever you seem to think he is! He'll play you like a fucking violin if you're not careful.'

Amanda glanced up at her sister's pale, sweating face. 'Do you need more painkillers?'

Emma passed a hand across her forehead. 'I don't know. Do I?' For a moment she seemed confused and exhausted. Marna watched her from under her lashes, afraid to stare directly in case it sparked off another wave of fury.

Amanda rose and left the room. Emma pulled a face and lay back on the sofa as gently as she could. 'My sister tells me you have a lot of property in Dublin,' she said in a low, tired voice.

'I own one or two apartments,' Marna said carefully. 'Well, I paid the deposits and I have them rented out; I don't exactly own them.'

'I think it's more like five.' Emma flashed her shark's smile.

Marna gave a noncommittal shrug. Emma might be Amanda's sister, but it was none of her business how many apartments Marna owned. She felt Emma's eyes on her and wished she hadn't come here. She was even starting to worry about her own safety. Emma was like a loose cannon, ready to go off at any second.

'Can I give you some free advice?'

'If you want.'

'Get rid of them. Sell them and take your money. Get out while you can.'

Marna forced a smile. 'They're investments. In a few years they'll be worth a fortune.' She took a sip of her beer. 'That's why I bought the bloody things in the first place.'

'In a few years you won't have them to sell. One thing I did learn from that bitch cop is that the CAB is growing more powerful every day. They have more power than the taxman and even less fucking heart. You could lose everything you own, just like that.' Emma clicked her fingers, then dropped them as if the effort had been too much for her. 'They don't give a shit whether you rent them out or not.'

'I'm not a big enough fish for them.'

'Don't fucking kid yourself.' Emma took a deep breath and rubbed her hands over her face. Marna saw how exhausted and hollow she looked, and wondered what she had been like before all this –

what two years of living a double life had done to her. 'Marna,' Emma said quietly, 'personally, I don't give a shit what you do; I don't know you, and quite frankly I don't want you here. But my sister thinks you're all right, so I'm giving you the best advice I can.'

'Thanks.'

'Don't hang around, Marna. The CAB will confiscate your money quicker than you can say "illegal earnings".' She snorted and lit another cigarette. 'I can see you don't believe me, but I'm telling you, it can and will happen. And then what will you do? Don't think we'll help you out if you lose it all. My sister seems to think she owes you, but believe me, she owes nothing to anyone.'

'Thanks for the advice,' Marna said sweetly, giving Emma a dirty look of her own, 'but I don't need anything from you.'

Amanda returned, carrying the tablets and a glass of water, which she passed to Emma. 'Take these and go lie down. Marna and I are going out for a stroll.'

Emma rolled onto her side and fixed Marna with a cold stare. 'Remember what I told you,' she said pleasantly. 'Look out for number one.'

Amanda put her sunglasses back on and tugged gently at Marna's wrist. 'Come on, Marna, let's go.'

They walked for two streets without a word. Then Amanda spotted a tapas bar and asked Marna if she'd like a coffee; Marna said she'd rather have a gin and tonic. She sat down outside while Amanda ordered. She felt numb and cold, even in the warm afternoon sunshine. Emma Harrington worried her.

'Your sister looks a lot like you, or you look like her,' she said, when Amanda came back out with the drinks.

'I know.' Amanda lit a cigarette and watched people strolling past from behind her oversized sunglasses. 'You must be angry with me,' she said eventually.

'I was when I heard about it first. I thought you trusted me.' Marna couldn't keep the hurt from her voice.

'I couldn't tell you—'

'How long were you and Emma planning this?'

Amanda gave a little half-smile. 'Since not long after my parents' funeral. Emma was home for a few weeks to help out with the arrangements. She was meant to go back to England, but when she saw the state of me she wouldn't leave me alone until I told her what was wrong. So I did. I told her everything.' Amanda smiled sadly. 'You don't know how good it was to talk to someone. I thought I was losing my mind.'

'You could have talked to me. Amanda, I knew he sent the Whale after you. I know they raped you.'

'You don't know about the tape he sent to Mum and Dad,' Amanda said softly. 'You don't know how upset my father was when he got it. He called me, Marna, crying – my father …' Her voice was steady, but her hands shook wildly. 'He was sobbing, begging me to tell him I hadn't been doing what Tricky said I'd been doing … They were dead two weeks later, you know. Gone. Gone.'

Marna took a sip of her G&T. 'You could have reported him, gone to the police.'

'And tell them what? Hello there, I'm a hooker and my former pimp sent a nasty video of me to my folks, who incidentally are dead now. And, by the way, after he had his goon attack me I won't be able to have children.' Amanda laughed bitterly. 'You know what would have happened to him? Nothing. A big fat fucking nothing.' She grabbed her cigarettes off the table, lit one and sucked on it as if her life depended on it.

'I knew then. I knew I was going to get that bastard if it was the last thing I did.'

'Whose idea was it to go after his money?'

'Mine. I knew that was the way to hit the bastard where it hurt, I just didn't know how.' She smiled coldly. 'But Emma did. She knew exactly how to get him, and with my background to help us, it was easier than we thought.'

'But why didn't you tell me? I could have helped you. I knew you were crushed when your parents died … You could have let me in.'

Amanda flicked the ash off her cigarette and picked at the skin around her chewed nails. 'I couldn't tell you anything – especially you. It wasn't your problem.'

Anger flushed through Marna's body at

Amanda's dismissive tone. 'Not my problem? Allen White was my problem. You could have fucking warned me about him. He nearly killed me – and if you're telling the truth about McCracken using him, you must have known he'd come for you sometime.'

'Marna …' Amanda turned in her chair and faced Marna at last. 'Don't say that. You don't know what the hell you're talking about. I swear I didn't know about White; I didn't know about the tape until after you were in hospital.'

'I believe *you* didn't know, but I'll bet your sister knew about that tape long before she went to the gardaí. What was she waiting for? What?'

Amanda took a long drag on her cigarette. 'Don't say that,' she said stiffly. 'You don't know what we've been through, and you don't know the first thing about Emma.'

Marna bit her tongue. Michael Dwyer had told her that, if Emma had come forward sooner with the video, they would have caught White before he could kill Tessa Byrne. Before he'd had a chance to attack her. By not revealing the tape sooner, Emma had put them all at risk, including her own sister.

'Oh, I know what you're thinking,' Amanda said wearily. 'She should have gone to the police about White. But what good would that have done? It's not like she was sure. And how could she have explained how she knew about him? My sister gave herself to Tricky for almost two years – putting up with his shite, winning his trust, fucking him …' The fingers holding the cigarette wobbled. 'So don't get on your high horse, Marna. In her position, you would have waited too.'

Marna shook her head. 'Stop it, Amanda. You're not like her.'

Amanda shook her head fiercely. 'You can think what you like, but she wasn't certain who killed those women. She didn't see the tape until the day before she went to the gardaí.'

'She only went to protect you,' Marna said. 'You told her what I said at the hospital, about him asking for you by name, and the next thing you know she's at the cop shop with the tape. She knew White was after you. She must have known Tricky sent him.'

Amanda grabbed Marna's arm. 'Shut up for a second and listen to me. Tricky wasn't after me, ever.'

'Yeah, right. He was using White to—'

'He wasn't using White for anything.'

Marna was opening her mouth to say something when the truth hit her straight between the eyes. She pulled away from Amanda and took a deep breath. 'What do you mean?'

'He wasn't using White for anything,' Amanda said softly. She glanced quickly at Marna, then away again. 'He wouldn't even have known where to begin.'

'But … he had the tape. And Grogan said he admitted it.' Marna tried to understand.

Amanda snorted and flicked her cigarette.

'Grogan would have said Tricky killed Elvis. He was blackmailing her, remember? She needed him to be the bad guy.'

'Then why did Emma bring the gardaí the tape?' Marna said in confusion. 'Was it to get him arrested? Was that it – get him out of the way so you two could run?'

Amanda glanced around at the other diners, some of whom were watching them with open interest. 'Keep your voice down.'

'Amanda, answer me! Why did—'

'Oh, please, give it a rest! Tricky was a bastard. He messed with all of us, made our lives a misery, and now you're acting like we did something wrong. He got his comeuppance. What do you care? We could have run any time; we waited to see justice done.'

'It wasn't, though, was it?' Marna said, horrified. 'Tricky didn't have anything to do with Sandy's death, or Tessa's, or the attack on me. Did he?'

'Marna—'

'White was working alone?'

'Shut up, goddammit!' Amanda snapped. She ran her fingers through her hair, ruining the sleek style. 'That bastard McCracken destroyed my life. We made him pay. We did what we had to do!'

'Regardless of what happened to anyone else, including me?'

Amanda's arm shot out suddenly. She grasped Marna's wrist and dug her fingers in, dragging her closer. With her other hand she ripped her

sunglasses off and threw them across the table.
Marna yelped in surprise and tried to pull back,
but Amanda's grip was like a steel trap.

'You're hurting my arm—'

'Don't waste your tears over that prick!
McCracken was going to kill us that night,'
Amanda hissed. 'We nearly didn't make it. My
sister's fucking deranged, and I'm—' She looked
into Marna's startled eyes and relaxed her grip.
'Emma's as mad as a fucking hatter. I think two
years of being Tricky's fuck-bunny warped her
mind. I don't think she'll ever be the same again –
and I'm not far behind her.' She banged Marna's
hand on the metal table. 'You think you can sit
there and pass judgement on me?'

Marna pulled her arm free and rubbed her
wrist. 'Why did you ask me to come here?'

'I don't expect you to understand.' Amanda's
face softened, and she tried a smile. 'I thought you
deserved an explanation. I thought you'd understand if you heard it from me.'

'Amanda, come on. If Emma knew about the
tape, she was playing with people's lives.'

'She didn't know.' Amanda looked away and
drew a deep breath. 'We came over here to lick our
wounds, but … I don't know. Things are so fucked
up … I don't feel like I've won; I feel cheated. I'm
supposed to be resting, thinking of making a new
life, but I can't … I can't even sleep at night. I don't
know what to do next. I've got all this money and

I'm … I feel so depressed. The past few months have been so fucking stressful.'

'What the hell did you expect?'

'Everything happened so fast. One minute we're planning to take his money and run, the next thing Sandy's dead and the gardaí are all over everything …'

Marna lowered her gaze and rubbed the red marks on her wrist. She couldn't bear to hear any more. She couldn't accept that Emma hadn't known about the tape sooner. And if Amanda had suspected … well, she knew her friend – the guilt would eat her alive.

'It hardly seems worth it any more,' Amanda said softly, and her self-pitying tone infuriated Marna. 'I don't think Emma's ever going to recover.'

'Emma seems tough enough to me,' Marna said, disgusted. 'McCracken's dead, you have his money and nobody knows where you are or what you've done. You've won, Amanda. Lap it up.'

Amanda gave a low, tortured laugh. 'Yeah, we've won. We've won. Isn't victory just great?' She lowered her head and put a hand over her eyes.

Marna looked at her sadly. 'What did you expect? Did you think you could walk off with Tricky's money and live happily ever after?'

'Oh, don't take the fucking moral high ground with me,' Amanda said wearily. 'What was there left for me in Ireland? What did you want me to do? Keep working, waiting for the next raid, waiting for my next trip to court to see if some judge would throw me in jail? What? I didn't have a life. It's all right for you; you can work for another few years, take your money and retire to Florida and pretend to your folks that you did well in whatever fake job you're supposed to be doing, and hope they don't ask too many questions. What had I got? What choice did I have?' She turned to Marna, tears rolling down her bruised cheek. 'I had nothing left, nothing but revenge, don't you see? He took *everything*. Do you know what my last words to my parents were? I told them to stop fucking crying and then I hung up. My God, Marna, I never even got a chance to say sorry.'

Marna shook her head and stared wonderingly at the woman she had spent so much of the last two years with. She searched Amanda's tormented face and shuddered. Whatever happened in the future, she never wanted to end up like this.

When was the time to quit? What price did you have to pay to leave the business? She glanced at Amanda again. Whatever she had paid, it was too much.

'This is a nice place to live, Marna,' Amanda said quietly, wiping her eyes with the hem of her sleeve. 'Anonymous. Nobody cares who we are or what we've done. It's a fresh start.'

'I was thinking that,' Marna said quietly, 'about fresh starts.'

'What about them?'

Marna looked at her. 'I hope it all works out for you.'

'Me too.' Amanda drained the last of her drink. 'Me too.'

The following Monday morning, Amanda waved Marna off at the airport and turned towards home. It had been great to see her, to explain, but secretly she was glad Marna was leaving. Marna was the past, and Amanda was only interested in the future.

Marna had been wrong about everything. She and Emma had made a decision that would affect the rest of their lives. But they weren't like other people. They had been born with a survival instinct so powerful it dwarfed every other instinct in their bodies. They would survive this situation; they would recover, both physically and mentally. They had made a stand against the Paul McCrackens and the Anthony O'Connors; they had won the game.

Amanda rubbed her arms and stared into the azure sky. She had cocked up so much of her life, it sickened her. But, now she was here, she had another chance at making something of her life. She could turn it around, hold her head up high. The nightmares would fade. She watched a plane depart and smiled. She had a life and a future; what she made of it was now up to her.

Acknowledgements

Writing a book is a solitary undertaking, and as a general rule I'm pretty comfortable in my own company. However, for the times when I am thoroughly sick of myself or I find I have run out of things to talk to myself about, there is a special group of people any person would be lucky to know. So, without further preamble, I'd like to name and shame them.

Thanks to Terry and Anne for all their love, kindness and words of encouragement. Anne was the first reader to skim my original, dog-eared and poorly spelled manuscript, and her genuine enthusiasm was much appreciated.

Thanks to Kathleen, Pat, Patrick, Gerard and Bernard for being family. I add a special nod to Patrick for letting me teach him the finer points of Spanish beer (and how to hold it). Thanks also to Anna, Antonia, Bryan, Mary K, Mark, Sarah, Tara, Valerie and Carlos, for being the sort of friends a girl needs: faithful, intelligent, unflappable and fabulous, always there at the other end of a phone call or e-mail. I consider myself lucky to have you all as friends.

Thanks to my agent, Faith O'Grady, for her unerring eye and commitment to this book. A big bow too for my publisher, Ciara Considine at Hodder Headline Ireland, for putting up with all the passed deadlines and ignored pleas for tardy re-writes.

Thanks to my daughter Jordan for making each and every day an interesting experience. I know you're nearly a teenager now and this sort of stuff makes you cringe and roll your eyes a little, but I love you and you make me very happy. I just wish you'd stop bringing home stray kittens.

Finally, and with great pleasure, I heartily, and with as much love as possible thrown in, thank my husband Andrew. Without his unfailing love and support, his coffee-making skills, his ability to ignore tantrums and run spell checks, his total one-hundred-per-cent belief in me, in fact his sheer all-round saintliness, this book would never have happened. I love you and someday I will get you a boat for fake fishing.